The CHARITY OF EBENEZER SCROOGE

12th Street Hill Press

The CHARITY OF EBENEZER SCROOGE

or

A CHRISTMAS CAROL II

A NOVEL BY

GLEN L. BLEDSOE

copyright 2009 by Glen L. Bledsoe
12th Street Hill Press | Salem. Oregon

COVER DESIGN: Gabriel S. Bledsoe

INTERIOR LAYOUT: Glen L. Bledsoe

ISBN 978-0-615-32502-6

For my wife and my mother

Acknowledgements

Without the help of these people this book would not be what it is: Anne Boyle, Jacqui Nydam, and of course my wife Karen. Their suggestions made this a much better read.

The devil tempts but doesn't force.

Guyanan proverb

———

He [Scrooge] had no further intercourse with Spirits, but lived upon the Total Abstinence Principle, ever afterwards; and it was always said of him, that he knew how to keep Christmas well, if any man alive possessed the knowledge.

Charles Dickens—A CHRISTMAS CAROL

But Mr. Dickens was wrong!

Prologue

IT WAS PRIVATE AS NO OTHER ROOM COULD EVER BE: NO DOORS, NO WIN-
dows, no stairways, nor any other architectural means of ingress or egress,
yet it could be reached—if the visitor were skilled in the Black Magic Arts.
Privacy was needed because the room's Occupant was inclined to engage in
practices which were distinctly unchristian while occupying a Christian
Time and a Christian Space.

Nor were the oddments strewn upon the tables and benches which ran
round the walls of the room likely to be found in a Christian dwelling:
assorted stone jars whose ill-fitting lids did little to prevent their mephitic
contents from oozing over their sides; discoloured pasteboard-boxes holding
the decayed teeth, hair and nail pairings of many of Europe's most infamous
villains; the mummified remains of creatures to which the most learned
natural philosopher could set no name nor even phylum.

These materials the Occupant put to astonishing uses. He once had used
them to raise a dead man, though strictly speaking it could not be said that
the man had *precisely* returned to life and the effect was, at all events, not of
significant duration. Disordered books, scrolls and papers leapt from dusty
shelves to the Occupant's hand at his slightest gesture. He could at will cause
the smiling faces of beautiful women to appear, although he hadn't any idea
who the women were or where (or even if) they lived.

The Occupant, however, was not satisfied with these elementary miracles.
He wanted more. The magic that he had thus far exercised, he felt, was only
marginally more accomplished than the level of a common stage magician.
The magic he practised was empty of true power.

To obtain what he sought he knew he would need to make a small sacrifice. A mere token: the little finger of his left hand. Removing it had been painful, but he hadn't ever much minded pain. If it got him what he wanted, it was small enough price to pay. The digit lay before him now wrapped in a blood-soaked handkerchief. It was his gift.

He was not so foolish as to believe that he could bend the Prince of Darkness to his will, but he knew that if he served the Beast well, there would be rewards—rewards at an unimaginable scale.

The Occupant chose Christmas Day for the Summoning. Easter, he believed, would have been the more profane, but in his enthusiasm he found he could not wait.

"Your servant," the Occupant said when at last the Unholy One, Satan, The Devil, The Beast, Old Nick, Scratch, Beelzebub, Lucifer, The Tempter, The Prince of Darkness and the possessor of a thousand other names appeared before him. The Occupant could scarce keep down his gorge from the stench of filth which accompanied the Prince. He swallowed, kept his eyes averted, head bowed. He held his gift in the palm of his left hand to better exhibit the sacrifice.

"I understand that pain is your friend," the Prince said. The voice was deep with a curious burr. Though the Occupant dared not look the Prince directly in the face, he sensed that it was tall and loose-limbed—a marionette animated by a malefic force. It was not, however, out of temper as he had feared. He felt the Beast almost sway with curiosity.

"I do not flinch from discomfort—even in the extreme," the Occupant replied, unable to suppress a smile.

"You are relentless."

Keeping his eyes downcast the Occupant gestured around the room. "None of this was honestly acquired," he said.

"You are cruel?"

"When it suits my purposes," the Occupant said, still gazing down at the floor.

"You wish for power?" the Prince said.

The hooves of the Beast scraped upon the stone floor leaving pale scratches. "I wish to serve you," said the Occupant. "Servitude is my sole desire."

"If I gave you the power to command storms and batter cities, would you take it?"

"That is not how the Darkness works," the Occupant replied.

"You do understand me well, then," said the Evil One.

"I understand that your ways are subtle. You gain power by undermining others."

The Prince laughed. "There will be little I can teach you," it said.

"There are not enough days in my life nor any other to learn all that you can teach me, My Master."

"You wish for immortality?"

"I wish to live for as long as you have use of me."

"That," the Prince said, "may not be for long. But...your answers are good."

"I am careful of my words."

"Are you now? We shall see."

"Will you accept this gift?" the Occupant said stretching his hand in the direction of the Prince.

"I will not."

"I am sorry if I have offended you, Master."

"You have not. It is that I prefer to take these gifts myself. It was selfish of you to inflict the pain upon yourself."

The Occupant said nothing, but bowed lower still. His hair hung to either side of his face. He hadn't anticipated this.

"However, the token is...appreciated," The Prince said.

The Occupant choked back a short gasp of relief.

The Prince lifted the gift wrapped in its bloodied cloth and tossed it indifferently across the room.

"It is well that you understand the nature of my power," the Beast said. "You are quite correct when you say that I gain power by undermining others."

"What service might I first perform, O Master?"

"There is a man here in London by the name of Ebenezer Scrooge. Do you know of him?"

The Occupant nodded. "Scrooge, the Money-Lender. Scrooge, Master of the Union Workhouses. Scrooge, the Counting-House Monster. Yes, I have heard of him. One of yours."

"No longer!"

The Occupant clutched his ears to mute the blast. Again foul vapours filled the room, and this time the Occupant could not prevent himself from vomiting.

"He has been Redeemed," the Beast continued, heedless of the Occupant's emetic reaction. "Worse than that. Far worse. It is clear to me that he will become the Symbol of Redemption, the living representation of Hope and Charity among the dwellers of this City. His story will ring far and wide from the lowest brothels to the most fashionable sitting rooms. Scrooge's Christmas tale will grow until it reaches mythic proportions. It will spread across all Christendom and every mind will think: 'If Scrooge can be turned from the path of Evil, then any man can.' This I can not permit. This I will not permit."

"You wish me to slay him?" said the Occupant kneeling uneasily in vomitus.

"No—no—no. I thought you understood the nature of my power. You disappoint me."

"I am imperfect."

"Death would only make of him a martyr and guarantee him his place in Heaven."

The Occupant's eyes glittered. "You wish for me to persuade him to return to the Dark Path—in my own special way."

The Darkness paused as if considering the suggestion. "Causing him pain will not change his mind. Not solely physical pain, at any rate. It will require more subtle methods. You must understand that Scrooge was never my servant. Not wittingly. Like many men and women, he perpetuated my will without being consciously aware of it. Whether he be *wooed* back to the Dark

Path or whether he drags himself suffering to my door matters little to me. I will leave that for my Servants to determine. However it is done, he will be mine once again. And when that is so, Scrooge becomes Redeemed to me, and his value as a symbol to mankind reverts to Hell. Scrooge will become the universal symbol of Weakness and Desperation, a symbol of the over-whelming power of Temptation. I will savour eating his soul and drinking his sweet blood."

The Occupant uncovered the back of his head with his hands. "However should I accomplish such a thing, O Master?"

"Why would you presume that I should rely upon you? So much respon-sibility cannot be given untested. This is far too important for that. However, your talent for creating these discrete spaces," it waved its claw at the room, "though trivial, might prove of some minor use." The Beast took several short steps away from the Occupant as if inspecting the room for flaws. The Occupant heard its horns scrape the ceiling. It continued:

"Scrooge's Redemption came about as a consequence of a visit by three Spirits of Christmas: Past, Present and Yet To Come. It was their persua-sion which turned him away from me. It is only fitting that three Demons should turn him back. These Demons however will not appear in a vision nor a dream of a single night's duration. They will appear to him in human form, and he will not know them from any other man or woman about him."

"This is a thing I would accomplish alone," the Occupant said, breathing rapidly. "I am quite sure of it. You must trust this only to me."

"Absolutely not, there is no more to be said on that point. Consider this your initiation into my services. A first, feeble step. The plot will be realised by divers minions of considerable cunning and power, and they in turn will have the assistance of mortal men and women who are mercenaries in my service such as yourself. They will perpetrate a scheme—long, devious and cunning—which would crush any man. Even one much younger and far more fearless than Scrooge. In the end he will come knowingly to me on his knees begging for my favour. Scrooge will learn that there are fates follow-ing death that are far worse than merely wandering the Earth as a remorseful spirit. Far, far worse."

"And when I have brought about Scrooge's destruction, what next might I expect? I wish to please you, Master. I am eager to make myself ever the more valuable to you," the Occupant said.

"When *you* bring about Scrooge's destruction? Such bumptiousness! Such audacity!" said the Prince. "Have you not heard a word I've said?"

The Occupant grovelled on his knees. *I have let my ambition trip me again*, he thought.

But then the Prince laughed. "First you indicate you would bring Scrooge down yourself without the aid of my Servants. Then, you are eager to accept a second commission without you have proved your fiddling worth in the first. But what should I expect? If you were not flawed, if you weren't a deviant—defective in both mind and spirit, an aberration of your kind— you would not call upon me, would you?"

The Occupant said nothing, but only held himself low and still.

"Perhaps I have chosen the wrong man," the Prince continued. "I am not perfect and make mistakes, but understand *I never pay for them*, Magician. If I have made an error in choosing you for this and you fail, *you* shall pay the price for *my* mistake. Your dalliance with pain which you have proudly alluded to could never prepare you for what would be your fate—your unending fate, I might add."

"I cannot imagine how one could fail with the assistance of three demons and the support of Satan himself," the Occupant stammered.

"Support? I have a small part to play—a cameo one might say—it is true, but I will not *support* you. Ha! Support you? Why not do the thing myself and be certain that it is done right? No, this is a time for you to prove yourself to me. Do your part well and you will rise in my esteem. Fail, and you will suffer. As for the Demons, they will care only for themselves and neglect you completely—you may depend upon it."

"In that case I should not suffer as a result should the demons fail to undo Scrooge," the Occupant protested.

"Suffer? My friend, *suffer* is not the word for it. If you fail me, if my demons should fail me, I shall come after you for your head."

CHAPTER 1

ଜଏ

Mr. Topper & Mr. Scrooge

Scrooge, who had not been expected, was the very first to arrive. Wearing his coat foolishly unbuttoned, collar open, carrying hat in hand and gloves in pocket, he fairly battered the door to kindling with his sharp knocks. The serving maid flung open the door to see his face flushed with excitement.

"Is your master at home, my dear?" he said.

"Yes, Sir," the frightened girl replied.

"Where is he, my love?" said Scrooge.

"He's in the dining room, Sir. Along with mistress. I'll show you upstairs, if you please."

"Bless you, sweet girl. He knows me," said Scrooge, his hand already on the dining-room door. He turned the handle gently, then sidled his face round the edge.

"Fred!" Scrooge bellowed and bounded into the room waving his arms frantically as if sounding an alarm of fire. Instead he shouted his Christmas Blessings to One and All!

The abruptness of his entry all but startled Lily off her footstool. She could not help sniffing his breath as he crossed the room to greet her. Finding him cold sober she was no less nonplussed. *Could this be the man who yesterday scorned our company?*

Scrooge simply could not sit still. One moment he was wringing the hand of his nephew as if he were intent on shaking it from its wrist. The next he was polishing a nest of apples on the table to the brightness of the silver. The next he was inquiring after the "lateness" of the other guests (who were not yet expected) as if he were their mothers and their fathers and all their unmarried aunts put together. The next he was hurrying behind Lily, offering advice, compliments, and suggestions on her preparations as if he had ever been anything but an old bachelor.

The rest of the guests arrived an hour or so after the setting of the winter sun. So deeply buried beneath woollen scarves, beaver caps, cotton bonnets, great coats, and rabbit-lined gloves that none could be recognised until those garments were removed. Every man and woman exhibited rosy cheeks, much the colour of the Christmas apples Scrooge had so industriously polished. Each eye twinkled with the promise of happiness known best on that day.

Fred's wife's seven sisters arrived as one. Being all dressed in a similar fashion and looking very much alike, Fred found them difficult to tell apart. To make matters more perplexing each had been christened with a name beginning with the letter L.

In order from eldest to youngest they were Lydia, Lottie (the only one with raven-black hair and silk-green eyes, unlike the rest with fair heads and eyes of lapis-lazuli), Lillian (that is, Mrs. Fred), Lucille (who would become engaged to a certain gentleman that very evening following a game of Blind-Man's Buff), Lucinda, Loretta, and lastly, Louisa. The eldest and the youngest were, of course, easy to distinguish—if not name; but, those born in between were, to poor Fred who had not been in the family so very long, of a single, blurred identity. He recognised Lottie (on account of her hair colour), Lucinda (on account of her plumpness), and Lily, of course (on account of her being Mrs. Fred).

After a savoury meal, the guests found themselves irresistibly drawn to the yellow, orange, and green tongues of flame gnawing at the previous year's blackened yule-log. The flames licked the bark of the log as they had licked their plates.

Fred told the tale of the talking Christmas goose while the sisters mopped their teary eyes and tittered softly behind their sleeves. The room boomed with Scrooge's loud laughter, an infection, which spread to the other men.

"A glass of wine with you, Sir," said a ruddy-faced gentleman to Scrooge, his ebullience exaggerated by similar pledges shared with several guests. "My name is Topper, Sir—Milton Alexander Topper—a long time friend of your nephew Fred."

"I am delighted to meet you, Mr. Topper," Scrooge said. "You are enjoying yourself this fine day?"

"Indeed, I am," Topper said sipping again at his glass.

They chattered on amiably thus for several minutes.

Topper squinted as if he were carefully weighing his next thought. "Now that we have a moment's private conversation and if I may be frank with you on this Holiday—my humour being so bright from drink and good company, in general, and a beautiful woman, in particular—I'm afraid I entertained a bad impression of you before your arrival at this lovely home this evening. 'Humbug!' I had been forewarned was your Christmas motto, and it was said you kept a tight-fisted attitude toward your fellow man— recommending prisons to shelter the poor.

"But now I see that this impression was just another of Fred's little jests. Ha! Opposites. Such as calling Jervis Thompson *Tiny*—he being the 6-foot coachman down Cox Court with arms the size of barrels. An humorous misstatement. And your nephew is a Master of it, Sir—Bless His Heart! Ha ha ha!"

Milton Topper had many ways of twisting his face into a smile. Like snow flakes, no two were identical. Every wrinkle of skin signalled a new variation —which is not to say it was an old face. One could see the boy in it plain: a time when the sandy head was not quite so spare, a time when the skin of his face needed not to be scraped clean of hair each morning, a time when the mind rattling about in that marvellous skull was filled with frogs and birds' nests.

Ebenezer Scrooge sat considering this very face a long moment. "Not at all, Mr. Topper. Fred was not joking in the least. He was not exercising any form of humorous misstatement for anyone's entertainment. My present good temper has been as much a surprise to him as it has been to you.

"Sir, I will be honest with you: I have conducted my life in the most miserly fashion. And now I am sorely ashamed of it and intend to amend it. I have sworn to change my ways and have changed them as of this very morning! Of this you may make no doubt. Few of my colleagues would know me as I sit here before you this evening, nor will they be less astonished when business begins on the morrow." Scrooge rubbed his knees with excitement.

"Truly, Sir?" said Topper. "What has happened, then, that you should be so altered as you say? You must enlighten me. No! I beg pardon, Sir. Clearly it is not my place to question a gentleman such as yourself—even on such a fine day as this."

"Indeed, Sir, by all that is Holy, I will speak to you the Truth, and you shall hear it." Scrooge turned to look him hard in the eyes and set his jaw. "On this day any man may speak honestly to any other regardless of his station, to be sure."

"Tell me then," Topper said, "what has changed your ways so quickly and so thoroughly." Then a broad smile creased his face. "Or rather should I ask: what would the gentlewoman's name be?—like the source of my great happiness this holiday."

Scrooge slashed the air with a dismissive gesture. "No woman at all, but Spirits!"

"Truly?! You shock me deeply, Mr. Scrooge." Topper sucked in his lower lip. "I should have smelt it on you." He sniffed noisily a moment, then scrubbed his nose with his handkerchief. Again he drew in the air. "Give me a moment to reflect, Sir." He hummed a low note and rolled his eyes. "No, no—too much spirits of a different nature in me now to judge properly, but I do see a bit of ectoplasm here at your knees, more at the elbows, and a wisp or two at the scruff of your neck."

Scrooge brushed vigourously at those sites as if they had gravy stains.

"They must have been of an extraordinary sort," Topper said. "Pray, tell me of them—but only if you've a mind."

"You will laugh at an old man's story," Scrooge replied.

Topper's face looked scholarly. "Laugh? Never in life! Members of my family has been in the profession of spiritual communication for many and many a generation. I call it a profession, but few of us have made our bread by it. Perhaps I should refer to it as our *calling*."

Topper bent his head forward and lowered his voice: "My Auntie Nellie, God Bless Her, has the Gift. True, she has spent the last eight years of her life bed-ridden, but that only has been a nurturing time for her powers. She can locate missing objects, run-away children, mislaid deeds, and even once identified a murderer—though her testimony was hardly acceptable in a court of law."

Topper raised his eyebrows. "The Gift was not passed to me, however, nor to my younger brother Thorne, now in America, nor the twins Ellen and Helena of my Aunt Betty. Cousin Lag—of whom you may have heard —is a proper fake. Does tricks by taking off his shoes and working black cords with his toes. An embarrassment to the family, but spiritual communication is thick with charlatans as I'm sure you're aware.

"Now," he said, "I have seen my share of ghosts, to be sure—that requires no gift. No English royalty, no Egyptian mummies, no vengeful abbots, no murdered heiresses—but significant spirits in their own way." He touched a glittering ring on his finger.

"An interesting design," Scrooge said, looking closely at the ring. "Did you have it made?"

"I did not, but you shall hear just how it did come to me. One summer night when I was just a lad I noticed Henry the Second, my pug dog, staring at a spot on the wall of my bedchamber. The hair along his back stood stiff as a boar's and his black lips curled to issue a gurgling growl and show his wicked teeth. His eyes were fixed on an oozing, scarlet stain." Topper pointed to a spot on the wall where, of course, there was no stain, though Scrooge stared as if one might appear at any moment.

"A ten year-old boy does not stand up brave and tall and demand: 'Who goes there?' but holds back beneath his bed-clothes, though he well knows they're little enough protection against mortal intruders, never mind supernatural agencies. But when you're seeing things you'd rather not and your eyelids are froze open, even such fragile things are enough to bury your frightened head.

"Henry switched his position this way and that, undecided which would afford the best advantage. I'd seen him face a half-dozen rats taking nary a scratch, but this was clearly something of a different order.

"The wall puckered and split like the skin of a mouldy orange, Mr Scrooge—Lord strike me dead if I'm lying. The hole spewed out a fog which chilled me to the bone. I expected the Red-Devil himself to dance out, skewer me and drag me back to Hell, but as I watched trembling beneath my bed-clothes, I saw three beautiful women wearing white dresses drift through the tear—angels without wings, they were. Just as the hole was about to seal itself, something else, some grumbling, scarcely visible abomination dashed out as a cat might before its mistress can close and bolt the door for the night.

"Unlike the ladies these creatures took immediate notice of me! There were two of them by my reckoning, trapped inside a thin sac. Demons! I couldn't see them clearly for the membrane was cloudy and distorted what little light passed through it, but I could see sharp talons, teeth, and other boney knob-ends pressed against the sac stretching it to its limits. The closer this bubble drifted near to my bed-side, the more furious they struggled to break free. The membrane thinned and would surely have split at any moment. One pin-prick was all they needed to be loose. Their claws were extended now, the skin acting like fine gloves, in a manner of speaking. They pressed their way toward my bed. The only thing which hampered them was a raging dispute over which was to dine on me first!

"Abruptly my fearless companion, Henry the Second, attacked, although he could lay no tooth to them. They turned their attentions from me to him and tossed the poor brute from one set of claws to another—him snapping at them to no avail—them howling and seething, trying to force him into their mouths, but the membrane prevented it. In their clumsiness the pug was dropped to the floor whereupon he retreated beneath my bed. His tail, usually curled close to his haunches, was now straight as a pin and remained so until his dying day.

"The Three Ladies in White at last took notice, the ruckus of the Demons drawing their attention. They waved their fingers as daintily as climbing-roses and wove a net of smoke and light. They gathered their net, snared the filthy beasts, and drew them back whence they had come with much snarling, hissing and cursing! Then the Ladies turned their attentions on me and sang a song with words which I could not understand, but were pure wonderful to hear."

Topper pulled his handkerchief and mopped his brow. The recollection had drawn a reaction which he had not experienced in years.

"Wonders! And the ring?" Scrooge asked.

Topper said, "Oh, yes, I'm not about to forget the most important part —that which makes my tale more than a mere Christmas ghost story.

"The Ladies in White then glided toward me, pointing at me, holding their mute mouths open like fishes out of water. Faint eye-brows sat high upon their smooth foreheads in a fixed expression which I could not read. Their eyes, like frosted-blue marbles, gazed at me for what seemed like hours, but surely could have been no more than a few seconds. They were so beautiful that I wept, Mr. Scrooge, as strange as that may seem. They were Spirits, Sir, and as to their purity and goodness there can be no question.

"I did not move—was incapable of movement. One of them glided forward, and something heavy fell from her extended palm—or perhaps through it—into my lap: this." Topper removed a silver ring from a thick finger and pressed it into Scrooge's hand.

"It has always fit my finger, Mr. Scrooge. No matter how small my hand as a boy, nor which finger I put it on now—it always fits perfectly."

Scrooge looked at it again with increased reverence. In spite of its large size, it seemed feminine off Topper's hand. Many finely-scribed, closely-spaced lines created a pattern of intricate knots and sprouting plants. There were no stones nor jewels to it, but it shone in a peculiar way.

Topper nodded at it. "It's the work of færies, my Auntie said. I've not seen another like it. Mother insisted that there must be some magic about it, but I've found none other than I seem to have more than my share of Good

Luck." He stared a long moment at Miss Lucille across the room. "After that the Spirits withdrew, and beyond that I've never discovered any more about it."

Scrooge returned the ring. As Topper replaced it, it snugged itself around his finger like a cat at the ankles of her master.

"Come join the rest of us, Mr. Topper," said Miss Lucille from across the room as she noticed his absence from the rest of their festive group. She was, however, glad to see Mr. Scrooge, such a prominent man of business, take keen interest in the man she hoped would soon be her husband. "And be sure to bring Mr. Scrooge with you," she added.

"Mr. Scrooge and I are engaged in a...er...discussion, Miss Lucille. Be there shortly," said Topper.

"I hope not politics!" She gave a dismissive cough of laughter. "If that be the case, then talk yourself dry of that topic before joining this happy group. We're about to play charades," she said with her yellow curls shaking in amusement. "Won't you come and join us? It shall be ever so much fun."

"Presently, Miss. Presently." Topper waved and smiled.

He continued to Scrooge in a whisper, "That young woman does enjoy her theatricals. She will have us all dressed in costume and parading about like silly children if we're not careful. Listen, Mr. Scrooge, as gentlemen of mutual understanding and respect, let's keep my experiences as a bit of confidence between the two of us. Miss Lucille doesn't like such talk and would rather have me speak of more polite matters."

"Certainly certainly, friend. Now, if you've the patience, I shall tell my tale."

Scrooge told Topper of his experiences with the Spirits of Christmas Past, Present & Yet To Come in quick whispers. As the story proceeded Topper nodded and grunted to convey that he did indeed believe it.

"The message of the Ghosts was clear, Mr. Topper," Scrooge said. "I have a short time to make my life over, make it over completely in substance, spirit, deed and act—and not merely for the single day of joy which we celebrate here to-day. Otherwise, Christmas next you will find my name on a cold gravestone, those who knew me will laugh at my memory, and I will find myself forever more wandering the earth dragging my cash-boxes behind me."

"Then you need perform some significant good deed," Topper said, "which only you can accomplish, Sir. Not a single act, but a goodness which perpetuates and grows itself. You might build a hospital or perhaps found a university."

"I have no knowledge of medicine nor education. My funds though generous are not of that order of magnitude," Scrooge said.

Topper scrubbed his chin in thought and clapped his hands together sharply as an idea slid into place like the bolt of a door. "I have it then. You shall found a charitable organisation," said he thoughtfully. "Can you imagine a better way to improve the lives of hundreds of people as well as your own?"

Scrooge's eyes widened at the idea.

"Charity..." he sighed. "I believe you have it, Sir. How better serve my fellow man than to see to their most fundamental needs by founding a charity? You are absolutely correct, Mr. Topper. The funding of such an organisation I shall gladly undertake. To undo the wickedness of my past I shall devote my every effort to it. I can imagine it now: *Ebenezer Scrooge's Charitable Aid And Victual Assistance To The Under-advantaged & Desperate.*"

Scrooge peered at Topper as if he were peering into his heart. "I believe it is no accident that on this day I am here and you are here and we have had this discussion. If I am to take on such a task I will need a capable assistant, a man to act as part personal secretary, part clerk, part day-to-day manager—someone whom I can trust, and—more than a little importantly someone—with a deeper understanding of the implications of the Spirits' message. Someone very much like yourself, Mr. Topper. Are you interested?"

Topper rocked back in his seat. "Well, Mr. Scrooge, I don't know. It's kind of you to ask, but, I doubt my skills would be useful to a man such as yourself. I'm but a simple clerk. And as such I know a bit about book-keeping, but I've no experience managing such a large affair as a charity."

"Can you tell an honest man by the look of his eye?" inquired Scrooge.

"I can do that," Topper said, and twisted the ring on his finger.

"Can you tell a family in dire need?"

"Certainly that, as well."

"Those will be vital skills beyond all others in our future undertakings. You must stick to these fundamental principles at all costs."

"Yes, Sir. Still my current employer pays well, and, if I may share a confidence with you, it is my intention to ask for Miss Lucille's hand in marriage to-night," Topper said.

"Then I give you joy, Sir," Scrooge said and wrung his arm in congratulations. "And I offer you dependable and morally uplifting employment to keep your new family." Scrooge made him an offer of wages in figures so handsome that it made Topper clamp his teeth.

"You do make it difficult for a man to say no, Mr. Scrooge. What precisely would my duties be?"

"Topper, Sir. You have it wrong. I ask you: what will *my* duties be?" said Scrooge.

Topper frowned. "I fear that I may have misrepresented myself to you, Mr. Scrooge. I am a common man with no more idea of God's Truth than any other man. When in doubt, I follow my heart."

"That is all that I will ever ask you to do," Scrooge said. "But even so, I have no doubt you shall more than earn your wages."

"Something about all this tells me we're in for a bit of adventure before we part our ways, Mr. Scrooge." Topper stretched his back.

"Life should be an adventure," said Scrooge, theatrically waving his arms.

They shook hands. "Here's to *Ebenezer Scrooge's Charitable Aid And Victual Assistance To The Under-advantaged & Desperate!*" Topper said. "Now, if you will excuse me." He rose from his stool. "The evening's plans call for a game of Blind-Man's Buff after which I have a proposal of a different sort to offer Miss Lucille."

CHAPTER 2

୨୧

The Yellow Door

SCROOGE POINTED WITH A GLOVED HAND. "THIS SECTION WAS PARTIALLY burned and sacked as a part of the Luddite riots the year the students at East India College in Hertford rose up against their masters. A decade later, along with a few outbuildings, it was acquired by Marley, my former partner, for a pittance, but even so he could make no return on it."

"Yes, Sir," Topper said. With a pencil freshly sharpened with a pen knife from his pocket he scribbled a few words in his notebook.

"Now it is my turn," Scrooge said, narrowing his eyes, "but it is not my purpose to spin gold from its dusty and mildewed straw."

"No, Sir." Topper said. He stomped his feet and pulled his collar tighter around his neck. He wrote: *Not spin gold from straw.*

"This is where I intend to establish my charity," Scrooge said. "It will take work, of course. For some time there's been no life within these walls except the kind whose eyes glitter red and whose tails grow no hair. The windows are out and the ceiling does little to keep the weather at bay. But we will put it right. This is where we shall care for, feed, and shelter those who cannot do for themselves."

"Yes, Sir," Topper said.

Scrooge said, "But mark me: word of my little charity will spread quickly. The poor will arrive twenty or thirty at a time—perhaps even more. The desperate need no formal invitation."

"I do believe you are right, Sir," Topper said. "We must give it our very best."

Scrooge said, "Napoleon may have been defeated at the Battle of Waterloo, but Britain's economy continues to reel, bruised by nearly two decades of war with the French."

"These are hard times, Sir, to be sure," Topper said.

"The ranks of the hungry and poor," Scrooge said, "have grown to the size of armies, Milton, in spite of Peel's measures to import cheap corn. If wealthy public figures as Scott and Lawrence have fallen to their financial knees gored on horns of economic disaster, how many more nameless of the lower and middle classes have been flung into heartless poverty, hunger, disease and crime?"

"Far too many, Sir," Topper said.

"Since the Peterloo Massacre common folk have grown to distrust the government as a whole, and especially the army."

"A terrible incident, to be sure," Topper said.

"We may not perform miracles, but neither are we helpless." Scrooge pulled up his collar. He said, "This is the time of year when winter storms descend upon London killing any man, woman or child caught overnight outside a shelter—freezing them alive and burying their corpses under mounds of snow where they are not discovered for days or perhaps weeks."

"I understand your sense of urgency," Topper said. He closed his notebook and slipped it and his pencil into his pocket.

Scrooge was quiet for some moments lost in his thoughts. Then at length he said, "I give you *carte blanche*, Milton, to turn my building into a proper charity."

"Sir?"

"Do whatever it takes, but if you cannot make this space wholesome for these people by midsummer, I will close it down and determine a better way to go about it."

"By midsummer? So soon? I am only a clerk, but I would guess that the renovation of such a building would take..."

"The clock is ticking for me, Milton," Scrooge said, sharply. "Time for me is the one commodity I do not possess in significant quantities. What I lack in time, I must compensate with money which—while I am not rich—I must confess that I have modest quantities of. No, it is absolutely vital I demonstrate that I am truly a changed man through and through by Christmas next or, I fear, you will find my name chiselled into a cold gravestone." Scrooge's memory of the vision sent his heart racing. "My charity will be the centre-piece of that demonstration."

"Yes, Sir," Topper said. "We will do our best."

"Yes, of course," Scrooge said. He inhaled deeply for a moment, then let it out in a quick burst. "I have hired you to do a job, and now I must stand aside and allow you to do it. As I have said, money is no object."

"I understand your determination," Topper said, "but you mustn't squander your funds, Mr. Scrooge."

Scrooge nodded and hugged himself against the cold. "I do not wish for you to be wasteful either as it would serve no purpose. But more importantly, I do not wish my charity to fail because of insufficient funds. It will operate under a trust from my counting house—lately and humanely managed by the steady hand of Bob Cratchit, my former clerk. No, Milton, I am confident that you are entirely capable of seeing this through—so much so that I have made the decision to leave you to supervise this undertaking alone while I am away."

"On my own? Whatever do you mean?" Topper said, in horror. "Where do you go, Sir, if I may make so bold as to ask?"

"There is a young man, a lame boy—the son of Bob Cratchit who, as I have said, now manages my counting house—who requires the aid of a physician. Otherwise the boy will die. I must at all costs see that he lives. To that end I have learned of a German physician, Professor Gebhard Friedrich, of Berlin, who has developed a treatment for the disease which hobbles the boy. Tim—for that is the boy's name—and I will sail for Germany to-morrow. It is a promise I am bound to keep, and I cannot be dissuaded from it. I can't help but think that in some way the fates of Master Cratchit and me are intertwined."

"I see, Sir." Topper sighed. "I understand completely, and I do wish the boy every success in his treatment. You can, however, see that I am uneasy to take on this task alone. I am not convinced that I have the necessary skills or experience. If I were to fail you, I should never forgive myself."

"Pish! I have complete faith in your ability."

"I appreciate your confidence even if I worry that it is misplaced, Sir."

"Nonsense," Scrooge said. "You can see for yourself what needs to be done. You have access to my resources and have my blessing. It's simply a matter of hiring the right people and seeing that the job is done to finish. If all goes well I shall be back by the first day of Spring."

"Yes, Sir," Topper replied.

Scrooge said, "I beg your forgiveness and the forgiveness of God for leaving you at this time, but you do understand about the boy. I am much attached to him."

"Yes, Sir," Topper said, and after a paused added: "You will miss the wedding then, Sir."

"What's that?" Scrooge said turning on Topper abruptly.

"Our wedding. Mine and Lucille's. We became engaged at your nephew Fred's party on Christmas day. Do you remember? The date for our wedding is March 1st. You did receive our invitation, did you not?"

"Of course! Of course! How could I forget such a thing? I am sorry to say that I *shall* miss it, my friend. Naturally I cannot be in two places at once. But I shall make it up to you. You'll see."

"Yes, Sir," Topper said. "I understand that attending to Master Cratchit's health has priority."

"Thank you for your understanding, Milton, but I do give you joy, my friend and wish you the best of luck." Scrooge opened his heavy coat and pulled his watch. "Where does the time go? Two o'clock already! I must bid you good day for I have much to do." Scrooge nodded and left the building.

Topper followed him out and bowed as the carriage rolled away. He straightened and weighed as to how best to begin his task. He glanced back at the building. Years of London smoke and grit had stained its brick face the colour of peppered gravy. His eyes were drawn to the door of the former employment office whose appearance was particularly disreputable. Green paint bubbled and peeled from its scored surface. Topper blew warm air on his hands, drew out his pocket knife and pointed it at the door.

"Here is where we begin—before the bitterest descends upon us again and takes the flexibility out of my fingers," he said to no one in particular. Nevertheless a crowd of small children stood round him as he scraped away at the paint and the rot. An hour and more passed before he was satisfied with the results during which time the vigourous activity warmed him.

"Where is there a can of paint hereabouts?" he said more to himself than to any of the spectators, but as if in a dream someone handed him a can of the merriest shade of yellow he had ever seen.

"And a brush, dare I ask?" he said darting a look over his shoulder. "You fellows! Is there a brush nowhere to be found? Surely there must be brushes to go with this lovely paint?"

The boys with their cheeks red and lips blue scattered to search. At last one was produced. Stiff it was having been poorly cleaned after its last use, and its bristles had the appearance and having been gnawed by tiny teeth. Topper did not, however, criticise its condition nor doubt its utility. He used his pocket-knife to prise the lid off the can, squinted into its bright interior, stirred the contents with a stick, dipped his brush, and dabbed at the door as if it were a canvas and he were Thomas Gainsborough.

"There's a proper yellow door for you," he said upon completion with a smile of satisfaction (and no little paint) upon his face.

Ebenezer Scrooge's Charitable Aid And Victual Assistance To The Under-advantaged & Desperate—soon known to nearly everyone simply as Yellow Door— shone its new face onto the busy square.

༄༅

CHAPTER 3

Respice, Adspice, Prospice

THE AIR SHOULDN'T SMELL LIKE WINTER. NOT THIS LATE. WINTER SHOULD have blown itself out—yet heavy snow fell in the morning darkness as if the season had just begun in earnest.

The sky changed from inky black to sea-shell pink to wooly blue, as Topper tip-toed through ankle-deep snow. He stretched out his tongue desperate to catch a snow flake. He counted thus far three successes. Topper thrust his hands in his pockets, yawned (accidentally adding one more snowflake to his count) and thought of the beautiful woman whom he had married by license just ten days since. What a morning *that* had been! Could his life be any better now? He doubted it.

Cook and Miss Goosegrass, Yellow Door's new school mistress, would already be inside preparing breakfast, of course, but it was up to him to officially open the bright yellow door to the world each morning. Those who did not live within the shelter but took their meals inside depended upon him.

Topper rounded the corner and saw them huddled together, stamping their feet to drive away the cold, but with smiles on their faces. They were tired, hungry, dirty, and ignorant, but always patient and grateful. And not without hope. No, not without hope.

"Lord Bless you, Captain," said Jemmy McCloud, putting a knuckle to his forehead.

"Good day to you, Mr. McCloud," replied Topper as he reached inside his breast pocket for the keys.

"Fine day for penguins, Sir." McCloud flipped his grey pigtail over a shoulder. He touched the jagged scar across his forehead as if something in the weather reminded him of that day he'd earned it sailing against the French in the man-of-war *HMS Cloud Dancer*.

"Indeed, it is, Sir," replied Topper in all sincerity, "I would hazard a guess that the snow and slush will all be run down the gutter by this afternoon. The sun will warm our backs this week. Or if not this week, then next."

"I expect you're right, Sir," McCloud agreed, nodding his head. "The glass is surely rising." But Topper saw that he doubted his own words.

"It's good to see you, Mr. Topper," said Mr. Crackers tugging lightly on Topper's sleeve. "Do you enjoy married life, Sir?"

"I do immensely, Mr. Crackers. Immensely. I have married the best woman in the world, I have. Make no doubt about it."

"I am pleased to hear you say that, Sir, I am, and that's a fact." Mr. Crackers replied with as broad a smile as would sit on his narrow face. "Makes the world go round."

"That it does, Mr. Crackers," said Topper.

"Won't be long till flowers is out, Mr. Topper," said Mrs. Blake whose teeth mostly were.

"No, indeed. I look forward to it," Topper said with a smile. "The first pretty bouquet I buy, I reserve for my wife—as is proper. The second, however, I shall give to you."

"Oh, Mr. Topper," Mrs. Blake said, blushing. "Now don't waste your hard-earned money on the likes o' me. You just think of your pretty wife is all."

They asked him how Mr. Scrooge did, and he told them that their benefactor did quite well—as did the Cratchit boy according to the latest letter received.

"I will see this yellow door flung open and directly you shall all have your breakfasts," he said, jingling the keys in his outstretched hand. He waited patiently as the queue swayed to one side and out of his way.

Topper distinctly heard the growl of a stomach and lifted his brows in comic surprise.

"Them's bears in there," said Mr. Porks pointing to his sunken mid-section.

The line laughed.

"Lions, too, by the sound of it," Topper agreed. "But we shall tame them, Mr. Porks. We shall tame them—them and whatever else you have in your inner menagerie. Cook's vittles will make peaceable the wildest of beasts while leaving the stomach satisfyingly full and uplifting the soul of men, women and children alike. Victuals of this order are guaranteed to fill you with contentment and joy." He laughed merrily at the thought.

The keys jangled. A twist. The yellow door swung open. Topper shook his head as he pocketed the key. The locking mechanism had failed long ago. It wouldn't prevent a cat from entering so long as the cat could turn a door knob, but the residents of Yellow Door respected it as if it were the secure tumblers of the vaults at the Old Lady of Threadneedle Street.

The hungry flowed coursed round him like water round a rock.

Topper took a step toward the door and stumbled.

"Have a care, Sir," said a small voice.

Topper swivelled in a complete circle unable to determine its source. From the corner of his eye, however, he saw a huddled form at his feet—a legless boy as white as the snow surrounding him on a low cart. Topper, however, pretended not to see the boy.

"Who's there?" Topper said putting a hand to his brow and absurdly scanning the horizon. "Who calls to me? Oh, an invisible spirit! What do you wish to tell me? Is there a will which would grant your dear sister her due fortune, and you want me to discover where it has been hidden? Or perhaps you have been murdered, and you wish me to find your body so that you may rest in peace?"

The boy giggled and said, "You're having me on, Sir."

Topper looked down, leapt back and dug his fists theatrically into his hips. "What's this?" he sang as if he were in an opera.

The boy's small hands fluttered in applause. "You should be in the theatre, Sir," said he. Topper looked into the boy's face and was reminded of Revelation 1:14. *His head and hair were white like wool, as white as snow. His eyes like a flame of fire.* The boy was an albino. His long white hair gave him the appearance of great age—yet his skin was free of creases and wrinkles and his pink eyes glittered like stars. So white was he that he seemed to shine with a light of his own.

Topper said, "I do not believe audiences would long sit for any meagre entertainment I might provide, young master..?"

"My name is John Forest, though some call me Jack Frost," said the boy.

Topper reached down to shake the boy's icy hand. "I am Milton Topper," he said. "I am most pleased to make your acquaintance."

"And I am pleased to make yours," said Jack.

"Tell me, son, if I may ask," said Topper, "what has happened to your legs that you must propel yourself about on that cart of yours."

"These sad peepers of mine," said Jack pointing to his crossed eyes, "have never steered me right. I had an accident. Foolish of me, but I walked in front of a carriage and was run down near on a year and a half ago. Lucky, I was."

"Lucky?" said Topper who could see no luck in it.

Jack smiled up in his face. "Lucky I wasn't killed, Sir."

"Well, yes. There is that to be said," Topper agreed. "And now, as the weather grows increasingly hostile, let me ask you: Is there anything I can help you with?"

"Well, yes," Jack said, "I am in search of suitable employment, and I was wondering if you knew anything of this charity."

"I do," Topper replied with a swift smile.

"I was hoping that I could get a job cleaning up. I can wash dishes, sweep, haul rubbish."

Topper looked at him doubtfully.

"Don't let appearances fool you, Mr. Topper," Jack said. "I am quite strong of arm. You might be surprised at what I am capable of."

Topper said, "You have already impressed me as being a rather remarkable young man. I am, in fact, in need of someone—a young man of about your age—to act as my page. He might also run a few errands—generally help out in the day-to-day functions of the charity. He must have a noble bearing..." Topper suppressed a chuckle as he watched the boy puff up his chest, "...be responsible and tidy in appearance. To your knowledge is there such a young gentleman as that who might be interested in earning...? " and Topper named a liberal sum. "Someone whom you would personally recommend?"

"There is only one person fitting the requirements which you have set forth among all my acquaintances," Jack said.

"And who might that be?" Topper asked.

"Me," the boy said tapping a thumb at his own chest.

"You would do such a thing?" Topper said. "I thought you preferred scrubbing and washing up."

"I would be honoured to serve as your page—would even prefer it to washing up," Jack said giving Topper a kind of bow.

"I can think of no one whom I should prefer," Topper said, reached down and shook the boy's hand again. "Won't you go in and have yourself some tea? After which keep yourself inside and make yourself available should I ring. Can you do that, Jack?"

"Oh yes, Sir. Thank you, Sir," Jack said and cleared his throat:

"Being your slave, what should I do but tend
Upon the hours and times of your desire?
I have no precious time at all to spend,
Nor services to do, till you require.
Nor dare I chide the world-without-end hour,
Whilst I, my sovereign, watch the clock for you,
Nor think the bitterness of absence sour
when you have bid your servant once adieu:
Nor dare I question with my jealous thought
Where you may be, or your affairs suppose,
But, like a sad slavey, stay and think of nought,
Save, were you are how happy you make those.
       So true a fool is love that in your will,
       Though you do anything, he think no ill."

"Why, that's beautiful, Jack. It's Shakespeare, isn't it?" Topper said.

"Yes, Sir—*Sonnet Fifty-Seven*," Jack replied.

"However did you find the time to memorise it?"

"It was no trouble whatsoever. I never forget a thing once I hear it, Sir. So help me," Jack said.

"What an amazing boy," Topper said.

"Thank you, Sir."

"Where did you get such a memory?"

"I couldn't say, Sir. All I know is that it's all locked up right here. Etched in stone, you might say," he said tapping his forehead. "Every sound I've ever heard has become a permanent record to be recalled whenever I wish."

"How is it then that you know this poem?" Topper said.

"My father is carpenter at the Palladium where I've spent many, many hours backstage. The recitation I just gave is based on a performance by Richard Collins, Wednesday evening, August 23rd, two years, five months and five days ago.

"I was examining a bucket of nails at the time. I can't honestly say that I normally spend much time studying nails, but my father had just brought me my lens, you see." He pulled the instrument proudly from a velvet-lined drawer in his cart and held it up for Topper to examine.

"It is very fine, indeed," Topper said looking it over quickly. He handed it back. "Your father sees to your every need, doesn't he? He loves you very much."

Jack nodded. "My lens was brand new to me. I, as you may well guess, do not see very well. Light, natural light—out of doors especially—hurts my eyes. Stage lights can absolutely blind me, so I spend my time in the shadows, among the folds of the curtains in the corners of the backstage. When Father procured this lens for me, I could see small things well for the first time. It was a wonder. To pick out the tiny flecks of rust on a bucket of nails utterly absorbed me for hours. Even now I can turn each nail from that bucket over and over in my mind. Count the ones which are bent, which are straight."

"That's quite all right, Jack. There's no need to tally crooked nails just now. I've heard enough to be impressed by your memory for detail."

"'The Devil,' as they say, Sir, 'is in the details,'" the boy said.

"So many talents. Who would ever guess? What should happen, Jack, when your head tries to hold more memories than you've room for?"

"I shall just grow me another head," Jack said without hesitation.

Topper burst out in laughter. "Two heads are better than one, I've heard tell," he said. "Well now, young Sir, run along and warm yourself indoors."

Topper turned and looked up at the sky which rather than clearing had turned a deep purple and now mixed rain with snow. He would have stepped into the shelter of the door, but Cook stood blocking his way with her fat arms folded across her bosom.

"Mr. Topper," she said.

Topper knew her only as Florence. Whether this was her given name or her surname, he couldn't say. She was a round woman, rather low to the ground with fierce black eyebrows and white hair pulled back tight against her head.

"Yes, ma'am," he said. "Is there anything I can do for you?"

"There is, Mr. Topper-Sir," she said. "Do you have any idea how many mouths we've to feed in there?"

"I could tell you in round numbers if I had my papers with me. Why?" he said.

"It is more than a woman can handle alone," she said.

"Then we shall need to get you help," Topper said.

She blinked her eyes at him as if she could not believe her ears. "But, Sir?" she said.

"What is it, Florence?"

"It's just that I didn't think..."

"Think what?"

"I didn't think that Mr. Scrooge could...I mean I didn't think Yellow Door had the money to hire..."

"Nonsense, Florence," said Topper. "While we don't splurge, we won't do things by half measures either."

"No, Sir. Of course not."

Topper closed one eye pointedly and said, "You wouldn't happen to know of someone who might act as your assistant—a kitchen-maid or whatever it is you need inasmuch as this appears to be a day when I am hiring new staff?" Topper gripped himself against the elements which spattered his clothing with increasing intensity.

"Funny you should ask, Sir," she said and put two fingers to her mouth and produced a whistle that painfully vibrated the back of his head. A moment later a young woman, taller than Cook (which wasn't saying much), broad-hipped, short-wasted, narrow-shouldered with a head covered with a mat of unruly hair and a jovial face which presented the merriest expression Topper could ever remember seeing. Her smiling cheeks nearly closed her eyes.

"This is Mary-Martha White," Cook said, placing a hand on the girl's shoulder and shoving her forward. "My sister's girl. Curtsey, Mary-Martha," she hissed, and the girl awkwardly obeyed.

"I am pleased to meet you, Mary-Martha," Topper said, clutched his coat collar against the wind and bowed slightly.

"I am pleased to know you, Sir," she said.

"I shall watch her close, Sir," Cook said. "Her mind does wander, but she's a strong back and a good temper—I can vouch for that. I'll keep her at her work. I knows I will—otherwise it's mine to do."

"Yes, well. I won't have her mistreated—but I know you'll handle her kindly. If I might make my way inside...?" Topper nodded toward the door.

"We've no time to stand about gossiping," Cook said, and gave Mary-Martha a gentle shove in. "We've got work to do." She spun on her heel and stomped inside.

But before Topper could pass through the doorway, he felt a light tap on his shoulder. He turned and found himself looking up at the tallest woman he had ever seen. She was fully two heads taller than he and wore a grey cloak with the hood pulled up over her head and down upon her brow. Her face was long with a straight nose, dark eyebrows and pale eyes which she held wide like a Grecian statue. Her expression though not unattractive was one of utter seriousness.

She pointed a long finger at him for a dozen heartbeats as if to accuse him of a crime, but instead she said in a rich contralto voice:

"Respice, adspice, prospice."

"I beg your pardon, Miss," said Topper, "but I don't understand your tongue."

"Sie heissen nicht Herr Scrooge."

"Something about Mr. Scrooge, yes? German, I should think, but I am afraid I only speak English, Miss," Topper said.

She opened her mouth again and a different string of sounds with a more familiar rhythm and cadence issued forth.

"You speak French, do you?" he said. Although he recognised the language from its sound, he couldn't understand a word of it.

The tall woman spoke a fourth time and raised one long arm slowly over her head as if she were a colossal statue. A fifth time, a sixth. Every new phrase she produced in a different tongue: Italian, Spanish, Portuguese, Russian—and other languages which Topper could not identify.

At last she finished. Both her arms hung calmly at her sides, lost in the loose folds of her cloak.

Topper applauded softly. "Bravo!" he said. "Very good. Very good, indeed. You are quite the talented linguist. And I should be very much surprised if the English language weren't listed among your accomplishments. I ask you then confident that I will be understood: how may I help you?"

"It is not I who am in need of help," she said in perfectly unaccented English.

"Indeed," said Topper, "and who then is?"

"You."

Topper struggled for a reply. "I beg your pardon," he said. "I don't believe that I heard you properly." The wind whipped around his head and deposited a spoonful of snow down his neck. He clasped his hand to his collar and waved the other to the door. "Will you not step inside out of the weather where we might hold a more comfortable discussion?"

"Of course," the woman said. "How rude of me. I do apologise." She nodded gravely, ducked her head and stepped through the door.

Topper closed the door softly behind. "You have quite a gift for languages, Miss....?"

"You may call me Miss Trellis, Miss Elizabeth Trellis," she said and widened her pale eyes. Topper found that he could not look directly into them long.

"I am delighted to meet you, Miss Trellis," Topper said bowing slightly. "My name is Milton Topper."

"So I understand," she said. "You are not Mr. Ebenezer Scrooge."

"No, I am not that beneficent gentleman, but merely his humble servant."

"Yes," the young woman said as if that were a detail that she understood but gave little importance to. Then she added: "Of course, he would have need of assistants to carry out his good works."

"That is my mission, Miss Trellis," Topper said, unbuttoning his coat. The air just inside the door was not perceptibly warmer than the air outside. Topper tested this by carefully exhaling and watched his steamy breath curl to the ceiling. The interior air did have one delicious quality which the air outside did not share: the smell of kippers, bacon, sausage, eggs, mushrooms and (a rare treat!) devilled kidneys. No gruel for this lot. Not from the larder of Ebenezer Scrooge!

Miss Trellis gripped his arm with a terrible strength and drew him to a corner. Topper blushed furiously, but did not twist away. She leaned down until her lips nearly touched his ear. Topper fidgeted as she sucked in her breath, then said in a hushed voice, "There are people lurking about here to-day, Mr. Topper. Watching you. Watching the movements of everyone here. Please have a care."

Topper gave her a nervous laugh. "Bonapartists I make no doubt. Those who would resurrect their emperor and export his revolution to the good lands of Britain."

"You mock me, Sir," she said, her voice startlingly low. She released his arm, stood upright and frowned.

"I mean you no insult, Miss Trellis. You will understand that it is only that I find it difficult to take your suggestion seriously. There is no evidence.

There is no reason why we should draw the attention of anyone but the needy."

"The League of the One-Eyed Demon," she said wagging a finger the size of a Bow Street truncheon in his face, "would know your secrets."

Topper withdrew from her carefully and stood tall—though he could only have matched her height had he stood on a chair. He spoke to her in a clear voice. "We have no secrets here, Miss Trellis. Anyone may come in or watch us, stare at us—if they have a mind to—secretly or in full view. We have nothing to hide," Topper said then quickly added: "Which is not to say we do not appreciate your diligence or concern for our well-being." And he handed her a coin.

"I'm no dog," she said. "I do not do tricks for sugar lumps."

"My dear lady, I did not wish to imply..."

She drew her grey cloak more tightly about her and let the coin drop to the floor with a clunk.

"I have misunderstood you then, Miss Trellis. And I do apologise." Topper bent to pick up the coin.

She blinked her eyes as if about to cast a curse upon him, but instead turned on heel and strode toward the door.

"Wait!" he cried. "One moment. Please."

She stopped and turned toward him, her face betraying no emotion.

"I mean to ask you, Miss, are you currently employed?" he asked.

She paused a moment as if she were considering the consequence of saying too much. "I am not currently employed, no."

"Capital! How lucky for us. Then I will tell you that Mr. Scrooge has granted me the right to hire help as I see fit and have need. We here at the charity often receive guests who speak languages we have no means of understanding. We have need of a talented linguist such as yourself. If you are not otherwise engaged, I would like to employ you should you find the terms of employment acceptable." And he described them to her.

From the look on her face he was convinced that in spite of the generous nature of his offer she would refuse. She did not.

"Mr. Topper, I accept your proposal, and I shall report here for work to-morrow, Sir. Till then..." she curtsied with surprising grace and walked out the door in a very business-like manner.

No sooner did the yellow door close than it flew open again and a young man dashed into the building as if shot from a cannon. Topper stepped aside to remove himself as an obstacle, but the boy had the identical notion. The collision left the boy sprawled upon the floor as injury-free as only the young can after such an impact. Topper sat down next to him with a grunt, the wind knocked out of him.

"What manner of demons give you chase, Patrick Coal?" Topper said, pressing his abdomen. "I believe they've passed you by and instead have taken their wickedness out upon me."

Patrick smiled elfishly. "Beg pardon, Guv," he said. "Is it too late for breakfast?"

"I opened the door not ten minutes since. If you're not too selective about what you eat, there are likely left-over slops."

Patrick's face turned the colour of ash.

"Do not take me seriously, boy." Topper said. "There are always victuals at Yellow Door for young men who enter the building like gentlemen."

"I suppose I deserved that," the boy said. He stood to his feet and brushed the seat of his britches.

"I suppose you do," Topper replied. "Give us a hand," he said. "I am ill-used to being run down and the wind knocked out of me. And it must be said that I am not so young as I once was." The boy helped Topper pick himself up from the floor.

Patrick lifted a penny-whistle to his lips. "I shall earn my redemption and forgiveness with this selection from Mozart's Cantata in E minor—no need to pay for this one, Sir. It's on me."

This was a misdirection inasmuch as he instead played "Rinse M'Mouth in Gin."

However, Patrick did not merely play the penny-whistle. Patrick sang, sighed, hooted, groaned through the instrument creating a variety of effects counter-point to the melody. He drummed his chest, slapped his thigh, waved his hat, shook and swayed his body in rhythm to the music as though the Devil himself tickled his Soul from the inside.

He finished to Topper's polite applause.

"Here, Mr. Topper. If I may have a moment more of your time, listen to this." He played a slow, thoughtful piece. Sad and beautiful it was all at once. It reminded Topper of the sky at dawn just as he had experienced it that very morning.

"It's lovely. What is it called?"

"Hain't got a name yet."

"Do not tell me it is of your own creation?" Topper said in astonishment.

"I do tell you, Sir. It is only one of many."

"You have a marvellous talent, young man. I do hope you realise that."

Patrick grinned.

"It is such a lovely melody. Perhaps if you were to write it down, you could have it published."

"Write it down?"

"Yes. That's what I said. Some people make a good living writing songs, you know. Popular tunes. Like 'Rinse M'Mouth in Gin.' Somebody wrote that and got paid for the effort."

"But you can't write down music," Patrick insisted. "Not this music."

"Oh, indeed, you can. You can write music just as you might write down words." Topper paused. He wasn't certain of the extent of Patrick's literacy skills. "Music notes on paper look like black goose eggs with flag-poles and waving banners. There are whole notes, half, quarter, eighth,—and faster notes like sixteenths and thirty-seconds." Topper traced a few in the air by way of example. "Sharps—flats! Keys major and minor. Modes! There are treble and bass clefs and staff lines: Every Good Boy Deserves Favour, and it is indeed a fine boy who deserves favour when he studies his music. You may not believe it to look at me now, but I took violin lessons myself when I was a young man." He tucked an imaginary instrument under his chin, bowed viciously, laughed, then looked down at his hands and shook his head. "That such thick fingers could have ever teased music from a fiddle— hard to believe. Yes, Mr. Coal, music can be written. Music is written down by masters, their students and common folk every day of the year."

"Not this music, Mr. Topper. No, Sir," Patrick said. "This music comes from my feelings, from my heart. The notes might be different to-morrow, but the feeling would be the same—or perhaps finer still. Or the notes will be the same, but the feeling will have changed. You can't write that down on paper. Not with all the ink in London."

Topper rubbed his index finger under his nose with thought. "Perhaps you are right. Still, it cannot hurt to improve one's understanding of the elements of music, can it?"

"Could this be written with a quill?" Patrick said and pressed a dented mouth organ to his lips. He tapped his foot, shook his body, hummed and blew all at once. To finish he threw the instrument into the air and caught it in the oversized patch-pocket of his coat. "Tell me what notation would record all that."

"None, I should think," Topper admitted. "That was, indeed, quite a performance." He tossed the lad the coin Miss Trellis refused.

"Many thanks to you, Sir," Patrick shouted and bolted out of Yellow Door.

"But what about your breakfast?" Topper shouted after him. How could the boy forget his stomach so easily? Topper moved toward the door to watch him run. As he did so he felt a hand grab him roughly by the upper sleeve of his coat. *Oh, now what!* Topper spun round surprised to see a handsome black man dressed in bright blue flowing robes.

"What can I do for you, my good man?" Topper demanded in the way that a normally patient man does when he is stretched to his limits.

The Black Man mutely handed Topper a sheet of paper which had been rolled like a scroll. A scrap of string held it closed. The outside was smudged, the corners dog-eared. The man gestured for Topper to open it.

Topper did so wondering if this were one of the men whom Miss Trellis had warned him of. He was stunned to see a finely drawn picture of Christ on the Cross. "Where did you get this?" he said.

The man shook his head and lifted an up-turned palm to indicate that he didn't understand.

Guessing that the man was offering the sheet for sale Topper reached into his pocket and withdrew several coins and held them out for the fellow.

The Black Man folded Topper's hand closed and pushed it away, shaking his head violently. With the white palms of his hands he sketched a large rectangle in the air with sweeping gestures, softly speaking words of a language which was entirely foreign to Topper's ear. There was passion in those phrases, Topper could tell, but he could not glean any meaning.

Topper reached a second time into his pocket and added several more coins to those in his hand thinking that the man wanted a higher price.

Again the Black closed Topper's hand and pushed it away. A second time he drew a fierce rectangle in the air large enough to be a door. He repeated the same phrase over and over.

Patrick Coal bolted back through the door with a hot bun in his hand. He drew up sharply when he saw the black man.

"Oh, there you are, Patrick," Topper said to the young boy. "I have need of you just now. If you hurry you'll see a rather tall woman not far from here. She can't be more than a block away. She wears a long, grey hooded-cloak. Bless you, she will not be hard to spot. Run along like a good fellow, and see if you can catch her up. If you can, send her my compliments and please tell her that Mr. Topper of the charity sends for her and has immediate need of her talents. Do you understand me?"

"Yes, Sir. What shall I do if I cannot find her?"

"If after half an hour's search you do not find her," Topper said tossing him a coin, "return here, and I shall have another coin for you. You can fill your other cheek with a bun to the match the one you've already tucked away—you squirrel."

"Right, Guv," Patrick said. "Any idea which way she might have gone?"

"None whatsoever. That's why I've hired you to find her," Topper pointed his finger at the boy and smiled.

"Me mates may know where she's gone," he said and slipped out the door.

Topper twisted the ring on his finger impatiently, and said to himself, "I do wish Miss Trellis would return. This is just the kind of thing we need her for."

Hardly had the words left his mouth when Miss Trellis opened the door and walked through, head held high. "You wish to see me?" she said casting an incurious eye at the black man.

"Patrick found you quickly enough, I must say. There's a bright young man for you. Yes, Miss Trellis—this fellow wants something, and for the life of me I cannot make out what it is. It is my hope that you will understand him and tell me what he wants and what if anything I can do for him."

"I shall be happy to try my best, Mr Topper," she answered.

There was a lengthy exchange between the two in a smattering of languages of which Topper recognised the tone and cadence of but a very few. Finally courtesies were exchanged in a language in which they had found common ground.

"He speaks Arabic, as you may have already guessed—actually Berber. He also speaks Portuguese passably well—learned from sailors, I should judge by his choice of words." She paused and briskly began asking him questions.

"His name is Al-Mustafa Ali," she said. "He says that he has the blood of many people in his veins: Berber, Arab, Ethiopian, French. He says that he once was one of the Blue People, but he says now he is a Christian. He asks, 'Do you know Christ died for your sins?'"

"Tell him that Britain is a Christian nation, that all men and women here well know of the Saviour."

She translated this message. The Black bobbed his head soberly. He slowly replied while Miss Trellis translated, "He says that he is from Morocco where there are too few Christians—except those in chains—that he is glad to be in a Christian land and is very pleased to meet you."

Topper said, "Ask him to explain what it was he was trying to tell me earlier of the drawing. Do you see it there in his hand?"

There ensued a long exchange in which Miss Trellis asked for many points of clarification. When she believed she had the story correct she explained:

"This will take some telling," Miss Trellis said, slowly. "He says that he grew up in Tangiers practising his trade as a carpenter—like nearly all

Moroccans he was a devotee of Islam. He worked for a wealthy merchant who traded between Europe and Africa. Generally the trade was limited to textiles, brass pitchers, platters and occasionally foodstuffs, but one day a shipment of Italian Art treasures—statues and paintings—bound for Spain found their way to the storehouse where Al-Mustafa worked. A rough sea voyage had damaged some of the packing crates, and Al-Mustafa was asked to replace or repair them.

"Al-Mustafa had never seen a painting nor a statue before in his entire life. He says that the human image is forbidden to the followers of the Islamic faith. There is much clever decorating with coloured bits of tile, but nothing like what was stored in the crates. When he first saw them he was awe-struck—he could not conceive that such things could be the product of human hands. They seemed flat and round, real and not real all at the same time. The paintings were mostly of landskips. He also recalls seeing a few portraits. None of these were much larger than the window of a house.

"Lastly, he set to repair a very large crate which held a painting of the Crucifixion. He removed the painting from its damaged crate and carefully set it aside to see if the painting had been in any way injured. He says that upon viewing it he immediately fell to his knees—for Christ had touched him. When he saw this painting his life was changed forever. He knew Christ's Agony, understood His pain, His suffering for those who were meek. He knew that he must find out more about this Jesus Christ, and more about the Art of making such paintings out of the oil paint. From that moment on he was a Christian though he admits that his understanding of his new religion is very shallow.

"There were not many in Morocco who could teach him about Christ, so he considered the prospects of leaving his home and travelling to a Christian nation. To this end he hired on a Portuguese merchant ship as a carpenter. He sailed to many ports—saw many new lands, but still searches for someone who can teach him to paint the Agony of Jesus. He wants very much to be able to make paintings such as the ones he examined in Tangiers. That is why he is here in London. To seek out our greatest painters and learn from them."

Topper said, "Although I do not run in those circles, I am given to understand that our great painters are some of the finest landskip painters in the world, but I'm not terribly knowledgeable about such things."

Miss Trellis interpreted Topper's comment and the Black's reply. "Al-Mustafa says that he has little interest in landskips. He says he wishes only to paint Christ in his agony."

"Tell him that although we are a Christian nation we prefer not to dwell on Christ's suffering. That is the difference between us and the Papists. He had probably been better off travelling to Italy to study among her masters."

Miss Trellis spent some minutes clarifying this message and responding to Al-Mustafa's many questions.

At last she said, "Al-Mustafa begs your pardon and apologises for wasting your time. He hopes that his ignorance does not offend you so very much. He says he will take his leave now."

"No, never. It was not my intention to make him feel unwelcome. That is what the charity is all about: making everyone feel welcome. Tell him, that although we do not paint crucifixions here, we have many fine painters from whom he might learn the craft. I am not sure if I can help him or no. The charity can supply food, clothing, shelter, but instruction in Art? That may stretch us beyond our abilities. Yet I will not say no without giving it a try. The Charity is not just Mr. Scrooge and myself. It is also the people we serve. Perhaps someone among us can help us make a connection. In the meanwhile, he will need a place to stay and something to eat."

In took several minutes for Miss Trellis to convey Topper's message. She clasped her hands before her and said, "He understands."

"Excellent. That will be all, Miss Trellis. I am grateful that you were able to come on such short notice."

Miss Trellis pulled the grey hood of her cloak over her dark hair without saying a word. She turned deliberately and glided slowly out the yellow door. Scarcely had her skirts crossed the door-sill than Patrick Coal burst in.

He pulled off his hat and held it apologetically in his hand. "I gave it my best, Sir, but I couldn't find her. I asked round, but no one's seen anything like her. No one like you described, tall and all."

"But Patrick," said Topper, "you just missed her. She walked out the door not a half-dozen heartbeats before you just came in. You would have had to pass her directly by on your way. Tell me you didn't see a tall woman so high." He held his hand over his head.

Patrick shook his head.

"Long, grey cloak?"

"Not that I saw."

"Well, I have it then," Topper said smacking his fist against his palm. "She's actually two midgets—one standing on the shoulders of the other and draped in a long garb."

Patrick said, "Mr. Topper, have you had your breakfast yet? A bit of indigestion might cause you to see things which ain't there."

"I shouldn't think so. Miss Trellis was real enough and will return to-morrow so that you may see her yourself with your very own eyes. Bless me. If I don't hurry, I'll miss my morning visit to the breakfasting, and that simply will not do. Care to join me?"

"Na-o, I've got me own 'pointments, Sir. A man's got 'is business to attend to. We can't all of us spend the day larking about."

"I am delighted to see you take such an industrious attitude," said Topper. "You must have eaten quite a number of buns to put you off your breakfast, though. I'll bet within the hour you'll have changed your mind. 'Hollow leg' as my mother used to call it. Howsomever, I must be on my way, and I shall see you later."

He strode down a corridor and up a short climb of three steps. As he grew closer the murmur of the happy assembly grew in his ears. His nose twitched at the tantalising breakfast aromas. He would not breakfast a second time, but he was sore tempted.

Topper stepped quietly into the dining area. He did not wish to disrupt their meals, nor draw attention to himself. He closed his eyes. He listened. The squeak of a chair backed away from the table. The clatter of a fork or a spoon or a knife on a plate. The clink of a water glass. The thump of a mug replaced on a table top. The aggregation of satisfied conversation and companionable tones—as soothing as the babble of a brook. Topper could not make out a single word, yet he knew there was peace here. This was civilisation at its highest. This was the mission that Scrooge had already fulfilled. There were greater goods, but this was a success which gave Topper intense satisfaction.

He turned and nearly broke his neck.

"Sir, have a care," said a small high voice from the floor.

Topper looked down.

"Twice in one day?" he said. "I do beg your pardon, Mr. Jack. I must make it a habit to watch where I'm going, mustn't I?" Topper said. "It doesn't do to walk about with one's eyes shut. I am such a fool. Have I injured you with my clumsy feet?"

"Not at all, Sir. I'm as right as rain."

At some point since they had last spoken, the boy found an old wig which he awkwardly draped over his head. Topper thought that in spite of any future attention, care and powder that Jack might give it, it would never match the whiteness of his natural hair.

"I've knocked your wig askew as well," Topper said, clucking in disgust at himself.

"I shall have to have Father add me a flag pole to my cart six feet high and fly the Union Jack from it," the boy said, rather seriously. He placed a hand on the top of his head and gave his wig a twist with as much dignity as he could muster.

Topper said, "That just might be enough to keep you safe from the stomping boots of Milton Topper."

"Yes, Sir. Before I forget: there's someone to see you, Sir," Jack said. "He sits in the waiting room."

"What sort of fellow is he?" Topper asked.

"I expect that he is a man of the cloth, Sir—an American from the sound of him," Jack said, his eyes shaking in the low light. "He murmurs verse beneath his breath."

"Very well. I shall see him directly—in my office (you do know where it is, yes? Good!) after I've been able to make my way there."

CHAPTER 4

༄

Gyrations

Topper eased himself into his chair as if his back hurt him — which it did after his collision with Patrick Coal. His eyes scanned the papers on his desk top. Receipts stacked neatly in one pile. Letters of correspondence in another. Bills which required his attention filled this slot. Appeals for grants and donations in the next. He set each stack square to the edge of the desk as was his habit, drew his appointment book forward and ran his finger down it until he found the list of this day's duties. There was nothing on it which couldn't be delayed a short while for an American visitor.

Topper listened to the sound of Jack's cart rolling down the corridor followed by soft footsteps. A rap at the door.

"Come in," Topper said.

The door opened, and Jack scooted in holding his head high. "Reverend Salvation Mitchell here to see you, Sir," he said gesturing toward the empty doorway.

"Very good, Mr. Forest," Topper replied, craning his neck as if somehow the visitor who was not present might be seen.

"Thank you, Sir," Jack said and after backing out of the room, gestured toward the unseen visitor.

Reverend Salvation Mitchell, a bulbous man with flapping jowls and pipe-stem arms and legs, charged into the room as if he were making a comic stage entrance. In height he was a mere imp of a man, hardly taller than a stripling. His cheeks flushed a delicate rose, his black hair glistened against his scalp, bags puckered beneath wide-set eyes. He danced like a man in his cups.

"I am the Volcano of HIM-HIM!" said the man in a frog-like voice which grated against back of Topper's head. The man vaulted himself to the tips of his toes like a ballerina and laughed as if he were about to tell an anecdote which he found too funny to deliver. His body shook. He quivered in the Ecstasy of Spirit.

Topper stood, walked round his desk and extended a hand in the gentleman's direction. He said, "I am Milton Topper. Mr. Scrooge's personal assistant. To what do I owe the pleasure of your visit, Sir?"

The Reverend stopped his agitation and looked suspiciously at Topper's hand. Rather than shake it, he bowed low from the waist.

"That is an unusual ring you have there, Friend," said he as he stood erect. "I don't believe I've seen anything like it. But then I've not seen much of the world outside my home. I am from the United States, you know."

"You have an interest in jewellery?" said Topper.

"None, Friend. None at all, but I recognise fine craftsmanship when I see it. Did you buy it hereabouts?"

"It was a gift," Topper said, and twisted the ring several times.

Then, as if this bit of conversation had never happened, the Reverend set about his gyrations once more.

"This day is perfect! Perfect!" said he. "How happy I am. I am!" The Reverend pranced about and pumped his arms as if he meant to fly.

Topper clasped his hands, cleared his throat and repeated. "To what do I owe the pleasure of your visit?"

The Reverend Mitchell inhibited his gyrations sufficiently to look Topper full in the eye. "Mr. Scrooge-Mr. Scrooge, have you seen it? Glory awaits us and the greater Glory of HIM!" The Reverend Mitchell pulled his lips into a tight smile all the while marching in place to an unheard beat. The veins in his neck bulged. His eyebrows were raised as if he were waiting for some signal from Topper.

"I am afraid, Sir, that there is some misunderstanding," Topper said. "I am not, as I have said, Ebenezer Scrooge."

"Would you be Marley, then?" he said.

"I would not. My name is Milton Topper. I am Mr. Scrooge's personal assistant. Mr. Scrooge is away at the moment. How may I help you?"

"Is there anything finer than Christian Charity, I ask, Friend?" said Mitchell.

"Charity is the finest of men's deeds," Topper said.

"When our people lack jobs, when our people suffer disease and ignorance, it is HIS test of their faith, would you not agree, Friend?"

It is a test of our society's failure to care for its own, Topper thought, but he said nothing of this. He returned only a blank look.

"Do you not see HIS mark everywhere?" Mitchell said.

"The world is not perfect, Sir, but the potential for goodness is at the heart of every man," Topper said. "We may rise to the level of angels or sink to the depths of Hell. We each of us are given choices."

"This is HIS challenge to us. We live in an imperfect world, Friend, and we must look carefully to determine HIS desires."

"We must work to make this a better world," Topper said. "That is the work of men."

"We are all instruments of HIM," Mitchell insisted.

Topper sighed. "What can I do for you, Reverend? Neither of us has the time to exchange aphorisms."

"No one is more aware of that than me, Friend." Mitchell slapped his hand on the top of Topper's desk. "I am here to help you," Mitchell said simply.

"You wish to make a donation?" Topper said, knowing full well that he did not.

"No-no-no-no-no," Mitchell said waving his hands. "I am here to offer my services."

"And what services might those be?" Topper said, his stomach sinking.

"Only this, Friend," Mitchell said with a cry and resumed his gyrations. "I wish to minister to the spiritually bereft of this fine charity. To prepare their souls for Him and their Reward of the Hereafter."

Topper paused, then said. "Can I offer you a seat, so that you might explain yourself at your ease?"

"Glory be to HIM. I cannot sit!" Mitchell said now bouncing on the balls of his feet.

"You test my patience, Sir. I believe it is time that you were shown the door," Topper said and made to leave the room. Mitchell stopped as if someone had dowsed his boiler.

"Let us talk, Friend," the Reverend said solemnly, and for the first time since he entered the room stood perfectly still. Topper nodded and pulled two chairs together.

Mitchell began, "Word has reached me that you are providing food, clothing and other necessities for the worthy poor."

"We do what we can for any unfortunate person who finds his or her way to us," Topper said. "Food, clothing and shelter may only be the beginning."

"Any person, do you say, Friend?" Mitchell said, pulling his chin thoughtfully.

Topper nodded. "The charity makes distinctions of neither class nor race among those it serves, although I will admit that we have had neither a Duke, a Count nor a Lord apply to us for help."

"You have a sense of humour about you, Friend. You do, indeed. You remind me of my daddy. A man of a fine sense of humour. A FINE sense of humour—rest his soul. No, I would imagine you don't have too many royal bloods to wait upon," Mitchell said. "Your resources are plentiful?"

"Our resources are modest compared to the need, I will not deny," Topper said. "We make do."

"Exactly, Friend, exactly," Mitchell nodded as if that was the answer he had been expecting. "You cannot feed every man, woman and child in London."

"Nor even every man, woman and child for three square miles. Not for any length of time, at any rate," Topper said.

"Then how do you decide who to feed and who to turn away?" Mitchell blinked his frog-like eyes. "Though far be it from me to tell you your business, of course. I'm just asking since I am interested in such things myself."

"We make no such decision," Topper said. "We feed all who apply."

"This is a Christian nation, Friend," Mitchell said.

"I said so myself not half an hour since."

The Reverend rubbed his forehead as if so rubbing cleared his mind. "Then charity must be reserved for those who have accepted Him as their saviour. Otherwise you are feeding souls who will one day be damned."

Topper felt his face hardening.

"I saw a Negro as I entered the building," Mitchell said. "Now I know a lot about Negroes as we have more than our share back at home. The United States are full of them. What was he doing here? Do you keep slaves?"

"He is from Morocco—and no he is not a slave. In Britain men are not made slaves because of the colour of their skin, nor for any other reasons, as they are in *some* countries."

"In the Miskatonic Valley in Massachusetts where I am from, we don't keep slaves either, though it must be admitted they are little more than innocent beasts. It is, however, a custom of our Southron brothers. They will not give up their peculiar institution in spite of all the blather they are given by the abolitionists. I too am opposed to slavery, but I cannot help but feel that the Negro benefits under the care of the white man. Why, they can scarcely clothe or feed themselves in their natural state. They can neither read nor write and think of anything but copulation—if you will excuse my saying so."

Topper closed his eyes angrily. "We in this country find the black men we meet as intelligent as men of any other race. White men raised as animals and treated no better might resemble your description of the slaves in the United States."

"P'raps so, p'raps so," Reverend Mitchell said. "But this one was from Africa do you say? Is he a heathen?"

"In fact, he is a Christian though he was born a Mussulman. He has converted."

"Then he deserves your kindness," the Reverend Mitchell said. "What does he do here?"

"He would receive our kindnesses," Topper said, sharply, "whether he were Christian, Jew, Buddhist, Hindu or Mussulman. The most Christian act I can imagine is to offer kindness to those in need who are not Christians."

"In a perfect world perhaps," Mitchell said, "with infinite resources—but our world is not perfect nor are your resources limitless."

"We make do."

"Mr. Topper, I have been sent here by HIM to convert unbelievers into the Faithful and to give sinners a chance at Redemption. Redemption, Sir —do you realise how important our Redemption is to Him? These are the services I offer. These are the services which you do not provide."

"We have no need here for your services, Reverend," Topper said.

"Is that your decision to make?" Mitchell asked.

Topper looked down. "No, I admit, it is not."

"Then I suggest that you perform your duty as *personal assistant* to Mr. Scrooge and take my offer to him. If he refuses..." Mitchell shrugged. "But I do not believe he will. He understands the value of spirituality. I promised my dear mother, Elizabeth Whately Mitchell, that I would spare no effort to bring every soul I can into His Flock, and I aim to keep that promise, Friend, I do."

"As you wish, but as I have said, Mr. Scrooge is absent at the moment. I am in charge in his stead." Topper said, stiffly. "Now if you will excuse me, I have other responsibilities to care for."

CHAPTER 5

லூ

Where is the Lively Gentleman?

THE WINDOW TO THE SITTING ROOM WAS RAISED JUST A LITTLE, BUT Scrooge found the cool air too much. He walked over to it, peered at the figures hurrying about on the quiet street below, and pushed it closed. The first day of Spring! He thrilled with the sense of renewal it brought him; it was a symbol of his own re-birth.

Scrooge slept well, had a good wash upon rising and would be ready to face the accumulated papers of his absence after a little breakfast. He took his seat at the table and his tea with a little buttered bread. When finished he wiped his hands and mouth on a linen napkin, flicked crumbs from his lap and pushed away from the table with a deep sense of satisfaction.

He let his eyes wander to his roll-top. The desk had seen hard use, but now it exuded feminine perfumes from bundles of letters written by women whom he had never met. Williams, who kept the house while Scrooge was away, had bundled them up and left them as a kind of sachet. Scrooge read only a few, but even so blushed violently at their provocative proposals.

He laughed at the thought that any woman should claim to love him. They could love his *money*, but they would never love *him*. Not that all members of the fair sex were uniformly rapacious, but he would never fool himself on that point. No. What few physical attractions he might have possessed as a young man had long since withered away. He had never been particularly handsome—more bone than meat—and age had done nothing to improve his appeal. His youth was long gone. Squandered. Lost. Opportunities of that sort were only offered to those with a blush to their cheeks and a thick head of hair. He had nothing to offer any good woman, and the thought made his heart heavy.

There had been a woman who had cared for him, of course. Cared deeply. Belle. Once. He was a different man then, another Ebenezer Scrooge—a tousle-headed youth with his whole life before him. That was so very long ago. Yet he could remember their time together with astonishing clarity. The way the wind rattled the branches of the Downy Birch as they took their long walks in Winter. The fading colours of the sun at day's end as they huddled together arm in arm, heads touching. The smell—no, the feel of the air. Cold. Clarifying. Their dreams—one together, inseparable.

He could hold the memory of it in his mind like he could hold a breath of air in his lungs. Those memories were precious. Nothing had greater value to him. Nothing he owned or could ever own would equal the memories of their time together.

"I wonder how she does," Scrooge said to himself in a hoarse whisper—a thought which he had pushed aside for decades.

Certainly she had married, but the thought pained Scrooge. He could not doubt that she had married well and was a mother, a very good mother, and perhaps by this time, a grey-haired grandmother with a round face and a half-dozen grandchildren to spoil.

No. Impossible! Belle would be forever young. He could imagine nothing else, could accept nothing else. Those wide, shining eyes. Her hair dark. Her lips full with a special smile which no other mouth could imitate.

Somewhere in time, in the past, he and Belle were together. Still very much in love. Whatever else there was left to him, Scrooge had this, and it would be enough.

But it was not enough and never could be. Of all the mistakes Scrooge had ever made, this stung him the most. *How in God's name could I have been so blind, so completely foolish?* She was ready to devote her life to him, whereas he dedicated his attention and energy only to business.

Business.

And what had business got him but loneliness? But grief? But bitterness?

Money had gotten Scrooge none of the things money could buy. Not happiness. Not security. Not well-being. Not Love. He only hoped he had money enough to pay for his sins.

The Spirits had opened Scrooge's heart to the Joy of Christmas, but in so doing they had also opened his heart to a larger set of emotions which he had steeled himself against for so long. Remorse. Regret. Previously his soul had been a hardened thing, a fortress against sorrow, proof against pain. No longer. In frustration Scrooge's eyes watered, his breathing quickened, and his appetite for all things faded.

But then—softly—*No, no*, he thought to himself. *I have been given a second chance, and I shall not let my past sins get the better of me. I am a new man capable of great good. There is Tim, there is my charity to prove it.*

Scrooge's heart grew calmer and something like peace (or perhaps only weariness) spread throughout his mind and body. Though he had been awake for only a short time, he found that he grew drowsy, and he willingly succumbed to sleep.

The clock hands moved the measure of quarter of an hour. Another. And another.

The timepiece chimed one o'clock.

A soft knock on the door. "Mr. Scrooge?"

Ebenezer Scrooge snapped awake, sat forward, and rubbed his face stupidly.

"Mr. Scrooge? Mr. Topper to see you, Sir." It was Williams, his man-servant.

Scrooge again rubbed his face hoping to wipe away the stale miasma which had permeated his mind and body.

Williams drew back from the door and Topper entered with his hat in his hand and a polite smile on his face. "Good day, Sir," he said.

"Oh, there you are, Milton." Scrooge sat forward as if he had been ruminating upon some abstruse puzzle. "Please come in. What will you have? Some tea? Coffee? Brandy?" Scrooge's eyes fell on the time-piece. "Is it so late already?"

"Nothing, thank you, Mr. Scrooge," Topper replied. "I hope your return voyage was a pleasant one and that the boy does well. I have read your letters of his treatment with great interest."

"Thank you, Milton. Yes, the trip was uneventful and might even be called relaxing as we were able to travel mostly over land. Berlin is not my idea of a city. It is certainly no London. I am happy to report that Professor Friedrich's ministrations have procured a positive effect on the boy. He walks now without a crutch, though he still does not have his natural strength back quite yet. He will. Give him time."

"That certainly is good news." Topper noted Scrooge's sleepy eyes. "I understand that travelling produces a strain. Our appointment was for one o'clock this afternoon, but if this is inconvenient for you, I can return at another time. I have no particularly pressing business to share which won't wait until you have recovered yourself."

"Heavens, no. I was expecting you. Of course, I was. I must have my report, you know. What news have you, Milton? What news?" he asked rubbing his hands together eagerly. "How does my charity do? Do we serve my people well? How does the construction go?" Then his expression changed and his good humour slipped. "Mr. Topper, you know my mind. I want this thing to be done right. It is very important to me, and I cannot help but bear in mind the message of the spirits: I will be judged by Christmas next and the success or failure of my charity will doubtless be one aspect of that judgement. I have seen a tombstone with my name upon it, Sir, and I will confess to you that it frightens and drives me like nothing else."

"But as a Christian, Sir," Topper said, "you cannot fear death."

"It is not death that I fear, but wandering the Earth forever afterward as a lost soul as is the fate of my former partner Marley. His wail was the most pitiful thing I've ever heard, I do assure you."

"Yes, Sir. No doubt. I am with my whole heart aware of your feelings and requirements on this subject," Topper said. "I assure you they occupy my every waking moment for I have no wish to fail you, Sir, nor the people who depend upon your charity for their lives. I give you my pledge that by June 21 your charity will be in such a state of operation that it is worthy of your name, and you may proudly take that reputation with you to your ever-lasting peace—when that remote time arrives—which is no time soon, I pray. We are slowly but steadily making improvements to the best of our ability in all ways to the property and organisation and to the lives of our people. To rest your mind on this matter—you will, of course, pay us a visit. I will then be happy to show you the progress we have made thus far."

"Unfortunately I will be unable to do that," Scrooge said. "You must surprise me when the day comes."

Topper blinked his eyes. "Why will you not come, Sir?" he said. "It would be an inspiration to the others. It would show that you take an interest in our endeavours. You may wish to make some small changes in the managements and arrangements I have instituted."

Scrooge did not immediately reply. At length he said, "I have made the boy a promise that should he recover sufficiently that I would take him to Italy to begin his education with a tour of Florence, Venice, and Rome. He is not strong so we shan't be so terribly long. I promise to return here by mid-summer's day."

"But, Sir. You place too much responsibility upon these narrow shoulders of mine. What if I should fail? We have needs of your talents here."

"My talents are the reverse of what you require at the moment," Scrooge said. "Milton, I have a long and inglorious history of creating poverty—of perpetuating misery—not expunging it. That is my experience and expertise. I am well-practised at putting profit above all other concerns, and as a consequence the damage I have done to my fellow human beings is inestimable. I do not say this with pride. These sins are deep stains upon my soul."

"You could not be more wrong, Sir," Topper said. "No man is perfect. No man is free of sin. A man may be judged not by the sins he has committed, but by his efforts to redeem himself. You are redeemed and forgiven by those whom you have sinned against. Of this I am quite certain, else I should not remain in your employ."

"But I must first forgive myself, Milton, and I have not yet done so."

Topper said, "The time to begin is now, Sir."

"And what of God's forgiveness?" said Scrooge.

"God's capacity for forgiveness is infinite."

"Perhaps, but my time isn't. I must see to the boy first. That much is clear. And in my stead, you will see to my charity—I am depending on you. I trust you implicitly. I know you can do that, and I have no doubt you have been doing just that these last weeks. When midsummer arrives I shall give my charity my undivided attention and energy."

"But Sir, I do not believe..."

"Mr. Topper! I cannot make it any plainer than I already have. I have an atonement to make in the form of saving a boy's life, and I mean to see that done. At this point in time were I to remain here, I at best would only be in the way. At worst, I could be very, very destructive. I know myself only too well. There is still wickedness in here!" Scrooge stabbed a finger at his chest.

"Surely not!"

"How can you know what lies in my heart?"

"I cannot and do not pretend to," Topper said. "I can only judge a man by his actions, and your actions only do you credit."

"No, Mr. Topper. Actions can deceive. False actions may mask the evil in men's hearts. A man may conduct himself in a perfectly moral fashion but harbour depraved thoughts and wishes. Before I can turn my full attention to my charity, I must purify myself of evil desires."

Topper gave him a resigned look.

"Professor Friedrich did more than make a lame boy walk, Milton. He introduced me to a wonderful method of achieving the spiritual purity which I require. He calls it the Total Abstinence Principle. I must purify myself with prayer. My every thought and reflection must be of Kindness, Light, and Goodness. There must be no vestige of wickedness anywhere in me—heart, mind, body or soul. I must cleanse my flesh and bones by consuming only chicken or mutton—no beef, no pig—and any vegetables I ingest must be taken raw. I must drink only tea or wine diluted by spring water in equal portions, and I must work myself so that the sweat of my exertions rids my body of its noisome humours. My only permitted vice will be bread and butter—not too heinous, I should think. While you prepare for me, I shall be preparing for you."

"Yes, Sir. I did not understand. Forgive me my lack of courage."

"I shall not forgive you because you have not lacked courage. You have followed a proper line of inquiry, but it has come to naught. Very well—so be it. We continue. Instead tell me how we have done. Tell me of the daily operations. Give me the flavour of your good work."

"Of course. As you wish, Sir. Our doors opened this morning at the usual hour, and we suffered no dearth of customers," Topper said, rather mechanically.

Scrooge leaned back in his chair. "Sad and happy, I am to hear it. Sad that so many should have fallen on hard times. Happy that we should be able to help them in our modest way. Go on. Tell me more. But make it quick as I don't have much time." He waved his hand impatiently.

"I have hired three new people to help at your charity: a young legless boy with white hair and pink eyes, a young woman to aid Cook, and a woman to help me," Topper said.

Scrooge said, "A legless boy? Can he work?"

"I have not found him wanting in any of the tasks I have charged him," Topper replied.

"And what tasks are those?"

"He performs the duties that any page might."

"How does he get himself up the stairs if he has no legs?"

"There are no stairs in your charity, Sir," Topper said. "We have not gotten so far in the rebuilding to put in a second level—though we would find the added space useful."

"I see. A second level would mean a great deal added expense. That can be something added at a later time, can it not?"

"Yes, Sir."

"And the woman? Not the one to help Cook, but the one that helps you. What would you have her do? Is she someone to assist in the cleaning up?" Without thinking he brushed at crumbs on his trousers which were no longer there.

"No, Sir. We have need of a linguist."

"A linguist!? You are paying for a linguist? Don't we all of us speak English?"

"No, Sir. Many of the people we serve come from foreign parts, and consequently speak languages with which few hereabouts are familiar—least of all me. It is vital that we should be able to communicate with them if only simply. Quite by chance this woman—who I must say is rather strikingly tall—revealed herself to be quite a gifted linguist. When I discovered her talent I offered her the job which she accepted. She has already handsomely proven her value many times over."

Scrooge said, "And what is her name?"

"She gave her name as Miss Trellis. Miss Elizabeth Trellis."

"'Gave her name?' You do not believe that to be her real name?" Scrooge said, steepling his fingers thoughtfully.

"Frankly, no."

"Do you have any idea why she should give us a false name?"

"I do not."

"Come, come, Milton. If there is more on your mind, let's have it." Scrooge snapped his fingers. "I have another appointment 'ere long. If you have something to say, spit it out. This shilly-shallying only wastes my time."

Topper cocked his head. "Yes, Sir. I may be wrong, but I had the impression that she did not know what her name was," he said.

"Really?" said Scrooge arching an eyebrow. "How interesting. Do you trust her?"

"Trust her, Sir? Trust her against doing what? Stealing from us? I don't know if you are aware of this, but the lock on your charity's door is broken—has been broken for some time. Yet no thief has ever done us harm, and I doubt ever will. Not that there aren't villains who would stoop to such a thing, but the outrage on the street would be too much. Anyone who commits a crime against Ebenezer Scrooge and his charity should expect swift justice from those whom you aid."

Scrooge nodded as if he agreed with this notion. "Let me say rather, do you believe she will betray us?"

"I keep no secrets, Sir, and to the best of my knowledge neither do you."

"You do believe in being perfectly transparent in all ways, do you not?"

"I do."

"The best way to keep a secret is to have no secrets, eh? That is why I hired you, Milton."

"Thank you, Mr. Scrooge."

"What else can you tell me about her?"

Topper hesitated. "She is quite possibly mad."

"Mad, indeed? Not half-mad? Not merely eccentric? What interesting news you have to share this afternoon, Milton. I should have been bored without it. And pray tell, what form does this madness take?"

Topper shrugged. "She believes that your charity is being watched by a secret society of rogues and spies—or some such nonsense. Something about a one-eyed man. She came, in fact, not seeking employment, but to warn us."

"Well," Scrooge said, drumming his fingers thoughtfully, "that is not necessarily madness. It is not inconceivable that I might have made enemies in my past. The ladder of business often uses the backbones of men as rungs, I am very sorry to say. At all events she has good intentions even if she is mad."

"I do believe so."

"And her madness doesn't trouble you?"

"It does not. Madness, it seems to me, is only another way of thinking. I do not fear people who think or act differently than I."

Scrooge looked down at the table cloth and smoothed it with his fingers. After several moments of deep thought, he said, "I will trust your intuition in this. I am deeply disinclined to send anyone to Bedlam." He shivered involuntarily. His pushed away the plate upon which his bread had sat. He said, "Anything else?"

"Only one other thing, Sir: a visitor who desired to speak with you."

"There are many such. They would have overwhelmed me if I hadn't been abroad." Scrooge waved his hand at the packets of perfumed letters on the desk. "That is another reason I have hired you, Milton. To fend them off. To keep them at bay so I might maintain my program of prayer and reflection while I am here."

"Yes, Sir. However, I should add that the gentleman in question was a clergy."

"A clergy? Humbug! No doubt his church wants a new organ. Or perhaps a leak in the ceiling threatens to ruin their alter. He expects me to be his purse."

"I do not believe so, Sir."

"Did he give you any idea why he wished to see me?" Scrooge said.

"He said only that he wished to minister to the spiritual needs of the people of your charity."

Scrooge frowned thoughtfully, "I have never been a religious man. Not in the orthodox sense."

"Nor have I, Sir," Topper said.

"But I do believe in higher powers, higher orders of beings—shall we say spirits."

"Yes, Sir. You refer, of course, to your experiences of this past Christmas. I do know how that vision inspires you."

"Inspires? Milton, it frightens me to death. I shall never forget them."

"I would not imagine you would, Sir."

"Tell me about this man of the cloth. Is he an agreeable gentleman?"

"I would rather not make comment on that," Topper said slowly.

"Then you do not like this man who wishes to see me?"

Topper did not hesitate before answering. "I do not."

"And why should that be?"

"He maintains certain affectations which are troubling."

"Many men of the cloth are guilty of that, Milton. It is the way of our society that men dedicated to the pursuit of religion conduct themselves as if they were morally superior to all other men."

"It is no mere affectation of sanctity that I refer to."

Scrooge said, "Then what *do* you refer to?"

"He pretends to be mad when he is not."

It was several moments before Scrooge could reply. "You never cease to astonish me, Milton."

"I do not mean to astonish you, Sir."

"But you do. Far beyond the level of elementary entertainments, I promise you. You tell me you trust a woman who may well be mad, but do not trust a clergyman who pretends to be mad but is not."

"That is what I mean to say, Mr. Scrooge."

"In what way does he pretend to be mad?"

"He shook himself and danced about the room nearly the whole time he was in it. It was impossible to hold a proper conversation with him. When I made as if I would tolerate him no longer and was about to have him removed, he ceased his agitations all at once and made his proposal."

Scrooge frowned. "He wishes merely to preach the gospel to our people?"

"Perhaps. I believe he has other intentions."

"What?"

"I cannot say."

"Then do you believe he wishes to take my money? Wouldn't he suffer the same fate you've told me of as anyone else who would steal from me?"

"He is more concerned with matters of what I can only call policy than money. He wishes us to care *only* for those who are the *worthy poor*, as he calls them."

"We do care for the worthy poor."

"'Worthy poor' is a euphemism by which he means the Christian poor."

Scrooge clapped his hands together. "What could be wrong with that?"

"Sir, doesn't Christian charity extend to men and women of all faiths?"

"Milton—this is a Christian nation. You would be hard pressed to find anyone within miles who was not a Christian—well, more or less a Christian. Sinners can still be Christians and need only redemption. There are far more poor and desperate Christians in London that I can afford to feed, clothe and shelter. When was the last time, for example, we had an A-rab in my charity?"

"This past week, Sir. Though with Miss Trellis's assistance he explained to me that he is a Christian."

Scrooge said, "Well, there you are then."

"But what of Jews?" said Topper. "There are plenty of poor Jews in

London. Do we turn them away for their beliefs?"

Scrooge waved a hand in dismissal and hardened his jaw. "The Jews take care of their own."

"Yes, Sir. Mrs. Edelstein? Mr. Levy? Shall I send them on their way?"

"Who are they?"

"Jews whom your charity has sheltered these last six or so weeks. Mr. Levy is blind. Mrs. Edelstein is very old and is homeless."

"No, of course they may stay. I speak in the abstract when I say Jews take care of their own. I do not mean to turn out individual Jews from my charity. As a general policy we see to the needs of our own kind. That is all."

"Yes, Sir."

"Why should we care for Jews?! Next you will tell me that we are taking in Hindus. Have Jews ever cared for Gentiles? Are there Jewish Charities where a poor Christian might take a meal?"

"I couldn't say, Sir."

"Well, believe me there are none."

"Yes, Sir."

"What did you say this man's name was?"

Topper looked puzzled.

"The clergyman, I mean. The one who wishes to see me."

"I didn't say, Sir. His name is Reverend Salvation Mitchell."

"*Salvation* Mitchell? Are you quite sure of his given name?"

"It is the name he gave me."

"How unusual. Does he bring letters of recommendation?"

"He does not."

"Is he Church of England?"

"I don't believe so."

"Good heavens! He's not a Papist, is he?"

"He gives none of the signs. He is an American, Sir, if I have not said so already. He belongs to a sect which apparently does not believe in speaking the name of God, nor Christ aloud. They refer to our Lord only as He or Him."

"That's a novelty, eh?" Scrooge said. "The Lord's good name comes too easily to the lips of those who are little less than fools. Leave it to the Americans to elevate the level of piety a notch higher. Perhaps he was drawn to us when he heard of our efforts. Though there are charities aplenty, I make no doubt my having opened a charity has caused quite a few tongues to wag."

"No doubt you are right, Sir."

"Of course, I am," said Scrooge. "A clergyman could provide a service which neither you nor I can: the spiritual. We can clothe them, put soup in their bellies and give them a warm bed to sleep in, but we cannot feed the needs of their souls."

"Yes, Sir."

"Did he mention anything about what he expects in return?"

"I do believe he means to offer his services freely, Sir," Topper said.

"But you are not happy with this idea, are you, Milton?"

"No, Sir."

"What is wrong? Don't you believe that our people need spiritual counselling?"

"I do, but I would rather give them counselling of a more practical sort," said Topper.

"What do you mean?" said Scrooge.

"Would it not be better if we were to give them an education, Sir? Teach them to read and write. Teach them a skill with which they could better themselves. If we only give them food, then we make them dependent upon us."

"Milton, I know you have their best interests at heart, but surely these people are poor for a reason. They are a mixed lot: ignorant and lazy. There's no denying it. It's their nature," Scrooge said. "There is nothing we can do to change the way God has made them."

"I agree with you that these people are poor for a reason, although that reason has little to do with their nature or God's plans for them and more to do with our nation's economy."

Scrooge said, "Well, yes. I won't disagree with that. The trouble is that there are so many of them. If the poor would only stop having children, they would make their burden lighter for themselves. The fewer there were, the more charities like mine could help them."

"In a world where all things are denied to them," Topper said rather warmly, "who can blame them for wanting the only thing that is left to them and only natural to all of us? Who does not wish to have a family?"

Scrooge felt Topper's words cut deep into his heart. He had wanted a family for so very long, and yet he had pushed it out of his mind, had pretended that such things weren't for him.

"Mr. Scrooge, are you all right?" Topper said, when he noticed Scrooge clutching at his breast.

"Now do you see why I must have a care with what I eat?" he said and gave a deep cough. "Some bit of indigestion is all."

"Can I get you something?" Topper said.

"No—nothing. It has passed. Well then," Scrooge said, clearing his throat, "before we conclude our meeting for the day, let me see the books. You did bring them, didn't you? How much money I am spending may be less important than where I spend it. I have rather a great deal of experience dealing with merchants, and I'll wager I can find you better prices than you're getting for any number of items. Economise is the key word! Let me ask you this: How many of the people at my charity are helping with its reconstruction?"

"How many?" Topper repeated.

"Yes, certainly you are reducing the cost of labour by enlisting the young and the strong who eat my food and sleep in my beds."

"But, Sir, you never said... They haven't the skills..."

"Don't you know anything about money management?" Scrooge said, rather coldly.

"I do not and have never pretended to," Topper replied forcing his voice to remain even. "That has been my contention all along. This is why I wish you were available to approve or disapprove of the actions I take. Without your direction..."

Scrooge said, "Haven't you noticed the expense, for heaven's sake?" His voice was sharp.

"I have, but you told me on several occasions that you had given me *carte blanche*, but if I have misunderstood you, Sir, I do apologise. I do not believe that I have used your money extravagantly. If you find my work unsatisfactory, I will terminate my employment at your charity with nothing further said."

"No, Milton—I wouldn't have you leave. I need you to do this for me. Perhaps I have not made myself clear. I must insist that no more money is spent on such labours when we have so many strong backs lying idle."

Topper stared straight ahead and said nothing.

Scrooge leaned to one side and peered intently at Topper. "You are acting very strangely, this afternoon, Milton. Where is the happy, lively gentleman I met at my nephew's last Christmas? You are not your old self at all."

◉

"Jack Frost!" Topper bellowed out the door of his room, "a word with you!"

Moments later Topper heard the familiar sound of a low cart rolling toward his office.

"Yes, Sir," Jack said breathless. "What can I do for you?"

"Mr. Scrooge has directed me to use the people of Yellow Door in any way we can to help rebuild it."

"Yes, Sir," Jack said, "it only stands to reason."

"It would stand to reason if we had men who were skilled and able. Still I suppose Mr. Scrooge is right. Any skills that our people might learn in the work involved would only improve their chances at finding future employment. For me that is the purpose of our being here."

"Yes, Sir," Jack said.

"To that end I have made this poster to hang in the dining room. A simple announcement is all it is. It directs anyone who has had experience with a hammer and saw and are willing to work to see me directly."

"May I see it, Sir?" Jack said.

"I mean for you to take it and have it hung," Topper said handing it to him. "You will need help, of course. It wouldn't do to have it hung too low."

Jack took it without replying. He pulled his lens from a drawer in his cart and held it over the paper.

"Your spelling is good, Sir," Jacks said after several moments examination.

Topper smiled. "I thank you for the compliment," he said. "but I did not mean for you to check over my writing. Please post it as it stands without revision."

"But your writing tells me more," he said. "Notice this stroke here and here." Jack pointed with an alabaster finger. "It shows strength of character and an inherent happiness. This crossed 't' indicates a growing sense of frustration, however."

"Yes, well—there's enough about my handwriting, Jack. Next time I shall have you write it for me. Go along with you and see if you can get someone to help you post that. There may be a number of our people who cannot read, so if you would be so kind as to read it aloud before you hang it, I would appreciate it. Send any interested parties to me straight away. Do you understand? The sooner we do this, the better."

"Yes, Sir," Jack said, and after a second's hesitation he added: "Do I not recall that Al-Mustafa is a carpenter?"

"He is, indeed," Topper said with a shake of his head. "That's the irony of the thing. Just when we need someone with his woodworking skills, I have found him an apprenticeship with a painter of some reputation. Mr. Charles Carlson may not paint crucifixions, but he is a portrait painter in demand by high society. Besides training Al-Mustafa in the fine art of portraiture he will introduce him to all the right people, and soon our black friend will be painting steadily and making more money than me. I could not ask him to give that up to do carpentry for us. It will all work out in the end. Have no fear."

Jack put his glass away and solemnly rolled off still squinting at Topper's handwriting.

◉

Topper heard a knock at his door.

"Come in," he said.

The door squealed open and a balding man with a long face stood just outside with his cap in his hand.

"I've come about the poster, Sir," he said.

Topper rose briskly from his seat. "Excellent, please come in, Sir," he said.

The man modestly stepped into the room and looked around approvingly.

"Have a seat. What is your name?" Topper dipped his pen in his ink pot and prepared to write.

"My name is Billings, Sir. Ned Billings."

Topper made the note and said, "I am pleased to make your acquaintance, Mr. Billings. Do you have skills which might prove to be useful to us in our reconstruction work?"

Billings nodded. "I believe so, Sir. I was a carpenter—more a cabinet maker—before I fell on hard times."

"That is capital. I mean your skills, of course—not that you've fallen on hard times."

"Yes, Sir. I take your meaning, Sir," Billings said.

"How is it, Mr. Billings, that you find yourself here? Surely a man with your skills should be able to find work quite easily," Topper said.

"I've no tools, Sir," Billings said. "Mine are gone."

"Have they been stolen?" Topper asked and set down his pen.

"No, Sir. They've been burnt."

Topper sat back in his chair. "Burned?"

"Yes, Sir. Burnt. By my wife. Though I don't know that she meant to burn them, but they was destroyed when she burnt the house."

"Your wife burned your house? Whyever for, Sir?" Topper said.

Billings blinked his eyes but said nothing.

"Did she mean to?" asked Topper. "Burn your house, I mean?"

"Oh, she meant to burn it all right. But she took the children out first."

"You are lucky for that, Sir." Topper said, "Where is she and the children now?"

"I couldn't say, Sir. Perhaps in America. She's relations there, you know."

"Was it an accident?"

"No, Sir, I don't believe it was. She did it of a purpose." Billings rubbed his knees uneasily. "It may have been that she was in a bit of a rage."

"I have no doubt, Sir, but rage over what? I do not pretend this is any of my business, of course. You may choose not to answer me if you've no mind to."

Billings bobbed his head amiably. "She's a good woman, Sir. Don't let this small thing colour your image of her. Good-hearted she is. I am devoted to her even so."

"She had a momentary fit, perhaps? Hysteria?" Topper suggested.

"It might be a fit of a kind, Sir. But not hysteria. Something closer to jealousy, I should think."

"You need not tell me another word, Mr. Billings," Topper said.

"Irene is a beautiful young woman," Billings said.

"Your wife is named Irene? You miss her?"

"No, Sir. My wife is Betty."

Topper coughed. "Mr. Billings, I think you will do just fine. To-morrow morning at eight o'clock I would like to meet with you in the kitchen. Cook tells me the larder needs repairing. After that we will make a tour of the premises and determine what other work you might do for us. We will discuss terms then."

"Irene has the bluest eyes you have ever seen, Sir," Billings said dreamily. "A true beauty even for one so young."

"That will be all, Mr. Billings," Topper said and stood to his feet.

"She has the sweetest smile and lips as red as raspberries. She is not yet fourteen and yet you would think she was..."

Topper stood to the door and shouted, "Mr. Forest! Come quickly!" Topper waved a hand to silence Billings and was only too gratified to hear the sound of a low cart rumbling toward him.

The Son of Virginia

A PALE RECTANGLE OF LIGHT FELL ON THE FLOOR FROM A SMALL WINDOW. Topper's attention was drawn by it to a scattered pile of sawdust and a broom whose straws were curled from years of hard use. They told a confused story: "This is where Billings fell the first day after the Sabbath, this April 15th," they said. "This is where the carpenter broke his leg and broke it badly." Had he slipped on a nail? Had he stumbled over a hammer? Had he simply tripped over his own feet? The answer made little difference now. Hard times and more than a little foolishness had driven Mr. Ned Billings, Master Carpenter, to Yellow Door, and now to make matters worse he had broken his leg. Bad luck clung to some people like the smell of moth balls.

Cold sweat broke out on Topper's brow. Midsummer was not so far away. What would be Scrooge's reaction to the news that the finishing work of his charity would be delayed unless a professional carpenter were hired— which he had expressly forbidden? He cringed at thought that Yellow Door might not pass his employer's inspection. Topper knew the matter was more important than merely his own continued employment. It would mean the end of food and shelter to the scores of the destitute whom he had grown to care for so very much—to say nothing of the eternal damnation of Mr. Scrooge's very soul.

"I must put my mind firmly to my task," he murmured to himself aloud. "I must not let my own worry and concern defeat me." Topper walked to the door, opened it and shouted: "Jack! Jack Forest! A word with you, young Sir!"

The clatter of Jack's cart grew from far to near. He rounded the corner, a broad grin stretched across his face, his wig askew. "Yes, Sir. What service can I perform for you this day?"

"Send my compliments to Reverend Mitchell, if you would. Ask him to meet me here at the soonest opportunity."

"Fetch the Yankee Kangaroo," Jack said repeating back his orders as he understood them. "Yes, Sir. Right away." Then his parchment-white skin flushed pink. "Ooops..." he gurgled and ducked as if he expected Topper to strike at him.

"Come again, Young Jack. What was that you said?" Topper said, hands-on-hips, knowing perfectly well what his page had let slip.

"Beggin' your pardon, Sir," Jack said. "I meant to say, 'Reverend Mitchell.'"

"We will have none of that. I will not tolerate any disrespect from you of your elders."

"Yes, Sir. Sorry, Sir," Jack said, "but it's not just me who says it. Not the first and not the only one, anyway. Everyone calls him that. You must admit he's earned it with his leaping about all the time."

Topper could not repress a smile. "Perhaps, but keep it to yourself, do you hear?"

"Yes, Sir."

"You are not even to repeat it behind his back. No good can come of mocking others. Mark my words, young master."

"Yes, Sir."

"I do not always find the man completely agreeable, I will admit, but I will not allow him to be disrespected here at Yellow Door. All men who come here will be received with the courtesy that is everyone's birthright. Rich or poor, clergy or laity, Gentile or Jew—they are all the same in the eyes of God."

"Yes, Sir—just as you say. Respect. I shall fetch him immediately."

"See that you do," Topper said.

With his usual clatter but faster-than-usual speed, Jack Forest disappeared out the door and down the passageway. In a few minutes the door flew open, and Topper was quite sure that if Mitchell were physically capable he would have entered the room doing cartwheels.

"Ain't it wonderful, wonderful!" he said spinning like a top. "My room for chapel is complete. Praise Be to our carpenter, and Praise Be to Him! Is the work of His Hammer and Saw not glorious? Have you ever seen such skill?"

"Have a care, Reverend. Already one man has broken his leg in this room to-day." Without rising Topper pointed to the disordered pile of sawdust as if Mitchell could read the signs as clearly as text. "I thought you should know we have a problem. The finishing work at Yellow Door has temporarily stopped."

Mitchell stopped his spinning, lost balance and thumped down on the bench next to Topper almost spilling them both over. "Bless me," Mitchell said. "I need to learn to contain myself."

"Caution, Sir. Yes, there are times," Topper said without any hint of sarcasm, "when we must tread carefully."

"What has happened here? What are you trying to tell me?"

"Only this: I fear our Mr. Billings has had a mishap and has broken his leg."

"Broken his leg?" the Reverend said. "How soon will he be able to return to his work?"

"He is in the care of our own Dr. Mipps, but I cannot speak to how long it will take for his leg to mend. No time soon, I fear," Topper said.

Mitchell clenched his hands and shook them at Topper as if he meant to strike him. "Our work must continue. We are losing souls for HIM with each stroke of the pendulum! Friend, I ask you! Who will take the responsibility?" He rose abruptly from the bench, but did not resume his dance. "That fool of a wood-worker is to blame."

"Mr. Billings did not break his leg to spite you, Reverend Mitchell, I can assure you. Believe me, he suffers far more than you as a consequence."

"He suffers? What do I care if he suffers or if he's broken his leg or his neck?"

Topper's eyes grew wide. "I must say, Sir, you shock me with such language."

"Shock? Let us not give this Billings fellow any further consideration. HE has other plans for him, Mr. Topper, Friend—you may be sure of it. They may be mysterious and unknowable to you and me, but they are HIS plans and who are we to question them? 'Who?' I say." Mitchell pursed his lips. "We, on the other hand, are on our own mission from HIM, and we SHALL NOT be diverted from it."

"Have you no concern for our Mr. Billings who has done so much for us?" Topper said growing angry. "Now that he is injured you cast him aside and can no longer be bothered with him?"

Mitchell screwed up his face and turned the idea in his round skull with the innocence of a school boy. Finally he said, "You mistake me, Friend. It is true that I am enthusiastic to see the physical condition of this good charity raised to the standards acceptable and charged to us by our Benefactor, Mr. Ebenezer Scrooge." He narrowed his eyes meaningfully at Topper. He bobbed his head and looked down at the floor. "Still, how do you propose we continue the Good Work remaining to us while our dear Mr. Billings recovers? There are funds to hire carpenters, are there not? Hasn't Mr. Scrooge given you a free hand to see to it that his charity is put in order? Surely in as large a city as London there are other carpenters who can finish HIS work."

Topper sighed. "Mr. Scrooge has made it clear that we should do this work ourselves to help improve our minds and spirits and expand our skills. Any savings we can incur by putting our own backs into it, the more we can have for food and clothing."

"Then let them work," Mitchell said wind-milling his arms. "Let them do HIS work. We will make do with the labour of HIS children. Every man can pound a hammer. Every man can draw the teeth of a saw across wood."

"Perhaps but without skill and proper guidance, Mr. Scrooge will not be pleased with the results. It will not do to produce work which is slipshod.

There is no one to show them what to do or how to it. We must wait until we find a skilled craftsman to direct the effort."

"You know, Mr. Topper," Mitchell said, shivering with indignation, "I am beginning to suspect that you do not wish for this beneficent institution for the relief of human suffering to be completed! Why do you stand in the way of my every suggestion?"

"I am merely tempering your enthusiasm with a caution for planning and measured action," Topper said. "If the execution of construction is bungled, there will be..."

"Stop! I don't wish to hear any more. I will go down myself to the dining room right now and gather the men I need," Mitchell said as if he were declaiming his intentions to the audience of a theatre.

Topper said, "But I have already done that. Haven't you listened to a word I've said? That is how I came to discover Mr. Billings. Surely we can't have a second carpenter in our midst and not know of it."

Mitchell did not reply, but bounded out of the room and down the passageway.

Topper followed after him slowly with his head down. Jack Forest joined him in the narrow corridor on his way.

"Sir," Jack said, "you do not look well."

"That man drains me, Jack, if I may be so bold as to say. We are at the same purpose here, yet..." He shook his head. They walked on without further comment.

Topper did not need to enter the room to listen to Mitchell's words which were clear though the walls of the dining hall were of a proper thickness. The room as yet had no ceiling to close it from the greater building, so all the clatter, the noise of chairs, the murmur of voices reverberated in that way peculiar to large public buildings.

"HE has a task for us to perform, O Children!" Mitchell shouted while spinning in place. "HE has chosen us as the instruments of HIS work!"

"Amen!" they replied just as Topper opened the door and entered.

The tables in the dining hall had been pushed aside. People sat in small groups—speaking a quiet word now and then to one another. Those who had been sleeping peacefully in the corners, rubbed their eyes and sat up at the noise.

Topper cast his eye around the room. Miss Trellis sat quietly speaking to Al-Mustafa. There were many faces he recognised, but a few he did not: two dark-skinned children who seemed to have no parents, but were clearly brother and sister. The girl, the elder of the two, held herself in an adult-like manner although she could be no more than ten years of age. *From India*, Topper thought.

Near the window was a tall, thin man dressed in clothes which were too tight across the shoulders, too short in the sleeves and much too voluminous at the waist. His face was covered with a thick but short black beard smeared high over his cheekbones and down the collar of his shirt. He caught Topper's eye and returned a nod of greeting. Topper was abashed at having been caught staring, but nodded hospitably in return.

"Who among you knows the use of the hammer and saw? Who among you follows the craft of your Saviour?" Mitchell demanded.

Every man, woman, and child cast one another curious, questioning looks. Several shook their heads.

"No tools," a toothless oldster said, "Just us fools." But no one thought the comment funny.

The bearded man whom Topper had been watching pulled his hands from his pocket, folded them across his chest and said, "I have some experience in that occupation, Sir. My father was a cabinet maker, though it has been a good many years since I was his assistant." There was a curious lilt to his voice which Topper instantly recognised as American.

"HE has sent me another Instrument of his Will. See, Mr. Topper, did I not tell you to have faith in HIM and not abandon the work that HE gives us? Did I not tell you?" Mitchell danced triumphantly with his hands held over his head.

"All that I hoped for was that we might find someone to help us in our work who was experienced in woodworking. That is all," Topper replied and tried to smile.

"What is your name, Friend?" Mitchell asked sidling toward the man with mincing steps.

"I am William Dawson—at your service, Sir. As you can doubtless hear, I am a son of Virginia, though I have spent many years in the western wilderness, living among the Indians in the Illinois and Indiana territories."

"I am from the United States myself, my Southron Friend. And what brings you to London?" Reverend Mitchell said. "How is it that you have found your way to this place at this time, I ask you?"

Dawson looked startled at the question, then replied softly, "Why, God does, Sir. What else?"

"Of course, my good man. Of course. What other explanation can there be?" Reverend Mitchell said.

"None whatsoever. Now why don't you tell me a little more what work you'd like for me to do?" Dawson said. "And what I should expect in exchange."

"I can do better than that, Friend! I can do better than that. I will take you directly to it as it lies inside these very facilities," Reverend Mitchell said.

"An excellent suggestion. You have only to lead, and I will follow," Dawson said bowing.

"Only too delighted! Only too delighted!" Reverend Mitchell said turning his back to Dawson and dancing toward the door. As he did so Topper noticed a dark expression pass over Dawson's face.

Topper followed after them with little energy. When he entered the unfinished room where Mitchell intended to hold his chapel services, he found Mitchell strangely still watching Dawson press his ear against a wall and squint with one eye as if listening for the heartbeat of the charity.

"Your wall is bowed," he said at last using the same tone a physician might in diagnosis. "Though I doubt very much that it will slow us down. It all depends on the level of craftsmanship you're willing to pay for."

"There is no money in this work," Topper said cutting off Mitchell before he could offer money which was not his to spend. "It will need to be accomplished as an act of charity. That is what Yellow Door is, Sir. A charity."

"But I know for a fact that Mr. Scrooge has given you..." Mitchell began but was cut off by a sharp wave of Topper's hand.

"We can, of course, repay you your room and board," Topper said.

Dawson nodded his head approvingly. "I understand you completely, Sir. For the poor, hungry and homeless. And more to the point: for myself. There is no grander thing in this world. All I ask is for the opportunity to work."

"We had the use of a skilled carpenter but mishap has fallen to him and we can no longer rely on his services. Perhaps you have been sent to us by God to take his place," Topper said.

Dawson bowed. "I cannot claim to be divinely inspired, but I am quite willing to take on this task. Are there tools?"

"There are," Topper replied.

"Are there materials?"

"You may have whatever you need to complete this job."

"I see that I have a goodly number of able-bodied assistants that I can call upon whenever I need them."

An old man who could barely stand erect took to his feet and turned his one good eye in their direction. "You may rely on me."

Many others of stouter frames echoed his sentiment: "Aye!"

"If you will but show me round and point out the particulars, I believe I can give you some estimate of the time and materials it will take. I believe that we can make this fair building presentable in short order—what with the good intentions of everyone present."

A cheer echoed throughout Yellow Door which reverberated far down the street.

CHAPTER 7

໑ལ໑

Visitation

ALREADY THE DAY PROMISED TO BE HOT. TOPPER COULD FEEL HIS NECK-
cloth stick to his freshly-shaven throat. The Day had come at last—hot or
no. Not that he had ever doubted it or the ability of the good people at
Yellow Door to bring it about. To-day for the first time since its inception
six months previous, Ebenezer Scrooge would be received by the charity
which his money had made possible and enjoy his official status as Grand
Benefactor.

Morning light sifted through the windows of sparkling glass upon a row
of six figures. Topper queued them as straight as they could manage. His
eyes ran down the line.

First was Miss Jane Goosegrass, school mistress. Her posture was plumb
to the ground and was, it must be said, without defect. She was of medium
build and in fine proportion—though she was of an age when many
women's figures began to lose the look of their youth. Her lips were finely
formed, her chin firm, and Topper thought she carried her head with its
copper-coloured hair as upright as a queen. Her voice was sonorous, her
words clearly pronounced.

Next in line was Cook. Topper noticed that she wore white spots of flour
on her chin, and he struggled with how he might find a polite way to tell her
of them. Miss Goosegrass saved him the trouble by reaching over with her
handkerchief and dabbing them away. Even so Cook wore an uneasy look
on her face—as if she were expecting to stand before the Magistrate rather

than their generous benefactor. Her flabby arms hung limply at her sides like great rolls of pastry dough. Topper tried to imagine what she had looked like as a young girl, but found it impossible.

Third in line was Mary-Martha White, kitchen-maid. Mary-Martha was six inches taller than Cook, though most of her height was below the waist. Topper had never seen her face not twisted in a grin. She spoke only when spoken to, but, Topper noticed, she often stumbled in simple day to day social interactions such as being wished Good Morning or accepting a compliment for completing a task assigned to her. She had never, however, neglected her work, and Topper liked her simple nature.

Fourth in the assembly was Ned Billings, crutch tucked under his arm, leaning three degrees from perpendicular. His long face beamed, but Topper noticed dark circles beneath his eyes. He had not slept a wink the night before, Topper was certain, worrying what Mr. Scrooge would make of their labours. Though Billings couldn't stand for any length of time, there was much work that he found he could do sitting.

Fifth was William Dawson. Taller than the rest, Dawson stood perfectly erect and looked as if he could remain so for hours. The heat seemed to have no effect on him other than to add colour to what little skin of his face his beard left exposed. His expression was patient. He had worked tirelessly over the past weeks—harder than any of them, yet rose each day as if he had just returned from holiday.

Last in line was Jack Forest, wig squared atop his head, fresh collar round his neck, squinting against the diffused light flooding the room. Topper, standing in shadow on the opposite side of the room, thought to relieve him.

"Jack," he said, "won't you come stay by my side? I will of a certainty have a multitude of errands for you to perform, and I do not wish to have to send for someone to fetch you."

"Yes, Sir," Jack said, and dutifully joined Topper. Even out of the direct light, though, Topper could tell that the sun hurt the boy's eyes.

The remaining five stood like a row of brown beer bottles on a shelf. Burnished, buffed, cleaned, pressed, combed they were until they were scarcely human. Soldiers could have done no better. There was Spit and

Polish about them in every way.

After weeks of hard labour, set-backs and sacrifice, Yellow Door had done its best. Yet in spite of the S & P, in spite of Yellow Door's glazed windows, its newly-patched roof, its newly-constructed labyrinth of corridors, its Spartan furniture, its whitewashed walls, its meticulously-swept earthen floors—even in spite of the feminine touches of curtains and lace doilies, Topper knew it was only just presentable.

Yellow Door still could not adequately feed all who came to its doorstep with bellies gurgling. It could humanely sleep only a dozen women and half a dozen men at any given time—although nights when the temperature dropped far below freezing they kept many times that number sat up on benches to keep them from dying at Winter's Cruel Hand.

What would Scrooge say? If Yellow Door met muster with him, would it also satisfy the Ghost of Christmas Yet To Come?

"Although your efforts are beyond reproach, there is much work left undone, I fear," Topper said to the Half-Dozen with a sad shake of his head. "Any deficiencies which Mr. Scrooge detects are mine and mine alone. You are to be celebrated and applauded regardless of the outcome of this visit. You are grand people—each and every one of you. I hope you know how much I appreciate your endeavours."

Miss Goosegrass, her hands clasped at waist-level and, glowing in her best dress which was much too heavy for the season, said, "You are too hard on yourself, Mr. Topper. Mr. Scrooge will find nothing to fault within these walls. You must prepare yourself for praise, Sir. Praise richly deserved."

"If there is praise to be delivered, I own I shall not be listed among the recipients. There are many men and women here far more deserving of Scrooge's praise, Miss Goosegrass—yourself included. My labour in all this is nothing compared to yours." Topper waved a hand at the row of people standing before him.

He pulled a piece of paper from his pocket, unfolded it and cast his eye down it while they protested softly. The itinerary has been written in Mrs. Goosegrass's graceful hand. He ran down the list ticking off the items in his head one by one.

"Everyone knows his part," Jack volunteered.

Topper looked down at the boy seated upon the rolling cart. What a precious human being he was! He was perfect in every way despite his physical differences.

"What was that you said, Jack?" Topper replied.

"I said, 'We have every word committed to memory,'" Jack Forest continued.

"Your speeches? Well, I've no doubt of it," Topper replied, "with a tireless tutor such as yourself."

"Where is the Gentleman at this moment?" said Miss Goosegrass, speaking in a voice which betrayed an anxiety which Topper would never have expected from her.

"As we speak he sits for Al-Mustafa in the artist's studio," Topper said, "in the south out-building. They work on preliminary sketches for a portrait which I have commissioned and will hang in the dining-room once completed. It will be only one of many great portraits which Al-Mustafa is destined to create, I am bound. We will in the end lose our black Moroccan, however. Once the cream of society has discovered this young man's talents, he will find himself showered with commissions. He will dress in the finest silks, shod his feet in the best boots, keep the sleekest hounds, and eat the savouriest foods our island nation has to offer. And we shall consider ourselves lucky to set our eyes upon him again—or to ever have set our eyes upon him whatsoever."

"That should give you a grand sense of satisfaction, Mr. Topper," Miss Goosegrass said.

"It does indeed. He is Yellow Door's first real success," Topper said.

"Not so, Mr. Topper," said Miss Goosegrass. "You must consider every man, woman and child among us a success. You have changed their lives for the better. Many of them owe you their very existence and are well aware of it."

"You are determined to make me blush, Miss," Topper said. "You must learn to save your praise for those to whom it will make a difference. Praising me will further neither you nor anyone else. Praising Mr. Scrooge, if done well, might enhance the future of our institution. I mean him no disrespect when I say that Mr. Scrooge will receive compliments from an attractive woman with far more relish than should they come from me."

"It is my turn to blush, Sir," said Miss Goosegrass and did just that. "I do hope I mistake the task you would have me undertake."

"I only mean to say that I believe that I can rely on your usual cordiality when our guest arrives," he said, looking up with raised eyebrows.

"You may for a certainty, Mr. Topper," she said, then frowned. "Is he not late?"

Topper pulled his watch from his pocket, eyed it and snapped it shut again. "I'd best hurry off to see how the sketching goes. I shall return with our honoured guest within half an hour. You will be prepared for us by then? Jack, I desire you to remain behind and lend whatever assistance may be required by Miss Goosegrass. Will you do that?"

"Yes, Sir!"

⊙

Topper rapped lightly on the door to the artists' studio, but he received no reply. Before knocking again he pressed an ear to the door, not to eavesdrop, but to determine whether or no Scrooge had yet made his departure.

He heard: "He says he cannot finish the drawing because you will not sit still. Each time you move he must rub it all out and begin again. He says his paper is no longer white, but the colour of the streets after the rain." The voice Topper recognised as belonging to Miss Trellis.

This translation was followed by a rapid stream of syllables which Topper identified as coming from Al-Mustafa—though he could make no sense of them. Topper felt that it was time for him to make his presence known, so he rapped the more sharply at the door. This time after a tumbling of sounds the door opened by the knobbly hand Ebenezer Scrooge himself wrapped in nothing more than a white sheet. Following him was a young boy with a charcoal stick in his fingers and a sketchbook tucked under his arm.

"Sir?" was the only word Topper could produce with his startled tongue.

"What are you staring at, Milton? Have you never seen a man in a toga before?" Scrooge said licking his lips.

Topper made a series of unintelligible sounds. He had never seen Scrooge dressed so before and hadn't imagined him to be so thin.

"Is something stuck in your throat, man?" Scrooge demanded and licked his lips again.

"No, Sir," Topper said.

"Certainly you understand the elements of French painting," Scrooge said, gesturing regally to the material draped over his shoulder.

"I'm afraid I do not, Sir," Topper replied. "My education included very little of French painting."

"The Emperor Napoleon himself was painted many times in the guise of a Roman Sovereign."

"Indeed, Sir," Topper said. "I've only read of Napoleon's military campaigns. There has been nothing in the newspapers that I've noticed regarding his portraits."

"Had he not been defeated, I fear we would have heard a great deal more of his portraits," said Scrooge. "Thank God for Wellington."

"Yes, Sir. And Long Live the King."

"I have not introduced to you Master Cratchit," Scrooge said ruffling the head of the boy who stood at his elbow. "He has learnt to draw during his time in Italy and to speak the tongue. I can make no sense of it, but he was speaking it like a native in just weeks. Just weeks! Can you imagine it? What a talent this boy is! Bob Cratchit has so much to be proud of. Tim will be returning to Italy with his sister Belinda in a few days. Quite the responsible girl Belinda is."

"I am please to meet you, young master," Topper said, shaking the boy's hand. "You look well."

"I am feeling strong, Sir, thanks to the kind attentions of Mr. Scrooge. If you will excuse me, I will leave you two gentlemen to your conversation and return to my lesson with Al-Mustafa. He teaches me perspective, but I believe he has it wrong. At least it is not how it is done in Italy."

"Yes, run along, lad. Gather your things for we shall be headed to my charity shortly."

"Yes, Sir," Tim said and bounded back into the studio.

"I have called," Topper said, "to inquire as to when we should expect you to make your way to Yellow Door and to fetch you there when you are ready."

"Yellow Door? What is that?" Scrooge's stomach growled like a good-sized animal.

"Yellow Door is," Topper said, "what the people have come to call your charity, Sir. I am surprised that you have not heard the term used heretofore. It simply refers to the colour of paint on the door to..."

"Whose money pays for this charity, I ask you?"

Topper looked down at his feet. "Yours, Sir, without a doubt."

"Where is the dignity? What sort of name is *Yellow Door* for a charity, I ask you?"

"No sort of name whatsoever, but it's not a name that any one person has given it, but simply the name people use when they speak of it. Perhaps they found *Ebenezer Scrooge's Charitable Aid And Victual Assistance To The Under-advantaged & Desperate* too long to speak easily, although it is far more descriptive, dignified, and proper. But you will pardon me. I have neglected the most rudimentary rule of a host," said Topper remembering Scrooge's protesting stomach. "I have not seen to your personal comfort. Can I get you something to eat, Sir?"

"What do you say?" Scrooge appeared startled by the question.

"Can I get you something to eat? Refreshment of some kind? Some buttered toast or a biscuit perhaps?"

"You tempt me from my regimen?"

"No, Sir. I only wish for you to be at your ease."

"It is not a question of my being at my ease. I have been fasting, Milton. Every Tuesday and Friday. You should try it. It purifies the spirit wonderfully."

"Yes, Sir. I see."

"However, you said refreshments, did you not?"

Topper said, "Yes, Sir. Cook has prepared refreshments for your visit. I believe she mentioned cake. But, of course, if you are fasting..."

"Cake?"

"Yes, Sir. Cake."

"Refreshments are not indulgences." Scrooge said, and it was clear to Topper that an inner dialogue of some complexity now pre-occupied his employer.

"Shall I send word to say that you are on your way?" Topper said.

"You do not expect me to attend the reception dressed like this, do you?" Scrooge said.

"No, Sir. I do not."

"Then please allow me to withdraw for a few minutes to shift my clothes, if you will."

"By all means. I shall await you out-of-doors."

Scrooge closed the door smartly in Topper's face.

◉

"How kind of you to pay us a visit, Mr. Scrooge," Topper said clasping a hand to his bosom and bowing. "And we are delighted that you have brought with you young master Cratchit. I trust that he is enjoying himself."

"Oh yes, Sir," TIm said. "*Sto esercitandosi in nel mio Italiano.*"

"Come again?" Topper said.

"He tells us that he is practising his Italian," Miss Trellis said from behind. Topper hadn't even noticed that she was in the room.

"Well, Sir, welcome back to England," Topper said. Then he turned to Scrooge. "We have long awaited this day." He gestured to the group of six queued before them in their practised formation.

Scrooge returned the bow in kind and said, "You are generous to include Master Cratchit and me in the celebration of the success of my charity. I certainly can see how busy you have been. Why the last time I saw this space, I could never have dreamed it could be turned out so. Such dedication! Such commitment! You—all of you—have outdone yourselves and are worthy of praise far beyond the faint words I can give you."

Topper's six beamed steadily back.

Topper's face showed a great weight lifted from his shoulders. He cleared his throat. "May I begin introductions? You have met Miss Trellis—and Mr. Mustafa several hours since."

"Yes, I have had that pleasure," Scrooge said, arching an eyebrow.

"Mr. Scrooge," Miss Trellis said and curtsied very prettily. She said something quickly in Italian which Tim briefly answered.

"Might I take Master Cratchit back to the studio?" she said. "His leg gives him some little pain, and perhaps he could spend the time practising his drawing seated just now. I believe that Al-Mustafa has set up a still life for him to work from."

"By all means. I will call for him when I am finished here," Scrooge said.

Miss Trellis walked over and took the boy's small hand in her giant fist. Tim looked up into her face and smiled.

"Handsomely, handsomely," she said to Tim as she slowly led him out of the room.

"I am delighted to see the boy doing so well!" Scrooge said.

"As am I," Topper replied. "But let us continue if I may. Next, I should like to introduce to you Miss Jane Goosegrass, a vital member of our staff. She instructs the children in their spelling and sums. She also gives freely of her time to those who even as adults have not had the opportunity to learn to read and write."

"Ah yes. I am familiar with your interest in education, Mr. Topper," Scrooge said and accepted the hand of the woman who stood before him. "I am delighted to meet you, Miss Goosegrass," he said.

The school-mistress curtsied, and blushed violently as she did so. Topper noticed that she could not bring herself to meet Scrooge's eyes, but looked down at her feet instead.

"I hope you are pleased by what you see here to-day, Sir," she said, softly. "The men, women and children—all of us—have worked very hard to make your vision of a haven for the needy come true. If there is any fault in it, it is due to a lack of our will and personal strength and not of your support, nor of Mr. Topper's leadership."

"Nonsense. Nonsense," Scrooge said. "I can see now that you have performed miracles with the inadequate funding I have provided." He bowed. "But you speak of the children. You must lead me to them. Are they kept in a separate room? Why are you hiding them from me? Come, quickly. Where are they, I say?"

"If you are finished your review of the staff, I will take you to them directly," Topper said. "We do have other wonders to share with you."

"No, of course, I am not finished with these good people," Scrooge said stamping his foot impatiently. "I have many questions to ask them and many compliments to pay."

"Which they are eager to receive, though they are an exceedingly modest lot as a whole," Topper said. "I must needs then continue with the introductions."

"By all means. I mean to meet every man, woman and child in this building, I do."

"They will be disappointed if you do not, but we do not intend to make the task an onerous one," Topper said.

"And in no way will it. In no way, at all, Sir. I assure you. It shall be my pleasure."

Topper looked up and caught an expression on Miss Goosegrass's face: She was smitten with Scrooge! Miss Goosegrass then noticed Topper's gaze and made yet another pretence at finding something of interest on the floor just beneath her skirts. Topper supposed that many women found themselves enamoured of Scrooge. Scrooge had indeed become quite the talk of the town. His conversion from miser to philanthropist had won him invitations for every night of the week to highest levels of society all over London. But he had no time to accept any of them—except for the occasional visit he made to the Cratchit's.

"There are two gentlemen in particular I should like to present to you today," Topper said.

"Is the Reverend Mitchell not among you?" Scrooge asked looking about.

"I fear not. Regrettably he has been drawn away at the last moment to tend to one of his flock who has taken ill."

"I am sorry to hear that. I was so looking forward to meeting him."

Topper continued: "It is my privilege to introduce to you two gentlemen, as I have said, without whose help this charity would not be the sound, stolid building it is this day. Allow me to introduce to you Mr. Ned Billings and Mr. William Dawson. Both Christian Heroes and Craftsmen of the highest order."

Billings hobbled forward on his crutch and managed a bow of sorts.

"A crutch?" said Scrooge.

"Yes, Sir. Very kind of you to notice. I am afraid I broke my leg when I slipped upon a nail some weeks since," Billings said.

"I pray you are recovering quickly?"

"Very quickly, indeed, Sir."

Topper knew that the doctor was concerned that Billings wasn't healing quickly enough.

"I know a German doctor who can perform wonders for the lame," Scrooge said. "If you are not wholly recovered within, say, six weeks, I'll have you sent to him."

"Yes, Sir. Thank you, Sir. That is very good of you."

"And who is this with so much fuzz all over his face?" said Scrooge stepping before the next in line.

The American made a bow of a depth to compensate for Billings's inability. "Allow me to introduce myself. My name is William Dawson. Your servant, Sir," Dawson said.

"You are an American, I detect," Scrooge said.

"I am a Son of Virginia, Sir," Dawson replied.

"He comes to us from a considerable distance," Topper said, "but he has made himself more than welcome here and no little useful."

"The gentleman exaggerates my utility," Dawson said. "Though I am far from my native land, I have made so many new friendships, that I consider this to be one of the richest chapters of my life."

"What brings you here from America?" said Scrooge.

"Why, I have been blown here by the wind. It is purely God's Will that adds me to the convocation of fine instruments who together aid in the construction of the charity which bears your name."

"Have you family, Sir?"

Dawson's smooth demeanour vanished. His face turned the colour of ash.

"I...I...I do not. I am afraid that I am an orphan in this old world," he said. "My parents died of consumption some time ago. I have been wandering ever since."

"So you have found a family here with us," Scrooge said.

"Yes, that is very well put, Sir," Dawson replied. "You might indeed say that I have found my family here. But enough talk of me, Mr. Scrooge. When you have a moment's ease, I would take a sliver of it to share some of the ideas which we have for the further improvement of your splendid charity."

"Indeed, it is not complete? I should have thought the execution of my will done to perfection," said Scrooge.

Topper said. "We have discussed, among others, the advantages of having, for instance, a proper wooden floor. Packed earth is rather cold in the winter."

Dawson said, "The ceiling is high enough that we should consider adding a second floor in the interior. With a second floor we could create a large sleeping facility to accommodate two-score men and as many women—the men and women, of course, would be kept separate as you'd expect in a Christian facility such as this—except in the case of families. We would like to add some small apartments in the back for them."

"So many?" said Scrooge.

"We would not, even so, service half of all those who are in need," Topper said.

"I shall give your notion deep thought, Sirs. I will do that. I will have more questions for you," Scrooge said, "as time passes."

Scrooge moved on down the line. He bowed and spoke to Cook: "I have heard a great deal of you, ma'am."

She darted a puzzled look in Mr. Topper's direction, but replaced it with a cordial expression. "You mustn't believe everything you hear, Sir," she said and gave a nervous laugh.

"Your cake, ma'am. I've been told you've baked me a cake."

"Oh, that, Sir. Of course. I should have knowed what you meant. I *have* baked you a cake. And there's lemon squash to wash it down."

"Lemon squash, do you say?"

"Yes, Sir, I do. Or barley water, if you'd prefer."

"It's been a very long time since I've had lemon squash."

"On a day like this, it will quench you like no other."

Scrooge nodded pleasantly and looked to the next person in line.

"And who might this be?" he asked.

"Mary-Martha White. She is kitchen-maid," Topper said.

"Good day to you, Mary-Martha," Scrooge said and pinched her cheek.

She curtsied and said in a bright and practised voice, "Good day to you, Sir. I hope you are enjoying your visit. We've spent a great many hours in preparation for your arrival."

He stepped down the line again. As he did so the door burst open and Patrick Coal bolted into the room. He slid to a stop just next to Jack.

"And who is this young man who finds running indoors preferable to walking?" Scrooge said.

"I am Patrick Coal, Sir, and I am to provide you a short diversion if you wish," the boy said.

"By all means. Should I expect a race against a horse?"

"No Sir, I shall sing for you," the boy replied.

"Sing for me? Excellent. What a wonderful surprise."

Patrick drew a penny-whistle from his pocket and piped a mournful melody. He withdrew the instrument from his lips and sang:

> 'Tis the last rose of summer,
> Left blooming alone;
> All her lovely companions are faded and gone;
> No flow'r of her kindred,
> No rosebud is nigh
> To reflect back her blushes,
> Or give sigh for sigh.

I'll not leave thee, thou lone one,
To pine on the stem;
Since the lovely are sleeping,
Go, sleep thou with them;
Thus kindly I scatter
Thy leaves o'er the bed
Where thy mates of the garden
Lie scentless and dead.
So soon may I follow,
When friendships decay,
And from love's shining circle
The gems drop away!
When true hearts lie wither'd,
And fond ones are flown,

Oh! who would inhabit
This bleak world alone?

"That was excellent young man. Beautiful! Beautiful! You have quite a remarkable voice."

"Thank you very much, Sir," Patrick said, doing his best to restrain a smile of pride.

Scrooge looked down at the pale huddled form on the cart next in line at his feet. "And who are you, young Sir? What is your talent?"

"My name is John Forest, Sir. I am Mr. Topper's page. If you have a taste for recitation, you will enjoy this, Sir." He stopped and cleared his voice and declared:

In Xanadu did Kubla Khan
A stately pleasure-dome decree :
Where Alph, the sacred river, ran
Though caverns measureless to man
        Down to a sunless sea.
So twice five miles of fertile ground
With walls and towers were girdled round :
And there were gardens bright with sinuous rills,
Where blossomed many an incense-bearing tree ;
And here were forests ancients as the hills,
Enfolding sunny spots of greenery.

> But oh ! that deep romantic chasm which slanted
> Down the green hill athwart a cedarn cover !
> A savage place ! as holy and enchanted
> As e'er beneath a waning moon was haunted
> By woman wailing for her demon-lover !
> And from this chasm, with ceaseless turmoil

seething...

"Boy, what is this you recite? Is this Christian Charity which bears my name to become a pleasure dome? Is that the plan? Is this how my money is to be spent!?" cried Scrooge. "And what is all this nonsense of demon lovers?"

"It is 'Kubla Khan—Or, A Vision In A Dream. A Fragment' by Samuel Coleridge, Sir. But I've not finished it yet."

"Who has taught you this horrible thing?" Scrooge said, turned on Miss Goosegrass, and glared at her with burning eyes. She struggled to compose a reply—but managed only to widen her eyes in shock. "Is this what passes for learning at my charity?" he hissed.

"One moment, Mr. Scrooge..." Topper said.

"No, Sir. I heard it recited on the stage," Jack said.

"You heard it recited on the stage? Do not lie to me, boy. Who would allow a young boy to hear such a thing? Even if you were audience to it, you don't mean to tell me you heard it one time and you've remembered it whole cloth! Such a thing would take many hours to learn."

Topper said, "Mr. Scrooge, if you will just listen..."

"Mr. Scrooge, if you are suggesting that the curriculum I have taught here is in any way..." Miss Goosegrass found her voice at last.

Topper stepped forward. "If I may explain, Sir. Mr. Forest here has a rather extraordinary talent."

"I have not had my word, Mr. Topper, if you please," Miss Goosegrass continued. "I may have no connections, but that is no reason for this man to speak to me in that fashion."

Topper said, "Begging your pardon, Miss Goosegrass, but I believe that Mr. Scrooge, once he hears what I..."

She dismissed him with a slash of her hand in the air. "My honour has been sullied and if you will not step forward to defend it, I will do so on my own. Mr. Scrooge, I ask you: do you mean to blackguard me and my lessons before one and all?" She stepped forward and stood nose to nose with said gentleman with hands on her hips.

"Please, Miss Goosegrass..." Topper said attempting to pour oil on the water, but she would have none of it.

"I am waiting for the gentleman to answer me inasmuch as I am quite certain that he has a tongue and knows the use of it. As a lady, I am entitled to an answer to my query."

Topper judged it was time to withdraw and let the battle play itself out.

Scrooge, for the first time, looked Miss Goosegrass squarely in the eye. He had no fear of sharp tongues insofar as he owned one with a razor's edge himself. The pale blue of her eye, the lid, the lashes, the arch of the brow gave him pause. He followed the line of the nose, nostrils flaring angrily. How much time had passed, he could not say. His knees trembled, but not from fear. He was conscious that a word was required of him, but could not find one—nor could he recall the question. At length he found a very short one.

"I..." he said.

"That is not good enough, Sir. Not good enough for a Christian woman with an education. You can do better. Follow your subject with a verb, and we shall judge the depth of your answer again," Miss Goosegrass said.

"I beg your forgiveness."

"You do?" she said in a brittle whisper. A brief look of triumph swept cross her face only to be washed away by an expression which broke Scrooge's heart. "You will excuse me, Sir," she said and bolted out of the room.

Topper cleared his throat, took Scrooge's arm and turned him back toward Jack. He said, "Once young Jack hears a thing, he can never forget it. There appears to be no limit to the capacity of his recollections. He is just one of the many wonders who are sheltered by your great charity, Sir."

With a brave face stained by tears, Jack rapidly repeated every word of conversation which had been spoken since he had entered the room—

including the tongue lashing which Scrooge had just received.

Scrooge still shaken looked down at Jack. "You will excuse me, dear boy. I have never met such a one as you before. Perfectly dazzling display, young man."

"I did not wish to offend you, Mr. Scrooge," Jack said. "It is poetry, Sir. Surely a man of your refinements has an appreciation of poetry. It was my way of receiving you. To show you that we are not idle creatures only worthy of pity."

Scrooge sucked in his breath. "Of course, you didn't, and of course you aren't. I have only myself to blame. If I had been here all along and gotten to know each of you, I would not be so unappreciative. My temper has made a muck of things." He spread his arms in exasperation.

"You have been busy, Sir," Topper said. "We do not expect you to devote so much of your time as well as being so generous with your funds..."

"No, Mr. Topper, you will not make excuses for me. My duty has been to be here all along. *Noblesse oblige*, one might say." Scrooge hesitated and looked nervously at the door through which Miss Goosegrass had made such a hasty exit. "Do you believe..." he said.

"I believe Miss Goosegrass will be fine, Sir. Now may I take you to the children. They will bring you great joy. I guarantee it."

"Yes, Milton. Let me see the children. I believe I may find myself on better footing with them."

◉

It would have been Miss Goosegrass's job to show Scrooge the children, but as she was at the moment indisposed, Cook guided Scrooge in her stead. She said, "I expect you'll wish to see the orphans first, Sir."

"By all means, let us see the orphans. Are they many?" Scrooge said.

Cook said, "They are only two in number at the moment, Sir. We had three more, but they run off last week."

"Only two? How delightful. Are they two girls? Two boys?"

"Or perhaps they was carried away by their uncle."

"And what are the names of our two orphans?"

"Their uncle was released from prison, you see, the day before. That's what makes me think they was carried off by him."

"Or is it a boy and a girl?" Scrooge asked.

"What? Oh, them. Our orphans! Yes, they's a boy and girl. Brother and sister, I should say. Bombay Blacks, they are."

"Good Heavens! Are they Christians?"

"They can quote you scripture, but that don't make them Christians. Hindoos they was born and Hindoos they'll be till the day they die. Beautiful children, they are, though, Sir. The little girl prettier than a pansy, but too proud for her own good."

Cook knocked and opened the door to a small apartment. Two children with dark skin and simple clothing looked up at them.

"Who is this man?" the eldest, a girl of perhaps ten years, said. "What are you doing in our room?"

Cook said, "This is Mr. Scrooge, young mistress Rajani. He has come to see you."

"I do not care for the look of his pedigree," the girl said curling her lip and turning away. "He is old, and he is full of himself, I judge."

"Watch your tongue, young lady, or you'll find your ears boxed, you will," Cook said.

"You may box me if it makes you feel superior, old woman!" Rajani said.

The boy looked up from stacking odd blocks of wood. He saw Scrooge and said, "Oh, Sir! Oh, Sir! Watch what I am doing. Watch what I am doing!" But instead of stacking blocks, the boy pressed his head against the floor, positioned his arms to steady himself and stood on his head.

"Their father was an acrobat. Their mother, too, but they died of consumption three months since," Cook said.

"You poor creatures," Scrooge said, feeling his eyes sting.

The boy dropped back to his feet. "My father is stronger than you are, Sir. He can run faster and jump higher."

Scrooge nodded. "Fathers are always stronger. They are always faster and jump higher. You may depend upon it, young man."

"Would you like to feel of my muscle?" the boy said and hurried to

Scrooge's side. He bent his arm at a right angle, gritted his teeth and flexed his arm. His entire body shook with the effort.

"That is the strongest muscle I have ever felt," said Scrooge.

"Ha!" the boy said, "I am even stronger than you. You are an old man."

"Yes, I am old, and I have no doubt that you are stronger than me. Because you are so strong I will pay you to be my guard. Would you like that?"

"Ha, I can't guard you. I am just a little boy. You are a silly man."

"Yes, I suppose I am."

"Why do you not leave us now?" Rajani said. "Or throw us into the streets if you wish. Do you expect me to beg you to give us food? I will not."

"Cook, may I ask you to leave until I call for you?" Scrooge said.

"Yes, Sir, Mr. Scrooge. You needn't worry. I won't tell a soul." She backed out of the room as if Scrooge were royalty.

"You will beat us now," the girl said.

Scrooge slowly lowered himself to the floor to sit beside the girl, but did not touch her or try to catch her eye. He said: "I spent a very long time being angry because my father left me when I was very young. He hadn't died, but sent me away. I loved him so very much, but I also hated him with a great fury. I can never forgive him. My heart will never let me."

"I do not need a father or mother," Rajani said.

"Whether you do or not, they are gone and cannot be replaced." Scrooge looked at the dark, pretty face and saw tears streaming down it. He pulled his handkerchief from his pocket and handed it to her. "You will never have another mother and father, and they will stay in your heart forever and will never be forgotten. You must hold them there because there will be times in life when you will need to feel the comfort they can still provide. You have the advantage of me. My father chose to send me away. Your father and mother did not wish to leave you."

The girl covered her face with her hands. Her brother sat by her side and put his arm around her. He said, "Do not be so sad, Rajani. You have me."

"You do, indeed, have your brother, young lady, as I had my sister," Scrooge said. "His courage will never fail you. And..." Scrooge hesitated

"...you have me. I am not your father, nor your mother, nor your brother. But I am your friend."

"You are not our friend," the girl said her voice trembling.

"You are not ready for friends now. I understand. But do not wait until you are old—as I did—before you are ready."

The girl turned her head and blinked her large, wet, black eyes at him.

Scrooge awkwardly made his way back to his feet. He said, "I will come back when you are ready." He walked out of the room.

◉

Miss Goosegrass had more things than she could fit in her pasteboard valise. She drew out a few things which she felt she could live without. These she would leave behind. Perhaps whoever it was who would take her place would have use for them.

She had little idea where she might go. Could she find employment as Governess again? Perhaps she could find a position on the continent. It would be a difficult thing, however, without references from Yellow Door, but she had others.

She looked in the mirror on her bureau. Her face was red and her eyes puffy. A piece of cake which was brought to her a half hour since sat untouched looking less appetising every second.

A knock at the door, cut short her sniffling, and she asked, "Who is it?"

"Ebenezer Scrooge," was the reply. "I would like a word with you, if I may."

Had he returned to give her a final taste of his anger before she left? A small sound of fear escaped her throat. "One moment," she said, stood before the mirror and examined the redness of her eyes and face in the mirror. *How can I see anyone looking like this?* She dabbed at her nose, but saw how little good it did. Instead she drew on a pair of dark glasses. Three steps took her to the door which she opened swiftly. She said, "What can I do to help you?"

"Miss Goosegrass," Scrooge said, holding his hat in his hand.

"I was just packing...."

"Packing? Whatever for, Miss? You are not leaving on account of my peckishness, I should hope. I have come to beg your pardon and now that you tell me that you are leaving, I shall add the need to ask you to stay."

"I have found a position elsewhere I am afraid and cannot stay."

"You are truly leaving us?" he said.

"I am afraid so."

"I will offer you twice the salary of your new employer."

"You are too kind, but I could not possibly..."

"Three times, then. Please, I would have you stay. If you agree to remain here at my charity and continue to educate both children and adults, I shall pledge to leave this building and never darken its door again."

"That would never do, Mr. Scrooge. Your charity needs you here, has needed you here from the beginning."

Scrooge said, "It appears that it cannot be both. You are needed much more desperately than I am."

Miss Goosegrass shook her head. "I will stay only on one condition," she said.

Scrooge said, "You have only to name it."

"You must visit your charity every day of the week. You must show yourself to the people who depend so entirely upon you—unless you are ill."

"What if I am drawn away on business?" Scrooge said.

"You are quite right, Sir. I have no right to make demands upon you. Please forgive me. If you will excuse me, I must resume my packing."

"You have no right to make demands, perhaps, but equally you have no right to deny any pledge which I mean to make wholly of my own free will. I make this pledge: I will visit at my charity every day of the week, except those days when I am too ill to rise from my bed—or if I am drawn away on business, I will write a letter to my charity to be read aloud to one and all at the evening meal each day I am gone."

Miss Goosegrass pulled off her dark glasses and pressed her hands to her face. "With such a commitment from your noble self, Sir, I can hardly do less. I make the same pledge as yourself, although I very much doubt I shall often be drawn away upon business."

Scrooge smiled at her. "Until we meet again, Good Lady," he said and bowed deeply. He glanced at the cake on her bureau top. "I see you have not eaten your cake..." he said.

Long after he had left the room she stared at the empty plate.

CHAPTER 8

≈

To Serve Man

TOPPER SQUINTED AT HIS OWN REFLECTION IN THE WINDOW. HE LIFTED A finger to his forelock and lifted it gingerly. His hairline ebbed like the tide. Unlike the tide, his hairline was not likely to return.

No matter, he thought. *I caught me a beautiful bride already. But I shall not lose her by growing me a belly. I promise that much. I'll not end up like my father—too round to fit through the door.*

He turned, took a step and stumbled.

"Jack, bless you, boy," he said, careful to keep his voice kindly. "have you ever thought of wearing a bell like the friendly cat or pasture bovine?"

"I shall give it serious consideration," said Jack, pulling himself back upon his cart. "Should I live so long. However, I am not certain what good it would do. I spoke your name several times, and you made no reply."

Topper's hand went unconsciously to his hair again. "Lost in reverie, Jack, I'm afraid. It happens when you grow old as I have."

"You're not old, Sir," Jack said. "Not like Mr. Scrooge."

"Now there, Mr. Forest. He is not so old as all that. His health is good and he is in excellent spirits. I would expect Mr. Scrooge to have many decades of life ahead of him," Topper said with a thin smile. "Now what can I do for you?"

"It is Miss Trellis. She sends her compliments and wishes you would visit her in Al-Mustafa's studio at your soonest opportunity."

Topper frowned. "Is there a problem?"

"Vandals, Sir. Someone has spoilt Mr. Scrooge's portrait."

"You may tell her that I will be there directly," Topper said grabbing his hat. "Never mind, Jack. I shall tell her myself as I'm on my way."

◎

Topper bent forward with his hands clasped behind him careful not to touch anything. Fresh paint glistened on the surface of the stretched linen frame whose lead white priming was covered in broad strokes of umber, grey and a muddy shade of green. Topper found the aroma of linseed oil not unpleasant, almost delicious in a peculiar sort of way.

To the right on the rectangular canvas stood a man with his arms clasped over his breast. None but the most basic shapes were evident except for the sitter's face. Al-Mustafa had spent his efforts on the most important part of any portrait, the eyes.

Topper said, with an approving nod, "It's an extraordinary likeness." The gaze was incisive, commanding yet with that spark of humanity which only the best portrait painters can portray.

The comment sent Al-Mustafa into convulsive sobs.

Topper's eyes scanned the painting for signs of vandalism that Jack had mentioned, but could find no tear in the fabric, nor any defacement of the subject.

"Tell Mr. Ali, that I cannot find the damage of which he complains," Topper said. "Though I am no connoisseur in such matters I can find no fault in the painting whatsoever."

"Can you not see it?" Miss Trellis translated. "It is horrible."

"Perhaps if he could direct my eyes," Topper said.

Al-Mustafa approached the canvas as one might approach a poisonous snake. At some distance he pointed to an area in the background which Topper had not paid particular attention.

Topper knit his brows, but could see nothing. He gripped the easel and turned the painting so that he could see the surface in a raking light. What Topper had taken only to be murky strokes of paint took form.

"It looks like a large eye," Topper said. "Is this an early attempt at painting one of Mr. Scrooge's eyes which was later painted over?"

Miss Trellis said, "Al-Mustafa says that he has never painted an eye anywhere on the panel except where Mr. Scrooge's two eyes are currently located."

"It's some sort of prank then. Someone has slipped into your studio when you've been out and dabbed it in. Nothing more. You needn't worry. I was concerned that someone had damaged the canvas in some permanent manner."

Al-Mustafa sat on the edge of a crate with his head in his hands muttering to himself. Miss Trellis spoke softly to him, but the painter merely shook his head.

Miss Trellis translated. "Al-Mustafa says that the eye was painted by no human agency. The craftsmanship of the eye is superior to his own—to any he has ever witnessed. He believes that the eye is evil, that it portends danger."

"Surely he exaggerates and his experience of the levels of craftsmanship which our English painters are capable is not broad. Tell Mr. Ali that I am instructing him to paint it over and continue with the portrait. If he is concerned that the vandal will return I'll have someone watch the studio night and day if need be," Topper said.

"Al-Mustafa says he cannot continue the portrait. He refuses," Miss Trellis said.

Topper lifted his hands in exasperation. "Whyever not? If Mr. Ali refuses to paint Mr. Scrooge's picture now, what will our benefactor think? He is sure to take offence. This could jeopardise the charity's funding. Oh my Lord! How many times have I pointed to Mr. Ali's success as a shining example of the good works we've accomplished at Yellow Door. What shall I do now?"

Miss Trellis translated. Al-Mustafa hung his head and made fearful sounds.

"He says he is frightened," Miss Trellis said. "But he does not repeat his refusal to finish the portrait."

Topper said, "Ask him if he would be less frightened if I were to increase his fee for the portrait."

A rapid conversation ensued.

"Al-Mustafa explains that he is not a man easily frightened. His Christian faith steels him to face danger and the unknown. He hopes you do not consider him a superstitious and ignorant man," Miss Trellis said.

"Can I take that to mean yes?" Topper said.

"I would believe that is a correct interpretation."

⊙

There is a pleasing effect upon the eye when hammer, nail, saw, and wood are used to build a harmonious living space or to produce an article of furniture. It must be said, however, that these same tools in concert produce rather less delight upon the ear. Scrooge muted the noise of a dozen hammers and saws at their play by pressing balls of wax into his auditory canals—though that sensation wasn't entirely agreeable either. He could not, however, block the scent of sawdust and fresh paint which hung in the air. Nor would he want to. Scrooge thought it the sweetest smell a man could inhale—not so intoxicating as a woman's perfume perhaps, but gratifying in a manly way nevertheless.

Taking care not to pick up a splinter, he ran his fingers over the top of a table of rough lumber he had knocked together himself. He was as proud of it as any piece in exotic hardwood built by master cabinet-makers he had ever owned.

His table wobbled in a corner room between two bow windows—the only ones of their kind in his charity thus far. The room was not large as far as executive offices went, but it was his and was not used for any other purpose.

A ledger in Topper's neat hand displayed these column entries: "Due," "Projected Expenses," "Food," "Building Materials," "Clothing," and several others. Scrooge meant to adhere closely to the budget he'd prepared for his charity, but it was not an ungenerous one. He would see to further building improvements in the near future if the banging of hammers did not drive him to madness first.

Scrooge's quill danced lightly as a mayfly over the columns of figures calculating their sums, their differences, their products and quotients. Organising finances was his skill. Numbers talked to him. He played them like cards. Scrooge applied them as deftly to paper as a painter applied oils to canvas. Make no mistake: money was Scrooge's medium.

Scrooge paused to look out his bow window. Roiling clouds blotted away the blue of the sky. A summer storm brewed. He stood, stretched, removed the wax from his ears, and was immediately greeted with the sound of hissing rain. Mercifully the din of construction had ended—at least temporarily.

A polite rap at the door drew his attention.

"Yes, come in," he said. A low peal of thunder rattled the windows followed by a flash of lightning.

The door opened and a head poked in.

"Ah, Mr. Scrooge, I've found you at last. Am I interrupting important work?"

"No, Sir. Please come in. Who do I have the pleasure of addressing, and what can I do for you?"

A round figure in a dark suit stepped forward, reached for Scrooge's hand and delivered a firm handshake. "My name is Salvation Mitchell. I'm afraid I wasn't able to attend your reception last week, and I am sorry. Unfortunately, it couldn't be helped. One of my flock was ill—terminally so, I'm sorry to say, and I needed to remain by her bedside until the end."

"I am grieved hear of it. Was it a painful end?" said Scrooge.

"Yes, it was," Mitchell said, lowering his eyes. "Whenever one of the members of my humble church leaves this world, I am by their side. I should explain myself. Sometimes I get rattled and forget to include all the details needed to make myself perfectly clear."

He smiled and smoothed the hair on his head. "I should say that a small number of those who cling to the same faith as I followed me here from our previous location in the United States. They do not belong in your charity, Mr. Scrooge. They are not in need financially speaking, but neither are they what you might call wealthy. It is their spiritual wealth which concerns them, and so I have not brought them round as it would not be appropriate.

We live a rather reclusive life some distance from here. It's not extravagant, but we are comfortable in our simple pursuits."

Scrooge said, "I understand. I am nevertheless glad you were able to stop by, Reverend. Mr. Topper has told me a great deal about you."

"No doubt he has. *Ebenezer Scrooge's Charitable Aid And Victual Assistance To The Under-advantaged & Desperate* has become such a large part of my thoughts and heart. Mr. Topper and I have become fast friends. Practically brothers."

"I have been rude. Won't you have a seat?" Scrooge said.

"That is kindly of you." The Reverend Mitchell lowered himself stiffly onto the crate which temporarily served as a chair and hissed as if he were sitting himself in hot bath-water. "These knees are not what they once were. There are times when I can hardly rise in the morning. Well, you don't want to hear about my aches and pains. I understand you will be visiting us far more frequently now."

"Yes," Scrooge said, "every day—so long as I am fit and able. I will never again separate myself from the charity which bears my name. I shall devote myself to it with my whole heart."

Mitchell's eyes sparkled as he said, "That's wonderful news. That can't help but inspire us to work all the harder."

"You must look to God, Reverend. Do not depend upon an old sinner like Ebenezer Scrooge for inspiration. I could not coax a fly to buzz."

"You are too modest, Sir."

"Never mind me. Where do you call home, Sir? America, no doubt, but from which city?"

"From a rather rural area of Pennsylvania, Mr. Scrooge. Little more than farmers, cows and gentle Indians. I'm sure you've never heard of it," Mitchell said, calmly folding his hands in his lap.

Scrooge watched him carefully. Mitchell didn't exhibit any of the eccentric qualities which Topper had described. He was not dancing at his feet, nor did he seem able to. He, in fact, appeared entirely sensible. Could this be the same man Topper referred to?

"Tell me more about your faith, Sir. You are not Church of England."

"No, I am not, Mr. Scrooge. Though I have no doubt that the members of that illustrious organisation have a deep-felt faith and believe it to be their way. However, it is not mine. We call ourselves simply 'The Church of Him.'"

"'The Church of Him!' I cannot say that I have ever heard of it."

"Our numbers are small, but our hearts are big."

"Your faith is unique in what way, Sir?" Scrooge said. "What activities do your beliefs deny you? Do you disbelieve in dance or drink or tobacco or the wearing of red or merry-making?" Scrooge said.

"A system of belief should not be founded on a list of thou-shalt-not's," Mitchell said. "We have no prohibitions against any of *those* things nor any others. With one exception. We do not speak His name lightly. There are too many people for whom His name comes far too quickly to the lips. His name is sacred. Not to be issued frivolously. We reserve His name for our private prayer. Otherwise we believe that we should each of us follow our hearts to make decisions about our social and moral behaviours. We cannot know the mind of Him, so we must rely on our own consciences to guide us."

"I am in complete agreement with you, Sir," Scrooge said. "Really. I find that refreshing. Too many faiths have been based on denial. What is it exactly that you base your faith upon?"

The Reverend Mitchell squinted thoughtfully. He said, "Compassion, Trust, Hope. Peace. Above all—to serve Him and in so doing to serve Man."

Scrooge sat forward. "Very reasonable. But let us get to the primary issue which I have struggled with for some time. Why should I select you to minister to the people of my charity? You belong to no recognised religious faith. You bring us no added income, nor sources of materials nor man-power."

Mitchell's face took on a stung appearance, but he inhaled and replied evenly, "You are, of course, under no obligation to do more than see me to the door. I am here only on your approval. If you wish me to leave, all you need do is ask. You are quite correct in your estimations. I bring no earthly value to your charity. I have none to offer and don't possess the connections or influence for others to do so in my stead."

Scrooge tapped a sharp finger on the table. "I will need someone here at my charity who knows the local people," Scrooge said and tapped a second time. "Knows the area. Knows its history. I need someone who understands the distinction between the classes. You, being an American, can't possibly know anything of this."

"You are of course correct, Mr. Scrooge," Mitchell said. "You need someone local, that's for sure. I can see that now. There's no sense to bothering you any further. I will gather my things and leave by to-morrow. I thank you, however, for the opportunity you've given me to get to know the people here." Mitchell reached out his hand again to grip Scrooge's hand in farewell, but Scrooge did not take it.

Instead he said sharply, "I have not finished, Reverend Mitchell. Wait until you have heard me out."

Mitchell frowned and withdrew his hand.

Scrooge said, "Tell me, Sir, what should we do with Mrs. Edelstein and Mr. Levy?"

"What shall we do with them? We—or rather you—need to make them as comfortable as we can. They are part of your charity as much as any of the others." Reverend Mitchell's face crinkled in spite of his effort to smile.

"But they are Jews, are they not?" Scrooge said.

"They are, but you do not mean to turn them out because of their religious convictions, do you?" Mitchell said. "Maybe that's a thing done in England, but in America..."

Scrooge raised his voice to a commanding pitch and said, "Reverend Mitchell, how should my charity deal with those who do not share our Christian faith? What should we do with the Jews? What shall we do with the Hindus?"

"I must beg my leave of you, Mr. Scrooge," Mitchell said and stood up quickly. "I will take no part in what you are suggesting. The most spiritual act of any faith is to offer mercy and compassion regardless of the ethnic or religious background of those in need."

Scrooge laughed with relief. "I am only too glad to hear you say that, my dear Reverend. I must therefore beg you *not* to leave your post. In spite of any shortcomings of your background, I am convinced that you will do very well. You are what we need here. I'm not at all certain that the Church of England could supply us with a clergy with such a fresh perspective as yours. We must be open to new ideas—values and notions from other peoples. We must not be judgmental in our attempt to learn more about each other. You have a permanent home here, Reverend, should you wish it."

CHAPTER 9

ගුව

Charades

"My darling," Topper said, holding his wife closely. "If you don't leave go of me, I cannot shave. And if I cannot shave, I will not be presentable before the people of Yellow Door. And if I am not presentable to the people of Yellow Door, I cannot command their respect. And if I cannot command their respect, I cannot help them to help themselves."

"And do you give me permission to help myself?" Lucille Topper said pressing her lips against his.

"Madame, you make my head spin," said Mr. Topper once she had withdrawn slightly.

"What difference would it make should you be thirty minutes late? Or an hour for that matter? They know we are newly married, and certainly they would understand."

"It would make all the difference in the world, my sweet. When I say that I will be at such and such a place at such and such a time, I mean for people to trust me to be then and there as I said."

"But just this one morning," Lucille said, breathing softly into his ear.

"You have made that same proposal every morning since our wedding," he said, gently pulling himself away. "And though I must say that it delights me to no end, I have my responsibilities. And there are such things as evenings, you know. Please, my love, stand aside for one moment. I need to set my shaving things out." Being bare to the waist, he pulled off his rings and set them on the washstand, placed a towel around his neck, lathered his face, stropped his razor to a frightful edge and drew it expertly across his chin.

"No," he said, seeing her furtively approach from behind in the glass. "This is no time for any of your funny business."

"But I wish only to see if you are ticklish. You tell me that you are not, but you will not let me test you," said Lucille.

"There is no need to test me. Would I have any reason to lie to you?" he said.

"You might," she said.

"Well, I have a razor in my hand which I've placed against my neck and if you wish me to spill my blood, now is the time to perform your experiment because if you make a lunge at me I will surely from pure reflex jerk my hand and make a horrible gash in my throat. Have I made myself clear?"

She said, "You have, dear. I wouldn't want your throat cut on my account."

"I am delighted to hear that," said he, mopping the soapy residue from his face.

She took his wedding ring, slipped it on his finger and brought his hand to her face. The sensation of her brushing his fingers against her lips sent a pleasant rush down his spine.

"And now I must go," he said pulling gently away and slipping on his shirt. "I shall see you this evening. I won't be late. I promise."

She said, "Oh, I nearly forgot. I am afraid you've missed your opportunity. To-night you will not find me at home. I have received a note from Father saying that my mother is ill. You must eat and sleep alone to-night as I will be sitting at her side and nursing her."

"Oh my goodness. Milton the Bachelor is free to roam the street once again," he said wriggling his fingers sensually in the air.

She slapped his shoulder lightly. "Who knows, perhaps you'll see me at one of your old nightly haunts in the company of strange and exotic men."

His reply made him an hour late.

⊙

It would not be a proper classroom for some time. Students sat on the floor or upon wooden crates and practised their spelling and multiplication tables on a variety of materials—everything from half-sheets of paper when they could be had to slates to scraps of lumber with chalk. Yet learning was taking place, Miss Goosegrass could see it, could feel it in the pit of her stomach.

On some days there were more adults in school than children, though most preferred to be tutored by older students such as Miss Eustacia Hardy during the evening hours. Mr. Guild was the only adult with them to-day, but his difficulties in hearing kept him from understanding much of what was taught.

"Haresh, would you please take your seat?" Miss Goosegrass said for perhaps the twentieth time in the past hour. "If you do not sit, how will you learn?" she said.

"Ha!" said the boy. "I already know how to read and do my sums."

"Then would you like to teach other students what you already know?" Miss Goosegrass said.

"I would not. What is it that you would do then?" the boy said.

Rajani, the boy's sister said, "Sit down, you little monkey, before they beat you."

Haresh turned on his sister and said, "Miss Goosegrass will not beat me, Sister. I am stronger than she is."

The door to the room flew open and a voice boomed, "I am stronger than you!"

Haresh turned and planted his tiny fists on his hips. "No, old man. I am stronger than *you*."

This is the third time this week, Miss Goosegrass thought with a sigh.

"Perhaps a contest will prove which of us is the more powerful. Do you accept my challenge?" Scrooge said, twisting his face into his most heroic expression.

"I beat you yesterday. I will beat you again," Haresh said squinting and twisting his mouth.

The two combatants strode toward each other grimacing fiercely with every step. Scrooge made a series of strongman grunts which were echoed by Haresh.

Rajani said, "Haresh, stop this silliness and return to your studies. You are annoying Miss Goosegrass, and—worse—you are embarrassing me."

Haresh ignored her, but rushed forward to meet his enemy. Scrooge of necessity dropped to a knee to meet the boy face to face. Their first clash produced sparks and growls and howls of pain and delight. They grumbled and struggled, but soon Scrooge's face wore the signs of exhaustion and defeat. At length he collapsed to the floor and closed his eyes.

"I am afraid," he said, hardly moving, "that you have me again. But there is always to-morrow. I shall learn to read, do my sums accurately, exercise and eat what Cook puts before me, and if not to-morrow someday I shall defeat you."

Haresh put a triumphant foot on Scrooge's motionless body and raised his crooked arms for all to see.

"How am I ever to teach these students their lessons, Mr. Scrooge," Miss Goosegrass said, but not without humour, "when every day we are disrupted by your...your silly charades?"

Scrooge climbed as quickly as he could to his feet, straightened his clothes, brushed the dust from his shoulders and bowed elegantly.

"Miss Goosegrass, how fine you look to-day!"

"You will not charm me in that way, Mr. Scrooge," she said.

"In what way might I charm you, then?" said Scrooge.

"Mr. Scrooge," Miss Goosegrass said, but could find no way to conclude her sentence.

Every child (save Rajani) at that moment bolted from their crates and rushed as one at Scrooge. The tiny boys balled up their fists and pounded his thighs. The girls clung to his coat sleeves and tried with all their might to pull him down.

"You have turned these children against me," he said and wept.

"Bam bam bam," the boys said in chorus. Although Mr. Guild had not joined the students, even he could hear their noise and added shouts of encouragement of his own.

Slowly Scrooge slithered once again to the floor and lay motionless. All eight children leapt upon him, some choosing an arm or a leg to wrestle with, each growling in a unique manner.

"I am finished," Scrooge said with more than a little melodrama. "My days are at an end. I cannot match these children for their strength or their viciousness."

The boys stood boldly flexing their arms. The girls fell upon Scrooge patting his head, kissing his hands and trying to pull him upright.

"There, there," the girls said. "See what you boys have done?"

Miss Goosegrass knew not whether to laugh or be angry with him. She said in an even voice: "Are you quite finished, Mr. Scrooge?"

"Not quite," he said as the children pulled him to his feet for a second time.

"Children, please return to your seats," Miss Goosegrass said.

"Yes, children," said Scrooge. "Obey your teacher else I will have Mr. Topper in, and see that you are all beaten."

The children laughed rather sharply at that. Mr. Topper, they knew, was more likely to deliver sweets than punishment.

Scrooge pressed a finger to his lips, and they all grew instantly silent.

"Shall I tell you a story?" he said.

"Yes!" they shouted as one.

"You must sit quietly, then. And when I have left you are to return to your lessons and mind every word your teacher tells you, do you hear?"

The nodded eagerly.

"Excellent. Then allow me to begin: There once was an old crow. He had not had a happy life. His father had pushed him from his nest when he was but a juvenile. The Old Crow did not die, but learned the cruel ways of the world only too well. He survived and he prospered—though mostly at the expense of his fellow birds."

"He should be killed," Haresh said.

"Haresh! I will not have that kind of language in my classroom!" Miss Goosegrass said in her most authoritative tone.

"Your teacher is correct, young man," Scrooge said. "There is too much death in the world already to wish anyone to be killed—even in a story."

"I am sorry, Sir. I apologise," said the boy.

"Accepted. Let me continue: the Old Crow was visited by three færies and shown the error of his ways and the Old Crow changed in his heart. He now wished to help all the little animals in the kingdom. He started a home for those who could not find food to eat."

"As you have," said Billy Parker, his dirty face breaking into a wide grin.

Scrooge pulled his handkerchief from his pocket and dabbed at the boy's face. "Why, yes, as a matter of fact. He built a place much like Yellow Door."

Scrooge had never used the term Yellow Door before. Always it had been *his* charity. At this moment he knew that was no longer true. It was no longer *his* charity, but *theirs*—together.

"I believe I know the story, Mr. Scrooge, " said Miss Goosegrass. "But the version I heard differs somewhat in detail. The Old Crow was not so old in the version I have heard. But in fact was reborn in spite of his age as measured by the calendar."

"Who am I to disagree with a woman of your education and reading?" Scrooge said.

"How does the story end?" Haresh wanted to know.

"I don't know," Scrooge said, pursing his lips thoughtfully. "I will have to ponder upon it. Perhaps you could make up the ending for me."

"Oh yes, Sir. I will tell you the story. The Old Crow wants to marry the beautiful princess, but evil demons cast a spell upon him and turn him into a monster."

"That is not a very happy ending, young man," said Scrooge.

Miss Goosegrass gave Haresh a withering look.

"I shall have to make a happier one then," the boy said.

Scrooge led Haresh to the opposite side of the room. He sat down on a crate and spoke in a low voice. Although Miss Goosegrass pretended to be busy at her table, correcting papers, she could not help but overhear their conversation.

Scrooge said, "I have need of you to do me a favour. Can you do it?"

Haresh said, "Does it require great strength and bravery?"

"It surely does, my boy. More strength and bravery than I myself have to draw upon."

"Then I am your man," Haresh said. "What is it you wish me to do?"

"I wish for you to give something to your sister from me."

"Why cannot you give it to her yourself?" the boy asked. "She sits just there."

Scrooge said, "I am very much afraid that your sister does not like me very much."

The boy nodded.

"Please give this to her now. I will stay here." He handed him a small box wrapped in a ribbon.

"This pretty thing—I am thinking she will refuse it," Haresh said.

"Perhaps so. But try to give it to her nevertheless."

"You will not beat her if she throws it back at your feet?"

"I will not beat her if she throws it back at my feet or for any other reason —ever. I promise this with all my heart. I only beat wicked boys."

The boy again nodded. "Wait here. I will return in a moment." He strode boldly over to his sister who made a pretence of reading a pamphlet. He roughly took her hand and pressed the small box into it.

"What is this?" Rajani said.

"It is a gift from the old man. If you refuse it, I shall break both your arms."

Miss Goosegrass stood to her feet, her mouth opened about to protest.

"You could not break two twigs, Little Monkey," Rajani said. "If you do not stop this nonsense I will tell everyone you are in love with Eustacia."

"Sister, can you not keep a still tongue in your head?" the boy cried in alarm.

"My tongue takes its example from your own," she said.

"Never mind about that. Just open the box and be quick about it!" Haresh said.

"I shall open the box, but not because you have commanded me to. I shall open it because it was given to me by a gentleman."

"You are calling him a gentleman now?" Haresh said.

Rajani ignored her brother and opened the box. She pulled off the ribbon and lifted the lid. Inside nested in a layer of cotton was a silver necklace. Scrooge stepped quickly forward.

"It was my mother's," he said. "I want you to have it."

Two small tears formed in the corners of Rajani's eyes. She looked up into Scrooge's face. "I cannot accept your gift or your continued kindnesses," she said and held the box out for him.

"Whyever not?"

"Because you will leave us. I cannot trust you. I cannot give you my heart. We have been hurt already by those who loved us."

Scrooge said, "I will never leave you. I will be here for you as long as I live. You will never be friendless again."

"Why do you make this promise to us?" Rajani said.

"Because I am commanded to do so by my heart. I am helpless to disobey."

"You cannot be our father."

"I will be your friend and protector," Scrooge said.

She nodded. "Let me think about it. Return to-morrow, and I will have an answer for you."

Scrooge bowed to her deeply and turned to Miss Goosegrass who was fighting back tears of her own.

"I do not mean to ignore you, Miss Goosegrass. I own I owe you an apology for the chaos which I have brought to your class this day—all this week."

"There is no need..." she began.

"There is every need, Miss. Every need, indeed. There is much I wish to discuss with you on a variety of matters, but this is neither the time nor the place to do so. Would you do me the honour of having dinner with me this evening?"

◎

Topper placed a small hand mirror on his desk where he could study his own reflection. With the tips of his fingers he retracted the skin just below the corners of his eyes and noted how his crow's feet vanished. He had never noticed them before, although certainly they had been there for years.

On a slip of paper he wrote down his age and then his wife's. He calculated the difference and said, "Hhmmm." On the reverse side of the paper he had already performed the same mathematical operation several times and each time had circled the result.

Topper tipped his head so that the light from the window struck in at an angle. There it was. The mirror did not lie: a grey hair. Should he pluck it out? He took the offensive hair between the tips of his thumb and forefinger. It must go. A grey hair would stand out too much in front where everyone must surely look, but there were few enough companion follicles for him to make the sacrifice.

A knock at the door disturbed this meditation.

"Come in," Topper said, smoothing the hair down.

The door swung open and Jack rolled into the room.

"I didn't hear you approach, Jack," he said. "What can I do for you?"

"It's the vandals again, Sir. They've been at Mr. Scrooge's portrait!"

Topper leapt to his feet. "Lord, save my soul," he said.

◎

Topper found Al-Mustafa in his studio with a thin blanket over his head squeaking like a mouse. The man's body shook as if in a fever. Miss Trellis sat at his side with a great hand resting on his shoulder.

She said, "He has had a shock."

"Is it badly damaged?"

"It is not damaged whatsoever," she said.

"I don't understand."

"Have a look for yourself," Miss Trellis said. "It's been finished."

"That's certainly good news."

She shook her head, stood and withdrew the sheet which had been draped over the painting to keep dust from drying upon its surface.

The posture of Scrooge had not changed, but the rendering of his face was much improved. The lines of mouth now echoed the expression of the eyes. The flesh was painted in such a manner as to appear warm to the touch—as real as if Scrooge himself were standing behind a window glass and looking back at the viewer.

But the background...

The eye which Topper had personally seen Al-Mustafa paint out was back again, but this time it was not alone. Added to the background in vivid detail was the figure of a hellish creature, a hybrid containing features from both those of the insect world and man. A black carapace glistened red just behind Scrooge's right shoulder. The pincers of the beast's nearly human head were poised to jab themselves into Scrooge's neck.

At Scrooge's shoulder opposite an old woman with skin of grey-green laid her hand on his arm. Her expression suggested that she owned this prize as a man might own a horse. He was hers to do with as she pleased. Ram's horns bulged from her forehead.

Topper pressed the back of his wrist against his mouth.

"God save us! Can you not paint this out?" he said.

"He has sworn not to approach this unless to destroy it," Miss Trellis said.

"But the portrait of Scrooge himself is beautifully done. Surely it can be saved?" Topper said.

Al-Mustafa flung back his blanket, shrieked at a pitch which jolted Topper's spine, and attacked the picture with a sharp implement in either hand. The sound of tearing linen made Topper's knees tremble.

Miss Trellis made no move to stop the black man. She watched him with no more interest than if he were carving a bird for supper.

At length Al-Mustafa exhausted himself. He lay on the floor and spoke in an even voice which Miss Trellis translated:

"It is forbidden by the Koran to create images of men and women. Such an action can only lead to detestable pictures which are worshipped or glorified. My portrait of Scrooge was an act of idolatry, and now I am pursued by demons for my sin. I am punished! I am punished!"

Topper held his hands on either side of his head as if to stop it from exploding. "But as a Christian you must not believe that superstition."

Miss Trellis translated: "Why do you call me a Christian? I do not accept your Christ as saviour as he has done nothing to save me from these demons. Oh woe! I should never have left my home." The black man's eyes danced. "I must leave this place. It is cursed. I am going to find a ship, hire on as carpenter and sail back to Tangiers and never look back. I must beg Allah's forgiveness!"

The colour drained from Topper's face. "I shall increase your fee. Surely that will induce you to repair this painting and see it delivered as we contracted."

"Do not attempt to persuade me with your evil money. You cannot stop me. I must go before it is too late!" Al-Mustafa grabbed a cloth sack which held his personal things and bolted through the door.

"How will I ever explain this to Mr. Scrooge?" Topper said.

CHAPTER 10

৩৶৶

The Sleep of Reason Breeds Monsters

"A GENTLEMAN SETS THE HEEL DOWN BEFORE THE TOE. A GENTLEMAN SETS the heel down before the toe," Scrooge said softly to himself. Though he felt as if his feet hardly touched the ground, his boots kicked up dust and scattered pebbles with considerable zeal. Scrooge sizzled. Delighted he was. Giddy he was. When he had ever been happier, he couldn't say.

Along the shaded lane he rambled—face flushed with exercise, with sun, with thoughts of Miss Goosegrass. After leaving her classroom he had wrapped fruit, cheese, and a chunk of bread in a handkerchief and took himself directly to the road. He simply couldn't sit still for the excitement! He would at last have what he had secretly yearned for all his life—a family!

"Give you joy, old Scrooge!" He hugged himself and spun in a small circle.

He stopped, mopped his brow, wriggled his toes and heard the creak of honest boot leather. Casting his eyes from side to side to make certain that no one was watching him he drew up a pant leg and measured the growing thickness of his thigh with his hands. He chuckled with satisfaction upon the discovery that his hands would no longer wrap completely 'round. So much for fasting!

"Not bad for a man my age," he said aloud, and he took off again at a brisk pace. Scrooge's mind spun so that he scarcely knew where he was going.

That evening he would take the most important step of his life. *Within a handful of hours I will ask Miss Goosegrass to marry me*, he thought. Then he repeated it out loud (but not too loud) to see if it felt any better. It did. "If she will have me," he necessarily appended. The idea that she might not was a source of nervous excitement. He remembered the unfortunate misunderstanding they had when first they met. Surely she wouldn't allow that awkward moment to interfere with their happiness! Scrooge was certain that the sparkle in her eye when they met was a signal of her agreeability, perhaps even her fondness for him.

But no—what if she were only being polite? What if she were treating him as she would any employer, any gentleman of rank and station? With interest. With respect. With courtesy. He would propose marriage to her and perhaps embarrassment or shock would cloud her features.

Never! Perhaps she didn't precisely love him as yet, but she would not reject him. Her smile held too much warmth for her not to think favourably of him. At least a little.

A thought suddenly stung him: but what of supper? Where might they take their meal so as to cause no tongues to wag? Then a simple solution occurred to him: he would have Williams bring something over from *The Copper Swan* to the charity, and they would eat in the dining room after the others had left. Scrooge was not so interested in food after all, he had to admit to himself. He wished only to use the occasion as an opportunity to propose.

Scrooge scarcely dared think of the next stage of his fantasy: children. He and Miss Goosegrass might be too far long in their lives to have children of their own, but Scrooge hoped that Haresh and Rajani would agree to his adopting them. He would care for them. See to their every need. Have them brought up as a gentleman and a lady. Spoil them in all imaginable ways. But teach them, too. It was too glorious! So happy, so happy. Had anyone asked him a year since that he would soon have a family complete with a son and a daughter, Scrooge would have laughed in his face—and yet there it was.

Scrooge increased his pace until the wind whistled past his ears and streamed through his hair. Soon he was far from the City, the sun well past zenith. Another forty minutes of the Primary Exercise passed before he yielded and stepped from the rutted lane into the shade of an old oak. Scrooge hefted the stick which propelled him on his walks these past weeks. He rubbed his thumb with pride against the brass plate which read:

To E. Scrooge—With Our Deepest Admiration, The Cratchits.

What will Bob Cratchit think when he hears the news? He will dance for joy, he will. I know he will! Tim shall bear the ring—if I can tear him away from his Italian studies. And Bob, of course, will be Best Man—or perhaps Fred.

Scrooge squinted at the sky above and judged the yellow-grey clouds to pose little threat of rain.

Swallows swooped to feast on the insects frantic at that time of day. The shadows beneath the trees were unusually clear, a result of a dust-settling rain which had fallen at daybreak. Though the sun had largely dried the dark blades of grass, the air seemed moist, inviting the weary pedestrian to inhale deeply of it.

Scrooge retrieved his bread-crust, sour apple, and wedge of sticky cheese wrapped in his handkerchief from his pocket, and nestled down upon a grassy stretch. He first laid down his stick, covered it with a small square of plaid wool-blanket carried expressly for that purpose, and created a nest for himself. The water from a nearby brook cooled his throat and brow. In less time than it takes to tell the cheese, bread, and apple became the contents of his belly.

He pulled the pamphlet, "The Practical Art of Transportation By The Use of One's Own Feet" by Dr. Gebhard Friedrich (as translated from the German by Mr. John Tringham), from inside his hat, and smoothed it on his knees. It had been a gift of Reverend Mitchell just the day before. Scrooge re-read the opening pages perhaps for the third time:

A Gentleman sets down the heel before the toe in the stepping exercise. This is the Primary Rule for the Primary Exercise. The Savages in America point the toe in; the Heathen Chinese point it out. But not the European.

His foot is straight and true.

One's stride and staying power is greatly enhanced by the
use of a stick. Careful choice must be made as to its
individual properties since no two trees nor no two
branches are of identical strength, resilience, density
nor moisture. A seasoned cane makes for a seasoned
body.

The pamphlet went on at length to consider the qualities of the various
kinds of wood for walking sticks, their proper length, the best walking
surfaces, choices in boots and stockings, the proper stride, the requisite
clothing from cap to foundation garments.

The proper stride? Scrooge worked the exercise, but had difficulty not
pointing his toes out (like the Heathen Chinese), for this had been the
fashion of his youth. He had always thought it entirely proper, yet the
pamphlet declared it a Foreign Affectation. Ah, well...even this difficulty
would be overcome with practice, he was sure.

He thumbed ahead:

Old People have been called by so many names, sometimes
out of reverence and respect, at other times out of
intolerance, neglect or spite. If each Old Person could
fan his or her Flame of Life a bit brighter as I have
done, so that they too might be described as "lively,"
"spry," or "young at heart," would we all be the
happier? For sooner or later, we all will grow old and
should know the condition intimately. The only other
option is Endless Sleep. By adhering to the Total Abstinence Principle each and every one of us may live and
longer and more fruitful life.

The gift of the pamphlet had been a humble one. Yet it spoke volumes of
the simplicity, spirituality and practicality of Reverend Mitchell. Scrooge sat

it down on the grass. He found Mitchell an honest man, pure of heart, direct in his opinions as he heard Americans were. Scrooge could not puzzle out why Topper had misread him so. Certainly Topper didn't hold hard feelings against Mitchell because of his American birth. The Wars with America were long over. Could it possibly be that Topper feared that Scrooge would favour Mitchell over himself? Scrooge found it hard to imagine Milton Topper as a man guilty of the Sin of Jealousy, but what other explanation could there be? Scrooge felt confident that he could read any man alive, and he read Mitchell as entirely guileless. Topper would grow to know him as he did, he was certain.

Scrooge's mind returned to Miss Goosegrass without any specific new revelations, but was content to repeat the same comfortable themes over and over again.

Rajani's face was there, too. Her sad eyes, the flawless beauty of her skin, her hair. He had to confess that he needed the little girl and her brother desperately, although he could not say why these children and no others. Perhaps they appeared more helpless to him. Perhaps it was because of the fact that they were not Christians, he could see them simply as wonderful human beings. If he were entirely honest with himself he would have to admit that he needed them more than they needed him. Scrooge knew he could never really be their father, but he did so want the chance.

There was so much to prepare for before this evening. His best suit. His boots must be polished until they shone like...

His energy flagged all at once, and he felt himself sag. Exercise, food in the stomach, and a contented mind—the recipe for sleep.

"No, there's no time for napping," he murmured. "I must be up and on my way back."

Despite this thought his body went slack, and he could fend off sleep no longer. His eyes became too heavy to hold open another minute. Every muscle in his body went soft. His breathing evened, and he tumbled blissfully asleep. As his peace deepened he dreamed that men and women were both human and animal. Great parades of half-human, half-animal creatures passed him by shouting and growling as they went. Bounding toward him arms out-stretched was Haresh, part boy, part monkey riding on the back of a sleek she-panther as black as night. It turned its yellow eyes on Scrooge, and he realised the panther was Rajani. Though she was a beast, there was no violence in her. Pride. Spirit. Determination. Cunning. But nothing wicked. Nothing base.

And there was Miss Goosegrass. Her eyes were like the eyes of a doe. She came to him and nuzzled his face. So tame. So lovely. Absolutely beautiful.

"You and I, Ebenezer," she said. "Let us walk together."

They discussed the nature of teaching young people the magic of numbers, but at length a voice disturbed him. Scrooge opened his eyes and noticed with a start that the sun had travelled some distance.

"Beggin' your pardon, Squire. We hate to disturb your private musings and all, but me and Bop was hoping as how you might have a shilling or two to spare for two destitute men like us."

Scrooge sat upright in confusion. The last taste of the dream left him, and now he could remember none of it except for the sense of pleasure it gave him.

The man who had just spoken was tall, narrow-shouldered, but had only one working eye—his left, reminding Scrooge of the mythical Cyclops. The gaping cavity of the missing orb was not covered with the customary felt patch, but his long stringy hair, ever so much like an unrinsed mop, hung over it as his only modesty.

Scrooge took stock of the two men before him and forced himself to wear a smile on his face. He saw two creatures down on their luck, dirty, hungry, likely with no education. These were the very sort of people his charity served. Rather: *their* charity served. He knew the charity was bigger than he himself could ever be. Scrooge knew he had to look beneath their rough exteriors and into their hearts to find the humanity in them.

The Cyclops continued in a rough voice: "We're honest men, Squire. We've got naught but the rags on our backs, and little in our stomachs." He gripped himself about the middle and bent forward at the waist. As he did so the sun fell into Scrooge's eyes. For a brief moment the image of the Cyclops shimmered like smoke from a chimney.

Scrooge fished around in his waistcoat pocket until his fingers found two coins. Without a word he tossed them to the Cyclops. The money disappeared quickly into the folds of soiled rags, but there followed in return no word of thanks.

"Would you two like the opportunity to earn more?" Scrooge said getting to his feet and brushing himself off. "Does the prospect of steady work, regular meals, a bed to sleep upon, a roof to keep the rain off your heads, and spiritual nourishment appeal?"

Scrooge turned to make eye contact with the one called Bop, but Bop kept his eyes steady to the ground, muttering under his breath through broken, decayed teeth. Bop's shirt collar and left shoulder of his thread-bare coat where he kept his chin planted glistened with drool which leaked from the longest tongue Scrooge had ever seen in a man's mouth. Bop's hair, the colour of rusty water, was thick upon his head except in a few clumps which appeared to have been pulled out or worn away. Bop's ears stuck from the sides of his head and came nearly to a point.

"If it weren't for the bloody Magistrate we'd have property 'our own, Squire. Them's cheatin' folk what takes a man's family possessions," the Cyclops said, showing Scrooge an ugly frown.

Scrooge doubted that the man had ever owned much more than the rags on his back. "We can return the dignity then that has unjustly been wrest from you. You can have the opportunity and the support of a community of like souls whose purpose it is to better themselves with common toil, education, and spiritual study." Scrooge hooked a thumb to his waistcoat pocket. "Let's speak the Plain Truth, Sir. Do these prospects appeal? Would you face the challenge of honest labour with the same pluck as the many other Britons I have had the pleasure of aiding and assisting?"

"We very much doubt, Squire," said the Cyclops with heavy meaning, "that you know the meanin' of honest labour."

Bop, with a lunatic's expression, circled to Scrooge's backside sometimes semi-erect, sometimes on all fours.

Scrooge started at those last words delivered cold. He found he could no longer look the Cyclops in the face as he had moments before. He lowered his gaze from the Cyclops's torn eye to his own shaking knees. Scrooge strained his ears to ascertain Bop's whereabouts, but had no courage to turn and face him.

"And we doubt that your back has suffered purifying, manual labour under the boil of sun or bite of the winter wind." The Cyclops's eye raced madly as his voice dripped with venom. "You know nothing of real cruelty, Squire. But I am willing to teach you.

"Nor are we certain of the exact value of your frizzled, grey head, old man, but we're willing to explore. Them two coins as you flung us won't buy much recreation for sophisticated gentlemen such as ourselves. The girls demands extra when I brings Bop along. Seems they don't like his looks. Imagine! But they come 'round eventually—especially when Bop brings 'em poppies. Them girls have good dreams after they've had their poppies, Squire. Remember Annie, Bop? She's the one—ain't she, Bop?"

The creature was much startled at having been spoken directly to. To the Cyclops's chagrin, Bop seemed unable to remember the girl so named.

"Surely you remember Annie's...things, Boppie? Soft frilly things? Things that tickled your nose. Remember them things, eh Bop?" said the Cyclops.

To which Scrooge heard the only comprehendible sound the beast had yet made: a dull: "Nnnnnaaooo."

"You're common thieves, more likely poachers," Scrooge said between clenched teeth.

"'Poachers?' Did he say, 'Thieves,' Bop?" He cupped a dirty hand mockingly to his ear. "One moment he offers us his form of slavery which he calls 'work,' and the next he calls us the lowest sort of names because we don't accept."

Scrooge turned to see Bop nod without emotion. Absently the creature touched his chest and appeared startled to find it wet.

"Call him all the low names you like, Squire, but Bop don't like it when you call him a *murderer*." The Cyclops winked his sole eye. "Bop only kills when he has to." The Cyclops smiled. "Or when I tell him to. Ain't that right, Boppie?"

The air hissed, and a thick but rotted branch struck Scrooge hard across the back. He shuddered under its impact, felt the wind driven from his lungs, and fell to the ground. He drew in a quick half–breath as numbing fire spread across his shoulder.

Scrooge hissed between his teeth, "You shall pay dearly for this."

The Cyclops smiled coyly. "There's a bit of spirit, Squire. Good, I likes when my clients struggle a bit. Pain often brings out the best in us. But what's this, Boppie? Don't you know a good stout branch when you see one? Who'll teach you, Boppie? Who?"

The creature's small eyes blink in dread. He pointed timidly at the Cyclops.

"Too right you are, Boppie," the Cyclops said. "Shall we pick a better stick now?"

Bop gave a whimper like a scolded dog.

"Let me see what I might find—and me with only the one good eye." The Cyclops searched around until he found a branch as big around as his wrist.

"Let us test this branch for strength and fitness, Boppie," the Cyclops said. Bop whimpered and withdrew a couple steps.

"No, Boppie. Come. You knows the test, dearie."

Bop crept on all fours sideways toward the Cyclops, head down, eyes blinking.

The Cyclops lifted the branch and brought it down like an axe on Bops' back. The creature shuddered, squeezed its eyes closed and grimaced. It made no sound.

After half a dozen such blows, Cyclops said, "This is more like it. Most the rubbish hereabouts is more suitable for switching ill–behaved brats than for coshing full-grown, if somewhat agéd men. It takes something more reliable, doesn't it, Boppie?"

Scrooge saw pain in Bop's yellow eyes. The creature's panting was rapid, short and red.

Scrooge lay over his own stout walking stick beneath his coat and blanket. Although he had no strength to use it in his own defence, he feared they should find it and use it on him.

"Bop's temper was nothin' but trouble to him as a boy, Squire. Any boy what does his mother in, gains a certain reputation among his mates." The Cyclops retrieved the two coins from the filthy folds of his waistband and turned them thoughtfully in his hand. "Copper makes 'im purr though, ain't it Bop?! You're really just a big puppy, eh?"

Bop gave a low growl, scrabbled over the Cyclops and snatched the branch from his hands. Bop brought down it with all the strength his pain-racked body could muster. Scrooge rolled with the blow, but he felt a warm trickle creep down his back.

"Certainly you've been relieved of your purse before, Squire? Give us your coin so that we may be gentlemen again and take our tea fancy-like." The Cyclops sipped from an imaginary tea–cup with mock daintiness.

"I have no more coins with me," Scrooge declared with what little strength he had left. "I can get you more if you will allow me to return to my place of business. There I can guarantee you any amount you name." He sobbed and jabbed the back of his wrist to his mouth as Bop landed another blow to his ribs.

The Cyclops imitated Scrooge's gesture. "Coins? Money? Wealth? I NEVER told you I wished for such things. Surely, Squire, you can under-stand these earthly pleasures mean little to the likes of me. Perhaps you don't. Perhaps even now you don't understand just who it is who faces you. If I were in pursuit of such successes I would be livin' in the lap of luxury by now. No, Squire. Though copper and gold makes Bop purr, it does nothin' to gentle my frame of mind. I have been sent to this world to deliver justice. I am Pain. I am Violence. I am Suffering. I am Cruelty. I am War. I am an Instrument for this and nothing more." He fingered the ugly opening of his missing eye as a gentleman might pull thoughtfully on his lip.

He continued: "The world has gone quite mad, Squire, so we must rely on the Good Book for direction. What does the Bible say, Squire? 'An eye for an eye.'"

Scrooge's mind shrieked at the thought, and he tried to crawl away. The Cyclops placed a foot on Scrooge's chest.

"Squire, kindly direct your attentions to this handsome face before you." The Cyclops bent low and pulled Scrooge's chin up until their noses touched.

"Look carefully, Squire. Let your attention wander over these handsome features. Much like the rest o' your gentlemen friends, I dare say—square jaw, side-whiskers, Roman nose, clear brow—but look closer. Can you find anything amiss?"

"Your eye, Sir," Scrooge said. "Your eye suffers from an affliction."

The Cyclops spat in Scrooge's face and pushed him rudely away. As Scrooge rolled, his blanket shifted to expose half the length of his cane.

"Infliction, indeed," grunted the Cyclops. "Can't you see, Squire? They ain't no eye in that hole!" He pulled the lower eye-lid down for Scrooge to see, laughing madly. Then Scrooge's stick caught his attention.

"What have we here?" He stooped to examine the object. He muttered to himself as he peered like a bird at the small brass plate which bore the Cratchits' dedication. "I'm afraid I can't quite make this out. What do these words say, Squire?" His voice was almost kindly. He drew Scrooge to his knees and held the stick in front of him to see.

Scrooge realised that either the Cyclops did not know how to read, or because of the condition of his eye, was unable to. It also occurred to him these men had no idea who he was—which gave him a strange moment of peace. These were mad men, wantonly destroying anything in their path. If he should read the Crachits' name to them from the stick, what horrors would they bring to that family?

"It was dedicated to me for the years of service I gave to Charing Cross Hospital," Scrooge lied with conviction.

"A physician it is, then?!" the Cyclops rubbed along the length of the stick in his hand as if his fingers would tell him more. "Liar! This is not the stick of a physician, and you are no healer. I know that sort only too well. No, you've the look of a banker or a money lender about you. Someone with a head for numbers and profit."

Scrooge would answer their questions no more. To continue this conversation would only increase their pleasure. Scrooge could well guess what they would do with him, and no amount of talking would save him. There was no point in giving them the pleasure of watching him beg for his life. He must maintain his dignity.

The Cyclops drew a short–bladed knife from somewhere inside his clothing. He pried loose the brass cap which fit over the business end of the stick and began to shave it as one might a pencil.

"An eye for an eye," the Cyclops repeated and spat. Bop examined Scrooge carefully, feeling the weave of Scrooge's coat.

"Shall we make him squeal, Bop?" said the Cyclops innocently. At these words Bop grew excited and raced about in tight circles. "Shall we make him squeal, Bop?" he asked over and over. The drooling Bop rolled on the ground and struck at empty air with massive fists. Again and again like a Master teasing his dog with a fetching stick, the Cyclops goaded him until the beast, his own pain forgotten, throbbed with madness.

"Bop," said Cyclops, "tie his hands behind." He drew a piece of mildewed rope from around his waist and threw it at Scrooge's feet. Bop tended to his work with rough enthusiasm. A pause.

Scrooge flinched. Behind him a hiss of something heavy whipped through the air. A bone smashing blow struck Scrooge on the shoulder, and he collapsed to the ground. He reached out to catch himself, but being bound neither arm would obey. He struck the earth face first.

Scrooge murmured but one word: "Rajani..."

A blow struck Scrooge across the temple. His world went black and dull, then drew painfully back into diamond-sharp consciousness.

"No one will hear you scream, Squire. There is no other soul about for miles."

Scrooge felt himself slipping away, giving up hope. The end could not be far off. This is not how he expected to die. Was this the vision that the Ghost of Christmas Yet To Come had shown him?

The bushes parted, and as if in a dream Scrooge saw a well-dressed and strikingly handsome young man step through to stare at them. He leaned upon an ebony cane and gawked as if marvelling at an exhibit in a Cabinet of Curiosities.

"Begad! If it ain't a picnic," the Gentleman said. "Don't the quaintness of it overwhelm? Such rustic sensibilities! I should paint this scene just so if I were a painter. I should paint it now before the need for crimson lake becomes too demandin'. Crimson for sickness, for madness, pain, and...blood. Sadly, my mean talent would never answer. The only brushes I own are the ones which Clarence uses to groom my hair." He wagged his head doubtfully. "Who would do it justice? Goya, I'm thinkin'. Something from the 'Atrocities of War.'" He placed a hand on his hip and tapped thoughtfully on his chin. "'The Sleep of Reason Breeds Monsters.'"

Scrooge's head throbbed. He rolled over on his side. Would this gentleman prove his saviour or would he walk away?

"What the Hell..." the Cyclops grunted.

"Hell, indeed. Damn me, but you are an ugly soul, Sir. Positively beastly. You've the look of Satan's arse-lick about you. Haven't you a patch for that ghastly hole in your head?"

The Cyclops blinked his eye rapidly and fumbled at words caught between lies and threats. "We was just picking him up, the poor gentleman. Been waylaid, 'e has. We was a'just helping him, the poor soul, to his feet. Ain't that right, Squire? These woods is just filled with poachers and thiefs. We musta scared 'em off when we come by."

The Cyclops lifted Scrooge gently to his feet, but his legs wouldn't hold. Doubled forward he could find no strength to do more than gasp and vomit.

"Perhaps your hearin' ain't too good, Sir," the Gentleman said. "I shall ask you again: haven't you a patch for that damned eye?"

"Well, no, Sir, you see I was robbed..."

"Damn me, I've always said that it's the lowest sort of villain who takes a man's eye patch," the Gentleman said.

"If I had half a rag, Sir, I could bind it, I could. My eye would offend no one then."

Scrooge opened his mouth and coughed up blood. He thought: *And if thy right eye offends thee, pluck it out, and cast it from thee: for it is profitable for thee that one of thy members should perish, and not that thy whole body should be cast into Hell.* Had the Cyclops plucked out his eye to save his body from Hell?

"That would never do. Half a rag? Even a whole rag would be a stretch. Somethin' on the order of an awning or a tent might cover it, I'm thinkin'."

"We must make do with what the Good Lord pervides, Sir," the Cyclops said.

All the while the Cyclops spoke Scrooge could see Bop slipping back into the trees and working his way behind the Gentleman. Scrooge lifted his hand and pointed, but could make no sound. The Gentleman took no notice.

"It won't do at all. A rag will not go with your new suit of clothes—now will it, my good friend?"

"New suit, Sir? Bless me, are you offering to buy me new clothes? That's too kind of you."

The Gentleman did not answer, but smiled and reached into his coat.

"Ah, I sees you have a taste for nice things. Pretty things, Sir," Cyclops said. Scrooge knew that he only wanted to distract the Gentleman from noticing Bop. "Fine clothes you are wearing."

The Gentleman paused his rummaging and looked surprised. "Clothes? A taste for clothes? Perhaps. I really couldn't say. One should carefully choose the cut of one's clothes, put them on with care, and forget them. Now where did I put...?"

"There's no need to bother. Really. We ain't worthy," said the Cyclops, folding his hands together.

"Ah, here 'tis," he said, and drew a pistol from within his coat and pointed it directly at Bop without bothering to face him. "Take another step closer, and I shall blow off your ugly head," he said.

Bop simply stopped moving.

"I wouldn't suppose the Gentleman can fire his weapon, reload it and fire it again before either Boppie or me could crush his head. Boppie, do care that we don't muss his clothes. I have a notion that I could find a patch to match that waistcoat of his. I know just the thing."

The gentleman swivelled the weapon around and pointed it at the Cyclops's chest.

Cyclops didn't flinch. Never moved a muscle.

The Gentleman pulled the trigger and the hammer clicked into place. There was no other sound.

"The demmed thing ain't loaded," the Gentleman said with a sad shake of his head. "That should come as no surprise to a thinkin' man. One wouldn't keep a such a lethal thing tucked in one's garments primed with black powder, now would one?"

"GET HIM, BOP! NOW!" shrieked the Cyclops, his arms flailing in the air madly.

The sound of a gunshot cracked over Scrooge's head. He watched Bop jerk back suddenly and clutch his shoulder. Red ran between his fingers. Bop made a sound which was indistinguishable from that of a wounded dog. Scrooge watched in dull fascination as the huge beast dropped to all fours and scurried into the trees. Scrooge swivelled his head toward the Cyclops, but caught just a glimpse of him crashing into the woods in the direction opposite.

"Let him go, Clarence," the Gentleman said. "He'll not bother us again any time soon."

Scrooge watched a tall man with a bare head at the edge of the trees walk easily in their direction. He had a fowling piece under his arm. As he approached he carefully set the gun down and reached down to help Scrooge to his feet.

"Easy does it, Sir," Clarence said. "Put an arm around my neck, and I'll support. Never you worry, Sir. We'll get you back all right."

"I am no physician, Sir," the Gentleman said, "but I might look to see how badly you been treated by those ruffians before we move you. I would not have you walk any distance if you're not fit."

Scrooge made to strip off his coat, but it proved too painful.

"Just sit yourself down, Sir. And I'll help you off with your coat," said Clarence.

"You were right to remain hidden, Clarence," the Gentleman said. "We owe you our lives."

"Never, Sir," Clarence said, "You would have found a way to deal with them. The likes of that filth are only brave when they're two on one."

Clarence carefully removed Scrooge's coat and stood aside for his master to make an examination.

"You'll be purple to-morrow. I cannot say for a certainty, but I don't believe anythin' is broken. I have a home not far from here—Owlpen Hall. We shall carry you there directly, and I'll send for a physician."

"You mustn't bother," Scrooge said, with a feeble wave of his hand.

"'Tis no bother, Sir. I am duty bound to help."

Scrooge took the Gentleman's hand in his own. Tears filled his eyes as he said, "I thank you, Sir, for saving my life. I should not like to have died that way."

"Nor should I. But we have not had the opportunity to introduce ourselves. I am James Weston, and as a novelty I am at the moment currently out of debt." He gripped Scrooge's hand, but gently. "My friends call me Wespie, though I can't say why. You may follow their example if you wish."

"I am Ebenezer Scrooge."

"Your servant, Sir. Now let me put this blanket around your shoulders. Clarence and I will get you to a shelter as painlessly as we can."

Scrooge could say no more, but passed out.

CHAPTER 11

ややや

A Scoundrel, a Bounder and a Blackguard

MILTON ALEXANDER TOPPER HELD HIS HEAD THOUGHTFULLY. HE TAPPED an impatient finger against his desk, dipped his pen in an ink pot and wrote:

Dear Mr. Carlson,

I make no doubt that you are presently engaged on a good many portraits of important peoples of this great city. However, the student to whom you were giving instruction, Mr. Al-Mustafa Ali, has left us to return to the country of his origin and the portrait which we commissioned of him is unfini...

Topper laid down his pen, the sentence unfinished.

"Scrooge," he said, although he couldn't have said why his employer's name should seem important just now. He stood up, pushed his chair under the table, hooked a finger around the back of it as if to draw it out again, then impatiently dragged it to the other side of the room. He clasped his hands behind his back to pace but caught his toe on a leg of the table and fell painfully to his knees.

Where was Scrooge?

Topper rose, impatiently brushed his trousers, then stepped from his room into the dim passageway. Scrooge should be in his office—or more likely he would find him in the school-room. Topper would check there first.

Just outside the school-room door he heard Miss Goosegrass humming tunelessly to herself. Topper flung open the door to the room without knocking and nearly startled her into the next world.

"Mr. Topper," she said. Her hands flew to her mouth as if she had been caught eating candy.

"I beg your pardon, ma'am, but have you seen Mr. Scrooge?" he said, his words tripping over one another. "It is rather important that I should speak with him."

"Why yes, I have," she said pressing a hand to her bosom to regain her composure. "He has been here with the children."

"And when was this?"

"Four or five hours since. Why do you ask?" she said.

Topper said, "Do you know where he is now?"

"He spoke of going for a walk. But that was shortly before noon. I suspect he is back in his office. He and I..." She broke off with the colour rising in her cheeks.

Topper nodded and without bidding the woman good-day, stepped quickly out of the school-room and down the passageway to Scrooge's office. He felt her following just at his heels.

Topper reached the room, knocked, and without waiting for a reply opened the door knowing full well no one would be inside—yet he needed to confirm it in his own mind. The clock on the sideboard showed nearly half-past four. Scrooge should have been back long ago. He turned, collided with Miss Goosegrass, and held her by the waist only long enough to keep her from falling.

"I beg your pardon," he said, but did not meet her eyes. He stepped away from her and shouted, "Jack! Jack Forest, I say. A word with you!"

"What is wrong, Mr. Topper? Where is Mr. Scrooge?" she said, taking him by the arm and drawing him near.

"That is what I'm trying to determine," he said and gently pulled away.

Miss Goosegrass stared after him her face growing darker by the moment. Topper thought she would burst into tears. Instead she gathered her skirts and rushed out of the room.

"Miss Goosegrass, where do you go?" he shouted after her, but if she heard him she gave no sign.

A moment later he heard the clatter he knew to be the wheels of Jack Forest's cart. The boy swung round the corner so swiftly that his wig fell over his eyes. Jack stopped the cart just short of Topper's ankles, pushed his wig back and breathlessly said: "Yes, Sir!"

"Have you seen Mr. Scrooge?"

Jack blinked his pink eyes. "Do you mean to-day?"

"Yes, Jack. Have you seen him?"

"This morning?"

"No, for the love of God, Jack. I know that you saw him this morning as did we all. Have you seen Mr. Scrooge this afternoon—since his walk?"

"No, Sir, I have not. He has not returned to the best of my knowledge. I expect he draws near even as we speak. He's given to having his daily stroll, you know."

"Has he, to your knowledge, ever been so late as this?"

"No, Sir. He's nearly always been back by half-past two."

Topper's eyes darted left and right.

"I fear the worst, Jack. I fear that he does not draw near—not at this late hour. I need for you to collect as many people of the charity as you can find. Gather them in the dining-room. I shall meet you there directly. Do you understand me?"

"Yes, Sir! 'Gather everyone I can find in the dining-room, and you shall meet them there directly.' Yes, Sir." Jack wheeled his cart around and careened down the narrow passageway shouting as loudly as his high voice would allow.

◎

"I wonder at the utility of leeches," James Weston said dabbing at the welts embellishing Scrooge's back. "I once had a black eye that the creatures did wonders for. Vile things, for all that."

A door whispered open.

"I've sent Bertram for the doctor, Sir."

"Very good, Clarence. There's nothin' more to be done until he arrives except to make our guest as comfortable as possible."

Scrooge lay face down on cool linen sheets. He heard their words but stored them in his head to make sense of later. He could give the outer world none of his attention—not when his inner world charged such premiums in the currency of pain.

The physical being of Ebenezer Scrooge burned as if glowing coals were laid about it. His lower back gave him hateful stabs unless he placed his limbs just so—which he was careful to do. He drew up his right knee just a little where the pain was only throbbing. He turned his head to the right and supported it by tucking his left hand under the pillow. He wasn't aware of where his right arm was or what, if anything, it might be doing. In spite of the pain Scrooge fell asleep—though the difference to his waking world was not great.

In his dream he wandered down a country road, one which he had never seen before. The clouds overhead were purple and blue and black with a great deal of weather in them which they threatened to release at any moment. Far ahead lightning silently licked the earth. He winced at each strike expecting a *brrroommm* which never came. The air was in all ways still.

At length Scrooge arrived at a village with an inn tall and narrow as if all seven of its rooms were stacked one atop the other. He entered the inn and found a group of men waiting for him. They sang their greeting as a chorus.

"Have you seen, Mr. Topper?" Scrooge asked, and flinched at a sudden jab in his back.

They replied in song that they did not know the man, could Scrooge please describe him. Scrooge tried his best, but could not remember the particulars of Topper's face. He told them that Mr. Topper wore a full black beard on his cheeks, walked on crutches and had a little boy named Tim who wished him home for his supper. They sang that Mr. Topper—or a man very like the description—had left not twenty minutes since. If the gentleman should hurry, they sang-suggested, he might catch him up. Scrooge sped along as fast as his legs could carry him (which in the dream was agonisingly slow). Far ahead he believed he could just make out a figure which might be Topper—the twists and turns in the path, low tree limbs and grassy hills, however, made it difficult to see clearly. Try as he might, Scrooge could not shorten the distance between them. Hours passed, but the sun did not move in the sky nor did the threatening clouds produce rain.

Scrooge approached another inn painted the most remarkable shade of yellow. So yellow was it that it pained Scrooge's eyes to look upon it. Scrooge threw his left arm over his face and blundered through the doorway.

"Where has Topper gone?" he said. But the room was devoid of any living creature. A small panther carved of ebony, however, sat upon the hearth. Scrooge picked it up and turned it carefully in his hands.

"Will you beat me?" the carving said, its flickering yellow eyes stared up at Scrooge in the most pitiful fashion.

"No, I will not beat you. I have myself been beaten. I am tired, and I need to rest. Do you have a room for me?" Scrooge asked.

The panther told him that there were no beds at the inn, that he would have to make his pallet upon the kitchen table, and would he mind if dinner were laid out while he rested? Scrooge could stand no longer and asked to be carried to the table. The panther having no hands could do nothing to lift him, so Scrooge laid down on the floor and the panther dragged a sheet over his head to keep him warm.

"Sir, I am going to sit you up now. You may feel some pain," the panther said in his ear.

"Of course," Scrooge said as a new shower of agony washed the dream from his eyes.

"Help me with him, would you, Clarence?" The voice was not one which Scrooge was familiar with.

"Who?" Scrooge said and twisted his face into the blinding light to see the one who handled him.

"I am Dr. Fluch—Dr. Tobias Fluch. Mr. Weston here sent for me. I understand that you have been treated cruelly."

"I have been..." but Scrooge could not recall the source of his pain.

"Horses," he decided. "Horses ran me over. Can you help me?" Scrooge's eyes focused on the face of the man who held him gingerly. It was a face with little flesh upon it. Yellow eyes rolled loosely in dark sockets. Long shanks of glossy hair shot straight back from a high forehead and down over his shoulders. Scrooge drew back in terror.

"There, there. Mr. Scrooge. You've had a bad shock. Your injuries are painful, but not crippling, I think."

Scrooge looked again, saw no skull of horror, but instead the bewigged head of a physician.

"You will need salves, Sir. There will likely be some congestion in the lungs, and I will instruct Clarence here how to make a cabbage poultice and how to apply it." Dr. Fluch said laying a gloved hand on his arm. "Clarence: hear me."

"Yes, Sir."

"Mind! Never lay a poultice on open wounds."

"No, Sir."

"The effect we shall strive for is moist heat. Poultices can be kept warm by replacing them entirely or placing a warm brick on top of the pack. Do not allow poultices to become cold, and do not reuse them. Mark this down, Clarence. There's more."

Scrooge saw the man whom he took to be Clarence pull a leather pocket-book from his coat and mark it with a stub of a pencil.

"And a palliative is in order. Laudanum, I should think. The common Tincture of Opium. You will find it there on the table in that glass bottle tied over with leather. Thirty drops in a glass of water morning and night for the next two days," the physician said. "Another ten if the pain over-comes him. I will return at the end of that time and see how he does."

"I'll see to it," Clarence said, solemnly. "Shall I bring him his supper?"

"Supper!" Scrooge said, trying to sit up. "I must go back. I have an engagement, you see. There must be no delay. I mean to take my meal with..." But Scrooge could no longer remember whom he was to meet.

"Mr. Scrooge," Dr. Fluch said, "I am very much afraid that I shall have to confine you to your bed, and you will take your meals with Clarence here. I think thin gruel only. No beef nor mutton. Claret mixed with an equal part of water."

"Yes, Sir," Clarence said.

"There is someone..." Scrooge said and a stab of pain cut away the thought.

"Would you like for Mr. Weston to send word to your people?" the doctor said.

Scrooge nodded evenly.

"Where shall we send the message?"

"Yellow Door," Scrooge said.

"Begging your pardon, Sir. Could you repeat that?" Clarence said, pencil still held over the pocket-book.

Scrooge could not repeat it. Flashes of light blinded him. The panther drew back the cover from over his face and said, "Who has beaten you?"

"The one-eyed man," Scrooge said. "The one-eyed man beat me until my back is broke."

⊙

"Has any among you seen Mr. Scrooge at any time this afternoon?" Topper had to say it twice with so much noise in the room. He rubbed the back of his hand against his chin. Something was missing—as if he had left his home without his shoes, but he couldn't decide what. He brushed the feeling aside and repeated his question a third time. Although no one had a reply, they quieted.

Only a baker's dozen of Yellow Door's inhabitants were to be had at this time of the day: a mother with her two young sons who quarrelled without break; Messrs. Dawson and Billings leaning forward on their elbows, exchanging soft words about some wood-working bit; Jack Forest his head cocked as if listening to each conversation; Patrick Coal, tapping his knee, humming, lost in composition; Mrs. Edelstein and Mr. Levy lost in dreams of their childhood; Miss Goosegrass chewing her lower lip, eyes blotchy; Cook and Mary-Martha White uneasy with their unfinished duties; and the Reverend Mitchell.

"What is going on here, Mr. Topper?" Mitchell said. "I hope this is important. I have a long list of duties to be taken care of, and the day is nearly at its end."

"Please bear with me, Reverend. I hope that this can be quickly resolved," Topper said.

"I hope so. I have more work ahead of me than I can do in several days, never mind several hours."

"I would not collect everyone here unless I felt it were important."

"I cannot recall seeing Mr. Scrooge since yesterday, Mr. Topper," Dawson said scratching his chin. "I'm afraid I can be no help to you."

Cook, head hunched forward on her short neck, raised a hand as if she were in school. Topper acknowledged her with a nod. She stood and said, "He was by the kitchen before noon and wrapped him up a cheese slice, a chunk of bread, an apple, too, I think. He made he was going for a long walk, he did. That's the last I saw of him."

"Did he say where he was walking?" Topper asked.

"Na-o, nary a word. Happy as a robin on a spring morning he was though, Sir."

Topper said, "Think hard, woman. Did he say anything at all at the time? Did he say what he expected to see along the way?"

Cook swayed side to side in memory, cocking her eyes toward the ceiling as she spoke: "Just birdses. He had himself a book, you see, on walking—so he made to me that he would strike out and work the—what did he call it now?—the primate exercise, I believe he said. 'I points my toes out like a heathen Chinee,'—bless me if that ain't what he said."

"He does what, ma'am?" Topper said.

"He points his toes out when he does his walk. 'Hard habit to break at my age,' he says. 'Done it since I was a boy,' he says."

"Did he give you any notion of what direction he might have taken?" Topper said leaning toward the woman.

"None, Sir," Cook said.

"I gave Mr. Scrooge a pamphlet not a week ago titled 'The Practical Art of Transportation By The Use of One's Own Feet,'" Reverend Mitchell said. "It was just a small token of my gratitude toward him for allowing me to join in this glorious effort to do His work at this wonderful Charity which bears Mr. Scrooge's name."

"A pamphlet?" Topper said, "I see. Thank you for the information, Reverend. I'm sure Mr. Scrooge appreciated your kindness and generosity."

"Mr. Scrooge is a man of great kindness and generosity himself," Reverend Mitchell said.

"As I am only too aware," Topper said, and turned to the boy. "Patrick, you are our only hope. Will you put out word in the street that I will give a shilling to anyone who can bring me word that leads to the discovery of where Mr. Scrooge has gone. Surely some one among them has seen him to-day on his walk and can at least give us an idea of the direction he took."

"Yes, Sir," Patrick said then after a moment continued: "Are you certain that he's not gone shopping?" He held out his hand as if admiring a ring upon it.

"Whatever do you mean?" Topper said, sharply, and then softly. "I suppose it is possible though I can't imagine where he might have gone or what he would have a mind to purchase."

"Could he have gone to buy a piece of joowl-ree?" Patrick said, raising his eyebrows significantly.

Topper narrowed his eyes and flashed a look at Miss Goosegrass. His face relaxed into a smile which he couldn't keep.

"Miss Goosegrass," he said, "did Mr. Scrooge mention to you anything about buying jewellery?"

"He did not," she said and her face flushed in high colour.

"If I may pry just a little, ma'am. Do you have any notion of why he may have wanted to buy jewellery of any kind or description?"

"I cannot read another person's mind, Mr. Topper. Can you? I can tell you that Mr. Scrooge left the school-room feeling quite light-hearted and felicitous this morning. He made no mention of where he was going or how long he was to be away. I wished to God he had so that I might help."

"Is there nothing else you can add?" Topper said.

"I don't know how it will sound when I tell you this, Mr. Topper, but Mr.

Scrooge invited me to supper this evening. I do not know if he would wish me to reveal this publicly or no," she said, softly.

The room murmured.

"And you accepted his invitation?"

"I am a grown woman, Mr. Topper," she said.

"That is indeed troublesome news, Madam," Topper said.

"Whatever do you mean?" Miss Goosegrass said, angrily. "I do hope that you don't believe that I have taken any..."

Topper cut her off with a wave of his hand. "I mean, Miss Goosegrass, that if Mr. Scrooge had in mind to take his supper with a gentlewoman such as yourself, he would have returned long before now. To prepare himself, I should think. He is not the kind of man to disappoint a lady."

Miss Goosegrass burst into tears. "Of course. You will forgive me if I appear out of temper just now," she said between sobs.

"There, there, Miss Goosegrass. All will be well in the end. You may depend upon it," he replied.

Mr. Levy sat forward, his blind eyes rolling aimlessly. "The house which is not opened for charity, will be opened to the physician," he said.

"And what is that supposed to mean, Jew?" Reverend Mitchell said.

Mr. Levy sat mute. He traced letters in the air with a crooked finger.

"I asked you a question, Sir, and I expect an answer!"

"Reverend Mitchell. Please," Topper said. "Mr. Levy is quite elderly as I'm sure you can see for yourself. Our conversation doubtless has triggered some memory of his, and he has given tongue to some long forgotten line. That is all. Let us respect Mr. Levy for his age if nothing else."

"It seems to me that the Jews are a little too handy with giving us advice around here," said Mitchell.

Topper said, "I don't believe Mr. Levy meant to give us advice."

"You coddle these Jews too much, Mr. Topper. Mark my words. You'll be sorry for it. I wouldn't be the least surprised to learn that they aren't at the bottom of Mr. Scrooge's disappearance. They are likely holding him for ransom."

"I must say, Sir, you shock me deeply," Topper said. "I have never heard such nonsense in my life. What evidence do you have to base such far-fetched accusations? They are so far from reality that I hardly know how to reply to you."

Mitchell said, "Never mind the proof. Unless I receive an apology from that Jew that I will find it necessary to take my leave of this establishment."

Topper drew in his breath sharply, held it, then burst: "Reverend Mitchell, when you exhibit such coarse manners and unfit language, Sir, that cannot happen soon enough. If leaving Yellow Door is a decision which you find you cannot easily make on your own, let me assist you: you have until to-morrow morning to pack your things and never darken the door of this establishment again."

"When I go I will take my Flock with me!"

"'Take your flock with you?'" Topper said. "Sir, I have no idea what you mean. At what point did any of the people in the care of this institution become members of your flock?"

Mitchell moved closer. "The people here are His—not mine, not yours. They belong to Him and Him alone."

"Reverend Mitchell, you have distorted everything that our religion offers us. You have perverted it to mean something very different than Christ's teachings. You, Sir, are a villain of the worst kind."

Mitchell raised a gloved hand as if to strike Topper, but instead smote Mr. Levy full in the face sending both man and chair tumbling to the floor. Topper grabbed Mitchell by the lapels of his coat and pulled him toward him. Mitchell drew back his fist and punched Topper in the face, but there will little power in the blow.

The mother and her children, Cook, Mary-Martha, and Miss Goosegrass rushed out of the room like startled birds. Mr. Billings, balancing himself warily on his crutches guided Mr. Levy and Mrs. Edelstein to their feet and led them shuffling away.

Mr. Dawson rushed between Topper and Mitchell. "Gentlemen, gentlemen, please. For the sake of the women and children, will you not stop?

This is not a house of violence. The people who come here seek peace and protection."

"You are only too right," Topper said, pulling his clothing back into place. "I do apologise for my outburst. I don't know what overcame me."

Reverend Mitchell twice jabbed an iron finger into Topper's chest. "I know exactly what overcomes you, Mr. Topper: Jealousy. You are jealous of me and my influence over the good people here at *Ebenezer Scrooge's Charitable Aid And Victual Assistance To The Under-advantaged & Desperate*. Notice that I give this cherished institution it's proper name. You, in the interest of diminishing the grandeur of our benefactor, make to disown his crucial contribution to the establishment of his charity by perpetuating the name of 'Yellow Door.' No man created Yellow Door, but Ebenezer Scrooge created *Ebenezer Scrooge's Charitable Aid And Victual Assistance To The Under-advantaged & Desperate*, and you wish to deny him that small, small token of his work. It is not a sign of the Sin of Pride to give him this recognition."

"I deny no man his due," Topper said. "Certainly not Mr. Scrooge and not even you, Reverend Mitchell. However, let us put this aside for the moment. There is the work of finding Mr. Scrooge to be done, and we must not delay another moment."

"My question to you, Mr. Topper, is this: Just what do you do around here to earn your keep?" Mitchell said. "I've seen you receive a few visitors. Mr. Scrooge has you write letters for him, no doubt. But I have never seen you lift a hand with the real work around here, Friend. Not once. And I've never seen you make the slightest attempt to see to these people's spiritual needs, or push a broom or pound a nail. What I want to know is who serves the people in Mr. Scrooge's Charity better in every regard: you or me?"

An angry clot lodged in Topper's throat.

"Mr. Dawson, will you see this man out?" Topper said. "I will not speak with him again."

"Mr. Topper, do you think it wise to do this?" Dawson said. "I don't question your reasons—for he has behaved abominably. But shouldn't Mr. Scrooge be the one who turns him away? It will seem the more fitting, I would think."

"Perhaps you are right," Topper said, though fire sputtered in his eyes.

"I don't know that I am, Sir," Dawson said. "But I give you my thoughts honestly. Let Reverend Mitchell stand before Scrooge and repeat the words he has spoken before one and all and see how he is judged. He dare not deny a word he has said against the Jews with so many witnesses. And I will swear on my honour to every word he has spoken here to the best of my memory."

Reverend Mitchell darted forward again. "Yes, Mr. Topper, let us both stand before Mr. Scrooge, and let him decide who is the Jew-lover among us. I will certainly deny none of my words if you repeat yours exactly as you have spoken them here to-day. I am not afraid of His Truth."

"His Truth. You wouldn't know His Truth if He Himself were to sit you down and shout it in your ear," Topper said. "You, Sir, are a scoundrel, a bounder and a blackguard!"

Mitchell lurched forward again, but Dawson pressed them back apart. Topper saw Dawson strain to keep the small man at a distance.

Mitchell again drove a finger into Topper's chest. "You have defamed His Name before every ear in this room. For that you will not be excused, Sir. Not by Him and least of all by me. I challenge you to a duel, Sir. The custom is practised here on this side of the Atlantic, I presume."

"A duel? Are you mad? I will not duel with you," Topper said, disgust filling his voice.

"You will not blaspheme without paying the price. I demand satisfaction."

"And I shall not give it," Topper said, crisply. "Nor will I apologise for speaking the truth."

Mitchell brushed Dawson's arm aside as if it were made of straw, stepped forward, pulled off a glove and slapped Topper's face with it.

"I see you give me no choice," Topper said. "When and where will this thing take place?"

"To-morrow morning. I don't care where," Mitchell said. "You may choose the location."

"To-morrow morning?" said Topper. "That is impossible. We have Mr. Scrooge to find."

"Oh, now you are concerned for Mr. Scrooge. His well-being interests you when it suits your cowardly purposes."

Topper stood stiffly. "To-morrow morning at sunrise. If you and your second will present yourselves here at the Charity an hour before dawn, I will see that you are given directions to a suitable location where you will find me waiting."

"I do not fear death, Sir," Mitchell said. "I will let Him judge me and if I am found to be guileless, then I will depend upon Him to protect me. To demonstrate to you my faith in Him, I propose that we take alternate shots until one of us is dead. You, being the challenged, of course, have the honour of firing first. I will see you at dawn, Sir," Mitchell said, spun on his heel and glared at the blind man. "The Jews in London would do well to keep to themselves. The day comes when they will pay the price of His displeasure," he said and bolted from the room.

Topper said, unable to keep his voice steady, "Dawson, what I ask you is no honour, Sir, but would you act as my second?"

Dawson bowed deeply. "I will assist you in any way I can, Sir. However, don't you believe it wiser to offer the man an apology?"

Topper clutched his head. "Of course. You are right. It wasn't my intention to accept his challenge, but somehow the words burst from my throat without asking my permission."

"I have reasons that I should prefer that his life not be destroyed," Dawson said, softly.

"I do not wish him dead, either, Mr. Dawson. I do hope you believe me. This is not a thing which I choose to do."

"Mitchell deserves punishment," Dawson said, "though in the end it will come from God and not any human agency. But I must explain why his destruction is something which I do not desire at the moment.

Dawson licked his lips. "Mitchell has certain information which I am eager to know. I am reluctant to tell you more—and would say nothing of this at all if it could be helped."

"I do not understand you, Sir, but I trust you to decide what you believe is best," Topper said. "At all events I must think of some way of preventing this catastrophe."

Dawson rubbed his bearded face as if to scrub the hair off. "It is time for the truth, Mr. Topper. After these many weeks I know you to be an honourable man, and I owe you that much. I must apologise. I did not wander here, blown by the wind, as I have led you to believe, but I am here for a purpose which is close to my heart."

A buzzing grew in Topper's ears. He sat himself down untidily. "Forgive me. I am not quite myself. Give me a moment, and I will be able to better attend you," he said.

Dawson said, "Can I get you a glass of water?"

"No, thank you."

"Something stronger?"

Topper looked up into Dawson's face as if he hadn't been listening.

"'Would you like something stronger?" Dawson repeated.

"There is brandy in my room," Topper answered.

Several minutes later Dawson returned. "Drink this."

Topper leaned forward with his elbows on his knees and cradled his head. "You must think me less a man. But the thought of this duel sickens me. And I must confess, I am no little afraid."

"There is no shame in that."

"I have so much to lose, Mr. Dawson, and not a thing to gain by this. I must find a way out."

"I do understand you, Sir."

Topper scrubbed his fingers through his hair. "Do go on. You had something important which you wished to tell me."

"Yes, Sir. I do not mean to trivialise your problems by comparing my story to them, but it is something you should know." Dawson hesitated and cleared his throat. "To begin: my name is not William Dawson," he said in an American accent but without the trace of his former Virginian twang. "I was born Lincoln Trumbull in Pennsylvania. It concerns my sister Annie, Mr. Topper. Annie is five years my senior and the favourite of my late father. She's been missing for the last nearly two years. Perhaps missing isn't the proper word, but I will not try to frame it with a more accurate one for it would disgrace her. Mitchell, you see, knows where my sister is. I blush to say it, but he *keeps* her—if you understand me. Keeps her and perhaps a half-dozen more just like her. He calls them his Flock, but there are far coarser words to describe them. They are no longer innocent, young women, I fear."

Trumbull pulled up a chair next to him and sat himself. He said, "I followed Mitchell here from America in the hopes that I could trick him into revealing her whereabouts. If I can do so I mean to take her away even if it is against her will. For weeks I have been secretly following him each evening as he's left Yellow Door, but so far he's managed to elude me."

"How is it that Mitchell does not know you?" Topper said.

"He has not seen me since I was but a round-faced boy of fourteen years and completely clean-shaven. My false name, the Virginia accent I adopted appear to have deceived him. Thankfully, he took no particular interest in me at the time. I had it in my young head that I should live in the wilderness and learn the ways of the Indians, and that's just what I did. As a consequence I was out of contact with my family for some time. Only about a year ago did word of what had happened reach me. I vowed on my father's death bed that I'd find Annie and bring her back home. She's a stubborn woman, Mr. Topper. Proud and perhaps arrogant, too, I won't deny. She broke away from the family when my father pressed her for the shame that her associations brought upon her and us.

"A number of families who likewise lost their daughters to Mitchell gathered one fateful night and made a pact to see to his destruction, I am ashamed to admit. Shortly thereafter one dark night a party of men of which I was one, planned to catch Mitchell on his way to 'ministering' to his flock and see him tarred and feathered or perhaps even hung—for our tempers ran high. Somehow or other he heard of this and fled with his Flock to England. Once this was discovered I volunteered to find him, find his flock and release the women he keeps in it. I must find my sister, Mr. Topper. Little else really matters to me. I've lost all taste for revenge, but I will see her freed from his clutches if it is the last thing I accomplish on this mortal coil, I have sworn and so swear to you now."

"What an ugly turn events have taken," Topper said with a heavy sigh, his skin the colour of gruel. "If I prevail in this duel—which is highly doubtful since I haven't handled a gun for anything other than hunting and that not for a decade or more—then you will be unable to discover the whereabouts of your sister and I will likely be charged with murder. And if I do not prevail, my life is forfeit, my bride will be widowed, and the good name of Mr. Scrooge's Charity will be ruined—for scandal there will be once news of a duel spreads through the City."

"I will not have you throw your life away for my sister, Mr. Topper. She is more precious to me than anything in this world, but I cannot ask any man that. There must be another way," Trumbull said.

"Perhaps there is. My every instinct tells me Mr. Scrooge is in grave danger and requires my immediate assistance. Yet I am inexorably diverted from that purpose. How can I search for the man when the hour of my own certain destruction so speedily approaches? I am duty-bound to find him, yet I cannot. My remaining hours are too few."

"There may be a simple explanation as to Mr. Scrooge's whereabouts. In the end he may be visiting his nephew or cousin for all we know," Trumbull said.

Topper shook his head sadly. "You may have no doubt that Mr. Scrooge is indeed in mortal danger. In participating in this duel and not seeing to his safety I am sealing my employer's fate as well as my own. All of this you may equally have no doubt is no coincidence. This has been a cleverly orchestrated bit, and we have entered into it all too innocently.

"You will excuse me now. I cannot return to my home. My wife will not be in her bed and I feel, at all events, unclean. I shall spend the night here at Yellow Door in my room and get what little sleep I can. Meet me an hour before sunrise. Then I shall face my fate as best I can."

CHAPTER 12

ༀ

Black Pearls

Mitchell announced: "Allow me to introduce my second. This is Mr. Fleming. He is an associate of mine and a gentleman of great discretion —a quality which I believe you British value highly." His face glowed red with the light of the rising sun.

Topper bowed reflexively. He said, almost too faint to be heard: "And this is my second with whom you are already familiar. He is Mr. William Dawson, an American who also values discretion." His teeth chattered in spite of the warm breeze blowing from the wood.

Mr. Fleming bowed in return. Fleming's mud-coloured hair was clubbed back in a manner out of fashion for some time. He was tall, narrow-shouldered. A patch covered his right eye.

"Sirs," Fleming said, holding his head high. "The Right Reverend Salvation Mitchell wishes that this confrontation may be avoided. He is sad that your disagreement has come to this point and wonders if some kind of settlement cannot be made between the gentlemen."

"I would do anything for this to be settled peaceably," Topper said to Trumbull in a hoarse whisper.

Trumbull darted him a look and in his Virginia accent said, "Mr. Topper is also interested in settling this matter without violence."

"The Reverend Mitchell is delighted to hear him say so," Fleming said as if he were addressing a vast audience.

Trumbull said, "Of course, Mr. Topper would need to know the terms of the settlement, before agreeing."

"Certainly, Sir," Fleming said, again bowing low. "The terms are simple and direct, and Reverend Mitchell believes they are fair and entirely reasonable."

"And what might they be, Sir?" Trumbull said.

"Merely that Mr. Topper signs his name to this document," Fleming said holding up a sheet of folded paper.

"And what is the nature of the document which you offer?"

"It is a confession," Fleming said.

"A confession?! A confession to what?" Trumbull's voice broke angrily.

"A list of crimes: embezzlement, adultery, and sodomy top the list. There are others. Do you care to see?" Fleming extended the list toward Trumbull and blinked his single eye.

Trumbull took it carefully from his hand and looked to Topper.

Topper returned him a blank look, his ears filling with the beating of his own heart.

"Mr. Topper," Trumbull said, "are you willing to accept the Reverend's terms which require you to acknowledge heinous crimes which you did never commit?"

Topper shuddered as if he had received a blow and gave the slightest shake of his head. Trumbull slowly tore the paper into shreds.

"Mr. Topper does not accept your terms. These words are lies," Trumbull said. "Nothing less than extortion."

Fleming said, "The Reverend Mitchell grieves to see you respond so, Sir. There is no other choice than to settle this in the low way."

Trumbull made no reply, but continued to gaze fearlessly into the single-eye of the man who stood before him.

Fleming held out a box of a dark wood and lifted the lid. "Do you find these pistols suitable, Sir?"

Trumbull lifted the weapons from the velvet lining and examined them. "They are of fine workmanship."

Fleming nodded. "They are very fine, indeed. Choose one if you will while I pace out the distance. Will you say a dozen paces is acceptable?"

"A dozen paces? So close?"

"It is to the death, is it not?"

Trumbull did not immediately reply. He laid back one of the pistols and hefted the other. "This one will do," he said.

Fleming paced out the distance and set a pile of stones at each end.

"I have laid the line north and south so that neither party will have the advantage of the other as to the blinding rays of the sun. Is that agreeable?" Fleming said.

"It is," Trumbull replied.

"If the gentlemen will take their places. Will Mr. Topper take the northern post or shall I flip a coin?"

"The northern position will suit," Trumbull said.

"Very good. It should be understood that the gentlemen shall alternate shots until one or the other them is mortally wounded."

"That is so."

"And it is also agreed that Mr. Topper shall have the first shot."

Trumbull merely nodded.

"The Reverend Mitchell would have this over and as quickly as possible," Fleming said, "for he has many duties to perform before noon. It would please us if Mr. Topper were to take his position."

Trumbull reached over to Topper and handed him the weapon. Topper took it as if he had been offered a dead rat. Trumbull escorted Topper to his spot and stepped to one side.

Fleming walked Mitchell to his southern post. "Whenever Mr. Topper is ready," he said as softly as if he were guiding a child's recitation.

Topper squeezed closed his eyes and probed his own chest with his left hand. Ribs were little more than twigs. Where, he wondered, will the ball enter? If Mitchell were a good shot it would be either his heart or his lungs. If not, then perhaps a shoulder wound or a ball in the abdomen and a slow painful death.

"How has it come to this?" he said as if he were alone talking to himself. "Not in my worst nightmares could I have foreseen the day when I might face a man in an empty grove to kill him or be killed. I am not a soldier. I am not even a hunter. I am a clerk."

Topper cocked back the hammer of the pistol and levelled it at Mitchell's chest.

"You, Sir, are a demon from Hell. Not because of anything you yourself have done, but for what you force me to do."

He hesitated, dropped his arm low and fired into the ground. "You cannot make me, Sir. You may kill me, but you cannot make me commit the crime for which I could never forgive myself."

"No, Mr. Topper, that will never do," Reverend Mitchell said, rushing forward. "That is entirely inadmissible. *The Code Duello of 1777*, which you are no doubt aware of, expressly forbids it."

"I have fired my shot, Sir," Topper replied and his arms to his side. "It is your turn. Do your worst."

"But you have *not* fired at me, Sir. That was the agreement. 'To fire at one another until one is mortally wounded.' You have dislodged your bullet into the ground where it can do no harm."

"I will not fire my weapon at you."

"Oh, Sir, but you must. It is your duty to do so, and my duty to see that it is done." Mitchell stepped briskly forward, slapped the discharged pistol from Topper's hand, and replaced it with his own. He pulled the gun into his own chest. "Here man, like this," he said.

Topper tried to pull away, but Mitchell in spite of his round shape and thin arms had the strength of a bear. Topper felt his finger forced against the trigger. The gun kicked. Smoke stung his eyes and burned his nose.

Mitchell staggered back; the smile on his face vanished. He doubled over, blood quickly spilling over his shirt and cloak.

"Oh, why force me to do this?" Topper cried flinging the pistol at a distance and lifting his hands over his head. "Why? Why? I do not want your death on my conscience."

Mitchell dropped to one knee, coughed, and dragged the back of a bloody hand against his head. He said, "You must feel what it is like to grant someone the gift of death. He is the One Who Takes Life. He is the One Who Owns the Darkness."

"Mr. Trumbull help me with him, if you would," Topper said. "Let us open his shirt and see to his wounds at once."

Trumbull rushed to his side, and they lowered Mitchell to the ground.

"Will you not help us?" Trumbull called to Fleming who had not moved since the shots were fired. Fleming made no reply, but to stand and watch.

"Where is he struck?" Topper said, pulling open the shirt. The blood which had flowed freely only moments before was gone. There was not a speck of crimson anywhere about him.

"Have you lost something, Mr. Topper?" Mitchell said. His eyes fluttered open and his mouth stretched in a sardonic grin. "Let me help you. It is a warm morning and I shan't need to wear this shirt for the business which I have in mind." The Reverend Mitchell stood to his feet and pulled cloak and shirt from his torso so that it was bare. The only markings were curious tattoos on his chest, shoulders and upper arms.

"You have suffered no harm?" Topper said, almost jubilantly. "You live?"

"No, I am not a living being as you understand it. I cannot be killed."

"What are you saying?" Trumbull said losing his Virginia drawl.

"I am saying when your band of friends decided to hang me back in Pennsylvania that had they laid hands upon me, they would have found no tree which would hold me. It would have been an interesting experience for them. But I could not stay. My Master had other plans for me. Other plans here on this side of the Atlantic."

Trumbull's face twitched.

"Did you believe that I didn't recognise you with your face full of whiskers? I know full well who you are, Lincoln Trumbull. You have come to rescue your sister, and I am of half a mind to give her to you inasmuch as she no longer pleases me. She is not so young nor pretty as she once was."

"I will see you dead, Sir," Trumbull said.

"I would have guessed by now you understood that such a thing is not possible. You still do not realise that I only wear the skin of a human. I am the living manifestation of Deceit and Racism. I am a demon under the command of the Prince of Darkness Himself. Why do you think that I never used the name of your god? When I referred to *Him* I referred to Satan,

Lucifer, the Prince of Darkness. He does not allow me to die. However, I idle away precious moments when there is a duel to be fought. I will remind you that it is my turn to shoot."

"Shoot? No!" Trumbull said.

Fleming stepped forward and handed Mitchell two loaded pistols.

Mitchell said, "I have given you two shots. And now I will take mine." He fired the first at arm's length into Topper's body and then the second into Trumbull's.

Topper braced to receive the kick of the lead ball. The impact knocked him back against a tree. His eyes dropped to his chest to see a dark pool spread, but the stain was not composed of his own blood. The blackness writhed. The blackness chittered.

"What in the name of God?" Topper shouted and swept away handfuls of black beetles swarming over his chest and arms.

"One might call them *Attagenus unicolour*," said Mitchell, "but we shall for the sake of simplicity call them the Black Pearls of Satan's Crown."

Just before the swarm completely covered his face, Topper heard Trumbull scream once clearly, a second cry was muffled. In two moments more, neither of them could speak, breathe, nor move for the blight which encased their bodies.

"Shall we not kill them?" Fleming said.

"It would bring me no greater pleasure, but we must put His goals above our need of personal gratification. No, they are of far, far greater value alive —if only for the moment. Dead, they become objects of pity. Alive, they will be known as thieves, unholy, a source of disgrace."

"What shall we do with them then?" Fleming said.

"We must keep them. We must keep them in a place where they may never be found. You know of the mortal Magician who also serves the Dark Prince. He practices the Art of creating chambers which no man may enter or escape by natural means. We shall load Mr. Topper and Mr. Trumbull in our wagon, cover them with a canvas sheet and drive them to the Magician. He will keep them in such a chamber until we have further use of them. But you must carry them to the Magician alone. I need to return to the Charity at the soonest opportunity. I have much to tell them, and there are many changes to make before the sun sets on this day."

 govj

Old Wounds and Joints

THE BENCH SQUEAKED AS COOK MADE WAY FOR MARY-MARTHA TO SIT beside her. The kitchen maid's perpetual smile was gone, and she held the hem of her apron to her mouth as if to hide missing teeth.

Miss Goosegrass entered the room but declined a seat offered her by Mr. McCloud. She spoke a few words in his ear before moving off toward the window where she crossed her arms and leaned against the wall like a pouting school girl.

A moment later Jack Forest rolled up the centre aisle. The brass wheels beneath him squeaked like demon mice. He pushed his cart into a corner and pulled himself onto the first pew next to Billings.

The last to enter was Miss Trellis, her cap brushing the lintel as she strode through the doorway. Several men stood and offered her their seat which she accepted with a "*Grazie.*" She pushed together their chairs and sat. Everyone at Yellow Door was now assembled in the room where chapel was usually held.

The room grew silent save for the sound of a fly colliding repeatedly against the window.

"I have very grave news to share with you this morning," The Reverend Mitchell said, his broad hips cocked to one side in a commanding fashion. "I am sorry to tear you away from your breakfasts so early, but the news I bring you cannot wait. If it were not so important, so vital to your future, I would let it pass for another time."

He smoothed his hair down on his forehead. "Most of you have heard by now," he said, unctuously, "that Mr. Topper and I had a disagreement here yesterday."

Those few who made any sound at all made monosyllabic protests.

Mitchell shamed them with a clucking tongue. "I do not believe in your postiche naïveté. I know how gossip travels in small communities such as yours. No, if you will be honest with me, I will be honest with you."

The Reverend Mitchell pulled a silk handkerchief from his pocket and used it to wipe his eyes. Briefly he held it across his face as if it were a mask, then returned it to his pocket unfolded.

"I do not deny it: Mr. Topper and I did have words. Gentlemen often have honest differences of opinion and the best of them learn to settle these differences with dignity and go about their business. They do not let it colour their work or their frame of mind." He paused, tilted back his head and stroked his chins for a moment before continuing.

"But sometimes the disagreement is not just a matter of a difference in opinion. There *are* higher Truths, are there not? Sometimes men become victims of their baser instincts. They grow to disbelieve in their own good, in their own professed principles. Please do not believe that when I say this I am referring only to Mr. Topper, but to the effect that institutions of power have on the well-being of our spiritual selves no matter how humble we may have been the day we were born. There's no denying that Mr. Topper is a troubled man, but I would like to believe that he could be saved if he were to apply the salve of His Grace upon his mortal soul."

The Reverend laid an elbow on the pulpit.

"How can I soften the blow to the gentle, brave-yet-needy collection of humanity which is assembled here this morning? Perhaps there *is* no softening the blow. Perhaps it must fall hard upon us as a lesson learned in pain. For it is with pain that I share this news."

He clasped his small pink hands together and rolled his bulging eyes skyward.

"Word reached me just moments ago," he said, "that a note was found in Mr. Topper's room, the contents of which will shock you all very, very deeply I am much afraid."

Jemmy McCloud, the old sailor, stood. "Say what you mean, Sir. We're not afraid of the truth,"

"No, I would be surprised if you were. You are all very brave and very deserving. It therefore grieves me to say that from the signs it appears that your Mr. Milton Topper has taken nearly all of the resources which were reserved for the maintenance of this institution. Stolen, rather! *Embezzled* I believe the legal term is. The complete assessment of this theft will take some investigation to reveal its full depth."

A horrified sound escaped three-score lips. Disbelief. Dismay. Anger.

Elizabeth Trellis rose to her full height, arched her prodigious spine then tumbled rearward like a felled oak. Her weight dropped atop a group of men who could not support her, and they sagged to the floor with a grunt. After a stunned moment they wriggled from beneath her iron bones and pressed their backs against the wall gasping for breath. Her eyelids fluttered, then drew wide to reveal orbs as white as hens' eggs. Her throat issued a low gurgling which gave even the bravest among them pause.

The Reverend scuddled sidewise in her direction, but kept a guilty distance. "Female hysteria," he pronounced.

Twenty-one heartbeats passed before Miss Trellis's right arm twitched. Two more and it darted snake-like at the Reverend Mitchell who danced away on small feet as nimbly as a ballerina, eyes wide with surprise.

In two more heartbeats all four of her limbs writhed madly as a single mass sweeping away chairs, tables, people—anything which stood within their range. Several young men leapt to her side to prevent her from doing herself harm. First one, then another, then the last of them flew through the air in an arc and landed with no thoughts of attempting to restrain her further.

At once, the shaking stopped. A haze rose above her body as vapour from a spent steam engine. No one approached her. No sound was heard until Mary-Martha began to hum—not a melody, but a single, unwavering tone. "Silly girl," said Cook. "This is no time to be amusing yourself."

Mary-Martha slumped from the bench to Cook's feet with a sound like a laundry bag hitting the floor. Her arms and legs flailed without purpose. Those who sat near jerked back as if a bowl of spiders had been dumped into their laps. In a moment she, too, was still.

"Female hysteria—it spreads," pronounced the Reverend a second time, but with little conviction.

From the first pew: "For the love of God, help me." Billings clutched a writhing Jack Forest protectively to his breast, but the boy tore at the man's face with his nails until half a dozen red trails glistened on his cheeks. "Lower him to the floor," said Billings. Strong hands lifted the boy and carefully set him down supine. Flecks of white foam appeared at the corners of his mouth, and his pink eyes shivered.

Miss Goosegrass dashed to Billings' side with a handkerchief. She drew away his hands from his face to dab his wounds, but found him unmarked.

"But, Mr. Billings?" she said.

He looked at his hands and felt his cheeks again. "How can this be?" he said, and rubbed his cheeks briskly in search of blood which was no longer there.

"What is this madness?" the Reverend muttered backing away and clutching at his neck-cloth.

Using his cane Billings lowered himself to Jack's side, placed his palm kindly on his shoulder and whispered, "What ails you, boy?"

Jack, like the others, stopped his contortions and lay completely still.

"Is he alive?" Reverend Mitchell asked.

Billings pressed an ear to the boy's chest. "His heart works, and he breathes," he said.

Miss Goosegrass picked up the boy's thin arm. "He is feverish," she said. "Someone get water." She ran her handkerchief over his brow and down his cheek. She gasped.

Jack opened his eyes as if he had only been lost in thought and sighed pleasantly.

"I do beg your pardon," the boy said. "No doubt we have disturbed these proceedings. The news Reverend Mitchell has given us, of course, has been a great shock. Please don't let us interrupt your presentation any further, Reverend. I believe I can apologise for us all." He sat up without help.

"You are well again?" Mitchell asked disbelieving.

"I would say so." He blinked his eyes and stretched as if he had just woken from a nap.

The Reverend Mitchell said, "Astonishing," and gave Jack a sidelong look.

Miss Trellis rose to her feet, dusted off her long skirts and pushed chairs and pews back into neat rows. Mary-Martha, also recovered, guided the people of Yellow Door back to their places.

"Do go on. We are anxious to hear all that you have to tell us, Reverend," Jack said.

The Reverend Mitchell cast him a suspicious look.

Jack said, "The assembly is attentive, Sir. What better time to finish your news?"

The Reverend said, "Perhaps you are right, boy. We seem to have recovered ourselves. I suppose one must expect this sort of thing when dealing with the needy in poor health. Yes. I will continue."

He turned his back to the assembly and adjusted his collar. When he turned back, his black eyes gleamed. He said.

"There is further bad news that I must share with you, though I will ask your forgiveness for the language I am forced to used to convey it. If you will cast your eyes around the assembly here you will notice that Mr. William Dawson is not to be found among us this morning either. It is for this reason: Mr. Dawson has been Mr. Topper's accomplice in this vile action against us."

A bleat of incredulity swept across the room.

"Perhaps you will believe that they have taken the money for a just purpose which only He may know—and if that lightens your heart in any way, then go on believing it. Far be it from me to steal small comforts from the minds of the distressed and unfortunate, but this note I hold here in my hand—this note filled with mockery and contempt for the worthy poor at our humble charity found pinned to the wall of Mr. Topper's room denies the comfort of such believe. It is with a heavy heart that I must tell you this news. I am not a gossip, my children, but I must blow the horn of alarm against those who would pollute our innocent flock with wickedness. Those men, I am obliged to tell you—because Truth is the only way—keep carnal desires for one another that neither could resist."

Women clasped their hands over the ears of their children, rose and huddled them from the room.

"Rather than following the natural path which He has created for us, Mr. Topper and Mr. Dawson have chosen to shun the world of decency and faith to live unnaturally together on value stolen from the mouths and backs of the down-trodden. May He have mercy on their souls."

The sob broke again, more anger than disbelief.

Miss Goosegrass stood to her feet, her face flushed. "I can hold my tongue no longer. You lie! You lie, Sir, as surely as the sun rose this morning. How can you stand there and express such filth, such unimaginably black slander against two people whose goodness we all know only too well. Why should I or anyone here believe you when you offer no proof other than your own word? There is no greater, gentler man than Mr. Topper and no kinder, helpful, selfless man than Mr. Dawson. Why you should cast such aspersions upon their characters is a mystery to me, but your baseless accusations violate their good reputations, and I will not have it!"

"Perhaps you would care to read this yourself!" The Reverend Mitchell said and wagged a folded sheet of foolscap in her direction. "There is every reason for you to believe what I have said because with even the most cursory examination you will find your name writ large in this disgraceful confession in Mr. Topper's own hand-writing. I would have spared you the disgrace, ma'am, were you to keep your silence, for I would not speak ill of a woman who has a past which she sought to leave undisturbed from the ken of decent folk, but since you have spoken up so boldly, let your face burn in shame at your Sins before these good people."

"Whatever do you mean, Sir?" Miss Goosegrass said, her eyes snapping angrily.

"Your sordid relations with these two men...and many others—not to put too fine a point on it," The Reverend Mitchell said walking rapidly toward her and shoved the paper into her bosom. "Read it. Shred it. Burn it. Do with it what you like for I have no desire to see it ever again and rue the day that I laid eyes upon its foulness."

Miss Goosegrass slapped his hand away and clenched her fists as if she meant to box him.

"No. That is unfair," the Reverend said. "I should be bigger than that. I offer you, Miss Goosegrass, my pity and my understanding. A woman who is well past her bloom and still unmarried is often driven by her desires into a hysteria which often involves—shall we say *abnormal*—practices and relationships with men and...with other women..."

Miss Goosegrass stomped her foot and said, "When Mr. Scrooge hears of how you have spoken here to-day, you will find yourself wishing that you had been born without a tongue."

"I am well aware of your designs upon Mr. Scrooge, Madam," The Reverend Mitchell said. "Your charms have had a strong effect upon him as they have had with many others before him as you know only too well. Far too strong in this instance. Unlike others who have fallen under your influence whose coarse hearts and thick skins protected them from feeling abuse both emotional and physical too deeply, Mr. Scrooge, I am afraid, has been unable to sustain the emotional burden which you have placed upon him. He is of a sensitive temper as anyone who knows him well can attest. He has broken down, ma'am, to put it simply. His reason is clouded, though I beg you not to repeat that to anyone, and he has only brief moments of lucidity from which he communicates with me his concerns and wishes." The Reverend Mitchell turned toward the assembly and raised his hands over his head. He said:

"Do not cave in to despair on his account, my Friends. Believe he will recover. Include your concern for his well-being in your prayers to Him. We can rejoice in the fact that he is under the care of a highly-skilled physician who will bring him round, I am quite certain, if we can only keep him in our thoughts and in our hearts."

"Where is he?" Miss Goosegrass said, in a voice which her students obeyed without fail. "I demand that you tell us immediately so that we can see that he is properly cared for. I would not trust the well-being of Mr. Scrooge to a wicked man filled with such lies as yourself."

The Reverend Mitchell tapped his nose. "That is information which I do not care to share. The temptation to run to his side would prove too powerful for you. I believe it to be in Mr. Scrooge's best interest if you two were to be kept apart. You will confine yourself to your duties at his charity. I forbid you in the strongest terms ever to see our great benefactor again. Do you understand me?"

Miss Goosegrass collapsed to the ground. She had not fainted but her body quivering in rage would not hold her.

"Would someone please remove her?" The Reverend Mitchell said, lifting his eyebrows. When nobody moved, The Reverend Mitchell gave a silent signal and the door to the room swung wide. Fleming stood in the opening. The Reverend Mitchell nodded at the heap which was Miss Goosegrass. Fleming stepped into the room and bent to gather her in his arms. Miss Goosegrass cuffed him sharply across the face knocking his eyepatch askew.

"Don't you ever lay a finger on me, do you understand? Not ever!" She rose to her feet and met the Reverend Mitchell eye to eye. "And as for you, you diseased creature, you filthy beast..." She drew back a cupped hand and struck him such a blow that he stumbled back against the wall.

"It is time for you to find employment elsewhere, Miss Goosegrass," The Reverend Mitchell pulled his hand away from his ear to see a trickle of red in his palm. "Your violence proves my point beyond any words I could have spoken. Even so, I cannot see it in my heart to send you before the Magistrate under the circumstances. There will be scandal enough surrounding Mr. Scrooge's charity in the coming weeks and months, and I will avoid adding to it in any way I can. We shall be pure of heart, and this innocence will shine a light which will bleach out the stain." The Reverend Mitchell lifted his thin arms over his porcine body, a tiny trickle of blood running from his ear.

Miss Goosegrass looked as if she would strike him again, but instead turned on heel and walked steadily to the door of the room with her head held high.

She turned and issued a final challenge: "If money has been embezzled, Reverend Mitchell, it is you who has done the deed—not Mr. Topper nor Mr. Trumbull."

"Why would I remain here and face the task of feeding, clothing and sheltering the needy if I were guilty of embezzlement? Wouldn't I run with the money and use it sinfully as have Topper and Dawson?"

"I know not what your motives are, but I am sure of one thing: You are a fiend. You may be certain that you have not heard the last of this yet." She stepped through the door and slammed it behind her.

"We shall not allow her to disturb us, Friends. No, we shall not. Instead you will allow me to introduce to you someone new to Mr. Scrooge's Charity. This is Mr. Fleming. Gentle as a lamb, he is."

A single, nervous guffaw broke from Fleming's lips.

The Reverend Mitchell made his face into a beneficent expression. "Mr. Fleming," he said, "has been known to give his last farthing to orphans."

Fleming pulled his eye-patch round where it covered the hole. He bowed low. As he did so the assembly felt old wounds ache and their joints stiffen.

"Mr. Fleming will be my assistant henceforth, and you will receive orders from him as you would me. Do not make too much of his missing eye— dear me, no. It was honourably lost in the war against the French Emperor."

Fleming walked slowly among them, nodding his ugly head.

"Before I can continue I need returned those women and children who earlier left us. Mr. Fleming, would you see to that?"

"Of course, Reverend," said Fleming. "I will have them returned here directly."

During an uncomfortable space of quarter of an hour while the Reverend Mitchell could be seen moving silently his lips, practising his delivery, the women ran their children in like wheelbarrows, never glancing up nor making eye contact with anyone. After all were seated and accounted for the Reverend Mitchell said:

"I carry with me a document in which Mr. Scrooge gives me full charge of his charity. Every word of it transcribed by my own hand during a recent moment of lucidity in which he begged me for help until the day should come when he is stronger and can return to his duties a wiser and better man for it. It is an obligation from which I will not shrink."

The Reverend Mitchell's eyes glittered preternaturally in the morning light. All heads were bowed save for three: Jack, Mary-Martha and Miss Trellis. All three faced him with expressions he could not read.

He said, "There are bound to be changes in the administration of an organisation such as this one when authority flows from a hand weak, corrupt, and sinful to one strong, decent and moral. The strong and moral must clean up after the mess which the weak and sinful have left behind."

The assembly responded with downcast eyes and silence. Again the only sound was that of a fly desperate to escape.

"To that end I have given directions that certain peoples under the care of this institution shall no longer be coddled. Those especially who do not share our faith must either accept Him into their lives or receive their hand-outs at another door. That may seem harsh, but after reflection I am quite certain you will see the wisdom of it. We offer our hearts filled with Faith, but if the heart which receives does not match the Faith, the gift is spoilt..." The Reverend Mitchell paused, clasped his hands together, and bowed his head as if in prayer. Then his head snapped suddenly up.

"Speaking of which where is that dark girl and her brother? The Indian children. Has anyone seen either of them this morning?"

No one offered a definitive answer though there was much murmuring.

"Well, can any of you get up off your lazy back-sides and go find them?"

Billings fetched Jack his cart and helped set him on it. Jack rolled himself toward Reverend Mitchell. Jack kept his eyes, full of fire and light, directly on Mitchell's who flinched under their gaze.

Jack said, "Here I am, Sir. I shall seek out the children and will return to you directly." Jack placed a hand to his breast and bowed with elegance. The cart seemed to swivel under a power of its own, and Jack left the room with uncommon grace.

After the boy left the Reverend Mitchell said, "It's about time that these two give up their heathen Hindu ways, learn His ways and join our Flock in more than lip service." The Reverend Mitchell crossed his arms and squinted his eyes.

"I have been watching them. Especially the girl. She does not do well here—not with her brother who needs discipline more than he needs a sister. She will require special instruction which she cannot receive in a charity which concerns itself more with filling bellies than filling souls. It is her soul which wants attention, and the only way to satiate a hungry soul is with reflection and prayer. How can that happen here with so many distractions? No, I will have the girl join the others of my Flock where she will learn the Arts of Prayer and Meditation."

Mr. Billings raised his hand.

"Yes, Sir," The Reverend Mitchell said, "You have a question?"

Billings stood to his feet with the aid of his cane. He said, "People here are saying that there was a duel between you and Mr. Topper. Is that so? Did you kill Mr. Topper? Is that why he isn't here?"

The Reverend flushed. "Let us put an end to that idea right now. I am the Shepherd of the Souls of my Flock. Do shepherds point guns at the members of their Flock and fire balls of iron into their chests? They most certainly do not! No, Mr. Topper has vanished—absconded with the life-blood of Mr. Scrooge's Charity. He is still alive unless he has come to some misadventure on his own in the meanwhile, and I am obviously alive, so there was no duel. I don't want to hear another word about it."

◎

The Panther grabbed the shoulder of Scrooge's jacket and pulled him into the brush.

"Will you eat me?" Scrooge said in a quivering voice. "If so, do it quickly, for I am in so much pain that I pray for release."

"I will not eat you, my father," the Panther said. "I will hide you for the moment. Here you will be safe while I search for those who would do you harm."

"Give me something for the pain," Scrooge said. "I cannot bear it."

Clarence said, "I dare not give you more Laudanum, Sir. The effect may be too strong."

"For the Love of God. More..."

Clarence poured him a glass of water and added eighty drops of the common Tincture of Opium. "Sit up, Sir, and drink this slowly."

⊙

Rajani heard a sharp rap at the door. Her brother looked up from the wood scraps he had been stacking, but said nothing.

"Who is it?" she said putting away her necklace. "Do come in."

Jack opened the door, rolled through and closed it softly behind. He said:

"Something is wrong. Terribly wrong. Mr. Scrooge has gone missing, and the Reverend Mitchell has taken charge of the Charity."

"I knew that we should not trust him. I knew that he would leave us," Rajani said, turning away.

"Gone missing? Where? He must be found," said Haresh. "Does not Mr. Topper know where he is?"

Jack said, "I am sorry to say, Mr. Topper is also missing along with Mr. Dawson, and the Reverend Mitchell has told terrible lies about them. The only one to defend them has been Miss Goosegrass. They are in as much danger as Mr. Scrooge."

Haresh stood and placed his hands on his hips. "They will be needing our help," he said. "At last I will prove how powerful I am."

"You cannot stay here," Jack said. "The Reverend Mitchell has sent me here to fetch you back. He means to teach you Christian ways whether you want them or not."

"I have felt him watching me for some time," Rajani said. "He does not wish to teach me Christianity. He is an evil man as I have never before seen," she said.

"We must find a safe place for you to stay," Jack said.

Rajani shrugged. "But run away to where? We know no one. That is why we are here to begin."

Jack smiled. "Do not worry yourselves about that just now," he said. "I will make the arrangements. For the moment gather your things and hide in the building where Al-Mustafa's kept his studio. I will send someone for you to take you to safety shortly. Do you understand?"

Rajani nodded. "Why do you help us? You are a Christian, are you not? Should you not obey the Reverend Mitchell?"

"No," Jack said. "The Reverend Mitchell in no way commands my obeisance. My master is far, far greater than he."

◎

Jack re-entered the chapel. "They are not in their rooms, Reverend," he said, truthfully. "No one else I've spoken to knows where they are either."

"What?" The Reverend Mitchell screamed and kicked over the pulpit. "How can this be? Who is in charge of watching them?"

No one said a word.

He continued, "That would have been Mary-Martha White's job, wouldn't it?"

"It's no one's job to watch the children, Sir," Jack said. "School is not held on Saturdays, and students may do as they wish."

"Silence, you worm!" Mitchell said and glared at Jack. But Jack did not flinch, did not look away. He only gave a shining smile which Mitchell could not meet.

"Mary-Martha," Mitchell said, "please come stand before me."

Mary-Martha rose to her feet, but did not take a step forward. She stood still, her arms hanging loosely at her sides. Her perpetual smile was once again as brilliant as the sun.

"Can you not hear me, woman?" he shouted and strode forward to stand directly before her. "I repeat: can you not hear me?"

"I can," Mary-Martha said, showing no sign of fear. "My ears are quite good."

"What?"

"Perhaps it is your ears which do not hear so well," she said.

"Some would call that reply disrespectful," The Reverend Mitchell said. "But I will rather call it spirit. I do like a girl with spirit."

"You may well call me spirited, Sir," she said keeping her expression just short of laughter.

The Reverend Mitchell returned the smile coyly.

"You may return to your duties in the kitchen. We will speak of this later, my child. I will call you to my room soon, and we will see just how spirited a girl you really are."

"Yes, Sir," Mary-Martha said and walked quickly away.

⊙

Light filled Scrooge's eyes even when shut. He covered them with his left arm as his right would not move. When he lowered it again it a trifle, he found the light more subdued, but still too bright.

"Where am I?" he said, sensing someone standing nearby.

"There, there, Sir. Do not trouble yourself to rise. I can fetch you anything you need. Please lie still."

It was a woman's voice.

"Where am I?" he repeated.

"You are a guest at Owlpen Hall, the home of Mr. James Weston. You have had quite a rough time of it, I am afraid, but you are passed the worst."

"Worst? What has happened to me?" said Scrooge.

"You've had a shock. A terrible shock, but you are in good hands now."

"A shock?"

"Do not distress yourself just now. You must take your ease, Sir, and not trouble yourself to stir."

Scrooge said, "Who—who are you? Do I know you?"

"You do not. My name is Mrs. Vivianna Claypoole."

"Mrs. Claypoole?" Scrooge said.

"You have been dreaming," she said.

"Yes, I have been dreaming," Scrooge said struggling to remember the particulars, but they had faded leaving only an emotional residue.

"The dreams have not been pleasant," Mrs. Claypoole said.

"They have not. You heard me cry out?"

Mrs. Claypoole said, "You have been restless."

Scrooge shuddered. "I would rather be awake. But please could you draw the blind?? The light hurts my eyes, I'm afraid. I cannot see you, and would like to."

"One moment," Mrs. Claypoole said, and Scrooge heard the sounds of curtains being drawn.

He lowered his arm bit by bit. "And would you move closer for my eyes are weak. You are too far away, and your face is blurry."

Scrooge felt a rustle of skirts draw near.

"Can you bend down a bit, please? Closer," he said, still unable to focus his eyes.

Her perfume filled his nose. His eyes worked hard to make sense of what he saw.

"Belle!" he gasped and quickly covered them again.

"What is it?" she said, and laid a gentle hand on his arm. "What has caused you to start so?"

"It is nothing," Scrooge said. "With my eyes so weak I mistook you for someone else."

"And this person was someone you cared for very much?" Mrs. Claypoole said.

Scrooge sighed. "She was, indeed, but that was a long time ago, and my life has changed much since then. Changed too much, I'm afraid."

"Changes are not always as happy as they might be," Mrs. Claypoole said.

"They are not, I admit," Scrooge said. "At times the thought makes me want to weep."

"In the end, the world is what we make of it," Mrs. Claypoole said. "Our lives are the result of decisions which we string together like a necklace of pearls."

"One moment. How is it, Madame, that you sit with me? Are you a nurse?"

"No, I am not. I am a friend of Mr. Weston's family. I have only recently returned from India and am by his good graces a guest here. When Mr. Weston and Clarence grew tired after sitting with you many nights, I volunteered to take their places."

"That is very kind of you," Scrooge said. "Could you bend down again to permit me to see your face. My eyes are still not entirely clear, and I would cherish a pleasant sight just now."

Again the woman bent over him, and Scrooge lowered his arm. It was a lovely face filled with light and charm. Not Belle's face as he first thought, but a wonderful face, indeed. Quite young, though.

"And where is your husband, Mrs. Claypoole?" Scrooge said. "Does he await you? You should return to him and leave me be."

"My husband? My husband is dead," Mrs. Claypoole said with a voice held steady only with great effort.

"I am very sorry to hear it," Scrooge said. "If I may ask, how did he die?"

"In India. Mr. Claypoole was a Colonel in the 13th Light Dragoons. Cholera swept through a small village in Tamil Nadu where he was stationed. I was away..." She could no longer suppress her emotions and a sob escaped her throat.

"There, there. I am sorry to have troubled you," Scrooge said.

"It is no matter," said Mrs. Claypoole. "I must be strong, and I have no financial concerns. I have much to live and be happy for."

"I make no doubt, ma'am," Scrooge said. "One as young and pretty as yourself cannot help but have a bright future ahead."

"Please do not speak so. I am no child. I am a fully grown woman who knows much of the ways of the world."

"No, you are no child."

A gentle knock was heard at the door. Scrooge said, "Come in."

A young man wearing a wig and a broad smile entered the room with his hands thrust mischievously in his pockets. "I stopped by to see how you do," he said.

Scrooge gave the man a questioning look.

"You remember me, do you not?" the man said.

"I am afraid I do not," Scrooge said. "There are so many things which I have difficulty calling to mind, so do not take it as a slight that I do not remember your face."

"That is not to be unexpected considering the acuteness of the shock you've received. I must therefore introduce myself a second time: I am Dr. Tobias Fluch."

"Oh, Dr. Fluch. I do believe I have heard your name mentioned at one time or another—perhaps I was half asleep—I cannot now recall. It seems that I owe you a great deal," Scrooge said. "Perhaps my very life."

Dr. Fluch said, "Oh, think nothing of it, old fellow. Your real well-being, of course, is the direct result of Mrs. Claypoole's attentions. She's the one who sits hour after hour by your side. I doubt that King George III received such care."

"Dr. Fluch," Mrs. Claypoole said, her eyebrows frowning, "members of my sex often take colour when men pay them such compliments. Is that your purpose? To see me blush?"

"By no means," the Doctor said. "I merely wish Mr. Scrooge to appreciate his good fortune in your visiting just now."

"I do, Doctor. Indeed, I do," said Scrooge, warmly.

"I fear we have already taxed him too much," Mrs. Claypoole said. "You may be the doctor, but I fear I must drive you away as our patient needs his rest more than we need to chatter in his ears."

She turned to Scrooge, tidied his pillow and said, "Lie back and say no more, Mr. Scrooge. You may sleep now and have no fear of troubling dreams. I promise it. Drink this draught. Close your eyes and awake a stronger man."

Scrooge did as he was told, closed his eyes and fell into a dreamless sleep.

◎

Topper opened his eyes and sat up to darkness. The nightmare had been horrible. The duel. The black beetles. He pressed his fingers to his neck, to his temples. His head throbbed. *What have I been drinking?*

He dropped his hands to his chest and found that he was fully clothed. "What in God's name?" he whispered to himself. The hand which he leaned upon felt the surface beneath him. It was rough wood.

I am dead, he thought. *This cannot be Heaven, and yet it does not resemble what I have been taught of Hell. Perhaps it is something else—a purgatory of sorts. Whatever it is, it is made like a packing crate.* The thought gave him a flicker of hope.

Rather than try to get to his feet he decided that it would be wiser to crawl slowly in one direction and locate a wall. This he did until he found a vertical surface of the same rough lumber. He steadied himself and stood to his feet. Carefully shuffling his feet so as not to stumble over a table or a chair he carefully measured its length: fifteen lengths of his foot until he reached a corner. He noticed nothing which might be a window nor a door. He followed the wall at the corner and paced out twenty-five foot lengths. Again no window nor door. Another wall of twenty-five steps. And another. And another. He was in a room with a floor-space laid out in a perfect square. Surely there was some way in and out, but he felt none.

There was little else to do than to explore the interior of the cube. Down on his knees again Topper carefully felt the way before him. His fingers brushed something. He felt of it. It was square—no, rectangular. His fingers climbed its vertical length. He gripped it lightly and tested its weight. It moved and made a distinctive sound. A table! He had hold of a leg of it.

Topper stood and ran his fingers over its surface. His fingers brushed something light and rectangular: a box of matches. He slid open the box and struck a match.

The flare from the match blinded him, but he did not shake the match out. He turned his face away, and through slitted eyes saw the shape of a body sprawled on the floor not ten steps away.

How could I not have tripped over it?

He feared the match would burn down to his fingers, but he was reluctant to drop it or put it out. How many more matches were in the box? He turned his face back to the table again. His eyes made the adjustment and the flame no longer hurt them. In the centre of the table was a candle and a candlestick. He set the match to the wick, placed the stick in its holder and lifted it into the air.

Topper stepped to the body and set the candle down. He touched it lightly with his fingers desperately hoping it would not be cold. It was warm. He turned it over and held the candle to its face. It was Lincoln Trumbull.

He shook him gently. "Mr. Trumbull. Mr. Trumbull. Can you hear me, Sir? Are you all right?"

A low moan escaped from Trumbull's lips. With difficulty he sat up.

"What?"

"We appear to be prisoners." Topper held up the candle and shed feeble light in their small cell. "How we were placed inside is a mystery. I see no doors nor windows. There must be some way to swing a section of the wall away. A secret panel."

"Who has imprisoned us?" Trumbull said.

"I cannot be sure. What is the last thing you can remember?" Topper said.

"A dream. Beetles running over my arms and chest. Up my neck and over my face. And then nothing. Just blackness."

"These are occult matters, I am very much afraid. Very much afraid, indeed."

Trumbull ran his fingers over the back of his neck. "Then we are helpless," he said.

"Perhaps," Topper said. "But then again, perhaps not." He reached to give his ring, the gift of the Ladies in White, a reassuring twist.

It was gone.

◎

Mrs. Claypoole lifted Scrooge and arranged the pillows which cushioned his head. "How do you do this morning, Mr. Scrooge?" she said, in a light, cheery tone.

"Better and better," Scrooge said, "though I do miss the use of my right arm."

"The doctor says you shall have it back in time. With care. He says I am to manipulate it for you so that it does not wither terribly. Would you object if I were to begin that exercise now?"

"By no means, ma'am," Scrooge said.

"This may cause you some pain," Mrs. Claypoole said.

"No matter. Please, begin. The sooner we begin, the sooner I will be whole again."

Mrs. Claypoole carefully lifted Scrooge's arm, and a sharp pain caused him to catch his breath.

"I do not like being the source of misery to you," she said.

"I am fine," Scrooge said. "I will let you know when I have had more than I can take."

Mrs. Claypoole gently lifted his arm. Scrooge watched her, but said nothing. She held his arm with one hand and softly ran her fingers along the length of it.

"Can you feel my touch?" she said.

"No," Scrooge said. "I am very sorry that I cannot."

"I will not give up so easily," said she. She took his arm in both her hands and rubbed his limp hand against her cheek. "And this? Will you tell me that you cannot feel this either?"

Although he could not feel her cheek the pleasure of the experience did not escape him entirely.

"It has been a very long time since I have known the touch of a woman. What a cruel thing to not to be able to experience it now when I am granted the gift," he said to her.

"Tell me about yourself, Mr. Scrooge," she said. "I have sat at your side now these many days and nights, and yet I know nothing of you. You are a respectable gentleman, so much is clear. But what are your interests and loves?"

"You ask me this to distract my mind from the pain," Scrooge said.

"I ask you this because I am curious to know," she said.

"I have been cruel," Scrooge said.

At this she laughed.

"No, I do not say such a thing to entertain you for it is quite true. I have been cruel, brutal, uncaring, ungenerous to my fellow man."

"I must say I find that very hard to believe, Mr. Scrooge. Your face belies the words you tell me. I see naught but kindness in your eyes and care in your face. I believe that you are being too hard on yourself."

"Not so!" Scrooge said.

"In this I will choose to trust what my eyes and heart tell me and disbelieve your lips."

Scrooge's eyes fluttered as her perfume engulfed him. "I am a changed man," was all that he could say.

"And I am glad of it," Mrs. Claypoole said. "I would hate to have aided in the recuperation of a villain."

"You no doubt have better things to do with your time than nurse an old man."

"Old man? You are not young, but neither are you old," she said. She brushed the hair off his forehead. "You, I take it, are not married?" she said.

"I am not."

"A widower?"

"Never."

"You must have a long list of admirers whose hearts beat rapidly at thoughts of you," Mrs. Claypoole said.

"No one," he said. *Is that right?* he thought to himself. There was a feeling in his bosom as if there had been someone. But who could it be? Someone in a dream perhaps? Belle?

"You have told me your first lie, Sir," she said. "And I am not so sure I like it. You are not so innocent as you pretend." She lifted his arm more sharply than previously, and the pain drove any answer he might have been forming from his mind.

"I believe I would like to rest now, Mrs. Claypoole. I thank you for your kindness. I can never repay you for all you've done for me."

She kissed his hand and she laid it carefully by his side. "You do not know what you have already done for me, Sir. It is I who am at a loss to know how to repay *you*," she said.

She stood and walked to the door, her skirts rustling pleasantly. She closed the door behind and Scrooge found he could no longer hold back sleep.

⊙

"There you are. We have been looking all over for you," Miss Trellis said in their native tongue. Though the loft was dark, she glowed with a soft light of her own. "We have been worried about you."

Rajani peered out from behind a canvas. The heat of the loft was stifling. "I am feeling very hungry," she said.

"No doubt you are, my dear child," Miss Trellis said. "You will never be hungry again. It is time for you to come with me. We have secured a safe haven for you and your brother."

Rajani crawled over to another canvas and tipped it away from the wall to reveal a sleeping Haresh. She shook his shoulder gently. "Where are we going?" she said.

Miss Trellis pointed a finger as if to direct Rajani to look, but she saw only darkness. "I have found a place where you can stay. You will not be alone. There you will be able to keep yourselves clean, fed and warm and you can make as much noise as you wish all day long."

Haresh said, "Will we be sleeping in proper beds?"

"Beds fit for a prince and a princess," Miss Trellis said.

CHAPTER 14

ು೪

Mrs. Topper & Miss Goosegrass

MISS JANE GOOSEGRASS SAT ON THE EDGE OF THE BED FOR WANT OF A chair. She had worked as governess for families with larger wardrobes than the room she now sat in, but it could be cleaned and made comfortable. Her meagre savings could afford no better shelter.

Miss Goosegrass made a mental list of her divers skills and talents with which to make a living and the many work experiences in her favour. References would not be forthcoming from Yellow Door, of course, which would be difficult to explain, but there was nothing that could be done about that. Her previous employers would vouch for her character, and she had not been with the charity for so very long. She would find honest and respectable work if she were patient.

She stood and stepped to her bureau upon which she had laid out her hair brushes. She had few possessions of value but these. If she grew too hungry she could pawn them to eat a few meals more. She had been that hungry before, but always managed to reclaim them once she found work.

Where is Mr. Scrooge? The thought flittered about her mind like a bat inside a cave. It prevented her from concentrating, from putting her best effort into finding new employment. She couldn't help feeling a pang of despair whenever the thought of him entered her mind—which was most of the time. She felt he must be in desperate need.

The Reverend Mitchell had accused her of having designs upon Mr. Scrooge. It was true that she had feelings of great depth for the man. The

Reverend Mitchell was correct about that, but she had no *designs* upon him as had been suggested, and certainly none of the other sordid claims he made as to her character had any truth about them. Her face burned at those accusations. If she had been a younger women with much less knowledge of the wider world, Mitchell's words might have driven her from her senses. Certainly there were laws preventing such slander, but she had no funds for legal recourse. She would need all her pennies just to eat.

But could the Reverend Mitchell be telling the truth about Mr. Topper and Mr. Trumbull? Could they be such villains? No. The idea was impossible. If King George IV himself would visit her and swear to the veracity of The Reverend Mitchell's statements, she would not believe them. The Reverend Mitchell was a liar and scoundrel of the worst kind. She would prove it, but to do that she must first find Mr. Scrooge.

That the Reverend had been able to produce documents for the Magistrate that indicated the truth of what he claimed regarding the issue of embezzlement proved nothing. Clever forgeries was all they were. Worthless sheets of paper. Fortunately the Magistrate found them suspicious as well. What was the name of the Constable who had interviewed her? *Cuff*, she recalled. Not a man of many words, but neither was he a man to be easily fooled.

She heard a knock at the door. *Who could that be? No one knows that I am here.* Could it be the Reverend Mitchell to accuse her of more crimes—more lies so bald, so outrageous that they were difficult to deny?

A second impatient knock sounded before Miss Goosegrass said, "Who is it?"

"I would like a word with you if I may," said a woman's voice which she didn't recognise.

Miss Goosegrass went to the door and opened it. There she met a woman of medium height and figure with fair hair and brilliant eyes.

"I am Mrs. Lucille Topper," the woman said. "Would you be Miss Jane Goosegrass?"

"Yes, I am she. Please do come in." She stood aside and let the woman enter the room. "How did you find me? I have sent word to no one that I am here."

Mrs. Topper pulled off her gloves. "I have been watching Yellow Door all this day and followed you here directly when I saw you leave. There are things which I am eager to learn, and I hope that you can help me."

"I see. This may take some time," Miss Goosegrass said. "I am afraid I can offer you no refreshment and no seat save for the edge of the bed. Or I am happy to stand if you like."

"I am looking for my husband," Mrs. Topper said, suppressing her full emotion.

"If you think that I have had any..."

"Do not misunderstand me, Miss Goosegrass. I am not accusing you of anything. I am only seeking your help."

"Of course. I will help you in any way that is in my power. What is it that you wish to know?" Miss Goosegrass said.

"What can you tell me of the disappearance of my husband?" Mrs. Topper said. She removed her hat and at last sat down on the edge of the bed with her back straight and her head held high.

"Nothing save that I am convinced that the accusations of the Reverend Mitchell are nothing but lies," Miss Goosegrass began.

"You will not find that I disagree with you on that, Miss Goosegrass," said Mrs. Topper. "However, our personal convictions shed no light upon the mystery which I am desperate to solve. Can you tell me when was the last time you saw Mr. Topper?"

Miss Goosegrass shifted her eyes in thought. "Mr. Topper came to me very upset three days since. He asked if I had seen Mr. Scrooge that day, and I told him Mr. Scrooge had been to visit the students earlier in the morning, but I had not seen him since."

"Was that the last you saw of Mr. Topper?" Mrs. Topper said.

"No, it was not. A short while thereafter Mr. Topper gathered all who were at Yellow Door into the dining room. He made inquiries into the absence of Mr. Scrooge. He asked me when I had last seen him, and I told him what I knew to the best of my ability."

"Then what happened?" Mrs. Topper said.

"Mr. Levy said something which I can no longer recall. Something about charity and doctors or some such thing. It sounded like biblical quotation, though I didn't recognise it. For some reason it drove Reverend Mitchell into a rage. He struck Mr. Levy which Mr. Topper wouldn't stand for. Words were exchanged and then blows. At which point I along with nearly everyone else made for our rooms."

"What happened following that?"

Miss Goosegrass averted her eyes. "Beyond that I have no direct experience, and I do not wish to repeat rumours."

"Rumours that my husband and the Reverend Mitchell duelled?" Mrs. Topper said.

"You have heard?"

"I have not been so very long married to my husband, but I find the idea of him engaging in a duel highly unlikely. Still, I do not discount it completely. He is a man of great humour, but inside every man there is a beast."

Miss Goosegrass said, "I do not believe Mr. Topper to be a beast of any sort."

"I only refer to the instinct in every man's breast to fight fiercely when backed into a corner. It is an instinct without which our race could not have survived."

"Of course," Miss Goosegrass said. "I only mean that I hold your husband in the highest regard."

"I understand you, Miss Goosegrass. It is to your credit that you defend him even against his wife! No. Do not apologise. I am unsuccessfully trying to make a small joke. This is not the time for levity."

Miss Goosegrass said, "If Mr. Topper and the Reverend Mitchell *have* duelled, do we look...I don't know how to say this."

"Look for Mr. Topper's body?"

"He may only be wounded and not dead," Miss Goosegrass said.

Mrs. Topper said, "I must hope and pray that he is neither. I have been told that Reverend Mitchell denies that a duel ever took place, and I will have to assume that is the truth. I cannot help but think that he knows where my husband is and is likely responsible for his disappearance. Now, let me pursue my line of questioning."

"You begin to sound like Constable Cuff," Miss Goosegrass said.

"And who is Constable Cuff?"

"Have the Robin Redbreasts not been to see you?"

"They have not," said Mrs. Topper.

"He is the Bow Street Runner who has been assigned to investigate the alleged crimes which the Reverend Mitchell has accused your husband of," said Miss Goosegrass. "He is rather more intelligent than what I would have expected in a thief-taker."

"Curious that he has not spoken with me. Then again, I can hardly say that anyone could have found me at home these last four-and-twenty hours. Never mind that just now. What can you tell me about Mr. Scrooge's interest in jewellery?" Mrs. Topper said.

Miss Goosegrass blushed. "I haven't any idea what you're talking about. Where did you hear mention of jewellery?"

Mrs. Topper gave her a severe look. "Miss Goosegrass, if I am to make any progress in locating my dear husband we are going to have to be candid with one another. Do you agree?"

"And if I am going to find Mr. Scrooge, I will need your help as well. Agreed. What can I tell you?" Miss Goosegrass said.

"You can explain nothing of the nature of the rumour concerning Mr. Scrooge and jewellery?"

Miss Goosegrass said, "He never mentioned anything to me regarding jewellery."

"He said nothing? Do you have any idea why someone might believe such a thing?"

Miss Goosegrass nodded ever so slightly.

"Yes?" Mrs. Topper said, with an encouraging wave of her hands.

"I do not mean to suggest that..." she paused and struggled to find the right word, "...that Mr. Scrooge and I had an *understanding*. He never said anything directly, but by his expressions and manner I believed that he wished to speak with me about..."

"You believe he meant to propose marriage to you?" Mrs. Topper finished without the slightest trace of sarcasm in her voice. "At supper?"

"He meant for us to have supper together—that is all I can say with any certainty."

Mrs. Topper hummed to herself a note of satisfaction.

"There was nothing dishonourable in his intentions, Mrs. Topper. A woman of my age and experience can tell," Miss Goosegrass said.

"I make no doubt. Let us assume you are correct, and I agree with you: a woman *can* tell these things. If Mr. Scrooge meant to marry you and someone found that out and wanted to prevent it, that might explain why he has disappeared. That must also relate to the disappearance of my husband and the slander that has blackened our name. The Reverend Mitchell is clearly involved, but there may be others of whom we do not know."

"But who would not wish Mr. Scrooge and I to be married?"

"That is what I need to find out. If I can discover that, I believe I will discover the whereabouts of my husband."

"Why would anyone not wish us married?" Miss Goosegrass said.

"Money must lie at the bottom of this. What else could it be? Mr. Scrooge has a great deal of money. Perhaps, there is someone else who would wish to lay hands upon it."

Miss Goosegrass narrowed her eyes. "I have no wish for Mr. Scrooge's money, if that's what you believe."

"Oh, I do not doubt you on that, Miss Goosegrass," Mrs. Topper said.

"Why do you say that?"

"Because if you had, you would have proclaimed loud and clear that Mr. Scrooge had proposed to you. Instead, you keep it a secret next to your heart which you have shared with no one except me under pressure. No, Miss Goosegrass. Have you no fear. I believe every word you have told me thus far."

"Bless you, ma'am," Miss Goosegrass said, with obvious relief. "I've had the feeling that no one would believe any word I uttered after the Reverend Mitchell besmirched me so completely."

"The Reverend Mitchell made a tireless enemy when he made an enemy of me, Miss Goosegrass. But we are doomed to failure should we pursue our goals separately," Mrs. Topper said. "If we join our forces together, perhaps we will be successful. What do you say?"

She paused and shook her head. "I certainly will do everything that is in my power to help you in any way that I can, but I am not a woman of independent means."

"You must stay with me," Mrs. Topper said. "There can be no question of that."

"I cannot accept charity," Miss Goosegrass said.

"And I offer you none. I cannot expect you to work and help me solve this mystery at the same time. Therefore I am hiring you to be my companion until such time as...until such time as..." Mrs. Topper could no longer hold back her tears.

"There, there," Miss Goosegrass said, touching her shoulder. "Have a good cry and let it out."

"It's just that Mr. Topper and I have not been married for so very long. It strikes me as being so unfair. We have had no children. People are spreading the cruellest lies about him. It is too much to bear."

"It is hard to be alone," Miss Goosegrass said. "I know. I've had to stand up for myself all my life."

"Will you help me?" Mrs. Topper said.

"I have no idea where to begin."

"Miss Goosegrass, you are the only other person whom I can turn to."

"Exactly what do we wish to accomplish?" Miss Goosegrass said.

Mrs. Topper held up a finger, "One, I wish to find Mr. Topper and put an end to the horrible accusations which have been levelled at him. I will not rest until my husband's good name and character has been re-established, and he is returned to my arms and our good home."

"Two," Miss Goosegrass continued, "And I will not rest until I have learned the whereabouts of Mr. Scrooge. I wish to ascertain that he is well and...and..."

"Let us be truthful," said Mrs. Topper. "You wish to find out where you stand in his heart?"

"No, Mrs. Topper. That is not a relevant issue here at this moment," Miss Goosegrass said.

"I believe it is relevant for many reasons," Mrs. Topper said, "but we need not go into them now. More importantly is what is to be our method of approach?"

"We have only one place to begin our investigation. That is with The Reverend Salvation Mitchell," said Miss Goosegrass. "The more we can find out about him, the closer we will be to the truth."

Mrs. Topper said, "What do you know of him?"

"He is an American only recently come over from the United States."

"Does he travel alone?"

"Yes," said Miss Goosegrass. "Well, no, now that you mention it. I am reminded that he has spoken of a flock which I took to mean other members of his faith."

"Are they at the Charity?" Mrs. Topper said.

"No. They keep themselves away from Yellow Door. He has never said just where. It is a place, he has said, where members remove themselves from the world for purposes of meditation and reflection."

Mrs. Topper said, "Then I suggest that our first goal is to locate that facility and have a look at it. Do you believe Constable Cuff would give us any assistance in that regard?"

"I would wait until we have evidence of some substance to give him," Miss Goosegrass said.

"Agreed," Mrs. Topper said. "At this point I am reluctant to bring anyone else into our confidence. Not just yet."

"I am sorry to be so prosaic on the issue, but what shall we do for money?" Miss Goosegrass said.

"I am not a woman of independent means, but Mr. Topper has a small annual income which will support us for as long as we need. If needs be, I'll become a charwoman. I am not too proud."

"I do hope that will not be necessary, unless... Mrs. Topper, you may have just given me an idea," said Miss Goosegrass with a smile.

☉

"Did the ring have sentimental value?" asked Trumbull.

"It was given to me under very special circumstances," Topper said. "It will seem hard to believe—well, perhaps not after what we've been through, but it was a gift from three Women in White—three spirits or ghosts, if you like."

"Yesterday I would have said you were mad, but just at the moment I have no other choice than to believe you," said Trumbull.

"My family has a long history of dealing with ghosts. Mediums and all that sort of thing. When I was a small boy, I was set upon by demons and three beautiful Women in White appeared out of nowhere. Such a sight they were! They gave me a ring which I've worn ever since. I've always believed it protected me against evil spirits after a fashion. Now when I've the greatest need for it, it has disappeared."

Trumbull said, "Could it be in your coat?"

Topper stood and slapped his pockets. Nothing. Then he turned pale, then blushed.

"What is it, man?" Trumbull said. "Has Mitchell destroyed it?"

"I should think not. I believe I've left it by my wash stand. Of all the sour luck."

"By the wash stand?"

"Yes, I took it off to shave and after I finished...I was distracted and left our home without it."

Trumbull half-closed his eyes. "Does your wife know anything of the nature of the ring?" he asked.

"She does not. Unfortunately, I never told her of it. She's never liked me speaking of such things, so I never discussed the ring with her. I'm very much afraid that any hope of rescue by that means is lost."

Trumbull pursed his lips thoughtfully and walked around the perimeter of the room running his hands along the boards. "Whoever built this room whether with hammer and saw or by magic knows nothing of proper carpentry."

"It will not help us to be critical just at this moment," said Topper.

"Perhaps not, but I can't help but believe if both of us were to put our shoulders to this corner of the room..." he pointed to the one nearest at hand, "...we would be able to prise it apart and see what lies just outside. There can't be more than five nails holding these two walls together."

◉

Bright lights no longer hurt Scrooge's eyes, although his vision was such that he found it difficult to see things at a distance. Reading proved very uncomfortable for him without a glass, and he found managing a glass while holding a book open all with one hand (his right still would not obey him) impossible.

Scrooge heard a light tapping at the door which set his heart racing.

"Come in," he said.

The door opened, and Mr. James Weston entered the room.

Scrooge's face fell, and Weston saw it.

"There's a look of disappointment if ever I saw one. You were expectin' someone else?" Weston said.

"Not at all. Happy I am to see you for this gives me the opportunity to convey my thanks for your kindnesses. I don't know what I would have done if it hadn't been for you."

"Call me Wespie," Weston said. "My friends all do."

"All right, then," Scrooge said. "I give you my thanks, Wespie."

"How does the patient do to-day?" Wespie said and folded his arms across his chest.

"Dr. Fluch tells me that I am recovering well, but not so quickly as I might have done if I were a young man."

"I shouldn't have thought your injuries were so serious as all that. You were knocked about a bit on one shoulder and back. A bump on the head, perhaps. Your coat was unfortunately utterly ruined."

Scrooge said, "When you are my age, you will feel differently about being knocked about a bit."

"I only meant that I felt that things could have been much worse," Wespie said.

"Of course. I don't mean to appear gruff when in fact I am only too grateful for your assistance. Without it, I should be dead. I am very fortunate to have had Mrs. Claypoole to care for me," said Scrooge.

"Yes," Weston said, and strode over to the window. "Dr. Fluch recommended her. She's devoted to you, ain't she?"

"Dr. Fluch recommended her? I believed her to be a friend of your family here on a visit."

Weston clasped his hands behind his back and stared out the window. Slowly he said, "Is that what she said? Well, I suppose that's true in a manner of speakin'. When does the doctor believe you will be on your feet?"

"He has not said. He is concerned over my loss of memory. He attributes it to the great shock which I have been through. I cannot remember anything in the least of the series of events which brought me here."

Wespie said, "Well, if the ministrations of Mrs. Claypoole don't put you right, I don't know what will."

"She is an Angel of Mercy from Heaven," Scrooge said with a sigh.

Wespie made a polite face. "I say, can you remember *nothin'* of the events which brought you here?" he said.

"None. Would you tell me what you know?" Scrooge said.

Weston turned to face Scrooge. "There's not much to tell. Clarence and I were huntin' when we heard a voice call out. We searched until we found you slumped to the ground, disoriented. You looked as if you had been runnin' through the brambles and had taken a hard fall from some height— I couldn't say where because the surroundin's where you were found were as flat as a dinner plate. I had Clarence bring round the cart, and we carried you here directly. You know the rest."

"There is a charity..." Scrooge said.

"You have only to name an amount, Sir. Let it never be said that Wespie is not a generous man," Weston murmured.

"I don't mean that," Scrooge said. "I mean that there is a charity which I myself am very much attached. I need to return to it as quickly as possible. I would like word sent to a dear friend of mine, Mr. Milton Topper, who is in charge of it. He must be worried terribly about me."

"I will have Clarence carry any message you like directly," Weston said. "Do you desire me to fetch you a pen and paper?"

"Yes, if you would be so kind. Have I been like this long?"

"These past ten days, Sir. These past ten days."

⊙

"It is not much of a disguise," Miss Goosegrass said, plucking at the dirty shawl about her shoulders.

Mrs. Topper clucked her tongue thoughtfully. "It will never do. Would you have any objection to dressing yourself like a man?"

"I do not believe any such disguise would be effective," Miss Goosegrass said, smoothing her dress over her figure. "My shape is too...too unman-like."

"I suppose you are right. I don't much fancy wearing a pair of musta-chios either," said Mrs. Topper, "or trousers. I am only too glad to be a woman when I think that every day men must wear such confining gar-ments."

"And I should imagine that side whiskers would tickle terribly," said Miss Goosegrass chuckling aloud.

Mrs. Topper sighed. "My, how I miss my husband in so many ways."

Before either woman had time for further speculations on the nature of men's facial hair, they heard a knock at the door.

"I've so come to dread that sound," Miss Goosegrass said. "I have a fear that it's the Reverend Mitchell come to hunt me down like a fox."

"We need not be bothered. Nancy will see who it is. If it's no one we care to see, we shall send them away."

A moment later Nancy knocked at the door. She said, "There is a gentle-man to see you, Mrs. Topper." She handed Mrs. Topper a card. "A thief-taker by the look of him."

"Here is your Constable Cuff after all, Miss Goosegrass. Better late than never, I should suppose. It would probably be best if he didn't see you here. Why not run upstairs, and I'll be with you when this interview is complete?"

Miss Goosegrass nodded and without a word left the room. Mrs. Topper could hear her light tread upon the stairs.

"Nancy, would you show Constable Cuff in now, please?" Mrs Topper said.

A moment later the Bow Street Runner stood before her with his hat in his hand.

"Constable Cuff, I have been expecting you," she said and looked directly into his eyes. He was in his mid-thirties. Rather plain-looking, dressed in clothes which had not been made for him.

"I thank you for taking the time to see me, Mrs. Topper. I can well imagine how you must feel."

"Can I offer you a cup of tea?" she said.

"Nothing, ma'am. I am not fond of tea.

"What are you fond of, Sir?" said she.

"I haven't much time to be fond of anything. Except perhaps roses. My father has a magnificent nursery garden. But never mind my predilections, ma'am. I don't wish to take up your precious time speaking of gardens. I just have a few questions which I'd like to ask you." The Constable removed a leather-covered book and a stub of a pencil from his pocket.

"Anything to have this all put to rights," she said.

"Yes, of course. I assume you've heard that there have been charges against your husband. The Reverend Mitchell has been to see the Magistrate, and I've been sent to bring your husband in."

Mrs. Topper said, "I have heard this."

"What have you to say about the charges?" Cuff said.

"I say in this great country of ours that a man is innocent until he is proved guilty," Mrs. Topper said.

"And do you believe that your husband is innocent?"

Mrs. Topper said, "I have no doubt whatsoever."

"Do you have any idea where your husband might be at this time?" Cuff said.

"None."

"If you did, would you tell me?"

"No. And you would not find me here now if I did. I would be with him."

Cuff said with a laugh, "You are an honest one."

"As is my husband," Mrs. Topper replied.

"Has your husband and Mr. Scrooge ever had any disagreements over the management of the charity?"

Mrs. Topper said, "My husband knows his place at the charity. Mr. Scrooge's directions were always followed to the letter. Mr. Topper never found any discrepancies between his understanding of moral character and the principles which Mr. Scrooge utilised to manage the Charity."

"I see," the Constable said running his pencil quickly over the pages. "Would you say that your husband is given to violent outbursts?"

"My husband is of a gentle character, Constable—as anyone who knows him will tell you. Do not take my word for it."

Cuff nodded noncommittally. "What do you believe your husband's opinion of the Reverend Mitchell is?"

"The Reverend Mitchell is a liar. What would you think my husband's opinion of him would be?"

"Has he ever been involved in any serious disagreements? Has he ever mentioned anything to you about duelling with anyone in the past?" Cuff said.

"My husband knows nothing about firearms, I dare say," Mrs. Topper said.

"Do you know Mr. William Dawson?"

"I have heard my husband mention the name," she said. "I have not met him."

"What would you say has been your husband's relationship with the gentleman?" Cuff said.

"I would say that Mr. Topper is grateful for what Mr. Dawson has done for the charity. Mr. Scrooge was anxious to have the building put to rights by mid-summer, and with Mr. Dawson's help this was done."

"Would you say Mr. Dawson and your husband were friends?"

"I know what you are hinting at, Constable. There is nothing in that allegation whatsoever. It is just another example of the filth which flows from The Reverend Mitchell's mouth. Lies. Slandering lies."

"Do you believe that your husband to be still alive?" Cuff said holding his pencil in the air.

Mrs. Topper burst into tears.

"I am very sorry to have upset you, Mrs. Topper," said he. "You do not have to answer the question if you'd rather not."

"I do not know what to believe, Constable. But I have every intention of finding out."

"I believe you do, ma'am. I believe you do."

◎

While lying on his back Scrooge balanced the book upon his drawn-up knees. They looked thin and boney to him even under the sheets. With some effort he managed to hold open the book with his elbow, rotate his wrist so that the magnifier was between his eyes and the text on the page. He read:

> I WAS BORN IN THE YEAR 1632, in the city of York, of a good family, though not of that country, my father being a foreigner of Bremen, who settled first at Hull. He got a good estate by merchandise, and leaving off his trade, lived afterwards at York, from whence he had married my mother, whose relations were named Robinson, a very good family in that country, and from whom I was called Robinson Kreutznaer; but, by the usual corruption of words in England, we are now called—nay we call ourselves and write our name—Crusoe; and so my companions always called me.

Before he could read any further the book slipped and fell to the floor with a clatter. In anger Scrooge flung his hand lens across the room where it struck a mirror and sent a shower of silvered glass to the floor.

The door flung open. "What is it? What has happened?" Mrs. Claypoole said.

"Now look at what I've done," said Scrooge slapping the pillow angrily beside him.

"I will ring for Clarence to clean this up," she said, and touched the bell-pull.

"I apologise," said Scrooge, clenching and unclenching his left fist.

"You have nothing to apologise for," Mrs. Claypoole said, softly.

"Don't I? What about the broken mirror?"

"You are not superstitious, are you?" she said, with a smile.

"Has anyone ever admitted to being superstitious when asked that question?"

"I suppose not," said Mrs. Claypoole.

"Mr. Weston has extended me the use of his library and brought this book. But I can't seem to manage to hold it open and read at the same time. Would you be so kind as to read it to me?" Scrooge said.

Mrs. Claypoole inhaled and held her breath for a moment. "What if I told you," she said, "that I cannot read?"

Scrooge sat stunned. "I beg your pardon, ma'am," he said. "I didn't know."

"Do you think less of me for it?"

"I do not," he said. "May I ask if it is because of a problem you have with your vision, or lack of opportunity?"

"Neither," she said. "You see I am merely an ignorant woman who has gotten her way for too terribly long."

"Would you like to learn to read?" Scrooge said.

"It is the thing which I want most in this world," she replied.

"Then I shall teach you," Scrooge said.

"Is there something I can do for you?" Clarence said. Scrooge started. He hadn't even noticed him entering the room.

"I apologise. In my clumsiness I have broken the mirror."

Clarence said, "These small accidents happen from time to time."

"It was no accident, I fear. I lost my temper. I hope it was of no value."

"Only sentimental, Sir. It belonged to Mr. Weston's mother."

Scrooge squeezed shut his eyes in self-disgust. "I must make amends. Where is Mr. Weston? I wish to speak with him."

"I'm afraid Mr. Weston's away just now."

Scrooge said, "But he stood just where you are not two hours since."

"That is so, but he is not at Owlpen Hall at this hour," Clarence said, "and I couldn't say where he has gone. He often leaves us with no notice. He might be gone for an hour, for a day, a fortnight. And when he returns he never gives us a word of explanation nor is it my place to ask."

"Of course, of course," Scrooge said. "A man must have his privacy. A time to be alone, to reflect."

"I'm sure you are right, Sir," Clarence said.

◎

"Wake up, my child," gentle voices said and softly shook the sleeping form of Mr. Levy.

"What is this?" the old Jew said, sitting up and clutching the blankets to his chin. His blind eyes searched perpetual darkness. "Who's there? What is it you want with me?"

"What do we want? We want to take you away from here. This is no place for you to be. You and Mrs. Edelstein will now come with us to where you will be safe. You have nothing to fear."

ｇɤ

The Right Hand of Ebenezer Scrooge

"Slovenly, I say, Mrs. Topper! More slovenly! You stand too tall and straight for a charwoman, and your hair is far too kempt," Miss Goosegrass said.

"Miss Goosegrass," Mrs. Topper said, "may I remind you that you are not directing an amateur theatrical. This is merely a disguise. No one will look twice at me once they identify my class. I will be as transparent as glass."

"Not so, Mrs. Topper," Miss Goosegrass said, "let us leave no detail undone. Should you be detected, I fear your life would be in grave danger. And just look at your nails."

"What is wrong with my nails?"

"Nothing. That is the problem."

"Must I really get dirt beneath my nails?"

"It would also lend effect if you were to break one or two of them. Your teeth are far too white and straight as well, but there's nothing to be done about that. Although we might find a way to discolour them. Temporarily, you understand."

"I might more simply avoid smiling. You really believe this is necessary?" said Mrs. Topper.

"I would not say so if I did not believe it. Do you intend to wear such fine rings as well? Some charwoman you'll make."

"My wedding ring? Surely even charwomen wear wedding rings?"

"None so fine as yours," Miss Goosegrass replied. "Cigar bands are more likely."

"Of course, you are right," said Mrs. Topper and twisted her wedding ring from her finger and set it upon the table where bits of various disguises were laid out.

"What is this second ring? I do not believe I've ever seen anything quite like it before."

Mrs. Topper held it up and peered at it as if she had never seen it before herself. "It is not my ring, but my husband's. He left it on the washstand the morning he disappeared. It's almost as if he wanted me to have it. I know it's silly of me, but I wear it for good luck. I will leave it behind if I must."

Miss Goosegrass said, "We are ever so lucky that The Reverend Mitchell has never seen you. He knows me far too well for me to take part in this."

Mrs. Topper nodded. "You will have your part soon enough, Miss Goosegrass. We will all of us have parts to test the depths of our characters."

"I pray that mine is not found wanting. I would not fail you. I value your love and devotion to your husband too much."

"Bless you," Mrs. Topper said, her eyes tearing up slightly. "Look what you've made me do. No doubt you will tell me charwomen have no tears to shed either."

"Very few, ma'am. Very few."

◉

Again and again the cane fell upon Scrooge's back. His eyes swam with blood. The air in his lungs escaped in short whimpers.

"You are having a nightmare, Mr. Scrooge," Mrs. Claypoole said, gently shaking his shoulder.

"No more," Scrooge hissed. And then "Rajani."

"Mr. Scrooge! Mr. Scrooge!" Mrs. Claypoole shook him more vigourously.

Coming to wakefulness was slow and laborious. Scrooge squinted until he could make out who sat beside him. "Mrs. Claypoole? How long have you been there?" he said, his words slurred.

"Not long. Two hours since—perhaps three."

"You are no doubt growing bored watching an old man wither away before your very eyes," Scrooge said. His lips and skin were bloodless.

Mrs. Claypoole gave him a rueful smile. "You do not wither away, kind Sir. You are strong and do not know it. I fear you have too little to live for. You have lost hope."

"Lost hope?" Scrooge said and feebly attempted to sit up. "Whatever do you mean?"

"I mean to say there is nothing that you care deeply for," she said. "Nothing to which you can devote your heart and soul. Perhaps if you had a favourite cat or a dog."

"Bah, I care nothing for animals," Scrooge said.

"What do you care for, Mr. Scrooge?" Mrs. Claypoole asked. "What is important in your life? What is worth living for?" Scrooge could not help but notice her heaving bosom.

At the edge of Scrooge's memory an image flitted. A face. A very young face with dark skin. But like a wisp of smoke he could not hold it long.

"My business keeps me occupied," he said finally.

"Then these drops are what you want," she said, dully and dribbled more of the contents of the leather-covered bottle into a glass. "Drink this. It will help your dreams." She held the glass to Scrooge's lips, and he drank.

◎

"We will be free from here in no time now," said Trumbull.

"I can only hope that you are right, Sir," said Topper. "But think: why give us candles—but no food, no water, nor chamber-pot? No, we were meant to escape from that room, Mr. Trumbull. But escape into what is the question."

"I am aware of but one way to test that, Mr. Topper. Shall we proceed?"

Topper said, "We have no other recourse."

Mr. Topper placed his shoulder against one wall near the corner. Trumbull pressed his back against one wall and his feet against the wall opposite.

"Mr. Topper, when I count three, push as if your very life depended upon it."

"As well it might," Topper said.

On three, they pushed until the veins stood on their necks. The sound of tortured nails was music to them. The walls smoothly separated for a space of six inches, then all at once tore free and fell back with a thud.

Trumbull held the candle to his lips and blew it out as he no longer had need of one. He said, "We appear to be inside another room. Bigger than the last, and perhaps more soundly constructed, but another room neverthe-less."

Topper looked about him and gasped in exasperation. "Another room," he said. "But this one, unlike the last, has a door. In fact it has three."

He crossed the floor and pulled open the first door. Inside was a small room with two beds. He closed it again with a frown. The second door revealed an equally small room in the centre of which was a table set for two and a delicious meal of baked chicken and potatoes laid out. The third door concealed an even smaller room with a wash stand, personal items such as combs, razors and so on, a chamber-pot and another door.

Topper rushed to it, twisted the knob and found it locked. He threw his weight against it. The door didn't give the impression that it was capable of being opened. He might as well have tried to move a granite boulder.

Topper rubbed his shoulder. "Well, Mr. Trumbull. I for one am famished. Let us eat our dinner or perhaps supper—I've lost track—and turn this thing over in our minds."

◎

Lucille Topper pushed something around in her bowl which might have once been a vegetable. The stew was thin with grit settled at the bottom—cornmeal, she preferred to believe. Meals had not been so meagre when her husband had been in charge—though she had to admit Milton never invited her to eat with him at his place of work. She did not blame Cook for the food, however. The woman did the best she could with what supplies she was given.

Mrs. Topper dunked a crust of bread into the grey liquid until it was saturated, raised it to her lips, tore off a chunk with her teeth and allowed it to dribble down her chin. She chewed with her mouth open and stared about her stupidly—and as a consequence no one paid her the least attention.

She recognised many of the people here from their wedding, but no one, fortunately, yet made the connection between Lucille Topper in a bridal gown, and Sally Ball in charwoman's rags. Her disguise was perfect.

Mrs. Topper had taken her meals at Yellow Door these last three days and only twice had she seen the Reverend Salvation Mitchell. He appeared and disappeared as if he were a ghost. Two days previous she had waited for him many hours just outside the charity in the long sun of a blistering day. Mrs. Topper would have enjoyed her role on stage, but in the street the only members of her audience were half a dozen flies. Her fair skin burnt, her head spun, but The Reverend Mitchell never appeared. Yesterday he was gone before she got there. To-day, she hoped, would be different.

Yellow Door was stifling. As soon as everyone finished their dinner they decamped just outside in the shade of the building where it was marginally cooler. Mrs. Topper joined the others and sat with her back against a faded-brick building on the opposite side of the street from where she could watch the front entrance. Would the Reverend Mitchell leave by another exit? She could only hope that he would not—or that she might spot him even so. Patience. She must be patient at all costs.

The sun undulated across the sky as slowly as a snail.

The light at this time of day blinded her, and as dark glasses were no part of her disguise, she closed one eye completely and squinted wickedly with the other. *Next time I do this*, she thought, *I shall have a pipe to clench between my teeth, and I shall expectorate on the streets...if necessary*, she hastily added. At the moment she had little to expectorate with.

Did charwomen carry parasols? They did wear shawls. Lucille drew the rag from her shoulders over her head, but doing so flooded her nose with the stench of cheap gin. Part of her disguise was to douse herself, but she had been perhaps too generous in applying her "perfume."

Another hour passed. She felt ill and wondered if it were the food or the sun. She was glad that Miss Goosegrass had suggested that she take an apple with her—perhaps taking a bite would settle her stomach. She pulled the apple now from a dirty pocket, but could find no segment of her garments clean enough to wipe it on. She gave it a token brush on her sleeve, bit into it and found it dry and tasteless. She had not thought to bring water (what would she have carried it in?), nor did she wish to leave her post long enough to re-enter Yellow Door to find some.

At length Mrs. Topper got to her feet. She rubbed her chin in a manner which she believed charwomen usually rubbed their chins and stepped back into the street in a way which she felt charwomen stepped.

It was just at this moment she noticed that her fellow loungers had all left. The shadow where they had taken their ease had shifted to the other side of the building, and they had drifted one by one with it.

With this realisation she made up her mind to step across the street and discreetly inquire after her quarry. Without wishing to appear too purposeful she wandered back to the bright yellow door, reached for the handle but before she could grip it, the door swung wide, and out stepped the Reverend Mitchell with a rubbery smile upon his lips. He bowed low with surprising grace. Mrs. Topper had not seen him so close before and found his watery, protuberant eyes exceedingly repellent.

"Peace to you, Missy," he said. He drew himself erect from his bow and examined her more closely. "There's a pretty girl under all that dirt," he said. He ran a finger beneath his nose and drew close enough to Mrs. Topper that she could see the stubble on his chin.

She dropped her eyes and covered her face with a hand as if shielding her eyes from the sun.

"Dirt's me job, Sir—cleaning," she said. "I cleans up, you see, by swabbing out people's houses with me petticoats." She gave him a coarse laugh.

The Reverend Mitchell looked as if he hadn't understood her. He gave her a sniff and wrinkled his nose. He said, "You are in your cups, dear lady," and strolled away without another word.

Dare she follow him now? She could not let him escape.

"Oh, Sir! Kind Sir!" she said pouring honey with her voice—anything to slow him down. "Could you spare..." How much did beggars ask for these days? "...a farthing for a poor, homeless soul?"

The Reverend Mitchell stopped and turned to look at her in surprise. "A farthing? A farthing? You'll want more than just a farthing, I'm guessing," said he, and he rubbed his fingers together meaningfully.

Mrs. Topper did not know how to reply to this. She grasped for words. "Children, I gots to feed 'um, you know." *Oh, a bit much*, she thought.

"I shouldn't have thought you had any children with your figure," Mitchell said eying her up and down appreciatively.

Mrs. Topper's first instinct was to slap his face. On second thought she replied, "Oh, ain't you the one," and she made a high-pitched bark of laughter.

"What is better than *Salvation*, ma'am?" said he. "*Salvation* is my business. You must permit me to introduce myself. I am The Reverend *Salvation* Mitchell." He made another low bow. "And what would your name be, my pretty, pretty, young petticoat?"

"Sally," she said, "at your service," and curtsied.

"Sally-at-your-service," the Reverend Mitchell repeated. "What a lovely name. And your husband's name? The one you share with him. You do have a husband, don't you? The father of the children you spoke of just moments ago?"

"'Course I got me a husband," Mrs. Topper snapped back. "He's a right handsome feller, Mr. Ball is, but he's run away just now—ain't he? And if'n I catch him up, I'll box his ears so's he won't know which way is round."

Mrs. Topper smiled at her own performance. *This is going better than expected.*

"There is no need to make excuses, ma'am," The Reverend said. "HE knows. HE sees into the hearts of all HIS children. You can hide nothing from HIM."

"HE can buy me a drink then," Mrs. Topper said without giving it much thought.

But the Reverend Mitchell did not take the bait. "The demon alcohol is perhaps the vilest of them all," he said jutting out his chin as if he dared her to punch it. Mrs. Topper balled up her fist and considered the angle.

"You don't expect me to drink...water," she said.

"There's lemon squash and barley water which is quenching if you truly are thirsty," he said.

"Salvation, you are a temptation, Sir, you are!" She gave him a poke in his chest with her index finger. "You'll take me some place quiet and special, will you?" She didn't know what she'd do if he said yes, but she desperately needed to find the location of Mitchell's so-called Flock.

"I will take you to a very special place, indeed," said The Reverend after musing a moment. "I will take you to a place of Hope and Opportunity."

"Hope and Opportunity?"

"Yes, Hope and Opportunity, Quiet and Meditation. Are you interested, ma'am?"

"If there's food and drink in it, I mights be," she said, "and adventure..."

"Will you walk with me, ma'am? Will you follow me where e'er I may lead?"

"The way you go on, Sir," Mrs. Topper said. "You promises a girl the world, you does."

"The world is not near enough for you, ma'am, or a hundred others just like you. You are promised much more by HIM."

"What does HE promise me, Love?" she said. *Adding "Love" wasn't too much, was it?*

"There is only one way for you to know," The Reverend Mitchell said. "You must come with me and discover for yourself."

"Lead on! Lead on!" she said, and gave him a broad smile.

The Reverend Salvation Mitchell turned and gave her a curious look. "I do believe, ma'am," said he, "that in spite of your layer of dirt you are not what you appear to be. Those teeth of yours are too white and straight for a woman of your station in life."

She immediately doused her grin. "Of course, I'm just ol' Sal. Who else would I be?"

"I believe that you are an actress in the hire of the Bow Street Runners—

an agent of the Magistrate investigating me for reasons I could not possibly guess being the guiltless soul that I am. Certainly you will find me innocent of any connection with the embezzlement of funds from Mr. Scrooge's charity," The Reverend Mitchell said.

Mrs. Topper's head buzzed. "You're bloody daft, you are," she said. "I'm no actress for the Magistrate. I keeps as far away from that gentleman as I can."

"Not near far enough by my reckoning," said Reverend Mitchell. "Well, I must leave you to your grease paint and be on my way, dearie. I wish you a good day."

"But, Sir," she said and for a lack of anything else to do Mrs. Topper made a gurgling sound and slumped to the street as if in a drunken stupor.

"I will leave you at the end of the first act with the curtains drawing together over your supine form, my dear clever actress," the Reverend said without impatience. "You may tell the Magistrate that his suspicions of The Reverend Mitchell are completely unfounded, but that I take no offence at his actions and consider them to be part of a proper investigation."

Mrs. Topper lay in the baking sun without moving. Her head throbbed. Her throat was parched. She counted slowly to three hundred and sat up as if waking from a stupor—which was not far from the truth. She stood to her feet and staggered in the direction she had heard him go.

"Wait a minute, Love," she said. "Wait for your Sally Ball." The banging in her head grew worse. She knew she should get into the shade and find something cool to drink, but she must not lose sight of him. Around a corner she stepped and spotted the Reverend Mitchell looking in a shop window two blocks down. He sauntered along with his hands in his pockets until her eyes could no longer find him.

Not too close.

She walked with as much speed as she could muster and did not stop until she reached the storefront he had passed. Lucille closed her eyes and fought a growing nausea. She sat down heavily and peered round.

Colour drained from her vision. The bricks in the building nearby faded to a rose-tinged grey. The sky grew so pale that it could hardly be called blue.

The street was oddly devoid of any movement. No pedestrians, nor idlers, nor horses. The only sound Mrs. Topper heard was the roar of her heart in her ears.

Where has he gone? Have I lost him?

She spotted him standing at the top of a stairwell to a half basement, removed his hat, pulled off his coat and threw it over his shoulder, mopped his brow with his handkerchief and descended. She waited until he disappeared before stepping into the street.

From the corner of her eye a movement caught her attention. A door opened just behind her. A figure stepped from it out into the street. She turned, stood aright and stared at it.

"Good afternoon, to you, Actress Sally Ball," the Reverend Mitchell said, tipping his hat. "I see that you have recovered yourself."

Mrs. Topper blurted a profanity. Her head spun for a long moment and when it settled, The Reverend Mitchell was gone. But where?

Shade. I must move to the shade. She blinked her eyes and staggered against a wall. Her cheek pressed against its gritty surface found it cool. Mrs. Topper squeezed shut her eyes and thought, *I mustn't faint.* She opened them, closed them and plunged face first toward the street. Before she struck, hands caught her and stood her on her feet.

"Have a care, Sally Ball. You might turn your pretty little ankle," the Reverend Mitchell said in a mellifluous voice.

Mrs. Topper twisted round to meet the source, but he was not there.

"You appear to be searching for someone," a voice said from behind her. The Reverend's arm wrapped companionably around her shoulder. "I am not sure if I can help you find your missing husband or not. Perhaps you would like to ask the people of this good neighbourhood if they've seen him," he said and waved his other arm toward the building on the opposite side of the street.

One by one the windows of the buildings opened as did the doors.

Through each the heads and shoulders of men could be seen peering out into the street. Each face, each set of shoulders were identical to those at her side. Twenty Reverend Mitchells stared at her.

Mrs. Topper found that she could not catch her breath. Consciousness left her body and sweet blackness enveloped her. She slid to the ground probed by two-score flickering eyes.

◉

"Try, Mr. Scrooge," Mrs. Claypoole said. "You must not give up hope."

"It is of no use," Scrooge said. "This arm of mine is gone. Dr. Fluch may as well take it off."

"How can you say such a thing, Sir? Our bodies are gifts to us from Him. They must be cared for." The light from the window behind her fell directly upon her bare neck and shoulders framing her in a soft aura.

"Very well, but it is a pointless exercise," he said. "Nothing will ever bring this arm back to life."

"I am going to place my fingers in the palm of your right hand. I want you to grasp them, Mr. Scrooge. I want you to grasp them, to feel of them, to caress them. Say you will, Ebenezer. Say you will."

Ebenezer! She calls me Ebenezer! Was it merely a slip of the tongue?

"I shall give it my utmost effort," Scrooge said licking his lips. He dare not called her Vivianna.

"Bless you, Sir. Bless you," Mrs. Claypoole said.

She laid her hand in his. He felt nothing. It was as if she had laid her hand upon the washstand.

"Do you feel me?" she said, passionately.

"I am afraid that I do not," Scrooge answered and turned his eyes away.

"You must believe that you can," she said. "You may close your eyes and turn your head away if you wish, but you must not give up trying. You must never give up hope."

"Mrs. Claypoole," Scrooge snapped. "I must ask you: why do you bother? Why do you waste your time on me? On me, a worthless old man. You should leave me and never come back nor think upon me again. Please leave me! Can't you see that I am at my end?"

"Ebenezer, why do you torment yourself so? What have you done that you cannot forgive yourself?" Mrs. Claypoole said, her voice pained.

"Forgive myself? Forgive myself? What have I done? I've grown old, you see—that's what I've done. I've placed myself in this ridiculous situation where you are forced to care for me."

Tears crept from the corners of Mrs. Claypoole's eyes. "Can't you see? I have cared for you because I wished to. No one commanded this service of me but my own heart."

"You are a liar, Mrs. Claypoole. No woman can harbour those kinds of feelings in her heart over an old man like me. No woman ever cared whether Ebenezer Scrooge lived or died. And no woman ever will!"

She reached for him. "Never. Never say such a thing for my heart yearns for you, if you'd only see it."

He lifted his hand and struck her across the face. His right hand.

⊙

"I shall never look down upon a charwoman again as long as I live," Mrs. Topper said.

Miss Goosegrass pressed a cool compress to Mrs. Topper's forehead.

"Were you able to find out where the Reverend Mitchell goes each day when he leaves Yellow Door?"

"No, I was not," Mrs. Topper said with a distracted look upon her face. "No, he eluded me, I am very much afraid." And then she told her friend the entire story.

"When I came to my senses he had taken his leave with no clue as to where he had gone," she said, with a sigh of exasperation.

"How is it that there were so many of him? Do you believe he hired actors to impersonate him? It seems unlikely," Miss Goosegrass said.

"There was only one Reverend Mitchell, Miss Goosegrass. It is only my silly intolerance of the sun which created the vision. Hallucinations!" She struck the sofa with her tiny clenched fist. "Why am I so frail?"

"You are not frail, Mrs. Topper. Not in the very least. You are brave and bold far beyond any woman I know," said Miss Goosegrass.

"Bravery will not serve me one whit. He knows me now. I cannot follow him again without incurring his suspicions. We are lost," she said, her voice trembling in frustration.

"I do not believe that we are without resources of our own," Miss Goosegrass said. "He may indeed know you in your charwoman guise, but do you believe he knows your true identity?"

Mrs. Topper removed the compress from her forehead and collected her thoughts. "He said something about my looking for my husband, and I thought that he knew me for who I was. But then he made a series of statements which leads me to believe he mistook me for an actress spying on him for the Magistrate."

Miss Goosegrass nodded. "Then we are fortunate. He does not know that we are watching him."

"Evidently not. I will find another costume. A wig perhaps. I can darken my skin if need be. I have learnt a little Spanish, perhaps I can pretend to be a woman of the..."

Miss Goosegrass held up a finger. "I believe I know of someone who might help us."

"Surely not Constable Cuff?" Mrs. Topper said.

"No, not just yet. Someone else."

Mrs. Topper sat up. "Well, speak. Don't keep me in suspense." Then she groaned. "My head bangs like a drum. Too much sun. Would you much mind if I were to put my feet up? I need to lie down. I do not feel a bit well."

"No, not at all. Do make yourself comfortable. You are rather red in the face."

Mrs. Topper stretched out upon the sofa, and Miss Goosegrass placed a cushion beneath her head.

She said, "Shall I ring for Nancy to bring you something to drink?"

"If you would be so kind," Mrs. Topper said rubbing her fingers on her temples. "Now tell me about this person who you believe will help us."

"Yes, of course," Miss Goosegrass said, after releasing the bell-pull.

"There are a number of young people who take their meals at Yellow Door. Many of them do not spend their nights there as they have family, honest poor, with whom they live. One lad among them in particular is quite intelligent. Remarkably resourceful."

"How can he help us?" Mrs. Topper said with her eyes closed.

"Patrick Coal—that is the boy's name—was my student. It is not unusual for young men of his age to have strong attachments to teachers of the fair sex. If I were to speak with him, I believe that he would agree to be our eyes and ears."

Mrs. Topper inhaled her breath and held it in thought. Then she released it. "How will that help? The Reverend Mitchell will elude your boy just as he did me. The man is a clever one."

"Young Mr. Coal," Miss Goosegrass said, "knows a great many people in the street. While the Reverend may notice a single person following him, he would be unable to spot a large network of young people scattered naturally about the street. He would not notice them following him because they wouldn't be. He would be moving through their territory as it were."

"Why should they co-operate with us?" Mrs. Topper said. "We have little money to offer them. While the young man may have the deepest admiration for you, Miss Goosegrass, I find it difficult to believe that an entire army of boys would be so struck."

Miss Goosegrass said, "Your point is well taken, but do not forget that your husband was well loved by the community which he served. Though a few may believe the lies which The Reverend Mitchell perpetuates, most believe the deeds and actions of their fellow men and care little for accusations. Mr. Scrooge and Mr. Topper offered the people of Yellow Door hope —and more than hope: respect. From what I've heard and what you've told me, under the management of The Reverend Mitchell and Mr. Fleming, the people of Yellow Door have been fed food of little nourishment, given little clothing, been subjected to strictures and rules without purpose, and have suffered countless slights and cruelties. No one has an ounce of love or respect for The Reverend Mitchell. I cannot help but believe they will do anything in their power to undo him."

"Exactly what are you proposing?" said Mrs. Topper.

"I am proposing that young Mr. Coal," Miss Goosegrass said, "organise a band of his friends to keep an eye out for Reverend Mitchell. Whenever he is spotted outside Yellow Door, they are to note where and when they have seen him. Eventually we shall learn of his daily habits and regular destinations."

"This will take some time," Mrs. Topper said, her voice faint.

"I am afraid it will," Miss Goosegrass agreed.

Nancy opened the door. "What can I do for you, ma'am?" she said.

"Mrs. Topper would like something cold to drink... Bless me, she's fainted. Fetch a doctor."

༄

CHAPTER 16

The Return of Ebenezer Scrooge

A CHAIR SCRITTED ACROSS THE FLOOR. A CUP THUNKED UPON THE TABLE. Spoons, forks and knives could not help but make some little sound.

But no one laughed.

No one bade anyone else Good Morning. No one asked for the salt to be passed, please. No one made the slightest whisper. Not if they wished to finish their meal. Not if they wished to continue eating at *Ebenezer Scrooge's Charitable Aid And Victual Assistance To The Under-advantaged & Desperate.* Those who finished their breakfast of thin gruel carried away their bowls, returned to their seats with eyes downcast waiting to be dismissed. They did not have long to wait.

The door to the dining room swung open and Fleming strode in riding crop tucked smartly beneath his arm. He swung his head side to side and cast his blood-shot eye upon each of them, piercing their very souls at a glance.

At length he settled upon Jemmy McCloud who stirred his gruel without appetite.

"Sailor Boy," Fleming said with arms folded across his chest. His elbows were close enough to brush Jemmy's head.

Jemmy did not shift away nor raise his eyes from his bowl.

"Can you not hear me, man?" Fleming said.

Jemmy turned to Mr. Crackers and said in a clear voice, "Would you hand me the salt, Sir?"

Mr. Crackers looked fearful. Jemmy repeated his request.

"But Mr. McCloud," Mr. Crackers said, "there ain't no salt on the table."

Jemmy gave a humourless laugh. "Are you blind, cannot you see it just there—on the other side of your plate?"

Mr. Crackers shook his head violently in the negative.

"Och, don't bother yourself with it then," Jemmy said, "I'll get it myself." He rose from his seat (brushing Fleming aside as he did so) reached across Mr. Crackers' bowl and lifted an object which was not there.

"It takes only a wee bit of salt to bring out the true flavour of a fine breakfast such as this one," he said shaking the imaginary saltcellar over his bowl.

Fleming's face lost its modicum of composure, and he slapped the bowl from the table whereupon it shattered into a thousand pieces on the floor.

"Clean it up!"

Jemmy looked as if he just noticed Fleming in the room. He stood slowly to his feet, ice in his eyes. "Why should I do that?" he said calmly. "'Tis your mess."

Fleming sputtered but could form no words. A sharp kick from his heel sent Jemmy's chair flying against the wall. With this release he was able to utter: "What did you say?"

"I don't know what you thought you heard me say," the old sailor said, "but I told you as clear as I can work my tongue that I wasn't cleaning up the mess *you* just made."

"How dare you?" Fleming gripped McCloud's arm which he found thick and hard in spite of the man's age.

"If you don't release me this very instant, you're going to find out something which only a few people know about me. You're going to find out that I don't much care if I get hurt or not. I've no very pretty face to wear, so I don't have much to lose. There's a lot of cutlery around here, Mr. Fleming. Plenty of knives and forks and things, and if you were just a wee bit careless, you might on accident put your eye out, Sir. And you've only one good left in that skull of yours from what I can see. It would be a terrible thing, so I'm just warning you to err on the side of caution. I would hate for you to be blind for the rest of your life—as short a time as that might be. You'd be just a little like poor Mr. Levy, now wouldn't you?"

"Your life is forfeit, Mr. McCloud," Fleming said.

"There's where you're wrong, Mr. Fleming. See, if I felt that you had any real notion of doing me serious harm, I'd see to it right here and now that couldn't happen. No, I'd make sure of that right in front of all these people. If you'd like to test me on this, you go right ahead and make the first move. I'll ask the rest of them to stay and bear witness as to who started it. Who knows, maybe a few of them might wish to join in the fun."

"Do you really believe that you can lay a hand on me?"

"I've lived a pretty hard life, Mr. Fleming. I've felt a lot of pain and given some, too. I have as yet to see the man whom I couldn't lay a hand on. I may not always come out on top, but the other feller remembers me real good the next day."

Fleming drew his cane from under his arm as if it were a sword. McCloud reached back and someone slipped a knife into his hand.

"Och no," he said looking at it, "not that one, Mikey. It doesn't need to have much of an edge on it. Not for what I want it for. Something dull will do quite well for Mr. Fleming here. I'm no surgeon, you understand."

But he took the knife after wiping it unnecessarily on his sleeve just the same.

"Fleming! You imbecile! What are you doing?"

Fleming hunched as if a bucket of ice water had been emptied down his neck.

"Reverend Mitchell," he said bowing reflexively. "The man's been disrespectful. I was only going to teach him his manners."

The Reverend Salvation Mitchell stood in the doorway with his arms folded. "What do you take this establishment for, Fleming?"

"Reverend Mitchell, the man has to be taught a lesson. We cannot have these people getting arrogant."

"I am as certain as the sun rises each day that this is all a simple misunderstanding," The Reverend Mitchell said.

"No misunderstanding to it at all," Jemmy said. "He took my bowl and tossed it on the floor. There was no call for it. I was still eating, and he just come up and did it. That's all. Just to provoke me." Jemmy held a hand to his throbbing scar, but never blinked on account of the pain.

"Is this true, Fleming?" The Reverend said.

"Well, Sir, it's like this..."

"Is this TRUE!"

"Well, yes, Sir. I may have done on accident. Not of a purpose, of course."

Mitchell silenced him with a wave of his hand. He bent down and picked up the pieces of the bowl and set them on the edge of the table. He bent down a second time and scooped up as much of the food on the floor as he could and deposited it on the table.

"Give me your handkerchief," The Reverend Mitchell said.

"What's that, Sir?" Fleming replied.

"I said, 'Give me your handkerchief.'"

"What do you need my handkerchief for?"

The Reverend Salvation Mitchell merely extended his hand in reply. Fleming pulled it from his bosom and handed it over. Mitchell wiped his fingers with it, returned it to him and said in a loud voice, "I am glad I found you all still here in the dining room as I have special news I am sure you are not going to want to miss."

For the first time that morning they could not contain their voices. The room filled with the buzz of the curious.

"As most of you know Mr. Scrooge has been ill these past three weeks. Many of us feared the worst, and I must admit that I was in no little distress myself. I have not revealed to anyone his location until he has had the opportunity to recover himself. I received word to-day, however, which is sure to lighten your hearts. It's here in my pocket, and it tells us that he will join us back at his charity, Monday next, in one week's time."

A huzzah burst from the throat of every man, woman and child in the room.

Once the shout settled, the Reverend Mitchell continued: "And he has a special announcement he will wish to make at that time. In fact, we both have special announcements."

◉

Though the day was not yet done the room was dark so that the Reverend Mitchell would have needed a candle lit to see—if seeing were a thing he wanted. The seat upon which he sat himself was supported by four thin, wrought-iron legs. It was painted with thick, green enamel and touches of gold gilt. Some attempt at a cushion had been made, but the covering was split and could no longer hold its stuffing.

Papers were strewn on the table before him. He gave them none of his attention but squeezed his eyes together—not in sleep, but in concentration. He sat perfectly motionless, not even the twitch of an eyelid. The only sound was the noise of his breathing—a hissing in his nose, a gurgling in his throat, a rattling in his chest. His thoughts were the thoughts of a spider. His ruminations were the ruminations of a snake.

A soft tap at the door. First one eye flickered open. Then the other.

"Who is it?" he said in his raspy voice.

"Mary-Martha," said the voice. "You wished to see me?"

The Reverend struck a match, held it to the candle, stood to his feet and walked over to the door. He moved to one side and opened it without looking at her. "Inside," he commanded and closed the door behind.

"Yes, Sir," Mary-Martha said, looking down. She curtsied and rustled in.

"Where have you been, Mary-Martha?" Mitchell said.

"Why, I have been with Cook, Sir," she said.

"I have been looking for you all day," he said.

"Perhaps you have not looked for me in the right places," she said. There was something different about her, he noticed. The same smiling cheeks, but now the eyes were not so closed. They were open wide. Quite lovely and a brighter shade of blue he had never seen. And she bore herself in a way he had never noticed in her before. Confident—as if she were privy to some secret.

"Do you know why I've asked you to come here?" the Reverend Salvation Mitchell said.

"No, Sir," Mary-Martha replied. "I've no idea, but I shouldn't be surprised if you were to inform me just now."

"Why yes, I was just about to do that," Mitchell said and blinked at her in surprise. "This may take some time, so won't you please sit down," he said and motioned her to the bed against the wall opposite.

"I will stand, thank you, Sir," she said, firmly. Mitchell had expected her voice to tremble, to shake ever so slightly with fear. But there was no fear.

"I mean to speak to you about your work here at Mr. Scrooge's charity."

"I understand you, Sir," she said. "Do you find my work wanting?"

"No, not at all. I've asked you here to give you my compliments. You know, I've been watching, and I believe I see potential in you."

"Thank you, Sir," she said. "You are too kind."

"Not by half, Miss. Not by half. Are you sure you wouldn't be more comfortable sitting down?"

"Perhaps I would," said she. Mary-Martha moved across the room and lightly sat herself down on the edge of the bed.

"Fall is upon us, ain't it? The mornings are cool, but the afternoons can still get hot, can't they?" The Reverend Salvation Mitchell said loosening his collar.

"If the gentleman is uncomfortable, he should do whatever he pleases to make himself at his ease," Mary-Martha said. Those bright eyes staring at him made his heart race.

"You are an intelligent girl, I'd say, Mary-Martha. Lots of sense behind those pretty blue eyes of yours. I must say that I don't believe I've heard you put three words together before to-day, but now that I've gotten to know you a bit better, I can see I've misjudged you. Underestimated you, you might say."

She patted the bed next to her and said in a strangely lower tone, "Come in. Come in and know me better, man."

The Reverend Mitchell's face grew a rictus of a smile. "I believe I'll just do that. I believe I will."

He turned his back to her, removed his coat, dropped it to the floor and undid his collar.

"I am in some difficulty with this last button, Miss. I wonder if you'd be so kind as to help me with it?" he said sweetly, but his eyes flashed like a snake's.

He turned around and found her gone.

"Fleming!" he shouted and threw open the door.

⊙

His long hair whipped his face in fury. Fleming lifted a chair above his head and making the sound of an angry bear flung it against the wall where it shattered into scraps. No one would take notice of the din he made any more than anyone took notice of the din anyone in this building made. Violence was common here. A drunk smashing up a few worthless sticks of furniture drew no one's attention.

Fleming dropped to his knees and sorted through the remainders until he found what he was looking for: a splintered chair leg. He squinted at it as if he were waiting for it to change shape.

"Am I not Sin brought to flesh and bone?" he snorted. He pulled a crudely-made knife from his belt and shaved a curl from one end of the leg. With increasing violence he drew the blade down its length until it was sharp and ugly. "McCloud must die!" he said, saliva dripping from his mouth. "Mitchell cannot deny me my revenge. He is not my master. No mortal can insult me and live to take his next piss."

Fleming had taken rooms—if these cockroach-infested chambers could be dignified with the term—far away from the Charity. Seven Dials, in fact. He wished to give himself the privacy he needed to "pursue his interests" as he called it.

"I, teacher of Vlad Tepes, know more than a little of the Art of Impaling," he said and whipped the crude stake over his head, each stroke singing through the air. "McCloud's death will be slow and exceptionally painful. But why should he only die once? I will bring him back again and again until his soul has no more substance than a flea." He laughed at the thought. Fleming strode over to the window and with a swing of his elbow smashed it out. He leapt onto the window sill snarling like a gargoyle and dropped lightly to the street.

"Bop!" he cried. A bulky figure lumbered obediently from the shadows. In a moment they were swallowed by the darkness.

⊙

A pounding on the front door jerked Mrs. Topper's head round from her book. She pushed back the curtain and looked out her window, but could see no one in the darkness.

"Nancy?" she called. But Nancy was out just now, she recalled, and she would have to get it herself. She stood from her chair and walked slowly to the door wondering who might be in such need of attention as to knock so tirelessly.

I cannot be frightened every time someone is at the door, she told herself, threw the bolt and opened the door braced for whatever she might find. With relief she saw that it was Miss Goosegrass.

"Won't you please come in?" said she, "I shall have to give you a key. Otherwise this door will need replacing before winter."

Miss Goosegrass did not wait to be invited in, but brushed her aside and dashed into the house. Mrs. Topper had the notion that someone might be following her, so she quickly closed the door behind and slid the bolt into place.

"What is it? What's upset you so?" said Mrs. Topper.

Miss Goosegrass's face flushed with colour. Her bosom rose and fell with great emotion.

"I bring news," she said.

"Do you bring good news or bad?" Mrs. Topper asked, but it was clear that Miss Goosegrass was in too great a state of agitation to answer. "Here, here, Miss Goosegrass. Brace yourself. Shall I get you some tea? Something stronger?"

"No. No, that won't be necessary. Just give me a moment to collect myself, and I shall be fine. A moment only, please." Her knees buckled, but

Mrs. Topper caught her before she hit the ground.

The next thing Miss Goosegrass knew was Mrs. Topper forcing brandy down her throat. She gurgled, found she could not swallow it lying flat on her back, sat up, swallowed, and turned ashen.

"You still do not look well," Mrs. Topper said and poured her another glass.

Miss Goosegrass pushed it away. "No, Mrs. Topper. Thank you, but no. I am myself once again."

"Tell me, woman. What is it? What news do you bring?"

Miss Goosegrass swallowed and spoke as evenly as she could manage. "I have had news from Patrick Coal."

"The young man whom you've had watch the Reverend Mitchell?" said Mrs. Topper growing in excitement.

"Yes, the very one. He brought me news not two hours since."

"Well, what is it, woman? Don't keep me in suspense."

"Mr. Scrooge is returning to the Charity."

Mrs. Topper stood and turned in a circle her skirts flaring out round her. "That is wonderful news. Absolutely wonderful."

Miss Goosegrass nodded, but bore a worried expression on her face. "Yes, I suppose it is, but what if..."

"What if Mr. Scrooge's good opinion of you has changed?" Mrs. Topper said.

"Yes, just so," Miss Goosegrass said, gravely.

"We do not yet know where he has been or truly why he has been away," Mrs. Topper said.

Miss Goosegrass answered with an uneasy sigh.

"You cannot know his mind either until you speak with him," Mrs. Topper said.

"That vile Mitchell has had poor Mr. Scrooge's ear and has doubtless filled it with his lies about me. He will turn me away, he will. I cannot bear it."

"If his heart be true, he will not believe him," Mrs. Topper said. "You must have faith, Jane."

Miss Goosegrass said, "Of course. It's just that I cannot help but feel as if something terrible has happened. I don't know why, but I feel it with all my heart."

Mrs. Topper said, "Nonsense."

Miss Goosegrass's eyes filled with tears.

Mrs. Topper cleared her throat. "Well, perhaps not *nonsense*," she said, "but there is little we can do now until you've had your chance to speak with him."

"How can I speak with him when I can go nowhere near Yellow Door?" Miss Goosegrass said.

"He doesn't live at Yellow Door, does he?" Mrs. Topper said.

"I think not."

"Where were you to take supper with him—that day he disappeared?"

"He never said."

"You would have followed him anywhere?" said Mrs. Topper with a smile.

"I suppose I would have," Miss Goosegrass said.

"If we cannot yet find out just where the Reverend Mitchell disappears to each day, I believe we shall have far less difficulty finding the whereabouts of Mr. Scrooge's apartments."

"Oh, Mrs. Topper, I don't know. I feel as if we would be invading his privacy."

"Is this the same woman who not long ago was ready to storm the Bastille for the man whom she loved?" Mrs. Topper said.

"Forgive me my insecurity."

"Once you have met with him and have had your say, I have no doubt that our little partnership will be broken apart, and I shall have to continue on my own."

"Oh, never, Mrs. Topper. Never. I would never abandon you. I will not rest until we find Mr. Topper. You must know that in your heart."

Mrs. Topper said, "Let us hope that soon we have word from Patrick Coal concerning our Reverend Mitchell."

"Yes, I most wholeheartedly agree. We must find out where he goes," Miss Goosegrass said.

"In the meanwhile, we shall track Mr. Scrooge down and arrange for you two to speak privately," Mrs. Topper said.

◉

Enveloped in a flowing cloak, a tall, narrow-shouldered figure walked purposefully down the centre of the street. A chill wind stirred rubbish and fallen leaves in his wake. At times he was indistinguishable from the thick fog which surrounded him. Loping after sometimes semi-erect, sometimes on all-fours was a scarcely human shape.

"Bop!" Fleming hissed when his companion wandered away to sniff and roll in something dead in the street. Bop crept forward hanging his head, but kept his distance.

"Bloody stupid beast!" He stumped over to Bop and struck him a flat-handed blow to the snout. Bop snapped his teeth on his master's wrist faster than thought. Fleming balled his fist of his other hand and slammed it into Bop's wet snout. Bop yipped and sat back hard on his haunches. Bop coiled. Bop sprang.

The two bodies rolled in the filthy street, hardly distinguishable. Bop ripped savage wounds on Fleming's face, arms and breast, but they healed instantly. Bop had no such ability and after taking as many wounds as he dared, he broke away and ran as fast as his torn body would allow.

"Damn him," Fleming said, wiping his streaked face with a torn sleeve. But there were other matters to attend to. There was vengeance to taste.

Fleming strode off into the darkness, but with a flawed sense of purpose. He approached a corner where burned a street light. A number of untidy men slouched against the building watching for any creature to exhibit some sign of weakness or fear.

The denizens of the street darted out of Fleming's way. Horses shied, their eyes wide with terror. At length he entered an area where the only lights visible were flickering candles placed in the occasional, unbroken window.

Fleming stopped before a colourless building and turned his eye upon it. Within the structure Fleming sensed many people without hope, wallowing in ignorance, living at the edge of death. He inhaled the scent of disease and fear and smiled. He scratched at the filth below his feet with his stake and made an unholy sign.

The door swung noiselessly open at his touch. He entered as a shadow and drifted up the stairs—a smear of black against black. As he passed down the narrow corridor old men groaned and babies cried. Nightmares filled the minds of those who slept.

He knew in which room McCloud kept his things, where he spent his nights. Like many of the poor, McCloud ate at the Charity, but preferred to take his rooms elsewhere. Bop, at Fleming's command, had followed him there and marked the spot in his special way.

Fleming scarcely contained his excitement. He tasted the blood, tasted the pain, tasted the fear. He choked back a giggle which threatened to give him away.

"Bless me," he whispered to himself, "Shall I kick the door in, or should I slip in quietly, practice my impaling arts over the remainder of the night, and then...?"

Quietly, he decided. Would McCloud soil himself in his fright? The thought tickled him. Would McCloud beg for his life? Would he beg for his death? Fleming would grant him neither.

He listened with the ears of an owl. Breathing. Slow, even, steady. McCloud was sleeping. He could hear it, feel it on his skin. The door to the room opened with a gesture, and Fleming darted in. The shuttered window allowed no glimmer from the outside, but Fleming needed no light, no sound to guide him. A pile of dirty clothes on the right in the corner. A torn playbill wedged into a chink of a draughty window. Several pale rectangles on the wall where pictures once hung. A shoe. A sock. A bed on the far corner to the left. In the bed huddled a shape in a grey blanket. Fleming saw them all without seeing.

McCloud was awake! Fleming was sure of it. *Capital!* he thought. Let fear permeate his being. Let his tissues swell with it.

Fleming darted forward swinging the stake high over his head and thrust it down into McCloud's mid-drift. He felt a shock as the wooden shaft passed easily through the blanket and the thin mattress beneath. Fleming whipped back the blanket and sucked in his breath.

Jemmy McCloud was gone.

◎

To fit another living soul in the dining room, he would have to be hung from the ceiling. The tables were carried away and the chairs filled. The remaining people squatted on the floor, leaned upon the wall or one another.

Scrooge would speak to them. He would appear after having been gone some five weeks. Scrooge was at last returned to his charity. His people were anxious to see him again. They pounded their feet and clapped their hands as one:

"Scrooge...Scrooge...SCROOGE....SCROOGE!"

At length the door opened, and The Reverend Salvation Mitchell appeared, face round and cheerful.

"If you cannot lower your voices," he said, then dropped his own to a whisper, "then I cannot permit, Mr. Scrooge to enter this room. I will not allow his delicate constitution to be abused."

The crowd quieted. They sat as still as children listening to a story.

The Reverend Mitchell spread his hands. "Mr. Scrooge is with us to-day," he said, "but I can not say that he is entirely recovered. As you well know he has suffered a terrible shock. It has affected him in both body and spirit. But his spirit is recovering, and as the spirit drives the body: he will be healed. Repeat that for me so I can hear what you believe!"

"He will be healed," they said as one.

"Yes, he will be healed. Our faith is pure, and his full recuperation is all but guaranteed."

"Guaranteed," the crowd echoed.

"Scrooge's Gift from Him is his talent for numbers and finances. He has used that Gift to improve the lives of each and every one of you. Your Gift to Him is your Faith. Let us all, each and every one of us, use that Gift of Faith, to return the blessing to Mr. Scrooge." The Reverend Mitchell's hand fluttered skyward.

"Amen," the crowd replied.

"And are we not grateful!?"

"We are grateful!"

"For the food!" the Reverend shouted.

"For the food!"

"For the clothing!"

"FOR THE CLOTHING!"

"For the shelter!"

"FOR THE SHELTER!"

The Reverend Mitchell stood with his head bowed and his hands clasped in front of him. He nodded his head slightly satisfied with the response.

"Then it is my honour, indeed, my pleasure to present to you the founder of this charity, the man whose name has become synonymous with generosity: Mr. Ebenezer Scrooge."

The door opened but it was not Scrooge who entered, but Fleming. Fleming backed into the room gently waving his arms at his sides as if to clear the path. Immediately behind him was an old man who took one careful step at a time, always leading with the same foot, never looking up but keeping his eyes fixed on the floor beneath him.

The crowd gasped. It was Scrooge. How he had changed since last they saw him. How he had aged!

The crowd gasped a second time as they saw a young woman follow him in, an angelic smile upon her lips, walking with infinite grace.

"A true lady," suggested someone in a whisper.

"His grand-daughter," said another.

"Naw, Scrooge ain't never been married," replied yet another disgusted at the other's ignorance.

"His niece then," satisfied them both.

"Who's that, mum?" a young female voice shouted. She pointed a tiny plump hand in the old man's direction.

Her mother answered her with a *ssshhhhh*, followed by "Don't be rude, Ellen."

The young woman touched Scrooge's elbow to guide him a little around a piece of furniture. He shook off her touch. He said, "I can do it. I can do it," with great impatience.

"Yes, my love," the woman said. "I have no doubt in your abilities whatever."

"Of course, of course," he said, patting her hand and smiling weakly.

Two more gentlemen entered the room. One was dressed in high fashion. The second wore the wig of a physician.

Scrooge moved to a spot where everyone could see him. He wavered for a moment collecting his thoughts. Absolute silence fell over the crowd.

A chair squeaked.

"Please take this, Sir," said Mrs. Smith whose swollen legs just held her. She pushed her chair in Scrooge's direction.

Scrooge accepted it with a smile. "It is not my custom to take a chair from a lady," he said. The crowd murmured their approval of this sentiment. "I cannot accept it, but I give you my deepest thanks."

A dozen young men stood up directly and pushed their chairs his way.

"I can only sit in one at a time," he said, and the crowd laughed.

He chose the nearest and lowered himself into it. "My, it is still warm," he said, and everyone again laughed their politest laugh.

Scrooge placed both hands on the head of his cane and squinted at the sampling of mankind wedged before him.

"It is most decent of you to meet me here like this," he said and gave them his best smile.

They gave him their best smile in return.

"I understand that there have been changes made in my absence. There have been those to whom I gave my trust and who disappointed me— disappointed me deeply."

The crowd murmured their agreement.

"And there are those who have taken responsibility when they saw their duty." Scrooge nodded in the direction of the Reverend Mitchell. "To those, I shall ever be grateful."

The crowd made no sound in reply.

"I am grateful to all of you for the trust you've placed in me." He pursed his lips sadly. "You see seated before you not the same Ebenezer Scrooge who last entered this charity, but an enfeebled old man who has had a terrible time of it. I had a shock the nature of which even now I do not completely understand—though it has been explained to me over and over again with great patience.

"Patience! What a wonderful virtue which some people of this world seem to have in such boundless supply. Patience and kindness and affection. With those three qualities all of mankind can be healed. Well, I have had those three qualities bountifully heaped upon my unworthy being these five weeks since. Far more than I deserve and far more than I have earned." Emotion choked Scrooge for a moment. He paused, blew his nose on his handkerchief, and continued in an unsteady voice.

"Many of you know—nay, all of you know—that I have not always been a kindly man, but that I was reformed. I must watch my nature closely to see that I do not return to my old ways. I have been harsh, uncaring, brutal. And if I am not careful, I will mistreat those who love and care for me. All that I can say in my own defence is that I am learning. With God's help I will learn and before the day I die I shall be at last at peace with myself and with those around me."

The crowd locked on his every word.

Scrooge shifted his weight to one side and leaned on an elbow to relieve the pain in his back. "I have not come here to-day to reveal to you my frailties though they are plain enough for anyone to see. I have come to make an announcement and to make a presentation. Several presentations, in fact."

The crowd made a single puzzled murmur.

"I have come to tell you that I am not abandoning you, nor am I abandoning this building which I have come to love so very dearly. The Reverend Mitchell has conveyed to me the financial conditions in which we find ourselves. The betrayal of certain people to whom I had given my complete financial trust has left us in jeopardy—I will not mince words with you. We do not have the funds to continue this institution in the manner which I had initially envisioned it."

The crowd cringed at the horror of this news.

"The Reverend Mitchell has made changes which neither he nor I would have approved of had our finances been in their original state. He has, with my approval, cut back on the services my charity provides and that has meant to you fewer meals, less clothing." He stiffened. "We have lost our teacher." He closed his eyes and sat back in the chair. Another pain shot across his face. "Discipline has had to be tightened. When discipline is lax, it is too easy for us to go astray. All these changes, I know, have caused you some unhappiness, but they have pained the Reverend Mitchell even more. More than you could ever imagine. He has opened his heart to me, and I have seen it for myself.

"Let no one, however, say that the Reverend Mitchell shirked his duty. He stood in when others failed us. He stood in and gave the helm of this wonderful ship a steady hand until its captain was recovered. Well, I am recovered now. Not completely. Not like I was. I shall never be that man again, but I am a man after a fashion. Old, crippled. But a man nevertheless.

"The Reverend Mitchell would like me to make an announcement for him. I fear that he is too emotionally involved to say these words himself, so I will say them for him. The Reverend Mitchell would like to announce that he is leaving my charity as of this day."

A gasp and a sudden uncontrolled murmur broke from the crowd which Scrooge put to rest with a wave of his hands.

"He wishes us all the best, but he intends to spend more time in prayer and meditation with his Flock. Isn't that so, Reverend?"

The Reverend Mitchell, his face clouded with emotion, could only nod his head in reply.

"We will not lose him as a friend—I can promise you that. I make no doubt that he would rush to my side should I have need of him. His generosity, as he has proven, knows no bounds.

"But he is not alone in his generosity, nor is he the only one among us to-day to whom I am deeply in debt. There are two more gentlemen I should like to present to you to-day before we go further."

Scrooge paused, and his audience shifted uneasily in their seats.

He continued: "The first man to whom I refer has been nothing less than my personal saviour during my recent difficulties. He graciously extended to me the use of his fine home while I recuperated from a severe emotional and physical shock which has left me the way you see me now, but I still live —thanks for the gentleman of whom I speak. There is no more gracious man to be found anywhere on British soil. I would like to present to you, Mr. James Weston of Owlpen Hall."

Polite applause bubbled in the room.

"Oh, you simply must call me *Wespie*," James Weston said striding to Scrooge's side. He clasped his hands behind his back, examined the toes of his highly polished boots and began:

"I must say this is as grand a collection as I've had the pleasure of ad-dressin' for some time," he said. "But you may remove your grave expres-sions as I'm not likely to deliver anythin' like a sermon to you, but have only popped by to wish you good cheer on the recovery of your benefactor. However, as the man babbles perpetually in his sleep, I have some rather interestin' stories to tell."

A look of horror swept across Scrooge's face.

Weston's face bore the expression of a young boy about to reveal his parents' dirty secrets. "I didn't sit with him as often as the others, yet I couldn't begin to tell you how many times while the man suffered deep in fever he expressed his concerns for your welfare. 'Oh, return me to my people!' he begged over and over. 'They need me.' It's clear to even a thick-headed gent like myself that the people of this charity are his first and foremost concern. You are very lucky to have someone so deeply attached to you, and I make no doubt that Mr. Scrooge is lucky to have you to care for him as well."

Applause erupted in the room.

"It's got me thinkin' about foundin' my own charity, but I've no head for figures I'm afraid," he said with a waggish smile and stepped away from Scrooge.

Scrooge reached back to clasp Weston's hand warmly. "No, please, Wespie. Stand here at my side."

"You'll forgive me. It won't do for a gentleman's face to show emotion when it spoils the effect of his clothes," he said and wiped an eye with his handkerchief. Miss Trellis appeared from a dark corner, bent and whispered something in his ear. "And now, Mr. Scrooge, you will excuse me. Miss Trellis here has business for me to attend to, and I cannot refuse so noble a woman," he said.

"Very well—I wish that you could stay with us. You will return soon and visit?" Scrooge said.

"You may be sure that I will darken your door much sooner than you might believe." Weston said with a wry smile.

Scrooge looked to the second gentleman and found him backing toward the door.

"Never, Dr. Fluch!" he shouted after the man. "You shall not exit this room until I have showered you in the glory you so richly deserve."

"What? Me? No, I have done nothing that any other physician wouldn't have done," Dr. Fluch said.

"You are too modest by half," Scrooge said.

"Mr. Scrooge," the medico said, "I really cannot stay. I am happy to see you recovered and reinstated among those who care so deeply for you. But I must tend to my duties. There are others who require my slight skills."

"Well, of course, I shall not detain you any longer than necessary, Doctor. But do join me for at least a moment and allow me to present the man to whom I owe my life."

The physician moved to Scrooge's side, blushed violently and bowed before the crowd which responded with warm applause.

"And now," Dr. Fluch said softly to Scrooge, "I really must be going. If you need me again, you only need call. Any hour of the day or night you shall find me at your service."

"You are too good, Sir. Too good," Scrooge said firmly grasping the man's hand. Dr. Fluch gently extracted himself from Scrooge's grip, bowed and left the room.

Scrooge inhaled and let a happy thought put a smile on his face. "But it is not only gentlemen which I present to you this day. I bring with me a member of the gentler sex for you to feast your eyes and share your hearts. Allow me to introduce to you a very important person in my life—the most important person in my life, I dare say. This graceful, young woman who has stood steadfastly by my side during these past few minutes and more importantly by my sick-bed these past five weeks is Mrs. Vivianna Claypoole."

Scrooge again had to quiet the excited buzz with the waving of both hands.

"Mrs. Claypoole, a widow of one of our young soldiers in service in India, has been my constant companion since my breakdown. It is only through her diligence and care that I am able to be here to-day. I do not mean to belittle the accomplishments of Dr. Fluch, nor the generosity of Mr. Weston, but I should hate to think of what I should be like if it weren't for this gentlewoman." Scrooge reached across with his right hand and gripped hers.

"I should like to announce that Mrs. Claypoole and I are engaged to be married. The ceremony is to take place on Christmas Day next."

No amount of waving of anyone's hands could quiet the crowd.

⊙

"Where is that girl? Mary-Martha—or whatever her name is?" the Reverend Mitchell said gnawing the bone of a ham.

"In the kitchen she's been all day," Fleming said. "I seen her there myself."

"Mary-Martha White...? I been through the kitchen a dozen times, and I've not seen her once."

"Maybe this one eye of mine sees straighter than your two," Fleming said with a laugh.

"I can't understand it." A hot sound sizzled in Mitchell's throat. "She slipped out of my own room just behind my back. I'll be damned if I can smoke how she did it." He paused and laughed at his own turn of phrase. "She'll not evade me long."

"It's not only kitchen maids what's been missing. Don't forget them Indian brats and the Jews," Fleming said. "Where've they gone?"

"No, no. I agree. I cannot forget the black girl." He licked his lips. "I so wanted to bring that tasty morsel into my Flock. And the Jews—well, they certainly can't have gotten very far on their own, now can they? The elderly, blind and feeble don't disappear without considerable assistance. The question is who could have done it? What about that fellow you were having a disagreement with earlier to-day?"

"McCloud?" Fleming said.

"Yes, that's him. He's a defiant one if ever there was."

"It wouldn't've been him," Fleming said. "He's gone missing as well."

"All the more reason for him to disappear if he's the one who has re-moved the Jews!" Mitchell said, then raised his eyebrows as a thought struck him. "Unless, of course... Did you sent Mr. McCloud packing in your own way, Mr. Fleming? That was naughty of you to do without asking me first. I am afraid I must forbid you your little pleasures until we have finished with our business here."

"You are not my master," said Fleming. "I don't need permission of you to so much as wipe my arse."

"Well, look at who's getting uppity now."

"What would Master say if he was to find out how you let these choice bits escape?" Fleming said, his lips curling into a sneer.

"He would say nothing and cannot be bothered with such trivial matters. They play no part in Scrooge's fate, as you well know," the Reverend Mitchell said, wiping his greasy lips on his sleeve. "Besides, I could find them if there were a compelling need."

Fleming said, "You are wrong about the Indian girl. She could have an important role in Scrooge's fate. He is attached to her and would do any-thing to save her."

Mitchell wiped his mouth again on his sleeve. "No, Scrooge's memories of her are gone—as are his memories of Miss Goosegrass. He remembers nothing of the people he met at the charity. There is only one now who tugs and pulls his heartstrings like a marionette—though his dance is not so pretty nor agile as it might once have been."

CHAPTER 17

৩৩৩

Ebenezer Scrooge and the Wise Man

SUMMER WAS SPENT. AT AUTUMN'S FIRST BLUSH THE TREES SHED YELLOW, tan, and orange flecks into liquid mirrors on the ground. When the sky cried, Scrooge's bones ached, and he felt a melancholy the hearth could not drive away. He watched the season from his window with a shawl thrown over his thin shoulders and a dull brown cap upon his head.

Only when he was with his Vivianna were his spirits restored.

"Read this to me," she said and held open the Good Book. She turned it upside down and giggled. "What does this say, my Ebenezer? To my eyes all these words might just as well be ants." They sat side by side on a sofa in the parlour of her home.

Scrooge gently took the book from her and demonstrated how to hold it respectfully. "We should begin your reading lesson to-day."

"Oh, not to-day, my sweet. You would spoil my mood, and you wouldn't wish that, I am sure," she said stroking his hand.

"Oh, very well. But we should start soon."

"Yes, my Ebenezer. One day you shall teach me to read. Not to-day," she said.

"You have picked an interesting passage, my love," he said glancing at the page. He read aloud: *"For unto every one that hath shall be given, and he shall have abundance: but for him that hath not shall be taken away even that which he hath."*

"I don't believe I understand what that means," Mrs. Claypoole said, clearing her throat delicately and looking down at her knees.

Scrooge reflected a moment and said, "Truer words have never been written." He put down the book and folded his hands in his lap. His collar was as white as a piano key and as stiff. "We observe this in the every day world of business. It all comes down to capital. Investments. Only certain members of our race bred for finance are able to reap its rewards."

Mrs. Claypoole ran a finger along the line of Scrooge's jaw. She said, "There's a French word I've heard. Something about nobles. You know it, don't you?"

"*Noblesse oblige*. Perhaps that is what you mean. It refers to the obligation of nobility to help the poor," Scrooge said.

Mrs. Claypoole clasped her hands in wonder. "You are so very, very clever," she said.

Scrooge pursed his lips and dismissed her compliment with a wave of his hand. "Thus it is that men who find themselves greatly advantaged—such as myself—create charities." He let his right arm rest. The change in the weather caused it to ache and throb.

"The poor are not suited for a life of leisure or intellectualism," mused Mrs. Claypoole. She rested her head against his shoulder and sighed. "The poor must eat simpler foods." She nibbled thoughtfully at her own knuckle. "Their digestions will not make use of the fine menu your charity has thus far provided them. Their bodies are strong and their stomachs and minds far too coarse to appreciate it. You do them injury, you wicked little boy."

Scrooge sighed. "How was I to know?" He gave a soft chuckle. "I am no master in the kitchen. I did not mean to spoil them."

She said, "Spoil them is just what you've done. The poor—the worthy poor, I should add—are a class apart from us, you know. Separate by birth. A different sort of creature, for all purposes. You must respect and understand that, Ebenezer. You will spoil them and ruin their lives. You will make them useless because they will not know their place and are not fit to raise themselves to any higher. This I saw in India. The work of the English soldier was to show the blacks their place."

"I will take your counsel, ma'am," Scrooge said, "take it to heart, I will. A man can be generous to a fault if he makes those whom he has pitied the lazier and more dependent for it."

Mrs. Claypoole batted her eyelashes. She pulled a tangle of gaudy wool from beside the sofa and fussed at it with a pair of knitting needles. "Your fault lies in your goodness of heart—not wickedness. A woman's practical touch is what *Ebenezer Scrooge's Charitable Aid And Victual Assistance To The Under-advantaged & Desperate* needs. Common sense. Frugality. Discipline. A gentle, but firm hand. This is what the poor want and need."

Scrooge said, "You believe then that I have spent too much on them?"

"Why Ebenezer! You could have operated your charity on half so much. A quarter! When you were younger, think! Were not the best times had at little expense?"

Scrooge slapped his thigh and laughed. He said, "Fezziwig could make merry for twenty friends or more on just three or four pounds."

"There—you see! Frugality is just the thing and no sign of meanness whatsoever."

"You put it so nicely, my love," said Scrooge. He closed his eyes. "Having you so near, so attentive makes me feel years younger. I crave the sight of you, the sound of your voice, your perfume, the expressions on your face. You help me to stand, to sit. You see to my clothes, my meals, my every need. You give me my medicine. I need you in so many ways. But now there is business to attend to, and I must leave you for a short time," he said.

"Oh, Ebenezer," she protested.

"No, my buttercup. There are things which men are meant to do alone. Perfectly boring things, you understand," he explained. "The sorts of things to add wrinkles to a young person's face. What? You doubt me. You need only look at mine to verify it. Scrooge and business go together like ham and eggs, you know."

She laughed prettily at him. "I shall send Anderson with you," she said. "He may help you to carry your...that is, should you have some small trifle which you mean to bring back, he will bear it for you." She gave him a smile.

⊙

Scrooge rattled down the street in his carriage frowning. There was the wedding and engagement rings upon which he needed to pay another instalment, of course, but his real purpose this day was the business of buying silk—silk for a wedding gown.

Scrooge examined a bolt of green at Wesley's. Pretty though it was he thought, *No, blue is what I am looking for. Blue to match her eyes.*

"Madame," Scrooge said, "would you have silk like this—only in blue? For a lady's dress. This shows a very fine sheen, it does."

"I believe so, Mr. Scrooge," the Shop-keeper said. "Mrs. Bunbridge had me put a bolt of blue away for her, but she's gone to Bath and won't be back for some time. I will order her another from Paris should you like it. Let me fetch it for you." She disappeared into the back room. Scrooge found a chair and painfully lowered himself into it.

He felt a touch at his sleeve and looked up into the not unattractive face of a middle-aged woman.

"Yes," he said. "How may I help you, ma'am?" He felt uncomfortable under her fixed gaze.

"Excuse me, Sir, but I do believe that you have dropped something," said she as if her words had fuller meaning.

"What do you say?"

"On the ground," she said, and stooped to his side. She handed him a slip of paper and as she did so her perfume disturbed him though he could not have said why. "It must have fallen from your pocket as you sat yourself down," she said. Without another word she handed it to him and with a quick step exited the store.

"Note?" Scrooge murmured to himself and unfolded the paper on his lap. His eyes were weak, and it was difficult for him to make it out though the penmanship was concise and well-formed. He turned it to the light and held it close to his eyes.

Meet me outside, was its simple message.

"What is all this nonsense?" he murmured to himself just as the Shop-keeper returned with the bolt of blue silk.

"What is that you say, Sir?" she said.

"Oh, nothing. Just thinking aloud on other matters." He picked up the silk and gave it a cursory glance. "This will do," said he. "It is to be a gift for someone special, and I mean for it to be a surprise. I will pay for it now, but you must keep it until I have it sent for. Is that clear?"

"Oh yes, Sir, Mr. Scrooge."

"How much did you say that was?" he asked, and she told him.

He flinched. Money. He was once its master. The betrayal he suffered at the hands of two men whom he had trusted drained him considerably. His counting house had lately seen a small reversal of its fortunes, and his investments did poorly. Scrooge could not blame Bob Cratchit for the state of England's economy, of course. His resources once so rich and diverse were all but exhausted. He would need to procure a loan. Something just to tide him over until times improved—which could not be long. He knew who to see.

"I seem to have left my purse behind," Scrooge said with a false smile which shopkeepers know only too well. "I will have you put it on my account, if you will."

The Shopkeeper gave him a knowing look. "Just as you wish, Sir. When do you expect to call for it? I should like to have it wrapped for you in advance, you understand."

"Soon. I can't say exactly when, but soon, I should think. To-morrow, perhaps. No later than Wednesday next." It depended, he knew, on how quickly he could secure a loan.

"It shall be ready for you, Sir," she said and carried it into the back room.

Scrooge leaned on his cane, drew the note to his eyes again and blinked at it. Nothing to do but see what lay behind it. He lifted his collar, buttoned his coat and stepped out of the shop. Rain and chill wind whipped round him.

"Anderson," he said.

"Yes, Sir," Anderson replied, smartly.

"I won't be needing you just now," Scrooge said.

"As you wish, Sir."

"Come back for me in..." he checked his pocket watch, "...in twenty minutes if you would."

"Yes, Sir."

"If you cannot find me, then go to the authorities. Do you understand me, Anderson?"

"I do indeed, Sir. In twenty minutes you desire me to return to collect you and take you home. If I do not find you here, I am to contact the Magistrate."

"That is correct, Anderson. Now go, and I'll expect you back here on time."

Scrooge watched Anderson walk briskly away, and as he did so the rain paused. After he was gone, Scrooge had no idea what to do next. Who was this mysterious stranger who wished to meet with him? Did he bring good news or threats or blackmail? He squinted again at the note when a shadow fell across it. He looked up into the face of the woman who had given it to him.

"Yes?" he said.

"May I have a word with you, Sir?" said she, simply.

"Who are you? What do you want with me?" Scrooge said.

"For the moment I would take your elbow and walk with you."

"And why should I do that?" Scrooge said.

"I am in no position to make demands upon anyone, Mr. Scrooge. It is merely a request of a lady you have the right to grant or deny."

Scrooge squeezed his eyes shut. "Oh, all right then. But let us be quick about it. The weather just now threatens to burst over our heads, and my health is none too good."

"Should it rain, we will get ourselves to shelter immediately. I would not have you take ill for the world."

"It is kind of you to say so, Miss...?"

"Mr. Scrooge, look into my face, and tell me if you have any recollection of its features."

"My eyes are poor. It may be that I know you. Turn so that the light falls upon you."

She drew so near to Scrooge's face that he could feel her warmth. He hastily withdrew with a blush.

"No," he answered at length. "I cannot say that I do. Should I?"

She did not immediately reply, but Scrooge felt her body quiver.

"My dear, I have upset you," he said, patting her hand.

"No," she said. "Not at all. It is just this wind which makes me shiver. I have kept you too long, Sir. Forgive me for intruding upon your peace, and I thank you for your time. It has been my pleasure to have this conversation."

"The pleasure is all mine," said Scrooge.

"Let us depart now. I wish you Godspeed," said she.

"Godspeed to you, good woman."

As she left Scrooge shouted after her: "Your name, woman! What is your name?"

If she heard him, she gave no sign but walked on steadily until Scrooge could see her no more.

◎

"He was polite if not entirely cordial," said Miss Goosegrass. She turned her eyes toward the window. Mrs. Topper could see she was fighting tears.

"But did he not give you any sign that he recognised you?" Mrs. Topper asked.

"Not a glimmer," Miss Goosegrass said.

"You say that he did not see well. Perhaps that is it."

Miss Goosegrass pulled off her hat and shook her head. "No, he saw me well enough, heard my voice. He did not know me in the least."

"Did you tell him who you were?" Mrs. Topper said.

"I did not. Surely he has been forewarned against his former employee who was the cause of his collapse. No. I did not wish to vex him unduly. He is not a well man. I wish to remember him as gently as I can. I have lost him, Mrs. Topper, and I do not know what I am to do." A single wet line glistened down each of her cheeks, but she made no sound.

"You shall just have to get him back, Miss Goosegrass. Is there any question of that?"

"How? You have heard the latest news as well as I. You know that he is engaged to be married to young and beautiful Mrs. Claypoole who I understand has an income of her own of ten thousand a year and more."

"Purity of heart will prevail," Mrs. Topper said. "Love will out."

"How do you know that she doesn't love him as mightily as I?" Miss Goosegrass said, twisting her mouth.

Mrs. Topper could make no suitable reply.

"Mr. Scrooge is an entirely agreeable man. I should think any woman could fall deeply in love with him," continued Miss Goosegrass, nasally. She raised both shoulders and looked out the window at the flying rain.

"I can only suppose you are right," Mrs. Topper said with a sigh.

"I must abandon all thoughts of him, and dedicate myself to aid you in the recovery of your own worthy husband," Miss Goosegrass said, sitting forward.

"No, you must think of yourself, dear Miss Goosegrass. You do have a life beyond my troubles."

"I shall take my leave of you, then," Miss Goosegrass said, softly, "if that is how you feel."

Mrs. Topper frowned. "No, never. I didn't mean that at all. Only you must not be so completely selfless."

"I only mean to never neglect my friends," Miss Goosegrass said.

"As you surely have not," Mrs. Topper said. "You have been too generous of your time and energy. You have been my unflagging companion since the beginning of this horrible series of events, and I can never thank you enough for the aid you have already given me. I am not abandoning you and never will, and hope you never wish to be rid of me."

Miss Goosegrass said, "I do not deserve your kindness."

"For the moment, kindness is all either of us has," Mrs. Topper replied.

⊙

Scrooge took the stairs one at a time, breathing heavily, resting often. Anderson waited outside and felt the full effect of the weather. What did Scrooge care, in or out of Parliament, whether by day's end Anderson was as wet as a drowned rat? Did not Scrooge himself suffer discomforts a hundred times worse? Didn't every step he take send a pain through his body which caused his teeth to grind and puckered his eyes?

Scrooge needed more money. He cursed the day he met Milton Topper and cursed his own inability to read the man's character. A deceiving thief was all the man had been.

"How could I possibly have given this man, a veritable stranger, such unfettered access to my money?" Scrooge grumbled to himself. "See where it has left me to blindly trust my fellow man? See what a little too much Christmas joy has done to a carefully planned financial empire! Let me never throw caution to the wind again so recklessly. For the Love of God, henceforth I shall forever more exercise the common sense that I was born with! If I can survive this, that is!"

Scrooge had been able to borrow small amounts from acquaintances, but nothing near what was required to keep his charity going and prepare for the wedding.

One man in all of London, he knew, could help him. That man was Saul Weissman, king of the Jewish moneylenders and no fool by anyone's measure.

He paused at the top of the stairs of Weissman's place of business and leaned against the wall waiting for the pain in his back and shoulder to ease. First one and then the other felt a modicum of relief, but never both together. Scrooge sucked in his breath and rapped against the door with the head of his cane.

He was shown into a room filled with rich furnishings: wall maps, Turkey rugs, tapestries, water-colours, rare coins, crystal lamps, silver tea settings. Weissman sat behind an elephantine desk of mahogany sipping coffee from a saucer.

He put it down, shook his head, stood and said, "Who would have thought that I, Saul Weissman, would ever have the honour of drinking coffee with the famous Ebenezer Scrooge in these humble offices?" He extended his hand.

"You do me a great courtesy to see me on such short notice, Mr. Weiss-man," Scrooge said and shook the hand warmly in return.

"I would prefer that you would call me Saul," said the Jew. "Perhaps if you were speaking with my father 'Mr. Weissman' would do. But my friends call me Saul, and so shall you."

Scrooge smiled. "You may call me Ebenezer, if you wish."

"Do you drink coffee, Ebenezer?" Weissman said. "I have been drinking it since I was a young boy, and I often assume that everyone has acquired the same habit."

"Coffee? Why, no thankee. I have had a great shock and my physician tells me that I should drink neither coffee nor tea. I must content myself with water—not too chilled."

"You are not well?"

"I am on the road to recovery." Scrooge grimaced under a stab of pain which belied his words. "With time and attention I shall one day be a whole man again. It is nothing really, but I thank you for your concern."

"I see. And what do I owe the pleasure of this visit? Surely you are not here to consult Saul on matters of medicine. I have a brother in Lisbon, however, who studies to become a surgeon, but me? I cannot tell you the difference between a man's knee and his elbow."

"No, I am not here for my health. I have come for a loan."

Weissman sat back in his chair and puffed out his cheeks. "This is a fine day! Indeed, when Ebenezer Scrooge comes borrowing money, it is a wise man who sits up and listens." He laughed at his own joke which Scrooge had no doubt he had repeated countless times. Then his face turned serious. "How much do you need?"

Scrooge named a sum.

"So much?" the Jew said wrinkling his face. He wrote the number on a slip of paper.

Scrooge twisted his mouth. "It is what I require. Can you do it?"

"These are hard times as you know. But perhaps. Perhaps for one of such elevated status as yourself this thing can be done. It may take some time, and I would have to call in a few favours."

"How much interest will you want?" Scrooge asked.

Weissman named a figure.

"So much?" said Scrooge, eyes drawing wide.

"I must cover my risk. Surely you understand the nature of business risks?"

"There is no risk in this," said Scrooge.

"Call it 'the cost of doing business' then."

Scrooge twisted to one side as a jab of pain arced up his body.

"Are you sure there is nothing I can get you?" Weissman said noticing Scrooge's discomfort.

"Nothing. I need money," Scrooge gasped, his face white.

"Perhaps if you were to tell me the nature of your venture I might be able to lower my risk and therefore discount the interest that I must charge you."

Scrooge hunched forward. "You believe that I have special inside information, don't you? You believe that I am accumulating resources for an investment in a particular stock?"

"What other purpose could there be? If you could find it in your heart to share this information, spread the opportunity for Saul and his friends to earn a little money all round, it might help my ability to aid you."

"There is no stock. There are no investments."

"Really?" Weissman arched his brow doubtfully.

"Some of the money is needed for personal expenses."

Weissman lifted his brow in doubt again. "Personal expenses? Ebenezer Scrooge does not have the reputation for high living." He waved the slip of paper with the number Scrooge had named. "There must be more. Quite a bit more."

"There is," Scrooge said.

"Then you must tell me," the Jew said.

"Perhaps you have heard that I have founded a charity."

The Jew's expression gave Scrooge no hint as to his reaction. "Go on," Weissman said.

"Its operations consume much of my time and financial resources. Not to put too fine a point upon it, this charity has momentarily drained me as I have been swindled by a man whom I never should have trusted and have lost most of the money with which I intended to fund it. Saul, many people are dependent upon me. Many people eat because I put food in their mouths."

The Jew nodded extending his lower lip. "Although I am a man of business as you are, Ebenezer, I am not an ungenerous man," said he. "I have been known to make..." he shrugged "...donations to various charities in the past. Tell me about yours."

Scrooge did.

"Can you tell me, Ebenezer," Saul Weissman said standing up and walking around to the front of his desk, "do you care for Jews as well as Gentiles in this charity of yours?"

Scrooge put a hand to his forehead trying to wipe away the fog. "Jews? Yes. We had two Jews among us once," he said. "I think."

"Once? Where are they now?

"I couldn't say."

"I see." Weissman walked over to one of several windows which looked out over the busy street below. He clasped his hands behind his back, mulling over what he would say next. "I cannot help but have great respect for you, Ebenezer. I have heard your name praised for many years as a successful businessman. Even when some said you had gone too far, I knew that inside your chest was a heart of gold and that someday you would find the opportunity to show everyone your true nature."

"Thank you, Sir."

"But Ebenezer. Are there no Gentile moneylenders who might help you? It would be awkward for me to give so much money to an institution which does not share my faith. You can understand that, can't you? Each faith must take care of its own."

Scrooge put his weight upon his cane, but did not stand up. "I am afraid that I have been unable to secure the money I need from my usual business contacts. That's why I have come to you. It's only a short-term loan. My investments will turn around soon. There is almost no risk in it for you whatsoever. The market is bound to right itself before year end next."

The Jew turned and looked Scrooge directly in the eye. "No, I am afraid it is quite impossible, Mr. Scrooge. I wish you luck in your search, but it is beyond Saul's ability to help you. You must have other resources, relations who could loan you the money you need. Someone?"

"None," Scrooge said in a voice barely above a whisper. "Saul, you are turning away someone who only wishes to make life a little easier for his fellow man. I do not do this for myself, Saul. This is not money for investment. This is not money for my personal gain. Do you understand what I am telling you? Surely there is a spark of humanity in you?"

Saul poured coffee into his saucer from a silver pot, lifted it to his lips, blew gently and sipped. "I see. You state your case well, but still there is the risk. I cannot stay in business if I cannot cover my risk. Sometimes I make a little money. Sometimes I lose a little money. So long as I make a little more than I lose in the long run, I can stay in business. That is why I must charge interest. To keep the ink black. Tell me, Mr. Scrooge, what can you offer me in terms of collateral?"

Scrooge shrugged. "Collateral?"

"Properties? Certainly you have properties of some value?"

"None. All that was lost as I have said." Scrooge held his breath for a moment then spoke with his eyes closed: "I am to be married soon. My wife-to-be has an income of ten thousand a year."

"This is dependable information?"

"It is," Scrooge said. "She is devoted to me, Sir. Utterly devoted."

"Is she beautiful?"

"The most beautiful woman whom I have ever laid eyes upon," said Scrooge.

Weissman rubbed his chin in thought, although it was clear to Scrooge that he had already come to a decision. "You must consider yourself a lucky man. Perhaps I could see my way to lend you half the money you need, but I will need to double the interest."

"Double the interest?" Scrooge said sharply. "You have me at a disadvantage, Sir—you know that."

"It is the best that I can do, and I need to protect my investments. I have had several men default on their loans this month already. The holidays are fast approaching for Jew and Gentile alike, and you know how it is with those who cannot manage their own money wisely."

Scrooge sighed and nodded. "I agree to your terms as you have offered them," he said. "And I thank you for them, Saul."

"I will draw up the papers, Ebenezer," Weissman said. "And I wish you the best of luck. May your marriage bring you great joy."

◎

"Why is this door such an odious shade of yellow, Anderson? Can you answer me that?" Scrooge said, knocking his stick up against it.

"I couldn't say, Sir," said Anderson.

"This looks like nothing more than the yolk of an egg," Scrooge said. "Do they not make paint of different shades?—subtler colours which do not offend the eye so."

"I am certain they do."

"Can you think of anything wrong with the colour brown, Anderson?"

"None, Sir."

"It is the colour of honest English soil. Is honest English soil good enough for you, Anderson?"

"It is, Sir."

"Then for the love of God, have this door repainted brown immediately!" Scrooge kicked the door open and passed inside.

"As you wish, Sir."

CHAPTER 18

ༀ

Trust Me

Aɴᴅ ꜱᴏ ᴛʜᴇ ᴅᴀʏꜱ ɢᴀᴛʜᴇʀᴇᴅ ᴛʜᴇᴍꜱᴇʟᴠᴇꜱ ɪɴᴛᴏ ᴡᴇᴇᴋꜱ ᴜɴᴛɪʟ ᴏɴᴇ ᴅᴀʏ ᴛʜᴇ rain stopped, the clouds turned to steel, and it snowed. It fell quickly and melted as soon as it touched the ground, but it was omen of things to come all the same.

"This shade of blue is a perfect match for your eyes, my dear," said Scrooge holding the bolt of silk out to Mrs. Claypoole at her home.

"Why, Mr. Scrooge! A present for me?" she said, her voice sparkling with delight. "How thoughtful of you. I have something for you as well."

"Really, what would that be?" he said.

"These letters to your charity. You asked me to bring anything of import to you directly."

Scrooge smiled, took the bills and patted her hand reassuringly. "I shall take care of these presently," he said. He fought back the emotions of what the envelopes held for him. Disaster. Ruin. Despair. When she left the room he would throw them into the fire unopened knowing what little good it would do. There was only one thing which would keep him out of the workhouse: his future wife's ten thousand a year. Even so the thought did not console him in any way.

"The silk is for your wedding dress," Scrooge said. He still owed money on it, of course, but the Shopkeeper had let him have it after he promised to pay the balance after the New Year.

"Where did you ever find such fine fabric?" she said. "Paris? No! It must be from China or India. When I was in India I saw how silk was made, you know. Small girls with the most cunning hands ran these charming little looms. A pity how steam has taken that job away from so many of our textile workers here in our own land."

"India?" Scrooge repeated. "Young Indian girls, you say?"

"Yes, why do you ask? Have you been to India?"

"No. Never. It reminded me of something," he said, his eyes not focusing. "Something in my dreams. A young girl. Indian, as you say. But she is not weaving silk. She is sometimes a panther and sometimes merely a girl,"

"Have you been reading those dreadful myths of India? Were-tigers and were-panthers and all that superstitious rubbish," she said. "It's no wonder I've never taken the time to learn to read. Novels will be the downfall of man, I make no doubt."

"I have not read any such thing. All that I have read of recent, I have read to you aloud."

"Then your dreams have returned," she said.

"They are not so bad. Nothing you should concern yourself about."

"Will you ever know peace, my love? What instruments of destruction women can be!" said Mrs. Claypoole. "I blush at the poisonous nature of so many members of my own sex. That a mere school mistress should cause you such grief and ruin to your health, leaves me trembling with rage."

"It occurs to me to wonder why it is that an emotional shock such as I have suffered should cause me such pains as are in my back," Scrooge said softly. "It is more like I have been beaten with a cane rather than suffered emotional stress."

"You will rest better with more drops, dear," she said. "To-night, I promise, you will get your much needed rest."

"Yes, I will need to be well-rested for the wedding. That is one day I do so want to be at my best."

"I do so look forward to the day, my love," she said. "I have never felt time move more slowly."

"Nor have I."

"Do you know the number of days?" said she.

"I do not. How many?" Scrooge said, realising he could not remember the last time he had looked at a calendar.

"Twenty-five. Not so very many, but they do trickle by."

"Twenty-five? So few. We haven't chosen our new home. There are several properties which I wish for you to look at. Perhaps we could start by renting a small house—something modest."

She waved away his suggestion and tugged lightly on his chin. She said, "Not now, dear. Let us put that all aside for the moment and discuss the arrangements for our wedding. We must be wedded first, yes? The ball simply must be the most magnificent thing ever done."

"The ball?" said Scrooge. "You leave me puzzled, my rose petal."

"The ball on Christmas eve. Have you not listened to a single word I have spoken to you, my silly plum?"

"Well, of course I have, but perhaps I have forgotten." Scrooge's eyes shifted with the thought: How shall I raise money for a ball? "I shall see to it, my love. I shall see to it," said he. "Have no fear."

She laid a hand on his arm. "You really haven't been listening, have you? That won't be necessary, my dearest. As I've told you, arrangements have already been made. Someone I know, a very good friend, offers us the use of his home and grounds."

"But surely my charity would do. There is room enough."

"No, I think not. You will be pleased, my Ebenezer. Let it be a surprise. Trust me."

CHAPTER 19

\ᦓᦓ

Two Letters

DEAREST LUCILLE,

I write this letter under the most unusual of circumstances. I know full well that I shall never be able to post it, nor will your eyes ever read it. But write it I must, my dearest. There is little else to occupy my time.

I am a prisoner, you see—a prisoner of the Reverend Mitchell, occult creature that he is, in an unknown chamber with the good Mr. William Dawson who, as it turns out, is not named Dawson at all but Mr. Lincoln Trumbull. (I will reserve the telling of that story for another time!) He is with me now—the only other soul I've seen in a long while. I cannot say just how long as we have no clocks and neither can we see the sun. He and I have had many extensive conversations, and have learnt to tolerate one another to the best of our abilities—which is not to say that we are always in perfect harmony.

Our prison, I must admit, does not much resemble a prison. There are no bars to it. We are not forced to spend our time in filth. We suffer no pain. We are neither too cold nor too warm, and we have little reason to be hungry. (In fact we eat quite well from a table which replenishes itself while we sleep—I have made such a glutton of myself that I believe I have grown quite stout. I should not be surprised to learn that I weigh 15 stone now!)

In spite of all this, have no doubt that we are tormented in horrible ways which I will reveal at length.

Let me first describe our chamber of confinement: It is a room large enough to hold a rather extensive ball with space enough for refreshment tables, chairs, musicians and their instruments, and, of course, a sizeable dance floor.

In shape it is rather longer than it is wide, and in height is unbounded so far as I can perceive—as if we were sitting at the bottom of a deep shaft. The room is filled perpetually with a light bright enough that we have no need of candles to read. The source of the illumination, however, does not come from above, nor does it appear to originate from any source nearby. The most uncommon thing about it is that the light is so even that no shadows are cast anywhere within the chamber. Above us, starting at perhaps twenty feet, however, there are nothing but shadows.

In this inky blackness I am deluded that I see shapeless things creeping slowly—as if trying not to attract attention to themselves. I imagine them to be giant spiders though that cannot be quite right. Yet they are something like spiders—perhaps more horrible than spiders could ever be. We are being watched by them.

Far worse than the darkness above are the walls. I wish desperately to batter my way through them to freedom, but I will not so much as lay a finger upon their surfaces. I do not mean to say that the walls are pro-hibitively thick. In fact, I have stared at them for many hours, and in thickness I perceive them as rather less than any of the walls of Yellow Door, almost delicate. They are soft and wobble a little from time to time.

Why have I not tested the walls' strength? Because, my dear wife, each wall is covered in short, light-coloured hair. I believe that I can detect a slight but steady throbbing just beneath their surface—which is perhaps the walls' most revealing feature. Though the room be a rectangular prism, it is no room at all. It is a living thing (or perhaps the insides of a living thing), and the throbbing of its surface is the beating of its abominable heart. Like Jonah of the Bible, we are living in the gut of some leviathan, the true nature of which I cannot begin to guess. No. I will not attack these walls for I have no idea what the consequences would be, and I am not so desperate —yet.

I have said that we are tormented and by that I do not refer to our uncertain knowledge of the essential nature of the chamber where we are being held against our will. I refer not to being ill-used in any way whatever *while we are awake.*

We *are*, however, bedevilled in our sleep—or perhaps it is only near-sleep.

None of the dreams we have had since becoming prisoners here have been anything like natural. No fanciful dreams of flying or of peacefully walking in the wood or of meeting loved ones. These dreams are always dark and depressing in the extreme. Mr. Trumbull, I need add, experiences them as well as I.

In our rigid states of somnolence incubi sit at our knees and relate to us horrible things which we then clearly understand. Yet when we wake we cannot remember anything of save for a residue of disagreeable emotions.

In other dreams creatures of quite a different kind speak to us at length in words we cannot understand—yet long after we wake we can recall the sounds clearly, could repeat them aloud should we have a mind to.

While we sleep there is a constant procession of men, beasts, creatures of impossible shapes who give us no rest. They try to persuade us to commit appalling acts, boast of their own detestable deeds and describe to us in terrible detail the end of our kind on our world.

For hours we are showered in colours which I can give no name to—neither red, nor green, nor blue, nor any other hue, texture or timbre viewed with sane eyes. We hear sounds which have never before reverberated in a human ear—sounds of astonishing clarity, coolness, colour and precise, almost geometric, location. Taste, touch, smell—all the senses are a confusion of unnatural sensations until we are left on the very brink of madness. We wake up exhausted—or worse into yet another dream. And always the dreams are shared—as if we were of one mind.

I cannot now say that we are not mad. Nor can I say that we are still alive. We may be dead. If so, this is certainly not Heaven but a Hell which I could never have imagined.

Your Loving Husband,
Milton

⊙

MY DEAREST LUCY,

The dreams have stopped. I begin to think clearly again, and in fact have time to read. There is not much variety in our library: two books. One is *Paradise Lost*—which was laid upon one bed and evidently meant for me, and the second was *Robinson Crusoe*. I have now read *Paradise Lost* three times and *Robinson Crusoe* twice. I shouldn't wish to read either book ever again, and if I were granted a small wish, it might be that our books were replenished as often as our food.

Our latest awakening (I cannot call it morning) a most curious thing occurred. We found our old clothes gone. Since I should not like to lounge around in my natural state, I donned the clothing left for me. I have only a small shaving mirror to study, but I should imagine that I look like something from the House of Lords. They are finer clothes than I have ever worn or could ever hope to afford. Boots made of the softest leather. Waistcoats made of the shiniest red silks you've ever seen and linen shirts and wool coats cut in the latest fashion from Paris! Far too grand for me. Mr. Trumbull wears fine clothes as well and his thin frame is also filling out on our steady diet of cakes and so on.

But on a more important topic—we have not been married so very long, my sweet, but surely you have noticed a ring that I usually wear on my right hand. I may have told you that it was a gift from relatives of mine, but that isn't strictly true.

My family has had experiences of a sort not common among most. We are sensitive to elements of the spiritual world, if I may put it plainly. I have not told you of this before because I feared you would not take to the idea and that you might think less of my Aunt Nellie whom you've twice met. You remember her? She is the bed-ridden one. She has a way of locating things which is most amazing.

All this is to say that the ring which I just mentioned was given to me by spirits—or perhaps angels. I do not know what to call them. And as such the ring must have significance. The ring may have protected me against Mitchell's wickedness had I not been so foolish as to leave it on the washstand my last morning at home. Though it cannot offer me protection wherever it is I am at the moment, I hope you will find it and wear it and be protected. It is all that I can offer you now.

Your Faithful Husband,
Milton

CHAPTER 20

ശ്ര

We Are Not Ghosts

Mrs. Lucille Topper declined her sister Lillian's invitation to Christmas Eve stating that she had been invited to their sister Lottie's home. Mrs. Lucille Topper declined her sister Lottie's invitation to Christmas Eve stating that she had been invited to their sister Lillian's home. The sisters being communicative in the extreme quickly detected the cheat.

"If she will not visit us on this fine holiday evening, then *I* shall visit *her*," exclaimed Lottie to her husband with a shake of her great black curls. "'Tis a terrible thing that her husband should be away on their first Christmas," she said. "And I will not allow her to suffer it alone and joyless."

"But what of my reputation?" her husband said. "You know what her husband's been accused of."

"You needn't worry about your reputation, Arthur. You can stay home and watch the children," Lottie commanded and so Arthur obeyed.

And thus it was that Lottie and Louisa, their youngest sister, entered the Topper parlour on the evening of December 24th, just as heavy snow began to fall.

"I should like to introduce you both to my friend, Miss Goosegrass," Mrs. Topper said after her sisters had hung up their coats and scarves.

Lottie (who among all the sisters was known not only for her dark hair, but also for her frankness and boldness of expression) said, "She does not have the face of an adulteress."

"Sister!" Mrs. Topper said. "This is my friend, and I would have you treat her with kindness."

"I have," Lottie said. "I have just proclaimed her innocent and have accepted her into my circle of friends. How can that be unkind?"

Mrs. Topper said, "And I ask you to have a care what you say in front of Louisa. You may be wise to the ways of the world, but she is but an innocent fourteen years."

"At fourteen she undoubtedly knows more of the world than either you or I at that age," Lottie said.

Mrs. Topper said, "I doubt that very much. I have heard too many stories of you and your young men."

"Sister, you cause me to blush," Lottie said, but there was no red upon her face which hadn't been applied with a brush. "Do not believe what jealousy may cause others to say."

Miss Goosegrass cleared her throat. "I am pleased to meet you," she said, reaching out and shaking first Lottie's and then Louisa's hands. "And I appreciate your good opinion of me. I promise you none of the accusations which The Reverend Mitchell has circulated about me are in the slightest way true."

"A wolf in sheep's clothing is what he is," Lottie said. "Men like him are not to be trusted. The more pious they behave, the more likely they are to try to get under a girl's skirts."

Louisa blushed violently.

Mrs. Topper said, "I should have invited the gentlemen to our little soirée —if for no other reason than to keep a civil tongue in our sister's mouth."

They all laughed heartily.

Miss Goosegrass listened to the conversation between Lottie and Mrs. Topper. Neither she nor Louisa had a chance to get a word in, but that didn't matter. Miss Goosegrass was content to listen. She turned her head to the window and watched the snow fall faster and faster grateful that she did not have to venture out that evening.

A soft knock. The door opened and Nancy appeared. "A boy to see you, ma'am," she said.

Mrs. Topper and Miss Goosegrass exchanged a quick glance. "If you'll excuse us a moment," she said to her sisters. "Miss Goosegrass, if you'd come with me..."

The two women stood and left the room with a swish of their skirts.

"Perhaps it is your young man with news," said Mrs. Topper as they walked down the short passageway.

A moment later Nancy escorted Patrick Coal into the library and sat him down before the fire.

Miss Goosegrass stood, walked over to the boy and said, "What is it, Patrick? What brings you here this Christmas Eve? You are, of course, welcome here now as at any time, but do you bring us news in addition to the season's greetings?"

"Well, ma'am," said the dark-haired youth looking down at his toes, "you will recall as how you asked me and me mates to spy on The Reverend Salvation Mitchell."

"Yes, Patrick," said Miss Goosegrass. "You know how much we appreciate your efforts. You have been more dedicated than we could possibly have hoped for."

"It takes a young man of your resources and intellect to succeed where others fail," said Mrs. Topper. "Even if you never bring us any useful information, we will be forever grateful for your courage and diligence."

Patrick's chest swelled with pride. "And it is at last that I do bring you the useful information you seek. A Christmas gift as it were."

"Patrick! What are you telling us?" Miss Goosegrass said.

"I've always said he was a clever boy," Mrs. Topper said.

"We have fixed the location of Reverend M's secret destination."

"Oh, Patrick," Mrs. Topper said, her eyes filling with tears. "You don't know what this means to us."

"Tell us where it is," Miss Goosegrass said. "Can you?"

"Well, yes and no," the young Coal said.

"Patrick, whatever do you mean by that?" Mrs. Topper said.

"I mean that I could, but that I shouldn't."

"Patrick, you are compounding mystery upon mystery. Explain yourself immediately," Miss Goosegrass said with an authority that only school mistresses possess.

"The Reverend M does not keep himself at a respectable part of town, and I would be ill-advised to take any lady there or tell her of its location even if I were sworn to do so," said he.

"That is a lot of nonsense, Patrick," Miss Goosegrass said. "Just tell us where he is, and your duty will have been fulfilled and you may go on your way feeling that you have aided a just cause."

"No, ma'am."

"You refuse?" Miss Goosegrass kept the anger out of her voice. "Do you mean to tease us?"

Patrick looked at his hands.

"Are you wanting something in exchange? Money? If it's money you want, just say so and it shall be yours...if reasonable."

"No, ma'am, I couldn't take money from you. I shan't tell you and that's that."

"You put yourself rather bluntly, young man," said Miss Goosegrass. "You trespass upon rudeness."

"I've made up my mind."

Miss Goosegrass said, "This doesn't make the slightest bit of sense. You spend all your time watching Reverend Mitchell's activities and just when you've discovered something useful, you refuse to share it with us. I must say I am disappointed in you, young man. Your sense of chivalry is defective."

"Do you understand that we need this information to help locate Mr. Topper?" said Mrs. Topper.

"Oh, Mr. Topper ain't in there. Nor Mr. Dawson."

"How can you be so certain?" Miss Goosegrass said.

"Neither Mr. Topper nor Mr. Dawson would be caught dead in such a place."

"Patrick, would you please just tell us where he is?" Mrs. Topper said, growing steadily impatient.

"No, this is a matter for the Magistrate," Patrick said.

Miss Goosegrass moved to his side and placed a hand around his shoulders. "Why Patrick. You don't believe we would take these matters into our own hands, do you?" she said, quietly.

"I believe you might," said he.

"Nothing could be further from the truth, dear boy," Miss Goosegrass said. "We are modern women, it is true, but we do know our limitations."

"I could not agree more," said he.

"When you tell us where the Reverend stays," said Miss Goosegrass, "I will take that information to a private thief-taker. We won't bother the Magistrate until we have more than suspicions and accusations. This is surely work for a man."

"I may be a mere boy, but I've accomplished what ten men couldn't," he said, proudly.

Miss Goosegrass nodded. "Surely you have, young man. You have supplied the cunning, but the time has come when brute force may need application. Give yourself ten more years..." she saw his face darken, "...rather, five, and you'll find yourself a strapping young man fit to wrestle a bear. But just now, you've done your part, done it well, and you're finished. None of this detracts from your status as trusted scout and valiant hero." She gave him a light kiss on the top of his head.

Patrick grinned, "Of course, ma'am," he said. "Your servant, ma'am," he added with a bow and laughed.

"Tell me, Patrick, what I wish to know," Miss Goosegrass said drawing nearer.

He told her, and she sent him away with coins a'jingling in his pocket.

"Now," Mrs. Topper said to Miss Goosegrass, "We've got to make our excuses to my sisters and be off."

Topper threw down *Robinson Crusoe*. He had to admit he was having an easier time of it than that gentleman, but the fact gave him little satisfaction. He could not remember if it had been on a Friday when they awoke to find themselves so confined. *Time has no meaning in this room*, he thought. *It is so very like death.*

"Trumbull," he shouted, "is there any more of that sliced ham upon the table? I have grown lethargic, and I find that I cannot rise from bed so quick following a long read."

"Don't trouble yourself. One moment, and I'll see," Trumbull replied. "Yes, there is plenty. Do you wish me to bring you a slice?"

"If you would be so kind," Topper said. He heard Trumbull who had been pacing the room open a door and then another.

Trumbull said, "Mr. Topper, come here quickly!"

"What is it, Trumbull?"

"You must see for yourself."

Topper rolled off the bed to his feet and followed the sound of the voice. Topper looked into the room where could be found their table-of-plenty, but Trumbull was not there. Again, he heard: "Mr. Topper, you should see this. I came in here to wash the knife."

Topper entered the room with their washstand. He saw Trumbull with his hand on the exit door.

It stood slightly ajar.

"How did you ever open it?" Topper said.

"I didn't. I found it that way when I entered the room."

"It appears that our prison term has ended. We are about to be set free."

Trumbull shook his head but said nothing.

"Do we have any choice but to venture through?"

"I wouldn't care to speculate as to the results either way," Trumbull said.

"Come, come! Where is your sense of adventure? We shall never be free so long as we sit in these rooms. We've been given fine clothes, good food— we have little to complain of, I should say. You shall take that silk hat, and I shall take the other and we shall see where this door leads. Never go bare-headed into mystery, I always say."

"We may be only leaving one room for another," Trumbull said. "Rooms inside of rooms inside of rooms. I would suggest that we carry at least a few pieces of fruit or slices of bread to take with us should our destination not be so well-supplied as this."

"An excellent suggestion, Trumbull," Topper said. "Will you stay here and see that the door stays open while I go and fetch us our victuals?"

"Of course," Trumbull said still reluctant to open the door any further. He slid his foot between the door and its frame.

A moment later it was Topper's turn to shout, "Mr. Trumbull. Come quickly, you will never believe what I have found!"

"Should I leave my post at the door?" Trumbull said.

"No, on second thought I shall come to you," Topper said. He entered the room with great fistfuls of money. "There must be several hundred pounds here. Can there be any doubt of it, Mr. Trumbull? Whoever it is who has been holding us offers us recompense for our trouble."

"I don't like the look of it, Mr. Topper," said Trumbull. "There's something just not right about all this."

"Nor do I honestly, Mr. Trumbull, but foolish we would be to leave it behind, I dare say." He held the money up for a moment, and then with a sigh added: "Perhaps you are right. It is much too good to be true. I shall put it all back on the table where I found it."

"Might not the money do Yellow Door good?" Trumbull said.

"No doubt it would," Topper replied.

"Then, let us take it with us and give it to charity. Our time spent here will not have been so complete a waste."

"Capital idea, Mr. Trumbull. Capital idea," said Topper. "I believe it is a good sign. Why give us money if we are only intended to be shunted into another room?"

"To build up our hopes only to crush them," Trumbull suggested.

"There is that possibility," Topper said, soberly, "but I'd rather put the best face upon it. Let us boldly venture forth into the unknown and see where we land."

"After you, Mr. Topper," Trumbull said.

Trumbull pulled the door wide. He was surprised that it moved so effortlessly. Topper bent forward to examine the bolt which had held them fast for so long and found none. He rubbed the edge of the door next to the knob, but could feel nothing which would have held it so fixedly.

They stepped through the open door with their fine clothes, their pockets stuffed with apples, pears, strawberries, carrots, and celery sticks. They divided the money between them and filled their hats full with it.

Trumbull turned to close the door behind out of habit, but there was no door to be closed—only solid wall.

Topper said, "I hope that I may never set foot again in that room so long as I live."

They found themselves in a passageway, dark but not without a grey light of its own. Through the walls Topper believed he could hear noises. The sounds of a large number of people, loudly speaking.

The passageway had no other doors but travelled along at short lengths before bending at right angles.

"Where do we go?" said Topper aloud. "To Freedom! To Freedom, I say!"

"Just ahead, Sir," Trumbull said, "What do you make out?"

"If it isn't a door, bless my soul," Topper said. "A door, and I could care less if it is locked or no, for I shall batter it to pieces with my feet and bare hands. I can taste the Freedom, Trumbull, can you not also? We were meant to be released now. Our gaoler had judged us innocent or feels we have served our time. I cannot wait to see my dear wife."

"I hope that you won't be disappointed, Sir," Trumbull said.

"Only time will tell us." Topper placed his hand upon the door at the end of the passage. "There is no where else to go."

"I suppose not, Sir," Trumbull agreed.

The knob yielded easily to Topper's hand. A broad smile creased his face. "It won't be long now. We will make our way home directly," he said, and swung open the door.

They stepped through the opening into the dining room at Yellow Door.

"There! You see, Trumbull? We are back! What did I tell you?" Topper stepped into the room and waved his arms over his head with joy. "We have returned, friends. We are not ghosts. Feel of us. We are real, and we have returned."

No one in the dining room at Yellow Door spoke a word and Topper sensed that something had gone terribly wrong while he had been away.

The grim expressions of their faces, the terrible silence, the air of joylessness was nothing like he had ever experienced in this room before. Many of the faces were new to him—the ones he recognised looked a decade older.

How long were we in confinement? he thought.

"What has happened here?" he said, his voice thick.

Topper glanced down at the soup bowl nearest him and saw it filled with a substance more suited to scrubbing floors than to filling bellies.

Several voices whispered, "Topper!"

A bulky stranger with a pock-marked face pushed back from his table, stood and said in a tone of distinct authority: "Who are you?"

The room broke into nervous babble.

"I am Milton Topper, and this is my friend..." Topper hesitated, careful not to reveal Trumbull's true identity, "...Mr. Dawson. Many here will recognise us. I am Mr. Scrooge's personal assistant, and I've overseen Yellow Door since its inception. And who may I ask are you?"

"You can call me Cox, and you've no need to put a Mister in front of it as no one else ever has," the man said. "I've heard of you and what you've done to us." Cox hooked his thumbs in his belt, closed an eye, cocked his head and stepped closer to Topper.

"This may sound fantastic, but until just moments ago, we were held captive against our will," Topper said aloud to all in the room, ignoring Cox.

But Cox would not be ignored. "I should say it does sound fantastic as you say, Mr. Topper. I should say it does. That's a right dandy pair of coat-skirts you've got at your backsides there. Mighty fine material, I'd say. Your prisoner rags?"

"I can explain all that," Topper said.

"As I have no doubt you can. No doubt at all. I see you've brought your *friend* with you as well," said Cox walking toward Trumbull and wiping his hands on his sides.

Topper said with a nervous laugh, "Yes, Mr. Trum..., ah Mr. Dawson and I have become only too well acquainted of recent."

"I'll bet you have," Cox said. "You don't look as if you've eaten on prison rations while you were gone, Sir." Cox walked back over to Topper, placed his hands on his hips and stared him square in the eye. "You're not a very bright one, now, are ye? Come back here to flaunt your pretty little selves. Did you think no one would notice? Where's the charity's money, Mr. Topper? Give it over. Or have you spent it all?"

"Money? I'm sure I have no idea what you're talking about," Topper said and turned to meet Trumbull's blank expression.

Trumbull said, "Someone's taken money from Yellow Door?"

"Yes, and you're the one who's nicked it, and I says give it over. We're hungry. We ain't had nothing but grey slops in months," Cox said.

Mr. Crackers stood from his table on the far side of the room. "Mr. Topper's an honest man, Cox. Leave him be. He didn't take Mr. Scrooge's money."

Some murmured in doubt, some in anger.

Cox turned on him. "Then who did?" A half-dozen chairs squeaked back and men stood threateningly. The women ushered their children out the door, their eyes dark, clutching their hands to their mouths.

"If there's a villain in all this, it's The Reverend Mitchell. He ain't half so pious as he makes out!" Crackers said. "Every man, woman, and child here knows that what it's been like here since he and Fleming took over."

"It's the villain who runs away, the way I see it," Cox said. "It's an honest man who stays behind and does his work. The Reverend does the best he can with what little money's left." Cox reached and knocked Topper's silk hat from atop his head.

Money flew in all directions.

Everyone in the dining room leapt to their feet with their arms wind-milling. Some grabbed for the bills darting madly through the air. Some grabbed at their neighbours' noses. Others wanted Topper—they wanted any piece of him that they could grab, no matter how big or how small.

"Wait! This is all a mistake. You must believe me. I've done you no wrong." Topper felt hands pulling at his clothes, at his hair. He bit one dirty hand which grabbed his ear.

They shall tear Trumbull and me to pieces, he thought. *No, it can't end this way.*

Topper felt the coat rip from his back. Apples, pears, strawberries and all the other foodstuffs from his pockets rolled across the floor and were smashed under foot of the raging crowd. One man had one of his arms and another man the other. They worked at cross purposes much to Topper's distress.

Topper could hear Trumbull fighting like a cat. Apparently he had spirit for this sort of thing because Topper saw many a man groan and sink to the floor after Trumbull battered his shins with a broken table leg.

Someone lifted a chair and hurled it at Trumbull. He ducked but as he did so someone kicked the chair leg from his hand.

Rough hands knocked Topper to the ground, curled around his throat and squeezed. He tried without success to twist from beneath the sweaty bulk crushing his chest. Consciousness was all but lost when he felt the weight dragged away. He gasped, sat up. Trumbull pulled him to his feet.

"Mr. Trumbull," Topper said, "I do believe you have yourself a blackened eye."

Trumbull touched his left eye gingerly. Around them pandemonium still raged. "Let's get out of here while we can," Trumbull said.

They pushed their way out of the hall and ran down the passageway. Topper pulled open the door which he was surprised to find was no longer yellow and stepped outside.

"Dear God," Topper said looking at the snow drifting down now shin deep. "How long have we been trapped in that room?"

⊙

The damp slithered down Mrs. Topper's collar and set her violently shivering in spite of her heavy shawl and thick layers of clothing. The gas lamp looming before the building of their interest was one of the few lights for them to focus their attention. All else was sheets of blowing snow.

"However shall we get in?" she said to Miss Goosegrass. They huddled between two tall stacks of crates in front of an abandoned building on the opposite side of the street. *How much longer can we take the cold?* she wondered.

"I've no idea," Miss Goosegrass replied, her frosty breath curling round her head. "Have faith. Something will come to us. Let us wait and watch."

Mrs. Topper flexed her numb fingers without patience and wondered just how much faith she had left. After watching several guilty-looking young men creep to the front door across the street, she abruptly said, "It's a bawdy house," and laughed.

"I do not see how you find that amusing," Miss Goosegrass said through chattering teeth. "Although I should expect no less of The Reverend Mitchell."

"I knew such horrid things existed, of course, but I didn't believe I should ever see such a thing," said Mrs. Topper.

"And now I expect you will wish to see it from the inside," Miss Goosegrass said.

"Well, of course. How else will we discover the Reverend's lair and free my husband?" Mrs. Topper said.

"What if we get inside and cannot find him?"

"Oh, I shall not give up," Mrs. Topper said, almost cheerily. "We can then chalk it up to yet another exciting life experience."

Miss Goosegrass shivered and stomped her feet. "I'd rather not, if it's all the same to you. Especially not on Christmas Eve. My idea of a desirable life experience just now is a cup of tea and a hot bath."

"Don't tell me you are backing out now that we are on the Reverend's door-step?" Mrs. Topper said, sharply.

"No, of course not," said Miss Goosegrass. "Not at all. We are a team, to be sure. You will forgive me my desire for creature comforts."

"You are forgiven. And I must ask your forgiveness when I seem impatient." She clenched her small fist and smacked it vigorously into the palm of her other hand. "I have not the forbearance for this standing around in such weather. I believe we should be bold, walk up to the door, beat upon it and demand to be let in. We might say that our husbands are inside, and we mean to see them home on Christmas Eve."

Miss Goosegrass said, "Yours may be."

"If it were only that simple," Mrs. Topper said. She peered out from her place of concealment and squinted hatefully at the building.

"And do you believe that they would let us in?" said Miss Goosegrass.

"Perhaps not," Mrs. Topper admitted. "Unless they are interested in chatting with a couple of frozen Esquimeaux women. We need a better plan."

An hour later they had one.

The wind died down, and the snow fell fine and wet—almost rain. The air warmed slightly, and Mrs. Topper stopped shivering though she was hardly less miserable.

"Wait a moment," said Miss Goosegrass pointing at a figure lurking below the gas lamp. "I believe I recognise that one. Isn't that Jimmy Hawk?"

"Who is Jimmy Hawk?" said Mrs. Topper who shivered herself all over again.

"One of my former pupils," said Miss Goosegrass. "And not a terribly shining example, either, I must admit."

"Do you believe he could help us get in?" Mrs. Topper said, twisting her hands anxiously.

"I couldn't guess, but it's worth a try. What shall I do? Call him?"

"Yes. You'd better do so quickly before he disappears inside," Mrs. Topper said.

Jimmy Hawk pulled his cap down on his head, folded his arms and looked back and forth as if he feared he might be watched. He scuffed the snow with his foot and began to wander away.

"He looks as if he's having second thoughts," Miss Goosegrass said. "There isn't a moment to lose." She stepped away from the crates and half-way across the street. "Jimmy! Jimmy Hawk!" she shouted hoarsely.

The young man's head snapped in her direction. He squinted his eyes against the lamplight and the snow.

"Who is it? How do you know my name?"

"I would like a word with you if I may," said Miss Goosegrass. Mrs. Topper stepped from behind her place of concealment and gave a wan smile which she wasn't certain he could see.

"Well, all right then," Jimmy said with the smile of a ladies' man, stuffed his hands in his pockets, and strode quickly in her direction. "What can I do for you two ladies on this Christmas Eve?"

"Do you know me?" said Miss Goosegrass. She turned her face to the light.

He squinted at her. "Miss Goosegrass! What are you doing 'ere?"

She took him by the arm and pulled him into the shelter between the crates. "Mrs. Topper, I would like you to meet a former student of mine, Jimmy Hawk."

"S'my pleasure, ma'am," Jimmy said touching his forelock respectfully.

"I'm pleased to meet you, Mr. Hawk," Mrs. Topper said.

"Jimmy, we have a favour to ask of you," Miss Goosegrass said.

"Certainly, Miss. But if I may be so bold as to ask, what brings you two respectable ladies out in this part of town on Christmas Eve? H'aint you got families to visit? Or is it charity? Delivering food to a needy family or some such?"

"Never mind that now, Jimmy," Miss Goosegrass said. "We have important business to attend to, and it can't wait."

"All right then. What can I do for you?"

"Can you get us inside that building?" Mrs. Topper said.

"That building over there?" Jimmy said nodding sceptically in the direction of the bawdy house.

"Yes, that building."

"What would a couple of respectable women like yourselves be interested in going into a place like that?" said he. "You got 'usbands inside? Is that it?"

"Well, no. I mean, yes," said Mrs. Topper. "Can you help us out?"

"I don't see as 'ow," Jimmy said.

"Couldn't you take us in with you? You know. A girl on each arm. Looking for a room?" said Mrs. Topper. She loosened a couple of buttons over her bosom and said, "Would this help?" When she felt the wind she quickly buttoned up again.

Jimmy looked down and shuffled his feet. "It don't work that way, it don't," said he.

"It doesn't work that way," Miss Goosegrass corrected.

"'It doesn't work that way,'" he repeated with a blush. "Pardon my grammar, Miss. It's me mates. They all talk like that. A bad 'abit like."

"Couldn't you go inside and unlatch the back door for us?" asked Mrs. Topper.

"You two ladies don't think I was going inside, do you?"

"No. Of course not. But if you could just help us out that much, I would be terribly grateful."

"Well, I'll see what I can do. Give me twenty minutes and scurry your-selves round to the backdoor. If I can manage it, it'll be open. If not. Then I've given it me best."

"You always were a resourceful boy," said Miss Goosegrass.

"I'll take that as a compliment, Miss G," Jimmy said. He put a knuckle to the bill of his cap and crossed the street.

"Twenty minutes," Mrs. Topper said and bit her lower lip. "That's a long time in this weather."

"It may take longer," Miss Goosegrass said.

"I hope not. what do you expect he's doing at this moment?"

"I'm sure I haven't the slightest idea," Miss Goosegrass said.

"Do you think it's been twenty minutes yet?"

"It hasn't been one."

"Of course. How silly of me," Mrs. Topper said. She leaned back against the cold brick of the wall behind her. She felt her stomach muscles tighten as if she anticipated being struck. There was no way to keep time, so she counted slowly to herself to sixty, twenty times.

"That should do it," she said. "Let's go."

They lifted their skirts and waded across the street, looking warily as they went. They stopped in the shadows, breathing hard and trying to catch the sound of being followed.

Nothing.

The space between the buildings was narrow enough that Mrs. Topper could touch both buildings at once, and she did so to keep her balance and to prevent from slipping on the ice. They stepped over dark heaps and around grey rotting masses which the snow did not cover until they reached the back. The clouds parted and a sliver of moon leaked a little light onto the space behind the building. The wind swept the snow low to the ground, and the two followed it through what might have once been a small garden long lost to anyone's attention. Several windows to the back of the building had lit windows, but most were black.

The two women gripped one another's hand and strode as purposefully toward the door as the snow would allow. Mrs. Topper felt her heart thumping in her chest, and she spun all sorts of explanations of varying likelihood as to why they were there should they be discovered. She wondered if she should share them with Miss Goosegrass so that they might not contradict one another should they become separated.

Too late for that now, she thought, and gripped the handle of the door. She twisted it and found that it moved freely. Mrs. Topper gave a gasp of satisfaction and pushed the door in. The door moved with such a groan that Mrs. Topper felt that even the dead should know of it. They waited and listened in the dark passageway just beyond. After counting to two hundred and hearing no other sound she whispered to Miss Goosegrass, "Let's go."

Mrs. Topper walked along, one hand gripping Miss Goosegrass's, the other feeling the wall. They moved rather swiftly for all the darkness. Her hand never detected a door nor a window as she went. The passage made a series of rapid right angles to the left or to the right, so that at length Mrs. Topper had no sense of which direction they had gone or if in some way they might be going in circles. The passageway at length grew warm enough that they were able to unbutton their coats.

At last they came to the end. Mrs. Topper with a sigh of relief clasped a door-handle. She squeezed Miss Goosegrass's hand as a message of reassurance which she did not herself feel, and swung the door in.

They were blinded by light and threw their arms up until their eyes had adjusted. Lowering their arms they found themselves standing in a small room with a chamber-pot, a wash stand, a small mirror, soap, men's razors, and other articles of toilet.

"This is no doubt a place where the men freshen themselves," Mrs.

Topper said, her bosom heaving with excitement. "That door should lead into the main passageway. If need be we will split up and search separately."

"I don't believe that is a good idea," Miss Goosegrass said.

"Why ever not? We may make the quickest search in such a way."

"What if one of us should be discovered?"

"Then the other may escape and get help. The Bow Street Runners will surely come if I tell them a school mistress is being held captive in a house of ill-repute against her will. The more so on the holiday evening."

Miss Goosegrass gave her a dark look.

"All right then. Let us stay together in the beginning," Mrs. Topper said, smiling in chagrin. "Now let us slip into the passageway and see where it leads us."

She opened the door, stepped through and was met by a curious sight. Rather than a passageway she found herself in a large room of a scale sufficient to give a ball. In the centre of the room was a smaller structure, as if it had been a room within a room. The walls of the structure had been knocked down, however, and much of the wood had been stacked in neat piles.

On the same wall through which they had entered were two other doors.

"This way," Mrs. Topper said, pulling on Miss Goosegrass's arm. "Perhaps one of these doors will take us where we want to go."

The first door she opened led into a small room with a table in the centre filled with food freshly laid out: turkeys, geese, game, poultry, cheese, ham, sausages, oysters, pies, puddings, fruit, and punch.

"Someone is preparing for their Christmas dinner," said Miss Goosegrass. It had been some hours since they had eaten.

"I do not believe you would offend anyone should you care to have a slice of that ham," said Mrs. Topper. She smiled at her companion weakly and stepped back out of the room. The third and last door was solemnly closed. *Surely it leads to a corridor.*

The handle yielded to her grip and she opened it. Her lungs gave a disappointed burst of air as she saw that the room contained only two beds, a couple of books and other personal items, and no way out. She dashed back into the room with the men's toiletries and twisted the knob of the door through which they had entered. It would not budge. She gave a cry of frustration.

"What is it?" Miss Goosegrass said, daintily nibbling a slice of ham.

"We're trapped," Mrs. Topper said with a moan. She stepped into the room to examine its contents.

"Look at this," Miss Goosegrass said. "*Robinson Crusoe*. I've not read that book in a good long while."

Mrs. Topper stepped into the room as if she had not heard her companion. A stack of papers sat squared to the edge of the table just as was her husband's habit. Her eyes moved over them and instantly she recognised the hand-writing. She scooped them up, read them and wept.

⊙

Topper's breath came in gasps. He clutched his side and panted, "I fear we have led the soft life for too long, Mr. Trumbull. We are in poor shape just now for a mad dash through the snow."

Mr. Trumbull could not catch his breath enough to make a reply before they were off again.

At length they ran into a narrow space between buildings, leaned forward and braced their hands on their knees out of fatigue.

"Do you believe we've been followed?" Mr. Trumbull said at last.

"Once word reaches The Reverend Mitchell that we're back, I have no doubt he will send word to the Magistrate. We can expect the Runners to be looking for us, and I, for one, do not intend to be found."

"Do you have any idea what the day is?" Trumbull said. "I was shocked to within an inch of my life to see snow. I didn't think we had been imprisoned more than a few weeks."

"I've no idea. My guess is that it is December at the very least. Perhaps later—the New Year. Wait, do you hear that?" Topper said cupping his hand to his ear.

"I'm sorry, but I can't hear anything for the sound of my gasping."

"Listen carefully. What do you hear?"

"Far away singing, but I can't distinguish any words," Trumbull said.

"I can tell you the words without hearing them," Topper said and sang in a rich baritone:

"Good King Wenceslas looked out on the feast of Stephen,
    When the snow lay round about deep and crisp and even.
    Brightly shone the moon that night though the frost was cruel,
    When a poor man came in sight gath'ring winter fuel."

Topper laughed. "They're singing Christmas carols! It must be Christmas or very near. It's hard for me to feel anything but cheerful when I hear that song, I must say."

"I'd feel a lot more cheerful if we could get out of this snow. We're not dressed for it," Trumbull said, hugging himself.

"Then we shall go to my abode," Topper said, grandly. "It is not so far from here."

"Do you think it's safe? It's likely to be the first place they'll look."

"I don't care if they do find me there. I must see my wife. I simply must."

Trumbull nodded. "I understand. Once we get warm and into dry clothes we can make other plans."

CHAPTER 21

ඉඈ

The Ball

"A COSTUME BALL? ON CHRISTMAS EVE? ON THE EVE OF OUR WEDDING?"
Scrooge said, shaking his head doubtfully. "I don't believe I've ever heard of
such before. Tongues will wag, I can promise you. We shall be the talk of the
town, Vivianna. Mark my words."

Mrs. Claypoole frowned at him. "Will you not get into the spirit of
things? For me. Could you not put on this simple costume? It is so small a
favour I ask of you."

"No," Scrooge said. "There are some things which I simply will not do. It
is not just beneath my dignity, for Heaven's sake, but it's Christmas Eve. I
thought we might stop by this ball your friend has been so kind as to throw
in our honour, have our punch, dance a dance or two, and make our way
back here for some quiet time together. We have much to reflect on. So
many plans to form for our future. You have not even begun to pack. If we
are to meet Tim Cratchit in Italy this week, we must prepare ourselves. The
wedding gifts! Think of all the wedding gifts you shall have to pack. Is it any
wonder that we should spend this evening in preparing ourselves?"

"Oh, Ebenezer," said Mrs. Claypoole. "We've servants to pack for us. To-
night is our night to have fun. To laugh. To dance. To be the centre of
everyone's attention and admiration."

"No, ma'am," he said, gazing at her fondly. "You shall be the centre of
attention. No one will look upon Ebenezer Scrooge with anything like the
intensity with which they will cast their eyes upon you." Scrooge lifted her

hand to his lips. He drank in her perfume dreamily. "At what time do you expect we should return?"

"Return? Ebenezer, this is our night together. We shall dance and dance and dance until the sun rises!"

"Until the sun rises? Dear me. I am not at all sure that these legs can hold me up so long, let alone dance, nor my eyes remain open. And look, here— here at the window. It snows! Can your driver manage your carriage through such drifts? We will be stranded and frozen before we can swear our nuptials. You wouldn't wish to delay our wedding, would you?"

"You worry far too much, my love. All will turn out well."

"Our wedding is to be held to-morrow at noon. Christmas Day. Our guests will be waiting, and where will we be?"

"They will not need wait upon us, my silly eager goose," said Mrs. Claypoole. "Come. Relax and join me. Or would you rather I go alone?"

"No no no. I shall accompany you. It is a husband's place in such matters," he said patting her hand. "I am eager to see you in your wedding dress. It will make a most handsome sight to my eyes. Most handsome." Scrooge's voice sparkled in anticipation.

"One does not wear a wedding dress to a costume ball, my darling. Not if one is a bride, that is. A wedding gown is not costume at all on such occasions."

Scrooge screwed his face curiously. "Then whatever shall you wear?" said he.

"Shall I surprise you?"

"No, tell me now."

"I shall go in costume as a shepherdess, and you shall be my flock."

"That is ridiculous," stammered Scrooge. "You expect me to pull on a fleece and prance about like some madman?"

"It is Christmas Eve, Love. Where is your spirit?" said Mrs. Claypoole.

"Spirit? This is not the kind of spirit I should expect on Christmas Eve."

"Very well, then," Mrs. Claypoole said, blinking her eyes agreeably. "You may wear whatever you wish. Far be it for me for people to say that Mrs. Scrooge will not permit her husband a mind of his own."

"Why don't you run along and put on your costume? I shall not be so humourless. Come! Let's see how you look."

"You won't be disappointed. Wait just one moment, and I shall return as your loving shepherdess." Mrs. Claypoole laughed lightly and dashed away up the stairs of her house.

Scrooge walked from window to window feeling the cold, watching the snow fall thick upon the ground. Yet the crackle of the fire in the hearth reassured him.

He thought back on that Christmas Eve just one year since. How different his life had been then. No promise. No hope. No one to care for. True enough, his health had been far better, but if he were asked to make his Life Sums he could not doubt that he would find himself to the good. Much to the good. Of course there were financial difficulties which were to be subtracted from his Life's Grand Total, but hadn't money been the source of his misery for so many years? Wasn't he happier now that debt threatened him? Perhaps not. The brightness in his heart came entirely in the form of a vividly beautiful young woman.

He heard the clatter of feet upon the stairs, their rapidity matched the beating of his heart. He swung round just as Mrs. Claypoole flew into the room and flung herself into his arms.

She drew herself back and gave him a glowing smile. "What do you think?"

Scrooge's eyes widened significantly. "How lovely you look! But...well, cut so low? You'll catch yourself a death of cold, I fear. There I go sounding harsh and critical again. I have no wish to spoil your fun, but, dear, be sure to wrap yourself well. I cannot but be anxious about the storm."

"That is why I love you so, Ebenezer. Such a practical man compared to myself. So protective and thoughtful. So much like my first husband, Robert."

Having mentioned his name, she grew silent and bit her lower lip.

"You were fond of him, weren't you?" he said, holding her close. "I know that I cannot possibly take his place, but I shall give to you my heart as unreservedly as he no doubt gave his to you. What man wouldn't, I should wonder?"

"You remind me of him in so many ways," she said, sadly.

◎

It had been summer the last time Topper had seen his home. A large elm had shaded the front step. Now, in the dark and snow, he shook as he approached it. Not from the cold, but from an incomprehensible fear. What would he find when he entered the house after being absent so long?

There were only five steps to the door, but he slipped on the third and fell to one knee. Trumbull grasped his arm and helped him to his feet. Topper's knee stung, and he saw that he had torn a hole in his pants.

He was forced to knock as he had no key, it having disappeared with his old suit of clothes. Two windows were lighted, but there was no sense of the cheer of the season. He waited for some time before he heard footsteps approach the door and saw the door cautiously open.

"Nancy," Topper said stepping through the door motioning Trumbull in behind. "How good to see you. Is your mistress in?"

He caught Nancy just before she hit the floor fainted dead away.

"Smelling salts?" Trumbull asked.

"I don't believe we have any. Perhaps if you'd grab a handful of snow just outside the door, I can bring her round."

Topper rubbed a small piece against her cheek. Nancy blinked her eyes and sat up.

"God love us, Mr. Topper, you're back," she said, her eyes filling with tears.

"Why thank you, Nancy," he said helping her to her feet. "Now tell me, where is Mrs. Topper?"

"She's gone out, Sir."

"Gone to her sister's?"

"I don't believe so, Mr. Topper. Her sisters were here earlier this evening to visit."

"Did she follow them back to either of their homes?"

"No, Sir," Nancy said. "The boy Patrick came to visit. After he left they seemed anxious to go. They made their excuses to Mrs. Conner and Miss Louisa and took their leave."

"*They?* Do you mean Mrs. Topper and one of her sisters?"

"No, Sir. Mrs. Topper and Miss Goosegrass."

"Miss Goosegrass? What was she doing here?"

"She's been staying with Mrs. Topper ever since you disappeared, Sir."

"Perhaps," Topper said, "you had better explain to me what's happened during my absence."

For half an hour Topper and Trumbull heard a detailed account of the events of the last few months.

"Do you have any idea what Patrick told them when he visited here?" Topper asked.

"I don't, but I know that he's been doing something for them since your disappearance."

"Looking for me, no doubt."

Nancy shook her head. "I couldn't say, Sir. I wouldn't be the sort of girl to listen at the door..."

"But if you were, dearest Nancy, what might you have heard?' Topper said, not unkindly.

"I would have heard, Sir..." she paused guiltily, "...that they have been trying to locate The Reverend Mitchell's late night destination."

"Oh, my God," Topper said, and Nancy drew back in horror. "We must find them immediately. Only young Patrick knows where she's gone. Where he stays at night I have no idea. He takes his breakfast at Yell... er, at the charity—beyond that I cannot say."

"He won't be hard to find to-night, Sir," Nancy said, cheerfully.

"How so?"

"He'll be singing his heart out at *The Copper Swan*."

"How do you know that, Nancy?"

"'Tis Christmas Eve, Sirs. He'll be there singing carols."

"Mr. Trumbull," Topper said, "we must get into dry things and make our way to *The Copper Swan*. There's not a moment to lose!"

◎

A sharp knock at the door startled Scrooge from his reverie. He heard the even tread of Anderson's step upon the thick carpet. Scrooge strained his ears, but detected no voices. A moment later Anderson appeared, his features without expression.

"Your coach has arrived, Mrs. Claypoole," he said and stood aside to allow them to pass.

Scrooge could think of no words to speak as he helped her on with her coat save, "My dear, my dear."

Scrooge and Mrs. Claypoole stepped through the door, and as they did so the wind howled. Scrooge pulled his collar high and stepped toward the carriage. Mrs. Claypoole fluttered to her seat as lightly as a bird, but Scrooge found he could not bend his knees in the cold to reach the first step. Any attempt to do so shot him white-hot stabs of pain so that he must clutch the carriage door to keep from doubling over.

"My dearest, what ails you?" Mrs. Claypoole said.

"'Tis nothing, dearest one. It is only these old knees. They do not want to bend in this weather." Scrooge felt strong hands grab him from behind and lift him into the carriage as if he were a mere child.

"Thankee," Scrooge turned to see whomever it was had aided him. Standing in the snow was the coachman, his face wrapped in a scarf so that only his glittering eyes shown. "Merry Christmas to you, Sir. Bless you," said Scrooge.

But the coachman made no reply to his holiday greetings. He pushed down the tall hat upon his head against the wind and climbed to his seat atop the carriage.

"Not many words to that fellow," Scrooge said to his companion. "No doubt he is ill-tempered in this weather, and who could blame him?" He leaned out the carriage window to look up at the man. Darkness had enveloped the driver and all that Scrooge could discern were his eyes.

Without a moment's notice, the driver flicked his whip and sent the horses flying. Scrooge and Mrs. Claypoole were flung back in their seats with a jolt, Scrooge grabbing for his hat, Mrs. Claypoole laughing in delight.

"What fun, Ebenezer," she said, "we shall party like this every night after we are married."

Scrooge could make no reply so intent was he at keeping himself in a single piece.

The snow flew by the windows of the coach obscuring Scrooge's view of the land. How odd it seemed to him, that the coach did not slide nor slip nor give any indication that the snow posed any sort of impediment to its progress. On they jumbled for twenty minutes, for forty, for one hour.

The coach stopped as abruptly as if it had struck a tree. Scrooge whose eyes had been squeezed tight, opened them and twisted his stiff neck toward the window. Outside were a pair of wrought-iron gates, black lines against the white snow. Scrooge whose eyes were not so strong gasped as he saw what appeared to be a wrought-iron devil flick its tail and turn its head toward him. Scrooge rubbed his eyes, but when his vision cleared the gate had been flung aside, and he could feel the coachman hoisting himself back to the driver's box.

The coach lurched on again, though this time Scrooge was braced for it. Past the window flashed snow-laden trees, frozen ponds, icy gardens, darkened out-buildings, columns and minarets from antiquity.

"These grounds are magnificent. And the building just ahead looks fit for a prince," said Scrooge to Mrs. Claypoole over his shoulder.

She placed a hand on his back and drew herself along side him. "He *is* a prince," she said.

"Surely, you jest. Prince of what land, I should ask."

"He is called Prince. Perhaps it is merely an honorific," she replied with a shrug.

"How do you know him?"

"He is a very, very old friend."

The coach pulled into a large circle before the main door and was met by a footman in a red velvet coat, matching knee pants, silk stockings, polished silver-buckle shoes and a powdered wig upon his head. He drew open the door of the coach and bowed gracefully.

"You are expected," he said, though Scrooge had difficulty making out his words, so thick was his accent.

"The Prince is here?" Mrs. Claypoole asked.

"Yes, Madame. He sends his compliments and asks to see you at your soonest convenience."

"You may send word that we will deliver ourselves to him directly. Please tell him that I have brought Mr. Scrooge with me. He will be pleased." She stepped down from the carriage, turned and offered Scrooge her hand.

"Thankee, my dear," Scrooge said. "It is a terrible thing to be so frail. However, a good woman will make a man reborn."

"Yes," said Mrs. Claypoole, coldly and looked toward the door. "When we are inside, there are a number of men...and women...I shall have to give my attention. You may wander where you wish. When it is time to meet the Prince, I shall find you. I won't be long."

"Of course, of course," said Scrooge. "It's just that on this evening... I don't suppose there will be guests here whom I... Well, no matter. Do not be concerned about me. I shall mix with the guests. Mill about, as they say."

The doorman clad identically to the footman only in green made way for them.

"Rather festive," Scrooge said to Mrs. Claypoole at his arm. "Those colours, I mean. Red and green."

Mrs. Claypoole showed him a smile which indicated she wasn't listening to him.

⊙

Lucille Topper pulled herself through the bramble, her face, hands, arms and legs covered in shallow wounds. Blood, sweat, and mucus stung her eyes. Her tongue was thick, her mouth dry.

A dog bayed in the distance. A pause. A second call, this time nearer.

Hide!

Moonlight glinted in the greasy pools at her sides. She squinted. A dark shape ahead. Solid. Motionless. Tall. She crept forward, touched it and felt rough texture beneath her fingers. Bark. A tree.

Climb!

She staggered to her feet, filth streaming from her hair, from the rags that had been her dress. Her fingernails skittered around the tree's girth seeking purchase. No branches. Not even a snag to lift herself had she the strength.

She circled the tree, stripping away clumps of bark in frustration. Her hands felt a change in shape and texture. No longer convex. A cavity. The tree was dead. The tree was hollow. Mrs. Topper squeezed into the hole, covered herself with mud, sticks, weeds, moss, gravel—anything she could lay hands on. She lay without moving, only listening. Beetles and termites squirmed at her backside.

A low, four-legged creature stepped carefully into the water to her right. Even with eyes squeezed shut, she knew it bristled. Could sense the upright fur at the nap of its neck. The smell of decay overpowered her for a moment. Breath held, she listened. Listened. Listened.

It moved tentatively toward her and then away. Then further away until she could no longer hear its pad. She waited thirty heartbeats. A hundred more, then a hundred more. No longer able to contain herself she wrenched forward, pulling away from the tree, muck flying. Then a rush of quick footsteps in the water in front of her. A dead weight struck her in the chest and drove her back.

Lucille Topper's throat tensed to scream, and she sat straight up in bed. Her nightmare dissolved as she blinked her eyes only to be replaced by another.

Standing over her was Salvation Mitchell. His leering face differed from when last she saw it, he then in his guise as the gentle Reverend. In his true form he was part man, part insect and part something to which she could put no name.

"You do not seem to be quite so plain a cow now, charwoman," said Mitchell, his teeth a confusion of razor edges.

Mrs. Topper's throat tensed again, and this time it produced sound, more battle-cry than token of fear. Miss Goosegrass, startled awake, flung her body protectively across her. Mitchell brushed the school mistress aside as if she weighed no more than a kitten.

"I am so happy you were able to accept my invitation," Mitchell said. "I hope you find the rooms acceptable as a clever associate of mine has gone to a great deal of trouble to see that they are private. It wouldn't do to have our little tête-à-tête subject to interruption."

Mitchell stared at her, running a lengthy tongue over his silvery lips.

"But look!" said he. "Two have joined the tryst, and I couldn't be more pleased. Two pretty little fish. You..." he pointed to Miss Goosegrass, "...I will throw you to Bop. He has a taste for women with your colour of hair, I am told." He rubbed his nose. "But you, my pretty, young Mrs. Topper, I shall keep for myself."

"Be not so sure, Reverend Mitchell." She thrust her hand against his bosom. "I have read my husband's letters and am aware of the significance of this ring."

The Reverend Mitchell drew back and howled in a voice not remotely human. The palm print of Mrs. Topper's hand burned through his shirt deep into the skin of his chest. She withdrew it, ring glittering on her middle finger, and held it before his eyes.

"Damn you!" Mitchell swore.

"How rude," Mrs. Topper said, her eyes snapped with a hellish light of their own. "When a lady offers you her ring, you must kiss it. Otherwise I am afraid we shall have to take our leave. Kindly open the door."

"No," said Mitchell, pulling smoking tatters of linen from his chest. "Never. The Ring of Three may prevent me from harming you, but you may not use it to force your will upon me. You are still very much my prisoner and will remain so until I choose to release you or you choose to capitulate to my desires."

Miss Goosegrass rushed to Mrs. Topper's side. Together they stood and drew nearer and nearer to Mitchell, Mrs. Topper's ring hand outstretched before her. The ring gave a pearly light which flickered in Mitchell's wide eyes.

Mitchell backed away from them like a trapped animal, out of the small bedroom into the larger room. His teeth glittered like a dog's. He snapped and lunged at the two, but never did he dare touch them and neither would they retreat.

Mrs. Topper pressed further and further until he was backed into a corner.

"Release us or I shall press this ring first to your heart and then against that hideous face of yours. Yield or suffer unimaginable pain!"

Mitchell coiled and lashed out—not at Mrs. Topper, but at Miss Goosegrass. The school mistress drew away with an awkward twist.

A pin-prick of light burst from the ring on Mrs. Topper's finger and struck Mitchell's left arm. It burst into flame. Mitchell flung himself against the wall, slapped at the tongues of fire and shouted, "Magician! Magician!"

The room shuddered as if in an earthquake. Mrs. Topper and Miss Goosegrass fell to the floor. Mrs. Topper sat up. She saw the wall behind him warp. A previously invisible orifice dilated, and he darted inside. It closed behind without a sound.

⊙

Scarcely had they stepped through the door when Mrs. Claypoole was whisked away by a dozen probing hands. Scrooge worked his face into a cordial smile while scores of elegant couples dressed in outrageous costumes rushed by on either side paying him not the slightest attention. Scrooge felt vulnerable as if his backsides were bare for all to see, so he retreated against the wall, found himself a chair and sat himself in it.

There were buffoons, there were *improvvisatori*, there were Pierrot, there were strolling musicians, there was wine. White-bearded men high upon stilts glided through the crowd throwing confetti and handfuls of gold coins. In the fountains lounged women with fish tails and teeth like sharks. Peacock-costumed figures in turquoise, aqua, and lapis cried "Help! Oh, help!" to one another and spread their shivering tails.

Every one of them, with Scrooge being the only exception, wore a masque of fantastic character. And every one of them staggered from drink.

The crowd at length cleared a space before him so that he could for the first time appreciate the scale of the room. So large he would have never guessed from the outside. The ceiling was lost in darkness, and wasn't the hearth at the opposite end of the hall the largest Scrooge had ever seen? He would need to climb a ladder to touch its mantel.

Scrooge grew curious. He stood and rotated in a small circle trying to take it all in. This friend of Mrs. Claypoole's must truly be a Prince for this hall was all Carrara marble, granite and other polished stones he could not identify. Which quarry did this come from with its stripes so like a tiger's? And where was stone quarried which is at first pink, then mauve a moment later, and then a moment later a dull ochre? And did his imagination play tricks or could he not make out the faces of weeping men in its dips and swirls?

The walls where they were not covered with heavy wool tapestries, held cracked oil-paintings twenty feet high and a hundred-twenty feet across with images of dark creatures, half-human, half-animal, scheming to end men's lives painfully and in tragedy.

Great gouts of crimson streamers fell to the ground from the ceiling moving in a wind from no direction to speak of. Gold and ormolu fixtures glittered in the torch light. Scrooge traced the number six hundred sixty-six set in onyx on the floor with the toe of his shoe and wondered at its significance.

A sound drew Scrooge's attention left. A man in a costume crested with arabesque feathers of blue, violet and pale yellow ran laughing up a twisting staircase with torch held high. As he rose, the flickering light revealed among the shifting shadows a snaking network without destination.

"What is this place?" Scrooge clasped his arms about him. "Wherever can Mrs. Claypoole be? I would counsel her not to stay here long."

"There you are, Scrooge," said Mrs. Claypoole, touching his arm. "I've looked all over for you."

"I've scarcely moved away from the door," he said, eyes still locked to the maze above him.

"So you have. So you have," she said. "I must teach you to not be so shy. Come with me. I have someone I wish you to meet, and he is no little interested in meeting you. He has spoken at great length of you more often than you could believe."

"The Prince?"

"Yes, the Prince. Come. Follow me. I will show you the way. It is just there. On the balcony. Do you see?"

Scrooge squinted at the wall opposite and saw seated upon the balcony a figure surrounded by a half-dozen girls clad in diaphanous garments.

"Vivianna," he said, "I don't believe we should stay. It grows late, and I must confess that my old pains have returned to me with a vengeance I can no longer ignore. Shall we leave?"

"I have no wish to offend the Prince. Do you?" said she.

"I have no wish to offend anyone, but these partygoers are rather too decadent for my tastes. And it's Christmas Eve, my love. I do believe in making merry with family and friends but this, this is nothing short of barbarous."

"Once the dancing starts you will soon change your mind." She gave him the smallest kiss upon the cheek. "Now let us be received by the Prince. Please don't disappoint me."

"Very well, my dear. I would not wish that. Let us go and give our greetings to your prince. Then I must insist that we leave. We have a long day before us on the morrow, and I would be better prepared for it if I get myself proper rest. Some drops might be in order for this night as I am afraid I have become agitated."

"The coach's ride was not the smoothest, I will admit. Can a return trip be any more pacific?" she asked. "Perhaps we would be better to stay the night."

Scrooge waved the idea aside. "No, I should think not. However, let us go to present ourselves to your friend now—wish him a Merry Christmas."

Mrs. Claypoole glided forward looking ever more beautiful in her shepherdess costume. Scrooge stumbled along at her side, tripping over the bodies of intoxicated guests—more than a few locked in passionate embraces.

"My dear," he said, "I think we really must go." But he followed her nevertheless as she guided him up the stairs, up step after painful step, to stand before the Prince. His retinue of girls disappeared at the wave of a hand, much to Scrooge's relief.

The Prince did not rise to greet them, but Scrooge noted that had he done so he would have been twice Scrooge's height. Yet the creature was as thin as a man made of twigs. His arms and legs were covered in a baggy suit of blue silk, as were the gloves upon his hands and the hood draped low over his brow. All that could be seen were two red sparks for eyes. To his lower face he held a scented scarf to match the rest of his garb. He bowed from his seat.

"You will forgive me if I do not rise," said the Prince. "This cloth," he shook his silk scarf lightly, "treats a condition." His voice was low with a bur which Scrooge could not place. "When you are as old as I am, you too will understand."

Scrooge placed his hand to his heart and bowed. "I am delighted to meet you, Your Royal Highness. It is kind of you to invite us here this Christmas Eve."

"Yes, yes," the Prince said, waving his other stick-like hand. "This is a very important occasion for us. We mean to celebrate, and we are a lot given to much sin. Surely a man of your experience will not bat an eye by anything which you might see here. I am sure you have seen and perhaps done much worse yourself."

"You are mistaken, Your Royal Highness, for I am a Christian man with Christian values."

"Of course, of course. I do not wish to offend you, but only wish to make small talk as one man to another, but I forget your bride who stands at your side. We have perhaps shocked her."

Mrs. Claypoole shook her head. "There is very little which shocks me, Your Royal Highness, as you should be aware."

The Prince laughed, his breath blowing past the scarf held before his face. The stench struck Scrooge's nose and his legs buckled with nausea.

"What do you think of these habiliments of mine?" said the Prince to Scrooge plucking at the bosom of his blouse. "This shade of blue. Have you ever seen anything like it? It is a perfect match to the colour of your bride's eyes, wouldn't you say?"

"They are very fine, Your Majesty," Scrooge said, but did not need to test the comparison. *Why has my bride given the Prince the silk for her dress?*

"Tell me, Mr. Scrooge," said the Prince, "how does it feel for an old bachelor like you to know that you will be married to-morrow? You will lie with a woman so young? How will you please her?"

Scrooge turned scarlet and tugged Mrs. Claypoole's arm to draw her away. "You will excuse us, Your Royal Highness," he said and turned.

"No, you are the honoured guests of the evening. You may not leave. I will not permit it. You must sit and at the very least watch the dance. Thereafter you may leave if you so wish. I will not stop you then." Two high-backed thrones were brought for Scrooge and Mrs. Claypoole to sit upon.

"It grows late," Scrooge insisted.

"Humbug! You will anger me if you do not allow me to entertain you with a simple dance. Surely you are not too frail to watch Christian men and women dance?" said the Prince.

"I am afraid I must insist," Scrooge said.

"Look! They have started. Sit quietly now, or I'll have you dragged to the floor, and you will dance among them like a puppet. You may not tell me no."

"A minuet performed with grace and distinction might prove an entertaining diversion at this moment," Scrooge said fixing his eyes angrily before him.

"You will see no minuets here this evening, Mr. Scrooge. This dance you will see has been called both vulgar and sinful by those who are in a position to know. I will let you yourself judge whether it is indecent or no. It is called a Waltz."

"I have not heard of it," Scrooge said.

"It is not unknown. Your King when he was Prince Regent included such a dance as this at a ball not long ago. If it suits one Prince, it will suit another," the Prince said with a philosophical wave of his hand.

The dance began and though no dancer himself Scrooge could not help but notice the voluptuous intertwining of the limbs, the intimate juxtaposition of the bodies of the dancers.

"It is the dance of adulteresses and prostitutes," Scrooge hissed.

The Prince nodded approvingly. "Just so, just so," he muttered.

Holding firmly to Mrs. Claypoole's hand, Scrooge hauled himself to his feet. "This dance display is complete?"

"Not for many hours. We have other dances to show you. From Buenos Aires. From Belize. I forget all where. We pick these things up as we travel, don't you see?"

"Nevertheless, Your Royal Highness, I have made my excuses many times to you this evening and do not need to repeat them. Mrs. Claypoole and I will now bid you good-night."

"Very well. As you wish," the Prince said, sitting back in his throne. After a heartbeat he held up a hand to stop them. "Oh, Mrs. Claypoole, I nearly forgot." He reached into the breast of his blouse and withdrew a thick piece of peach-coloured paper, folded in half and sealed with a blot of crimson wax.

"This came for you just before you arrived. You may wish to read it here and now as it may be of some importance," The Prince said.

Mrs. Claypoole gave Scrooge a questioning look. "Go on, read it," he said. "It won't take you more than a moment."

Mrs. Claypoole broke the seal and unfolded the thick sheath. Her lips moved as she read silently to herself. She spread her arms and shouted, "This is wonderful news, my love!"

"What is it, dearest? What news could possibly excite you so?" said he.

"It is a message from my husband."

Scrooge felt his knees buckle beneath him, and he clutched for the arms of the chair he had risen from just moments before.

"He is in London just now, having been carried over from India by the *Ulysses*," she explained with her cheeks flushed with delight.

"But, but...but he is dead."

"So I had thought, but this letter explains all. Shall I read it to you?"

"I thought you said that you couldn't read?" Scrooge said.

"Well, yes, but one can learn can't one? You didn't expect me to be ignorant forever, did you? Stop asking so many feckless questions, Scrooge, and attend me. It says here that he was left for dead—you remember the letter I spoke of to you when first we met which explained how he had died in service—but he was only gravely ill. An Indian girl heard him moan as his body was being stacked in a pile of corpses meant to be burned, you see, and so over a time of four months, it says, 'she has nursed me back to my good health, and it is just recently that I have been able to remember who I am.' Isn't that just wonderful, darling? My husband lives! Can you give me joy, I ask you? Can you think of a better thing that a woman could ever wish for upon a Christmas Eve?"

"I cannot," Scrooge said, and pulled himself to his feet. The Prince was nowhere to be seen. "I offer you and your husband best wishes, and if you'll excuse me, I must be leaving." Scrooge half-expected the touch of her hand to turn him back, but when he glanced round he found her gone. Gone too were the revellers who had filled the hall. The only remaining person was Ebenezer Scrooge.

◉

Topper removed his hat as they entered *The Copper Swan*. The warmth of the fire, the happy chatter of the crowd, and the smell of food and drink hit him and at once he felt himself grow sleepy.

He and Trumbull found an empty table and sat themselves. They ordered up chops and mulled wine, unbuttoned their coats and looked at one another with meaningful glances. They kept silent and listened to the conversations of others. Topper was eager for news, but didn't wish to appear to be ignorant.

When the serving girl sat their plates upon the table, Topper asked, "Will there be singing this evening? Isn't *The Copper Swan* known for its Christmas carols?"

"Oh yes, Sir," said she. "A boy sings here this evening, and if he ain't the one. Has the voice of a bird, he does." She smiled prettily at Trumbull who had caught her eye. "Patrick Coal, he is. He's just catching his supper in the kitchen, but he should be returned 'ere long."

"Patrick Coal?" Topper said, theatrically. "Do you mean the boy so high..." He held his hand at an appropriate level. "Dark hair and plays the most unusual array of musical instruments?"

"That would be the very same boy, Sir. Do you know him?" she said continuing to grace Trumbull with her best smiles.

"Do I know him? Indeed, I should say that I do. I know him quite well. In fact," he reached into his pocket and drew forth a coin which he slipped into her hand, "I would regard it as an honour if you were to give him a message for me. Please tell him that Mr. Topper sits in the audience and would like to have a word with him at his soonest opportunity. That's all. And bless you, girl."

She curtsied, blushed and looked as if she wished for something to say to Trumbull. Neither she nor he could think of anything but to smile at one another. A moment later someone shouted, "Molly, there's other customers, you know."

"If you kind gentlemen will excuse me," she said and hustled herself away.

"I believe she caught your eye," Topper said. "A charming young woman, I must say."

"Oh, I hadn't noticed," Trumbull said, lifting a cup to his face to cover his expression.

"My word," said Topper, "I believe I've caught you in a lie."

"This is not the time for me to charm young women," Trumbull said.

"No, it is not. To be sure. Still—you must take her attentions as a compliment, and perhaps when this is all over you can return here to have your dinner again."

Trumbull shrugged. "After I've found my sister."

"Mr. Topper!" a voice exclaimed and Topper looked up to see Patrick Coal making his way through the crowd toward them. Patrick was often stopped by men who slapped his back in congratulations and forced a coin into his palm. He wished them all Merry Christmas, but cheerfully broke away one after another until he stood by Topper's side.

"Mr. Topper," said Patrick, hardly able to suppress himself. "Mrs. Topper found you!"

"That's one of the reasons we are here this evening," Topper said, evenly.

"Something's wrong, isn't it?" Patrick's face grew serious.

"There may be," Topper said. "I recently returned home—I don't have time to explain the circumstances surrounding my absence—but Mrs. Topper has gone missing. I have reason to believe that you may know where she is."

Patrick's face reddened.

"What can you tell me, young man?" Topper said.

"Mrs. Topper and Miss Goosegrass asked me to do them a favour."

"What favour?" Topper said.

"They was trying to find you, Sir, and they reasoned that Reverend Mitchell was behind your disappearances. They tried following him to see where he went each evening, but always he slipped away from them."

"How well I know that," Trumbull said. "The man disappears like a ghost."

Patrick said, "Miss Goosegrass asked me if me and me mates could keep our eyes open. Not follow him exactly, but put out the word to watch for him and note when and where he's seen. It took months, but we finally found where he goes."

Topper said, "Where *does* he go then, boy?"

Patrick told him.

"Did you tell Mrs. Topper this?" Topper asked.

"Worse," Patrick said looking down in shame. "I took her there and came back here myself to sing."

"How could you?"

Patrick did not reply, but flushed a deep crimson.

Topper said, "There, there. Don't blame yourself, Patrick. Mrs. Topper can be a very persuasive person. I should know. And Miss Goosegrass as well. The thing to do is not fret over the past, but to take action now. Could you take us there?"

Patrick looked back over the crowd. "What do I do about them, Sir? They're expecting to sing Christmas carols."

Topper stroked his chin in thought. "Mr. Trumbull. How is your singing voice?"

"My what?" Trumbull said.

"Your singing voice. Your Christmas carols. Surely you know the words to at least a dozen."

"I wouldn't say that I am blessed with a very good singing voice," Trumbull said nervously.

"Nonsense, All you need do is open your mouth, give forth with a joyous sound, and the crowd will do the rest for you."

"I couldn't possibly," Trumbull said, his face flushing above his beard.

Just then the serving girl returned to their table.

"Is there anything else I can do for the gentlemen?" she said.

"No, I don't believe so," Topper said, "but thank you just the same."

She didn't leave, but stood there swaying slightly from side to side. "If there's anything else you'll be sure to let me know," she said.

Topper glanced knowingly at Trumbull. "If I may introduce my friend: this is Mr. Lincoln Trumbull," he said. "From America," he added.

Patrick gave him a puzzled look.

"My name is Milton Topper as I have said. Merry Christmas to you, Miss."

"Merry Christmas to you, Sir," she said. "My name is Molly Jones."

"My friend here is rather shy, but I believe it would be the jolliest thing if he would lead us all in holiday song. I am completely unable to persuade him, however," said Topper, "but perhaps you could...a Christmas carol?"

She grasped Trumbull lightly under the arm and lifted him as easily from his seat as if he were a feather. "Come, Sir. Step up with me to the front, and let us sing together. It is Christmas Eve!"

Trumbull gave Topper a sheepish look as he was pulled through the crowd. Before he had opened his mouth for the first song, Topper and Patrick Coal had left the protection of *The Copper Swan*.

⊙

Scrooge shuffled painfully to the door. His only wish was that a coach remained which could take him back to his own chambers. The door swung open before he touched its handle. Scrooge looked into the swirling snow and beheld the carriage which brought him and Mrs. Claypoole perhaps only an hour since. He crawled inside, this time without help, and the door closed behind of its own volition. The carriage lurched but Scrooge cared not a whit that he bounced against the upholstery like a billiard ball. Not a whit.

An hour later, the rig stopped not before his own home, nor in front of the charity. It stopped instead before his rooms of the previous year, before his redemption and meeting of the spirits.

He stepped from the carriage and even before he could swing its door to, it had bolted away spraying him with snow and slush.

He stepped to the front door and stared at the ornate knocker at its centre. Here he had seen a vision of Marley exactly one year ago. Would Marley return? If so, he would come this time to bring Scrooge his chains. But Marley's face did not appear.

How would he get in? He had no key and the rooms were no longer his. He would sit on the street and freeze. It was cold enough.

The door, however, swung open at his slightest touch, and Scrooge climbed the dark stairway which he could have done blind. He felt for the doorknob, twisted it and it opened to him as it had thousands of times before. This was his room impossibly as he had left it one year since.

He swung his hat onto a peg and held a burning match to the stub of a candle. He hung his coat in its place, and pulled on his gown where he had left it.

Something to eat, Scrooge thought. *It grows late, and I need my rest.*

The glow from the fire threw little light, so he filled his bowl by feel and warmed it a little over the coals. He dipped a wooden spoon into the gruel and tasted it.

In an instant he threw the spoon and the bowl into the fire. He covered his eyes and wept harder than he had ever wept in his life.

"I am ruined. There is nothing left for me. Nothing. I have no money. I will spend my few remaining years in debtor's prison beyond the care or aid of anyone who might remember who I once was."

Scrooge cried until there were no more tears to shed. He threw himself back in his old chair and clamped hard his jaw.

The spirits showed me no ruin like this. I need my drops.

Without his knowing how it had gotten there, he found the leather-covered bottle in his lap. He pulled the stopper and tipped the bottle to his lips.

Before he could swallow, a soft knock sounded at the door.

"Go away and leave me my peace!" He nearly threw the bottle at it until he remembered what the bottle contained. "Go away!"

"Won't you invite me in?" said a voice.

"No. Who is it?"

"I can help you, if you'll permit me."

The voice was familiar, yet Scrooge could not remember where he had heard it.

"What do you want?" he asked, this time more quietly.

"You will need to open the door to see for yourself."

Scrooge stood rapidly to his feet, but a shooting pain compelled him to drop to a knee. "One moment," he said, massaging his back. "One moment, or perhaps two before I can rise again." He gasped for his breath. Once. Twice. Thrice. And he held the third until the pain left him. He crawled to the door and hauled himself up.

The door swung open, and he saw a male face crested by a physician's wig.

"Dr. Fluch," said Scrooge. "What are you doing here?"

"If you allow me in, I can explain all."

Scrooge stood aside. The physician stepped into the room. He looked round, but held any comment about its furnishings he might have had. "I trust I find you well," he said.

"You do not. You have eyes and don't need me to tell you what you can see for yourself."

"Just as you say. Nevertheless, I am here to inform you that I have been told of your troubles by an interested party and would like to offer you my assistance."

"There is nothing anybody can do for me. I only wish to be left alone," Scrooge said. "No, that's not true. Give me a draught which will help me forget."

"There will be no need for you to forget, Sir."

"I don't understand you."

"Then you must listen. It is all very simple as I'm sure you will agree."

Scrooge twisted his head from side to side, but gave no reply.

"All of your difficulties may be summed up in one person, and you know who that one person is," Fluch said.

Scrooge thumped his forefinger into his own chest. "Me," he said and tipped a little liquid into his mouth.

"You will need to put that away, Mr. Scrooge, otherwise you will have no mind to understand what I am about to offer."

"Offer?" Scrooge pushed back the stopper and set the bottle on the table. "Go on," he said. "I'm listening."

"The cause of all your grief is Mrs. Claypoole, is that not so?"

"Perhaps," Scrooge said. "You're not proposing to... I have no taste for revenge—as low as I've fallen I am not so low."

"Murdering Vivianna would solve nothing, Mr. Scrooge—and I make no doubt that you would much prefer to possess her than destroy her."

"Go on."

"What if Mrs. Claypoole had never received the note from her husband this evening?"

"How can you know about that note? Were you there?" said Scrooge.

"Answer my question."

"I couldn't say. I suppose we would have left that horrible party and returned home. But that didn't happen."

Fluch sat down in a chair and spread his gloved fingers before Scrooge on the table. "Events might be arranged so that Mrs. Claypoole's husband— what was his name?"

"Robert, I think."

"Events might be arranged so that Mrs. Claypoole's husband Robert did never recover from his illness," Dr. Fluch said.

"The note is a forgery?"

"The note is not a forgery. Even now she lounges in his arms." Fluch drew his finger thoughtfully over the surface of the table.

"Then what in God's name are you proposing?" Scrooge said.

"Let us not put it that way. Let us not put it that way at all."

"If you cannot explain yourself more plainly than that I shall grab you by the collar and the seat of the pants and throw you out, no matter the cost in pain."

Dr. Fluch narrowed his eyes and his lips into something like a smile. "There are, as you know, higher beings. You, yourself, have experienced these higher beings—one year it has been since this very chamber was visited by three spirits who desired you to change your ways."

"That is so," Scrooge nodded. "Though how you can know so much is beyond my understanding."

"There are other spirits—other beings which would not have that change occur."

Scrooge coughed. "Why should any other...what other spirits do you speak of?"

"As there is light, there is dark."

"I am a fool," Scrooge said. "The Prince."

"Yes, the Prince, His Royal Highness," agreed Dr. Fluch. He pulled off his gloves, and Scrooge noticed that the little finger of his left hand was missing.

Scrooge said, "What does His Royal Highness wish in exchange for making certain that the late Robert Claypoole remains only a memory in his widowed wife's mind?"

"A small thing. A thing of virtually no substance whatsoever. You will not miss it. It is merely a traditional token of bargain. I shouldn't have to spell it out to you, man."

"I know, I know." Scrooge bobbed his head gravely. "I suppose I have known it all along. It is the only thing left to me and yet you want even it."

"It is a matter of business only. Surely you can understand that."

"Business," Scrooge muttered. "To Hell with Business."

Fluch raised his hand as if it held a drink. "To Hell with Business," he agreed with a smile.

"When do you want your decision?" Scrooge said, staring blankly ahead.

"Well, it would not do to go beyond noon on the morrow, I would say. Isn't that the time when you are to be married?"

"Yes, noon," Scrooge said. "If you can come by the stroke of noon, I shall have your answer for you."

"Do not disappoint me, Mr. Scrooge." Dr. Fluch gazed round the room as if inspecting for peeling wall paper. "I will see that you are not disturbed while you make this decision of your own free will. I have a knack at this sort of thing. You will be completely alone for," he pulled out his pocket watch, "for the next twelve hours."

Scrooge gathered himself to stand.

"Stay where you are," said Fluch. "I can show myself out. I know the way. No one else does."

In a moment, Scrooge was alone. He could keep his eyes open not a moment longer.

◎

"See here," Topper said, pointing to the footprints between the two crates. "They are small like women's feet. I believe that they stood here sheltered from the wind and blowing snow watching that house."

Patrick shrugged. "I'd best get back to *The Copper Swan*, Sirs. You will excuse me."

"I am cutting into your income this evening, I fear. And Christmas Eve must be one of the most profitable," Topper said.

"Never mind about that, Sir," Patrick said. "The important thing is to find Mrs. Topper."

"I shall make it up to you, Patrick." Topper handed him all the coins that he could find on his person.

"Thank you, Sir," Patrick said. "And best of luck to you. Shall I send Mr. Dawson—or Trumbull—or whatever his name is after you?"

"Yes, do. His name is Trumbull," Topper said. "At some point in the future I shall explain it all to you. With God's permission."

Patrick gave Topper a small salute, smiled and dashed away in his typical fashion.

Topper watched him go. The snow stopped falling and a stillness of a kind only to be heard with a layer snow on the ground filled his ears. He turned up his collar and jammed his fists into his pockets.

He pondered whether he should simply go to the front door and knock or search round for another way to enter. He crossed the street, snow soaking his shoes. It wouldn't be long before the sun would rise. An hour or two. He had no watch to tell.

Topper walked along the side of the house, his eyes to the ground. It was difficult to tell with so much new fallen snow, but he thought he could make out small footprints. Two sets. Did they belong to Mrs. Topper and Miss Goosegrass? He could only hope.

He tried the back door and found it unlocked. The door swung noiselessly in. He followed a long corridor only too familiar. It turned at right angles on itself and after awhile he opened the door and stepped inside a room. A half dozen steps took him to another door which he flung open, his heart racing in his chest.

"Lucille!" he cried, and his wife at long last was in his arms.

CHAPTER 22

ဖာ

The Clock Strikes One

THE CLOCK STRUCK ONE! SCROOGE WOKE TO THE SENSATION OF WATER dripping upon his cheeks. Warm water.

He blinked and beheld a lovely face—a woman's face lined with care—looking down at him.

"Mrs. Claypoole," he said, "how ever did you find me? How did you know to look here?"

He rubbed the back of his hand across his brow, and his vision cleared.

"Belle!" he cried, and his breath left him as if he had been kicked in the chest. "How can this be?" His face burned, and his heart raced as it had not done in years. He wept even though there were few tears left in him. He drew her arm to his lips and kissed it. But the flesh was not flesh.

"Ebenezer," Belle said, "my heart breaks again. You have twice wounded me. How can I ever forgive you?" She caressed his poor, white head, and dotted his cheeks with more of her tears.

"Mrs. Claypoole, do you mean? We are not to be married now. She has gone to her husband. It is over."

"No," Belle said and stood erect. She was transparent so that Scrooge looking through her apron could see the tie of it on her waist behind.

"You are dead?" Scrooge cried in disbelief.

"In childbirth fifteen years since."

"How horrible. I have found you only to lose you again."

"No—not horrible. My husband is a kind and just man. The boy I gave birth to is healthy and strong. I have not been forgotten by his father nor his older sister, and both remember me to him so often that he believes he knows me. There is no horror in that. To be well remembered is the highest achievement."

"I am so sorry." Scrooge clasped his hands before him.

"It is I who am sorry, Ebenezer," said the Ghost, "for I have watched you misled, abused and tortured until your judgement has been dulled and your reasoning confused. The care I felt for you so long ago did not desert me when I left for this side of the grave. That is why I am here. That is why I shed these tears over you."

"My life is forfeit," said Scrooge, "You are here to bring me my chains which my sins have earned me."

"No, you do not understand, Ebenezer. You have earned only my pity. On no account am I here to collect your soul nor to deal you punishment. You are guilty of no transgression against Good and Light. You are but a pawn in a terrible war which has endured since the beginning of time. Nations have fallen and races exterminated in such battles. No, Ebenezer, I am not an Avenging Angel. I am here to bring you Hope."

"Hope is what I am entirely lost to. Do you not understand, I am to sell my soul to the Dark One to-morrow noon?"

"You will not. There was no agreement made, no binding contract signed. You are still your own man. Your soul is your own."

"But I am an old man, Belle. Broken, penniless, without friends, without any mortal being who cares whether I live or die."

"Not so, there are many who care for you, many who love you deeply. In your pain you can not remember them, but they are there. They do not forget you, and you shall at length remember them as well."

"The pain." Scrooge ground his teeth. "It is constantly with me—never giving me a moment's ease. It will drive me mad."

"It is a thing which I can undo," said she and the Ghost moved her hands over his body. Scrooge felt himself flushed with light, with warmth, with gaiety. The pain drained from him like stagnant water. Scrooge stood, laughed and clapped his hands over his chest.

"Marvellous! You've done it," he said. "Spirits can do anything, as I should well-know. Belle, I love you. Bless you, bless you. I am whole again."

"I have done a small thing in removing your pain. You must complete a set of larger tasks to redeem yourself."

"You need only tell me what they are, and I shall put my whole being into them."

"First I must explain," Belle said. "As there are three Spirits of Christmas, three higher beings of Light, there are three lower beings of Evil created by the Dark One for the express purpose of laying you low."

"Laying me low? But why? Why should I be of any interest to Satan?" Scrooge shuddered. "I am not a king nor an influential man of state. My monetary resources when they existed were relatively small compared to many. I am no different than thousands of men who walk the earth every day, yet do not draw the attention of Lucifer."

"Dear Scrooge, how innocent you are. Are you completely unaware of the story which has spread word of mouth to nearly every ear in this land?"

"The story of the three spirits of Christmas?"

"Yes. You are a source of concern for the Dark One because you have become a symbol of the redemption of man in the Spirit of Goodness as represented by Christmas. As your story spreads it strengthens until it transforms men and women by the score who simply hear it."

"People have idealised me?" Scrooge said, "Impossible."

"It is so."

"But I am the epitome of misery and suffering—of man's inability to choose the right path or make the right decision. I am all that is weakness in man."

"This is what the Dark One wishes you to believe. This is what we must dispel."

"Who are these three lower beings of which you spoke?"

"Three demons are they with human aspects. They have been at your side for many months undermining you in every conceivable way."

"I know the first: Milton Topper," Scrooge said. "He is a scoundrel and a thief. He will come to justice, demon or no. The law will catch him up, and his fate will be decided in the courts. We will see how demons deal with Newgate."

"No, you are gravely mistaken." Belle gave a shake of her head. "Milton Topper—you have wronged him greatly in believing that he has stolen your money. His heart is free of greed, his soul is pure. He is to be trusted without reserve."

Scrooge held his head. "You see. I cannot determine so simple a thing as who are my friends and mine enemies. How can I represent anything to anyone other than tragedy?"

"You must not give in to despair," Belle said. "There are many people who depend upon you. Many are your friends and are in great need. There are generations who will know you and gain strength from your moral courage and the decisions you have already made and will make."

"Then who are these demon enemies you speak of?"

"Can you not guess?"

Scrooge shook his head.

"The Reverend Salvation Mitchell. He is powerful and destructive beyond imagination. He is the Sin of Deceit and Prejudice made into flesh and bone. It is he who stole Charity funds and made it appear as if Mr. Topper had stolen them. He has no need for your money, but only wished to separate you from those who were your strongest supporters."

Scrooge hissed through his nose. "And the second?"

"The second demon is Fleming. He is the Sin of Violence and Cruelty. He is the one-eyed monster who with the aid of an insane creature called Bop, beat and broke your body sending you into a downward spiral so that you were ready to give yourself over to the Dark One for all the pain you suffered."

"And the third demon is Dr. Fluch?"

"No, he is mortal, a magician eager to please the Dark Forces in return for power."

Scrooge looked down at his feet. "Then it is Mrs. Claypoole," said he. "I suppose I have known it all along."

"Yes, she was, among the three, the most powerful, the deadliest. She could do to you what neither Mitchell nor Fleming could. Whereas Mitchell poisoned your mind as to your friends and Fleming brought physical pain to your body, only Mrs. Claypoole could break your spirit."

"There is no Robert Claypoole?"

"No. A demon such as herself may not be brought to join a mortal man in Holy Matrimony. There is no Robert Claypoole. It was all part of a play staged by the Dark One himself. You sat by his side as his guest and watched it unfold."

"I cannot believe it, though I do not doubt you, my spirit." Me sighed. "I am such a fool."

"That you are still alive and have a whole mind is a token of the Dark One's weakness and fallibility. He can be defeated. You can defeat him and his host of demons."

"But how? I have just two arms, two legs and but one heart. I am no more than a man—though you have made me whole and free of pain."

"You have powerful resources."

Scrooge frowned. "I do? What are they?"

Belle said, "Those who love you. Your friends."

"My friends? Who are they? Yes, of course Topper, but help me to remember the others—if others there be. Help me to remember!"

"To remember you must revisit your dreams."

"The beatings. In my dreams I can remember the beatings," said Scrooge.

"You must go beyond the beatings. Go back. Isn't there something else you can recall?"

"Only a cat. A large jungle beast with yellow eyes and sleek black fur."

"Does the name *Rajani* mean anything to you?"

Scrooge's heart filled. "Rajani! Haresh! Where are they now? Are they safe?"

"They are," said Belle. "They are sheltered where they can come to no harm."

"Thank God," Scrooge wrung his hands together.

"There is another." She paused and looked at Scrooge with the same warm smile she had shown him when they were young. "Miss Jane Goosegrass. Do you know her?"

Scrooge walked in a small circle with his fingers interlaced behind him. "Miss Jane Goosegrass," he said over and over to himself. Finally he came to a rest before the Ghost. "She is to be my wife."

Belle nodded. "She is a good woman and loves you deeply."

"I must do everything I can to go to her! There's not a moment to lose."

"And when Dr. Fluch comes calling for you to-morrow at the stroke of twelve?"

"He shall find me gone."

"There are enchantments on these rooms which prevent any mortal man from entering or leaving," said Belle.

"What shall we do then?" said Scrooge. "I have no wish to be here when he arrives."

"Are you afraid?"

Scrooge closed his eyes in thought. "A little, perhaps. Can you not somehow circumvent the magic? Surely it is not so powerful or strong as yourself. I am impatient to find Miss Goosegrass and the children."

"I can, but consider this carefully, Ebenezer: will you run from Dr. Fluch or will you face him?" said Belle.

Scrooge thought for a moment then said, "I shall not leave until I have faced Dr. Fluch. It is time for Ebenezer Scrooge to turn the tables on those who would harm him and his friends."

Belle smiled. "You have made the correct choice. This is why you will become the stuff of legend. You choose to face your fears, your mistakes. You choose not to submit, but to persevere. For you it is never too late."

Scrooge covered his face. "For all that you have done to heal me, Belle, I am quite tired."

"Spend the night in happy dreams, Ebenezer. Rest and awake in the morning to do battle with your enemies and rescue your friends. When you have finished with Fluch, you may walk free from here."

CHAPTER 23

ဟဝ

Scrooge the Defiant

THE CLOCK STRUCK TWELVE NOON. THE DOOR SWUNG OPEN, AND DR. Tobias Fluch stepped inside the rooms of Ebenezer Scrooge.

"You did not knock," Scrooge said. He stood at the mantel, a cup of tea in his hand. "Where have you learned your manners, Doctor? This is England, after all."

The Doctor shrugged. "There is no other person whom it could have been—and you were expecting me."

"Had I? I'd forgotten. Forgive me. Remind me what was the nature of our business? You had some investments in mind? Or was it a sum of money you wished to borrow?"

Fluch gave Scrooge a puzzled expression. He glanced to the leather-covered bottle upon the table. "I should have taken that with me," said he.

"This?" Scrooge said, lifting the bottle and shaking it. "I have been told that fifty drops from this small container is just the thing for any man troubled by dreams. Are you troubled by dreams, Doctor?"

"I am not."

"You are able to sleep with a clear conscience, then?" Scrooge said.

"We are not here to discuss my health."

"Then why *are* you here?"

"It is a matter of your fate, Mr. Scrooge," Dr. Fluch said. "Have you accepted the Prince's offer?"

"The Prince? That palace of his is positively a nightmare. I would rather go to the opera than return to his cold chambers."

"Mr. Scrooge, I am not at all certain you appreciate the gravity of this situation. The Prince will not take kindly to any sort of game which you feel you are capable of playing. It is possible that he may even change his mind concerning the conditions of the offer made to you last night."

"Have you had your Christmas goose yet, Dr. Fluch? It might put you right. Your temper is not with the season, Sir. Not at all."

Dr. Fluch kicked the table, but Scrooge placed a hand upon it so steady it.

"Can I get you something? You need something to steady you. Coffee? Tea?" Scrooge held his cup as an example of the service offered.

"Let me remind you, Sir," Dr. Fluch said, perspiration beading on his forehead, "that without you marry Mrs. Claypoole, you are a broken man."

"Was she the one with the blue eyes?" asked Scrooge.

"You know damn well she was."

"Something about a husband, wasn't there? That is so often the case." Scrooge gave a sorry shake of the head. "I have had so many proposals, you see. I must be frank with you, however. I don't believe these women are attracted to me in the least, but to my money."

"Money? Mr. Scrooge, have you forgotten that you are penniless? Without Mrs. Claypoole's ten thousand a year you will spend the rest of your life in debtor's prison. But that money will not be yours so long as her husband survives his illness in India. The Prince can make certain he didn't."

"Precisely what disease did he suffer?"

"What difference should that make?"

Scrooge shrugged, "Oh, I don't know. I just thought as a medical man you might have had an interest."

"I didn't ask."

"What was the man's name again?" Scrooge said.

"Robert Claypoole."

"Are you quite sure? Perhaps it was Richard."

"Of course, I am."

"Claypoole is a common name, and I would be distressed to know that any decision of mine would possibly affect the life of an innocent man."

"Mr. Scrooge."

"After all, the name Trevor is nearly the same as Robert. Turn the letters round the other way and change b for v, and you'll see what I mean."

"Mr Scrooge!"

"Now that I think on it, if you'll grant me any wish I want, my first wish will be for three more wishes, and my second wish will be for ten more and so on until I might wish all day and all night and never come up short of wishes. Do you see what I mean?"

"You're mad!"

"Certainly I'm not happy with how I've been treated. You surely can understand that." Scrooge folded his hands calmly in front of him. "But I am a reasonable man who says, 'Live and let live.'"

"I won't remain here and tolerate this treatment for another moment," said Dr. Tobias Fluch. "You are raving, Sir. Absolutely raving."

"As you wish. You know the way out."

"Indeed I do as no other mortal man can."

Scrooge said, "How is that? I have been in and out of these rooms thousands of times. If I cannot find my way out, then no one can."

Dr. Fluch showed a cunning smile. "I have placed an enchantment on this room so that no one may leave or enter it without my knowledge and express permission."

"Now who is raving mad?" Scrooge wagged a finger at him as if scolding a small boy for throwing rocks. "You will soon see, that the spell you cast upon this room imprisons not *me* within these walls. It is *you* who may not leave."

The physician clucked in disbelief. "What is this you're saying? Impossible! I have cast no such enchantment. I may leave at any time I choose. It is you who are imprisoned, not I."

"There is the door, Doctor," said Scrooge. "You may attempt to leave whenever you wish."

Dr. Fluch strode over to the door, but could not open it, try as he might.

"I think you'll find these rooms comfortable," Scrooge said. "Though rather dark and sometimes draughty."

"What is the meaning of this?"

"It means you are my prisoner," Scrooge said. "But you will at length be rescued."

"And who would rescue me?" said Fluch.

"Why, your Master, of course. The Prince. The Dark One. And I wouldn't expect that he will be very pleased with you, either. That is the chance one takes when one makes a deal with the Devil after all."

Scrooge lifted his hat from its peg and placed it upon his head. He gave Dr. Tobias Fluch a friendly wave, stepped through the door and closed it softly behind.

CHAPTER 24

෨෨

Allies

EBENEZER SCROOGE SQUINTED AGAINST THE SUNLIGHT AS HE STEPPED FROM his doorway into the street walking stick in hand. The air which filled his nose was so unlike the stale air of his rooms.

Scrooge cupped a hand to his brow and peered both up and down the street. He had no idea which direction he should take nor even what his destination might best be.

"Merry Christmas," a passing gentleman bade Scrooge with a polite side-long glance.

"Yes, A Merry Christmas to you, Sir," Ebenezer Scrooge said with a wave in return. Although his face smiled, his mind was otherwise pre-occupied.

"Where to begin?" he muttered. He walked briskly first one direction and then another, hands clasped behind his back.

There's nothing for it but to face these demons head on, he thought. *After I have defeated them and it is safe, I will seek out Miss Goosegrass and the children.*

'After I have defeated them?' Whatever can I be thinking of? What can an old man like me do against creatures of pure evil? I could no more oppose three demons chosen by Lucifer himself than I could oppose the force of an earthquake or a tidal wave. What ever am I to do?

Scrooge paused, put his back against a cold brick wall, and squeezed closed his eyes.

I mustn't give up hope. I must trust to Belle. I must give her my complete faith. There is so much to lose if I don't try.

Scrooge's eyes snapped open. Had he heard his name called? He turned his head left, but noticed no one trying to catch his notice nor did he recognise a familiar face. He turned his head right and again heard his name. He felt a tap upon his left shoulder and turned to see young Patrick Coal.

"Patrick! How good to see you. Merry Christmas to you, my boy."

"You are looking remarkably well to-day, Sir," Patrick said with a look of surprise upon his face. "Merry Christmas to you." Then Patrick leaned in closer and whispered: "There is someone who wishes to speak to you, Mr. Scrooge. He stands over there between those to buildings. Do you see him? He waves a handkerchief just now to draw your attention."

"I do see him. It's Mr. Dawson, isn't it?"

Patrick twisted his mouth. "Dawson or Trumbull. One of them two names anyways. Will you come with me, Sir? It might seem a bit peculiar, but he means you no harm. He has information which I am sure you will be keen to learn."

"Certainly I will." Scrooge wondered if this diversion would help or hinder his mission. "Lead away." Scrooge stepped nimbly through the snow after Patrick and with a sideways glance in both directions to see that no one was watching slipped between the buildings.

"Mr. Dawson," Scrooge stepped forward with his hand outstretched, "I feel I owe you and Mr. Topper an apology. I have misjudged you."

Trumbull grasped his hand and gave it a hearty shake. "No apology is necessary, Mr. Scrooge. Never mind about that now—first things first. Mr. and Mrs. Topper are in grave danger, and I have reason to believe Miss Goosegrass is with them. I was on my way to see if I could help them."

"What?!" Scrooge narrowed his eyes. "Kindly explain to me what is going on."

Trumbull did so as quickly as possible. He also sketched out the story of his true identity and the reasons why he had hidden it.

"This is a far more tangled mystery than I could ever have guessed," said Scrooge with a shake of his head. "Do you know the location of this house where they've gone?"

"I don't, but Mr. Coal here was taking me there when we spotted you walking our way."

"Then we must continue without delay. Lead the way, young man," Scrooge said to Patrick, "and do not slacken your pace for me. Not in the least. Be on your way, and I shall do my very best to match you stride for stride. Let us go!"

"Yes, Sir. Right away, Sir," Patrick said.

"We must have a care, however," Scrooge said under his breath to Trumbull as Patrick set a stiff pace. "Though it is Christmas and full daylight I cannot help but believe that we may be in some jeopardy. As soon as we are within sight of our destination we must send Patrick on his way. This is no place for a boy."

Patrick opened his mouth to protest, but Trumbull clapped a hand on his shoulder.

"We can't all go in. We need someone to stay on the outside and get help if we're not back in a reasonable amount of time," he said.

Patrick nodded mutely in agreement.

They walked with determination shoulder-to-shoulder for some time before they arrived at their destination.

"There it is, Sirs," Patrick said. "That's the place where the Reverend disappears to every night. It is....a house of ill-repute, I'm sorry to say. Not that I would know anything about such places."

"Of course not. Very good, Patrick." Scrooge fished in his pocket for a coin. "You are a brave boy and have earned a greater reward than this coin. If all goes well, you will get that reward, I promise you."

"Patrick," said Trumbull, hesitating, "before you go. Could I ask a favour of you? I would like for you to carry a message for me."

"Of course, Sir. Who would you have me carry it to?" Patrick said, knowing full well who the intended recipient was.

"To Miss Molly Jones, if you would," Trumbull said in a soft voice. He wrote something on a slip of paper and folded it. "At *The Copper Swan*. And..." he paused, "it's of a personal nature."

"I know who she is." Patrick's face bore an amused expression. "Don't worry, Mr. Trumbull, your message is safe with me."

Scrooge gave Trumbull an odd look, but said nothing. Patrick bowed and dashed away clapping his cap to his head with his free hand.

"How do you believe we should try to get inside, Mr. Scrooge?" Trumbull said.

"What was it Nelson said?"

Trumbull gave him a puzzled look.

"'Never mind the manoeuvres—always go straight at 'em!' That is what we shall do, Sir. Go straight at 'em."

Scrooge arranged his face into its kindliest form, straightened the lapels on his coat and strode briskly across the street with Trumbull tagging at his heels. He walked directly up the few steps to the front door and knocked as if he meant to get an immediate answer.

The door swung open and without a pause Scrooge bowed low. "Merry Christmas to you," he said without hesitation. "I am Professor John Tringham, manufacturer of the household *nostrum remedium* 'Professor Tringham's Pectoral Drops,' a guaranteed universal panacea to remedy all your common complaints and ills." Then he did glance up and immediately recognised the pink eyes which looked back at him.

"Jack Forest? What in heaven's name are you doing here?" said he, straightening.

"We have been awaiting you, Sir." Jack rolled his cart to one side to allow Scrooge and Trumbull to enter. "Please come this way."

Scrooge's brow clouded. "You have betrayed me, Jack. You are in league with the demons," he said, his voice heavy with disgust. "All along I have trusted you, and now I find you in their lair."

"We have betrayed no one. Look into my face and tell me what you see. Tell me that you see evil," Jack said.

Scrooge did look, but found only kindness and goodness therein. He shook his head in confusion. "I do not. None of this makes sense to me. Cannot a rational mind follow these events?"

"All will become clear soon," Jack said. "At the moment we are to lead you to a battle which has been brewing for long. Do not fear. We will be at your side, but in the end the victory will be yours and yours alone."

We? thought Scrooge. He and Trumbull stepped through the doorway into the semidarkness just inside. Standing in a parlour immediately right of the entry way were Miss Trellis and Mary-Martha White.

"And here are my foot-soldiers?" Scrooge said with no small trace of irony.

Mary-Martha, however, seemed more mature than Scrooge remembered her, a young woman now. Her face shone peacefully as she greeted Scrooge and Trumbull.

"Merry Christmas, Sirs," she said and gave a graceful curtsey.

They returned the greeting in kind.

Miss Trellis, however, brooded over them. Her cloak covered her head and left her face entirely in shadow.

Scrooge said, "Why have you three come? I do appreciate your concern, but I cannot ask you to place your lives in peril." Scrooge wished that his allies had been broad of shoulder with hangers buckled at their sides—not a linguist (however tall and forbidding she might appear), a leg-less albino page and a kitchen-maid.

I must not question which companions have been chosen for me, he thought. *I must only play my part.*

He said, "Miss Trellis, do you know where Miss Goosegrass and Mr. and Mrs. Topper are? We must see to them without delay."

She nodded solemnly and pointed a long finger down a doorless passage-way.

"Lead on then," Scrooge said. "I would have my friends freed on this most holy of days and this struggle brought at last to an end."

The group of five stepped into the passageway single file: Miss Trellis in front, followed by Scrooge, next Mary-Martha, then Trumbull and Jack in the rear.

As they followed the corridor Scrooge noticed that it turned on itself at frequent right angles. After half a score such turns he lost all sense of direction. On they continued in silence. How much time passed he couldn't guess. It might have been minutes. It might have been hours.

At length the passageway terminated at a door which, though the light was dim, Scrooge could see was marked and gouged as if someone wished desperately to pass through but couldn't. Miss Trellis, however, opened it with a gesture.

The group stepped through into a small room and out into another, this one quite large and well lit.

Scrooge looked quickly round. In the middle of the room were neatly stacked piles of used lumber. On the wall through which they had just entered were two other doors—both closed. Miss Trellis pointed to one of these and from behind it Scrooge heard the sound of familiar voices.

Scrooge was so choked with emotion that he could make no sound. Tears rolled down his cheeks.

"Come, Mr. Scrooge," said Jack, softly. "They will be happy to see you. It is Christmas, and there can be no greater gift than for all of you to be together on this day. It is the gift we grant you."

Scrooge at last found his voice. "Exactly who are you, Jack? You are surely more than you seem."

Jack touched his sleeve. "This way. We shall give them a pleasant surprise."

Scrooge stepped slowly over to the door uncertain whether he should knock or simply open it. At last he decided to knock. He did so, and the conversation on the opposite side abruptly stopped. After a long pause a male voice which Scrooge recognised as Mr. Topper's said, "Who is there?"

"It is Ebenezer Scrooge."

The door swung open and Miss Goosegrass pushed past Mr. Topper. For a long moment she looked into Scrooge's eyes reading his expression. Scrooge knew she was trying to determine if he remembered her.

He tilted his head to one side and said, "Jane Goosegrass, will you marry me?"

Scrooge, his senses focused entirely on Miss Goosegrass, was only dimly aware of the gasp which escaped Mrs. Topper's lips.

Miss Goosegrass drew near and wrapped her arms around his shoulders. "Of course, Ebenezer. That is, if Mrs. Claypoole, your wife, makes no protest."

"Oh, am I limited to only one wife?" Scrooge said. "What of King Solomon? He had seven hundred official wives. I am modest in asking only for a pair."

Miss Goosegrass put her hands on her hips. Scrooge believed he was about to receive a tongue lashing, but to his surprise she laughed and then in a heartbeat, cried. She hugged him close and said, "I thought I'd lost you forever."

"I must tell you that I retain no affection for Mrs. Claypoole—if I ever had any," he said. "She was a demoness, a supernatural seductress, but that is no excuse for my being an old fool."

"None of that matters," said Miss Goosegrass. "What only matters is that we are together again."

They rocked slowly side to side. "Nothing will ever come between us," he said at last and kissed her gently. Then he gently drew away from her and turned to Mr. Topper.

"Milton, can you ever find it in your heart to forgive me?" Scrooge said, clasping Topper's hand in a tight grip.

Topper laid a hand on Scrooge's shoulder. "Do not be too hard on yourself, Sir. I cannot believe that I should have behaved any differently had I been in your shoes. You were deceived."

"No—no—no. This is all my fault. I must take responsibility. It is yet another example of my weakness and frailty of spirit."

A deep peal not unlike the sound of far-off thunder welled inside the room. All conversation ceased. Heads swivelled left and right and a look of fear crossed their faces.

"What was that?" Scrooge said. "The weather was clear and bright just before we entered the building. There are no thunderstorms during winter, at any rate."

Topper said, "I've no idea, but I believe, if it is still possible, that we should remove ourselves with all due speed."

The fur-lined walls bulged and wriggled. A susurration as if tons of sand were sifting just outside hissed in their ears. Scrooge desperately looked round for a weapon.

"Whatever it is we shall meet it and show no fear," he said. "We have cowered before this evil for far too long. It is time we stood like men and do what needs to be done."

The wall puckered, then split horizontally. Dark liquid spilled in. It took a heartbeat before Scrooge recognised the true nature of the substance: insects. He had no more time than to draw Miss Goosegrass near than the walls burst and a seething sea of black beetles engulfed them.

༄༅

CHAPTER 25

The Swamp, the Sister and the Wedding

LUCILLE TOPPER SAT UP, SPAT FILTH FROM HER MOUTH AND RAN THE BACK
of a hand over her brow. She saw little in the darkness, but knew this place.
The water, the mud, the scrub trees and brush. This was where Salvation
Mitchell had stalked her. It had only been a dream, but the dream had been
a mirror to reality when she woke. Her husband's ring protected her, but the
thought gave her little reassurance.

The ring?! She felt it on her middle finger and breathed a sigh of relief.

"Milton?" she said, softly and listened. Nothing.

Lucille got to her feet, mud streaming from her dress. She shivered
though the air was warm.

Dresses are not suited for this sort of activity, she mused, *and there is little reason for
modesty here.* She slid out of her dress, but decided to keep her foundation
garments.

Thunder rumbled in the distance, and she prayed that it did not mean
rain.

"We cannot be separated again. I must find him," she said. "He is here
somewhere. I know it. But which way?"

She turned in a slow circle trying to discern some point which she could
make a destination. There would be, she knew, no point in wandering
aimlessly.

There—just there—was a faint glow. A bluish light—probably nothing
more than a rotting log. She heard of such things glowing mysteriously in

swamps. Two quick strides took her out of the shallow pool, but mud caked on her bare feet with each miserable step. She walked for some time yet never seemed to draw any nearer to the flickering blue glow. As she walked she experienced an increasing sense of danger until at length she stopped. She felt exposed.

Nearby was the silhouette of a broken tree. Walking over she leaned her back against it and hugged herself. Her ears picked up very little. A slow steady drip. The trickle of running water. The rustle of a dead leaf. The creak of a tree limb.

She held her right hand before her face. The ring felt reassuring around her finger. She kissed it, straightened her back and walked toward the blue glow with an unwavering step.

"Oh, my God!" she moaned when she was at last close enough to see.

Milton Topper was tied to a tree twenty feet above with a length of shimmering rope. His torso was so bound that only his head and shoulders were revealed above and his hips and legs below.

"Milton!" Lucille shouted and broke into a run. There was no sign of life in him. His head lolled to one side. His legs dangled limply.

"Milton!" she screamed again and again. The tree possessed no branches, nor stubs, nor was it forked in such a way as to allow her to climb. She tried shimmying up, but succeeded only in breaking her nails and tearing the skin of her hands, arms and legs.

In frustration she struck the trunk with a stone as if she might thus fell it. All without effect.

Lucille dropped to her knees and began to weep, to pray.

"Lucille..." came a weak voice.

"Yes! Milton, you are alive!"

"I am dying, Lucille. I am dying."

"No, Milton. You will live. I will save you. All will be well. You'll see."

"It is no use," said Topper. "I cannot last long. I am being crushed." A hoarse whisper rattled from his throat. "Mitchell lurks in the darkness. Out there. I know not where. The only way to spare my life is to kill him. Only then will these enchanted bonds relax. Once he is dead, his power will be broken."

A fine rain spattered her face and hair. Thunder peeled once again, but much closer.

Lucille said, "I will do anything to save you. Anything at all. But how will I find him?"

"The ring," Topper said, "will take you to him. Follow it. It knows where he is."

"Can I not use the ring to free you first?"

"No, though the ring could undo the magic of the ropes, it could not free me before the life was crushed out of me. My only chance is for you to act quickly. You must bring Mitchell here. There is a coil of this rope he has left behind. Use it to bind him and return him to this spot. It is only appropriate that he will be brought to justice with his own magic. You must slay him in the presence of the bonds for the spell to be broken. Quickly, my love. Go quickly."

Lucille lifted the coil of rope to her shoulder, took a dozen steps and stopped. She held her outstretched hand before her face and turned counter-sun-wise in a slow circle remembering the glow the ring had given off when she had rested against the broken tree. The ring flickered and grew warm.

"I will find him, my darling," Lucille shouted back to Topper. "Your life will be saved if it is the last thing I do. Your ring will protect me against any harm Mitchell might attempt."

Blindly she ran. Roots, vines, brambles tripped her, cut her face and hands. Again and again she fell clawing the air, stones bruising her elbows, digging into her ribs. Her foot slipped, her ankle turned. Lucille crumbled to the ground with a sob. *Was it broken?* No. When she stood, however, it would not hold her.

"Lucille!" a voice hissed in the darkness.

She bit the back of her hand to keep from crying out. Mitchell!

"Is that you, Lucille?" the voice called out.

Lucille looked at the ring on her hand. It grew brighter and brighter by the moment. She buried it in the pit of her arm to keep its light from betraying her.

"This is horrible, Lucille. Horrible," Mitchell said.

Lucille pressed herself against the ground and watched a dark shape pass her by. She gasped and the figure twitched in her direction.

"Where are you?" Mitchell said.

Lucille gathered all her courage, pulled herself to her knees, and then stood with her weight resting on one foot.

"Monster!" She threw the coil in the direction of the shape.

In the darkness she watched it soar through the air, uncoil snake-like and wrap itself around Mitchell's body. The rope once dull, sizzled with a rainbow of colours.

Mitchell thrashed as the rope whipped round. At last only his pudgy nose, eyes, hips and legs were exposed. Lucille walked round his backside and kneed him. The ring glittered with blue fire.

"Move! Your life isn't worth much, but if I can use it to save my husband's, I will thank you for it."

Mitchell did not struggle. Instead he sobbed quietly.

"Where is your courage now, demon?" Lucille said, kneeing him again. "Do you see that light beyond?"

Mitchell nodded.

"Then you'd best make your way there as quickly as you are able. If you will release my husband from his bonds, then your life will be spared."

Mitchell walked calmly as if resigned to his fate. Lucille held one end of the rope and limped along behind him.

At length they drew near the tree where Topper was bound. As Lucille approached she struggled to see if there were signs of life left in her husband's body. Topper's head twisted to one side. He said:

"You have found him. I am saved."

"I have promised Mitchell I would spare him his life if he would release you."

Topper moaned. "He cannot be trusted. Quickly now! At the base of this tree you will find an axe. Use it to cleave his head. Nothing else will do. Save your husband's life."

"Release my husband now, demon, so that your life can be spared," Lucille said.

Mitchell's voice was muffled behind the ropes. "I cannot," he said.

"You see, Lucille. He refuses. As we wait these bonds squeeze what little life I have left out of me. Act now. Act now!" Topper said.

Lucille walked over to Mitchell and held the ring before his face. "If you do not co-operate I shall use this ring against you as I have already once done. Would you have me press this ring against your cheek?"

Mitchell made no reply but turned to face her full on.

"Do not waste your time with the ring, my darling," Topper said. "You must use the axe. See it below? Just there."

Lucille ignored her husband and looked into Mitchell's eyes.

"My God!" she said, trembling. She held up the ring, but he did not flinch.

"Now! Please, my darling. It squeezes me so. My life-spark is dwindling," Topper said.

"Before I cleave this demon asunder," Lucille said, "can you tell me the names of my sisters and the order of their births?"

"Have you gone mad? There is so little time. Why do you ask?"

"There is, as you have said repeatedly, so little time that I cannot explain. You would do best to simply answer my question," Lucille said.

"For God's Sake, please!"

Lucille folded her arms. "In order from eldest to youngest."

"Of course. Whatever you wish, my love. They are Lydia, Lottie, Lillian, Lucille—that's you, of course—Lucinda, Loretta, and Louisa."

"Are you quite sure?"

"Of course, I'm sure. They are my sisters-in-law, are they not?"

"Do you have the order correct?" said she.

"Yes, I am certain of it. Why should I not be?"

"Because Mr. Milton Topper, my husband, was not sure himself. He always got them confused—much to my on-going chagrin."

"I've since learnt their names and ages straight," Topper said.

"For a man whose life is being squeezed out of him, you certainly have had a lot to say."

Topper merely twitched in his ropes.

"I do not believe you are my husband, Sir," Lucille said. "And if you are not he, then I must wonder who it is I have trussed in these ropes. But I have little doubt that my ring will provide me the answer to my question."

She lifted her hand to the face of her prisoner but he did not draw back. The ring shimmered and blinding light flashed in her eyes. Yet she did not blink. She felt, rather than saw, the ropes drop to the ground. In less than a dozen heartbeats—there, before her, was Milton Topper, her husband. She rushed to his arms.

"I almost killed you," she said. "Why did you not speak up?"

"An enchantment sealed my lips. I had faith that you would not be fooled in the end."

The bonds holding the beast to the tree slipped away, and Salvation Mitchell slid to the ground.

"Damn you," Mitchell hissed and leapt into the air claws reaching for Lucille's throat.

A burst from her ring turned night into day, and Mitchell flew back as if struck by a club. The light drove him against the tree until his spine was jammed against it. Chips of bark flew as he was driven to his previous position twenty feet above ground.

Topper clutched his wife to his bosom. Neither had control of the ring any longer. Strands of fulgent energy gathered and circled round and around Mitchell binding him tighter and tighter. His body thrashed as the bands squeezed. Lucille heard a crack and buried her head against her husband's shoulder.

"There, there, now," said he. "This is none of our doing. This is the will of a higher force."

"Do not be concerned for his destruction, Mrs. Topper," a soft voice said, "for he was never alive. This is no worse than pulling down an old house before someone is hurt by it."

Lucille pulled away and looked down in wonder at the white hair, the alabaster face and the blazing eyes of Jack Forest.

⊙

Black beetles sizzled all round. He expected the foul creatures to flay him alive with their pincers, but in the few seconds he was immersed beneath them he felt no tear to his flesh. He pulled his coat over his head and lay face down upon the floor, lost to all sense of time.

"They are gone, Lincoln," said a voice at last. "You may stand now. Come. I have someone you will wish to speak to."

Trumbull cautiously drew back the coat from his head. Standing over him he saw Mary-Martha.

"Please, Sir," she said. "Give you a hand."

Trumbull reached out and was lifted to his feet with surprising strength.

"If you will come with me," Mary-Martha said. Trumbull followed her down a corridor—this one with doors, a rug underfoot and as straight as an arrow. Mary-Martha knocked softly at a door mired with hand-prints.

"Come in?" a voice said.

"You must go in alone," Mary-Martha said, folding her hands.

"Thank you." Trumbull felt like a child in a dream. He placed his hand upon the knob and twisted. It yielded and swung in gently.

A woman sat at a boudoir table with her back to him. He recognised her immediately. Annie! He trembled at the thought of knowing what to say to her.

"I will be with you in a moment." Her hand fussed at pins in her hair.

He fumbled at his neck-cloth for a moment before saying, "Sister."

Annie turned round and drew a hand to her mouth.

"What are you doing here?" she said. Trumbull searched her face. Did she wish to have no contact with him or was she simply surprised to find him at her door?

"I've come to take you home," he said, watching her eyes.

"You came all this way... How did you find me?" she said. Still no clue as to her meaning from either her voice or her eyes.

"It's a long story, and there's no time to tell it now," he said. "First we must get you out of here. I don't know how long it will be before I'm discovered."

Annie turned so that the light from the window fell full upon her face, and Trumbull noticed how she had aged. The corners of her eyes were crinkled. The circles beneath her eyes frightened him. Could this possibly be the same young girl who mercilessly teased him not so many years past?

"I cannot leave, Linc," she said, tears welling in her eyes. "I am unclean. I have seen and heard sinful acts and have been used in sinful practices. There is no saving me. You must believe me dead. Leave me now and never think of me again."

"That is the one thing I can never do. I have come a long way, and have made many sacrifices to be here. I won't be turned aside."

A heavy hand knocked at the door.

"Annie! It's me, Fleming," the voice said, "Open up. I'm back, and I've brought flowers—ain't that sweet o' me? Flowers in a manner of speaking. Poppies, they are."

Brother and sister exchanged quick looks.

"I've got a gentleman with me just now," Annie said in a pitched voice. "A customer. Can you come back later?"

"A gentleman?" Fleming said. "Who?"

"Mr. Smith—or is it Mr. Jones?" she said, "A private gentleman. You know how it is. We don't use names around here."

"Tell him to leave."

"We're almost done, honey." Trumbull shuddered to hear her use the term of endearment so easily. "Give us just a few minutes. Go on downstairs and wait like a good boy," she said. "I'll send someone down for you when I'm ready. I won't disappoint you. Go on now."

A lengthy pause followed. "Well, don't be long," he said. They heard his quick tread move away.

"Quick," Annie said, "your only hope is to escape through the window."

Trumbull grabbed her arm. "No, I'm not leaving without you. I promised father on his death-bed that I would bring you home, and that's just what I intend to do."

To his relief she made no effort to pull herself free. "Father is dead?" she said and her shoulders slumped.

"Yes, nearly two years ago. Do you have anything you wish to take with you?" Trumbull said, looking around at the diaphanous materials strewn over her changing screen, bed and sofa.

"No, I would leave these clothes on my back here if I could," she said.

Trumbull removed his coat and laid it across her shoulders. "Come— before it's too late."

He moved toward the window when it burst into a hundred thousand pieces. Reflexively Trumbull raised his arms to protect himself. The hot slashes he expected, however, were never felt.

Trumbull lowered his arms and squinted. The myriad glistening shards and slivers stood unmoving in the air like bark suspended in amber. Crouched behind on the window sill was Fleming, dirty hair hanging over his face, his single eye a mad beacon.

With a growl Fleming leapt down from the window and swept his great cloak to clear the glass from the air.

"Brother and sister reunion. What sweetness!" He laughed madly. "Have you yet sampled your sister's new skills? She is master of both pleasure and pain now. You will enjoy her."

"Fiend!" Trumbull swung his fist wildly and connected with Fleming's jaw. Fleming staggered back against the wall. He shook his head, surprised at the pain.

Before Trumbull could land another blow Fleming punched at Trumbull's head, missed, followed up with a second which glanced off Trumbull's uplifted shoulder.

Trumbull gasped for air. He was in poor physical condition after having spent so much time in confinement. If he could not quickly defeat his opponent he knew he would be lost.

In desperation Trumbull clasped Fleming awkwardly about the waist and hurled him back. Fleming stumbled over a chair and sat down hard on the floor with a curse. Trumbull leapt upon him knees first. Fleming grunted, squirmed from beneath him, and moving with the speed of a cat wrapped his hands around Trumbull's throat.

Annie at last found her voice and released an ear-splitting shriek. She grabbed the first thing she saw to use as a weapon: a silver-handled hand-mirror. She brought it down upon Fleming's head. The glass of the mirror fell out in three jagged chunks, and the handle twisted. Fleming jerked and loosened his grip on Trumbull. Again and again she struck him until he turned, blood running red down his face and slapped it from her hands.

"Bop! Bop!" Fleming shouted. "Help me! Your master calls! Come now!"

Trumbull heard his sister cursing Fleming, felt her pelt the demon with soft fists and feet. Fleming momentarily relaxed his grip and Trumbull twisted from beneath his weight. Trumbull staggered to his feet, scooped up a wrought iron chair, and brought it down hard on Fleming's head. It made a dull, yet satisfying *phlunk*. Fleming shuddered and his body went slack.

Heavy, quick footsteps sounded in the hall. Trumbull saw a new look of fear on his sister's face. The sound, however, strengthened Fleming. He pushed himself upright. "In here, Bop!" he cried.

Annie flung herself against the door and held the knob with one hand while feeling along the top of the wardrobe with the other.

"The key," she said. "Help me find it, Linc."

Trumbull dropped the chair and stumbled to the wardrobe, his hand searching blindly. Nothing. He turned and sat the chair upright and stood upon it. Amid the clumps of dust, pushed nearly to the wall was a large key.

"I found it," he said, and held it out. She snatched it from his hand, jammed it into the keyhole and twisted.

Trumbull felt the chair jerk beneath him. He fell, flattened a small table, and struck his head against the windowsill. Consciousness faded in and out several times until after a space of blackness his eyes focused. He saw Fleming hurl Annie to one side and twist the key in the lock. Before Fleming could open the door, however, Annie grabbed his coat tails and gave a vicious tug. Fleming snapped off his feet and onto his back.

Annie snatched up the poker from the small hearth and brought it down three times as if chopping wood. Fleming shuddered, shook away the pain, tore the poker from her hands.

The door burst on its hinges. Trumbull his head spinning couldn't see what shot through the opening except that its hair was rust-red. It might have been a dog or perhaps a kind of ape. The creature tore at Fleming's throat.

"Bop, no!" Fleming shouted.

Trumbull felt his sister pull him to his feet.

"We can't stay here, Linc," she said. They slid past the horror on the floor, down the passageway, down the short flight of stairs, out the door and into the street. A coach stood in front of the building. The last thing Trumbull saw before blackness overcame him was Mary-Martha motioning for them to enter the cab.

"You have done well," she said.

◎

Ebenezer Scrooge ostensibly watched an air bubble beneath the breast of his shirt, but in fact he ogled the curvaceous form of Mrs. Claypoole as she bobbed in the bath not ten feet from him. He wondered briefly why he should be fully dressed while soaking in this luxuriant therma when his bride-to-be was not clothed in so much as a blush. He tilted back his head, rested it on the bath's marble lip and squinted his eyes. He had never seen a cathedral soar so high. Could it possibly be clouds that he saw within its vaulted ceilings?

Perhaps it will rain, he thought with a laugh. *Then our guests will get as wet as we are.*

Lowering his eyes again Scrooge settled his attention on the statuary which surrounded the rim of the pool. The fanciful creatures carved in dark grey and green stone were of a form unlike anything Scrooge had ever seen before: neither Roman nor Greek—at times entirely unworldly.

The shape depicted nearest at hand was partly human with man-like hands and arms, but its chinless face more closely resembled that of a goat. Its lower trunk was a confusion of tentacles encompassing powerful, fur-covered legs and what might be the stub of a tail.

Scrooge's eye fell on the statue next to it. This figure was also generally man-like though its surface texture was more akin to that of the carapace of a crustacean. Its head was eye-less and elongated in the extreme. The tongue which burst from its fanged mouth finished in yet another set of needle-sharp teeth.

The other sculptures were no less bizarre: combinations of men and sea-creatures, men and birds, and others less easy to categorise. One, however, was different from the rest in style and depiction. Something of its posture, its imposing stature struck Scrooge as familiar and important. The stone figure was draped head to foot in a heavy robe so that no trace of its human form was visible save for one hand. While the other statues writhed in baroque alien worlds, this severe figure seemed aware of the room and its occupants. The statue's grey finger pointed directly, accusingly, Scrooge thought, at himself.

"Clever diversions," Scrooge murmured and splashed a little perfumed water on his face. Humming tunelessly he lifted one foot from the water to admire the polish of his shoes. Scrooge doubted that he had ever felt so good, so warm, so relaxed. Could life be any better?

A slight movement in the pews to the left and right at his rear drew his attention.

Oh yes, our guests.

He sat forward and twisted in their direction. So many red eyes and dark circles. Their clothing too was rather sober for a wedding—more suitable for a wake. The women were singularly unattractive, and the men looked guilty of unmentionable crimes. Scrooge believed he recognised more than a few of them from the Prince's party—when was it, the night before?

These are patient folk, however, Scrooge thought. *Waiting so still for a man to finish his wedding bath.*

One side he knew was reserved for the friends and family of the bride and the other for the groom's.

"I do not see anyone from my party," said he. "What do you believe has delayed them, my dearest apple blossom?"

"I cannot say," Mrs. Claypoole said, her hair a bed of seaweed surrounding her head. "Perhaps they have stopped to hunt a fox or a wench. How can I know? I am not their mother."

"Just so. Just so, my love," Scrooge said, tenderly. Then did he notice the solitary woman who sat on his side of the isle. Scrooge looked at her and believed he recognised her, though he couldn't place exactly where from. He drew himself up a bit higher in the water. His clothing weighed him down, and he felt the chill air. Still he could not place her.

"Vivianna, my sweet. Who is that woman who sits just there? You see her? The one who is bound with the coil of rope. The one with the dark hat."

Mrs. Claypoole rose to the waist out of the pool. Her bare skin glistened with tiny drops of water. "Where, dear?" she said. "They are all of them wearing dark hats."

Scrooge gave a little gasp, then checked himself. "I don't see how you can miss her. She's the only one sitting on my side."

"Oh yes," Mrs. Claypoole said, "I do see her now. She's one of yours, isn't she?"

"I know that. Do you know *who* she is? What is her name?"

"How do you expect me to know your friends when you yourself cannot remember who they are?"

"She does look familiar. I wonder if she is Milton's wife?" he said. "Funny that she should be gagged like that at a wedding. She can hardly be happy to sit about so."

Mrs. Claypoole splashed a little water in her face. "You know how some people are, dear: always blurting out."

Scrooge nodded and relaxed back into the water. The light streaming through the stained-glass windows coloured the guests in peculiar ways. Golden light tinted them blue. Green light tinted them orange. Blue light, a pearly pink. Only the red glass was true—guests who sat in its light turned the colour of blood.

"Don't you believe we should be getting on with it?" Scrooge said, at last.

"Whatever do you mean, dear?"

"The wedding, of course. I must confess that my skin is beginning to wrinkle more than it usually is." He chuckled at his bit of whimsy. "Water wrinkles the skin when you've been in too long, you understand."

"Must we to-day?"

"I suppose it isn't absolutely necessary, but our guests are all here and waiting for us to begin. We cannot disappoint them, can we?"

Mrs. Claypoole thrust out her lower lip. "I suppose not," she said. She half-swam, half-waded to the steps of the bath and rose out of the water. All eyes turned to her, and Scrooge felt a twinge of disapproval as both men and women hung out their tongues and shouted coarse obscenities.

"Have a care," he said to them, rising out of the water. "This is the woman who is to be my wife."

They responded to his reprimand with laughter, Mrs. Claypoole laughing loudest of all.

Scrooge made his way through the water until he, too, was able to ascend the stairs. Bath-water drained from his clothing creating a puddle beneath his feet. He removed his coat, shook it artfully, and put it back on. As he did so, he noticed Mrs. Claypoole had pulled on a black dress which looked as if it had been slashed with a razor. Even from a distance it smelt of mould.

"This is not your wedding gown," he said. "Where is the one made of silk to match your eyes? You remember? The bolt I gave to you not long since —what have you done with it?"

When she turned her eyes upon him, they were no longer any shade of blue, but an unnatural green.

A movement at the corner of his eye caused Scrooge to turn his head toward the statue with the accusing finger. It no longer pointed at the bath. It pointed directly at him.

"Vivianna, sweetest," he said, "what is the name of that figure? What does it portray? The rude one which jabs its finger at me so boldly."

Mrs. Claypoole turned her head and wrinkled her brow.

"Just there. You see it, don't you?" he said.

Mrs. Claypoole turned away and adjusted the torn bosom of her dress.

Scrooge looked back at the statue and breathed a sigh of relief. Its arm had dropped to its side. It no longer accused him of anything. He blinked his eyes, and it shifted its position.

"Vivianna, darling," he said, touching her arm.

She shook off his touch.

The statue now had one foot placed upon the floor, and blue sparks danced above its head.

An animal stench stung Scrooge's nose. He swung his head back round to remark upon it to Mrs. Claypoole when he saw the Prince cocked in a pulpit which had not been there the moment before.

"Let us begin our malediction," the Prince said, holding up a clawed talon. With his right he held a perfumed handkerchief to his mouth— though little good it did. As before a suit of blue silk covered his thin body like pyjamas on a puppet. Sat upon his head was a crown made of bone and horn and yellowed teeth. Though his face was deep in shadow, his eyes nevertheless burned with horrible light.

"Please join hands. Dearly despised: We are gathered here to-day to join this mortal man and this..." he hesitated and produced a short bark of laughter "ahem...woman..."

Someone struck Scrooge lightly between the shoulder blades with an apple core. He whirled round to see who had done such a thing and froze. The statue was three steps distant from its pedestal. It had been moving, but not in Scrooge's direction—rather away from him toward the guests.

"...into a state of aggrieved matrimony." The Prince gestured an epicene hand at the guests which began a chorus of hacking and coughing. "This unholy state requires from the groom a solemn but willing pledge of his very essence, his soul to me, the Prince of Darkness, the Fallen One. It is a pledge made only upon mature consideration and thought and should be treated with the utmost irreverence."

Scrooge turned his head at the noise, and found that the statue, though frozen at the moment had made its way half down the length of the aisle as if it were trying to escape. The guests were motionless save one: the woman trussed in ropes struggled as if her very life depended upon her freeing herself.

"We are here to celebrate the devotion which these two beings have for me and to recognise and witness their decision to desecrate themselves to become one with the Darkness," the Prince said.

Scrooge whirled round. The statue was within a few yards of the struggling woman.

"Have you come here freely and without reservation to give yourself to me in marriage?" Satan boomed.

"I beg your pardon," Scrooge said. "I'm afraid I was distracted."

"Do you take me to be your Master, your Lord, your Prince, your Everything?"

Scrooge gave the Prince a puzzled look.

"Will you devote your every breath to my service, to honour me, to worship me, forsaking all that is Holy, keeping yourself exclusively for me in all ways, so long as you shall live or die and your spirit be coherent?"

Scrooge mute with horror staggered back toward the guests. The hand of the statue, he saw, was poised high above the woman's head ready to drop like the blade of a guillotine.

"No!" Scrooge shouted, fear constricting his throat.

The arm fell. It brushed aside the woman's black hat revealing a mass of shivering curls. A single granite digit stroked the length of her torso, and the ropes which bound her snapped like threads. In a heartbeat the woman sprang to her feet and shouted a single word:

"Ebenezer!"

"Jane!" he cried in reply. He turned to Mrs. Claypoole remembering everything at once. The enchantment was broken.

"You foul beast," he said. She was no longer the beautiful young woman whom he had so strongly desired. Scrooge for the first time saw Mrs. Vivianna Claypoole for what she really was: a green-skinned hag with curving horns like a great ram. The bride of Ebenezer Scrooge opened her fanged mouth and hissed. Scrooge recoiled and fell backward into the bath. Water closed over his head. He stood to his feet sputtering.

Miss Trellis stood on the surface of the water as if it were solid as marble. She pulled Scrooge out of the bath and set him tenderly to one side.

Mrs. Vivianna Claypoole, bride-to-be, leapt at Scrooge with claws extended. Still a creature of stone, Miss Trellis swung her right arm with the weight and power of a granite column and struck the hag while still in the air. The thing which was Mrs. Claypoole skidded half-way across the cathedral floor and fetched up against the pulpit behind which the Prince silently stood.

The guests shouted, rose to their feet and ran in panic. The grand doors of the cathedral swung open at their approach revealing only blackness and cold and the pinpoints of stars. The guests spilled into the emptiness and tumbled away in silence like so much rubbish. The door swung smoothly back and closed with an audible click.

Miss Goosegrass rushed forward, grabbed Scrooge's hand, and they threw themselves under the first row of pews.

Up flew the hag's hands. She uttered a guttural curse which brought a rumbling from above. The stained-glass windows on all sides of the cathedral shattered. A thousand ebony shapes flittered down and enveloped Miss Trellis in a thick cloud. Bats! They shrieked at pitches which made Scrooge's teeth ache and his head throb. Faster and faster they spun round Miss Trellis their razor sharp teeth sparking gold and crimson against her stoney robes. Miss Trellis gestured with both hands and the cloud of bats became a flock of doves which wheeled and darted for the Prince.

Satan waved his claw in the tiniest gesture. All motion in the room stopped. He said:

"Ghost, you know this is not how I work."

"You must release Ebenezer and Jane. They are bound to you in no way,' she said.

"This battle will continue in another time and in another place," Satan said.

"In the end, you cannot win," Miss Trellis said.

Old Scratch said, "You know only the shadow of things as they *may* be, Ghost—not as they *will* be."

Miss Trellis pointed her long finger at Scrooge and Miss Goosegrass. "Release them," she said.

"Oh, very well," Satan said as if a spoiled child foiled in cruel play. He flicked his finger. Scrooge and Miss Goosegrass vanished from the cathedral.

Owlpen Hall

"I AM DELIGHTED TO SEE YOU IN SUCH GOOD HEALTH, SIR."

"Why thankee, Clarence. It is kind of you to say so," Scrooge said.

"Mr. Weston and I are only too pleased at your remarkable recovery," he replied. "I fear that you have only an unpleasant impression of Owlpen Hall, and who wouldn't under the circumstances? But I hope you will give us the opportunity to dispel the notion. Harsh memories do fade in the light of better times and wholesome company. And, I might add, in the light of Truth."

"I spent many days and nights in pain here." A chill ran down his back at the thought of Mrs. Claypoole's touch, her perfume. "Yet it was a haven of sorts, I suppose. All that is behind me now. I am ready to turn to the future."

"Yes, Sir," Clarence said. "And may I add that Mr. Levy and Mrs. Edelstein are resting comfortably in a cottage maintained by Mr. Weston. Mr. McCloud has gone away to see his brother."

"Mr. McCloud?"

"One of the people at your charity whose life was threatened by Mr. Fleming," Clarence said.

"Oh, I see," Scrooge said. "I'm afraid I don't know the man."

"A retired seaman. A Scot, I should think. And now, Sir, if you will come with me I will lead you to the children. When you have finished your visit, ring for me. We will all gather in the library."

Scrooge followed Clarence along a passageway lined with portrait paintings of bold-looking gentlemen and well-bred ladies from various ages.

"You will find them inside this room," Clarence said stopping before a door. He gave Scrooge a shallow bow. "I will be listening for the bell."

Clarence moved down the passageway with an ease which came of spending many years wandering fields and forests.

Scrooge did not knock upon the door until Clarence was out of sight and earshot. He drew his handkerchief from his pocket and blew his nose.

He rapped his knuckle against the door.

"Come in," said the voice of a young girl.

Scrooge turned the handle, swung the door inward, but did not immediately enter the room.

He cleared his throat. "If this isn't the prettiest little scene I've ever observed," he said.

Sat upon a chair cocked at an angle to the door was a young man in a tailored outfit. He posed with back straight, eyes narrowed as if concentrating on some puzzle. The boy's hair was glossy, combed precisely dividing his head in two.

"How good to see you, Sir," said he, eyes still averted.

"You are quite the young man," Scrooge said.

"Thank you, Sir," Haresh said turning his head toward Scrooge and rewarding him with a big smile.

"Please, brother," Rajani said, "how can I do you justice when you are moving?"

"Do you think that I am a statue?" Haresh said.

"You would be lucky to have the brains of a statue, Monkey Boy."

"The next time you need your pencil sharpened, don't bother me," Haresh said. "Use your tongue."

Rajani stood, and Scrooge wondered if she intended to give her brother a shove. Instead she floated across the room as gracefully as a dandelion seed and stopped before him.

She looked up in his face and tears filled her eyes. Scrooge pulled out his handkerchief and dabbed at his own eyes before handing it to her.

"I am happy to see you returned and well, Sir," she said.

"Rajani?"

Both she and Haresh bolted like lion cubs, leapt upon Scrooge hugging him, sometimes kissing him, sometimes biting his leg.

"I am stronger than you," Haresh said, his fists bouncing off Scrooge's shoulder.

"Oh, ow! Ouch!" Scrooge complained in a falsetto voice which caused Haresh to cackle like a fiend and redouble his efforts.

A moment later Rajani pulled her brother off Scrooge. "Enough now, Monkey Boy," said she. "We must treat him with respect." She leant over and gave Scrooge a kiss upon the cheek. "How do you do, father? We are so very happy that you have returned to us."

Scrooge put his arms around both his children and hugged them till they squealed with joy.

The window at their back exploded showering them in countless needles of glass. Scrooge whirled round and saw a creature perched on the sill—half man, half dog. In a heartbeat he recognised who it was—or who it had been at one time: Bop. The one who had beaten him. The one who had nearly ended his life. The one who had caused him such unbearable pain.

"Behind me, children," Scrooge said and moved between them and the beast. "You will not harm them," he said as calmly as if he were directing a clerk to correct an error. "There is nothing you can do to get around me. I fear no one and nothing. I especially am not afraid of you nor of anything you might attempt."

Bop growled low in his throat and crouched as if ready to spring.

"Damn you!" Scrooge shouted. He lifted the chair he had been sitting in and brought it down hard on the floor. From the remains he took a broken leg in each hand and raised them as if they were swords of iron.

Haresh grabbed a book fallen to the floor, raced forward, and pitched it at the beast's snout. The creature shivered and gathered strength to leap. Scrooge saw its body arch in the air.

Time for Scrooge slowed, the colour drained from his vision, and he felt himself move with a supernatural quickness. He drove first one, then the other of the stakes into the creature's belly as if guided by unseen hands. He felt with satisfaction the sensation of the wood pass deeply into the beast's bowels.

Rajani twisted aside as the creature crashed into the corner where she stood. Bop staggered erect to his hind legs and pulled the shafts from his body.

The beast drove Scrooge against the door causing pain to shoot up his torso. Scrooge brushed it aside, gripped the monster's jaws and pulled. He was aware that Haresh had wrapped his arms around one of the beast's legs and was biting it with all the energy the boy could muster. The creature shook its leg, and the boy flew against the wall.

Footsteps pounded the stairs. The door behind Scrooge's back thumped as Clarence tried to enter.

"Move aside, Sir! You're blocking the way," Clarence said. Scrooge wished he could comply.

The beast's forepaws clawed his chest. His coat tore, then his shirt. Scrooge felt talons rake his chest and blood run in warm trickles. Scrooge brought his right knee up into the beast's side twice, but without effect.

Something black shot through the air. Bop jerked as if hot coals had been poured onto his back. His claws lashed out so quickly that Scrooge perceived only a blur, but they met only emptiness. Scrooge heard a growl which was not the sound of the dog-man. It was the sound of a great cat.

A blur of shadow. Bop was lifted bodily and carried by the nape of its neck to the window by a creature which Scrooge had known in his dreams: a panther. In a heartbeat they were gone and Scrooge's ears were filled with the sound of the terrible battle just beyond his sight. He rushed over to Haresh who was struggling to his feet.

"Are you hurt, son?" he asked, but Haresh was not concerned with his own well-being. Haresh said, "Where is Rajani?"

Scrooge turned in a complete circle. She was gone. The door crashed open behind him, but Scrooge pushed past Clarence and dashed down the stairs. He flung himself at the front door, pulled it open and was through in a heartbeat. There at his feet was the lifeless form of Bop. Standing over him was Rajani, her face wet with tears.

"There, there, my girl," he said and picked her up in his arms. "Your new dress has been spoilt." He brushed off clumps of rust-coloured fur from her shoulders. "Let me take you in, my sweet. Don't worry. We shall buy you a new pretty dress." He pushed her jet black hair away from her face and kissed her gently on the forehead. "My dear little girl," he said. "My dear little girl."

◉

Jack Frost felt every eye turned upon him. He understood their curiosity, their wonder, their desire for the Truth. He smiled at every one in turn.

First was Mr. Scrooge in a spare suit of Weston's fashionable clothes. Scrooge was scratched, bruised, yet resilient with his back straight and his head held erect. Miss Goosegrass clung to his arm and gave him such attentions that Jack's heart was filled with joy. Scrooge, Jack knew, would finally know the happiness he had longed for, for so many decades.

Next Jack rolled to Lincoln Trumbull who took his hand and squeezed it with emotion but could produce no words.

His sister Annie said, "I can never thank you enough for reuniting my brother and I..." She finished her thought by twisting a handkerchief in her hands.

"You are concerned that you can never live down your shame," Jack said. "You must not let this experience destroy the natural goodness in your heart. You have been a victim, good woman. Blame lies with the criminal, not with the victim."

"No, it is not so simple," Annie said, her voice unsteady. "Each time I have been given a decision to make in my life, I have chosen whichever action I thought my father would disapprove of. I did so not because I hated him, but because of my pride. I believed that I knew better than he did, that I knew more than he did—but, of course, I knew nothing. And now he is lost to me, and I'll never see him again in this world. I never had the chance to tell him that I loved him."

Her brother put his hand on her arm. "He knew you loved him, Sister. He went to his grave knowing how much you cared for him."

"You are a poor liar, Brother," she said. "There is no need for you to protect my feelings."

"Father forgave you before he died. I heard him say so with my own ears."

"But I cannot forgive *myself*. If it weren't for you, my brother, I don't believe I could go on. Perhaps even so, it is too late for me."

Jack said, "Forgiving yourself will not come easy, but by degrees you will rediscover the goodness which lies within you. The first step is to cleanse your heart by good works, ma'am."

"I will dedicate my every waking moment to good works. I can promise that much," Annie said. "I swear that by the memory of my father."

"Then you have my blessing and the blessing of my two companions," he added nodding toward Mary-Martha and Elizabeth Trellis.

Jack moved next to Lucille. She removed herself from her seat and knelt before him.

"There is no need," Jack said. "Please rise and take your place beside your husband."

Instead Topper joined his wife on his knees before Jack. "One day, dear Jack," Topper said, "we will have a son, and I hope that he will be like you in every way."

Jack smiled and patted Topper's shoulder. "No doubt you will be blessed," he said. Topper wrapped his arms around the boy and hugged him as if he were his own. After a long moment, he returned with his wife to their chairs.

James Weston stood apart from the others. Silent. Arms crossed. He and Jack exchanged a look, but Weston's face remained dark.

Jack took his place in the centre of the room between his two companions.

A look of shock passed over the faces of the group.

"Be not sad nor afraid for us," said Jack. "Let me explain: There are beings of complex order: part Spirit, part Man. Just as Salvation Mitchell was the embodiment of Deceit and Prejudice, Fleming—Violence and Cruelty made into flesh and bone, and Mrs. Claypoole—the Deadly Sins of

- 362 -

Ignorance and Lust made corporeal, we three are the aspects of higher beings, beings Holy and Good being temporarily hosted by the bodies of Jack Forest, Mary-Martha White and Miss Elizabeth Trellis."

Jack saw Scrooge's eyes glitter and his mouth open to speak.

"No, Ebenezer," Jack said, "we are not purely the Spirits of Christmas Past, Present and Christmas Yet To Come. Nor, my friend Milton, are we purely the Three Ladies in White who visited you when you were just a boy. We are flesh and blood humans imbued with spiritual essence. We contain aspects of those Spiritual Trinities and others called by various names in divers cultures. We are, however, not all-powerful nor are we powerless."

"Are you Jack? Are you the boy who came to me looking for a job?" Topper said.

"No," the Spirit replied. "We subtly influenced Jack Forest, Mary-Martha White and Miss Elizabeth Trellis to make themselves a part of the Yellow Door community as these three humans have had an innate affinity with us since birth. We used their ears and eyes to monitor events. When Reverend Mitchell proclaimed his lies regarding Mr. Topper and the embezzlement of charity funds, we knew we had to take a more active role. We took possession of our hosts rather clumsily, I'm afraid."

Miss Goosegrass said, "You allowed Mr. Scrooge to be beaten?" Her face was unforgiving.

"We did not know that Mr. Scrooge had been beaten at that point," the Spirit in Jack said. "We did not see nor hear anything other than what our hosts were aware of. And please be reminded that the battle between good and evil must be played out among men, not spirits. We Spirits of Goodness can only act to return balance when Evil Spirits apply themselves to unsettle events and tip their outcome in Hell's direction. Ultimately it is mankind only who can settle the contest by their own deeds and decisions."

Scrooge said, "Where are Jack and the others then?"

"They are safe and will be returned to you after we are finished here," the Spirit in Jack said, softly. "They will return to you insensible of their roles as our hosts."

"Spirits of good and evil attend me, interfere on my behalf or plot my destruction. I find it difficult to believe I am so important a person to attract such interest," Scrooge said. "I am merely one man." The Spirit in Jack watched him grip the hand of Miss Goosegrass lovingly.

The Spirit in Mary-Martha said, "Lucifer was not concerned with Scrooge the Man, but feared Scrooge the Myth—the story of whom holds the power to change the hearts of millions by its example." She sat down beside Jack and set a hand on his shoulder.

The Spirit in Miss Trellis moved her right hand through the air as if she were tracing runes as she spoke: "At the instant of Ebenezer's redemption, Lucifer became aware and feared its power. He summoned his vilest allies and set them to undo our friend in the complex scheme which has been foiled by your efforts."

Mrs. Topper shook her head. "Without your help we should have all been damned to Hell."

"No," The Spirit in Jack said. "I must repeat: the actions of we three spirits are limited only to counter-balancing the power of evil, not to destroy it. The victory is yours. The demons were defeated by your love and devotion to one another and by the strengths of your own characters."

"Gad, but you must all believe me the worst sort of villain," James Weston said, interrupting the conversation like an unexpected blast of steam. "Consortin' with demons from Hell."

"Not at all, Mr. Weston," said Scrooge. "You have cared for my children while I was unable to. No villain would do such a thing. But please tell your story as you see fit."

Weston looked down at his boots as he spoke: "Then you must sit through a short history of my family, though I should have preferred to spare you—spared myself the tellin', for all that.

"My father was a good man in many ways—though he was careful in neither his clothes nor his financial investments. What little money my father inherited from his father, he 'invested' in cards. As a boy I could see panic take him as he watched our estate slide into ruin. Our family fortune, the great wealth that built this home, dwindled over the course of many generations and so my difficulties certainly can't be blamed *entirely* on my father. When he passed away, I inherited only his debts and as such have naturally long been desperate for ways to resolve those obligations and rebuild my ancestral home.

"One day a man comes to my door and wishes to see me. I can see by his wild manner of dress that he is clearly an eccentric, and I would see him to the door kindly, but he suggests he has a solution to my indebtedness if I will only give him five minutes of my time. I'm thinkin' I have only a few idle moments to lose, so I'm damned if I don't ask him to explain himself!

"He offers nothing less than to pay off my obligations and finance the reconstruction of Owlpen Hall if I will play only the smallest role in a caper he's contrived. I may be many things, but I am not so gullible as all that, so I dismissed him, of course, and quickly put the scheme out of mind.

"I often take me out to a hermit's hut on property I own not so great a distance from here to write...to write..." Weston paused and shifted his jaw, "...poetry. I would appreciate it if you would keep that piece of information to yourselves—some of my friends, I am sorry to say, find poetry-writin' a rather feckless pursuit. I would rather not be the butt of their jokes." He straightened his neck-cloth before continuing. "Sometimes I'm away—only me, an apple, a jug of wine and an ink-bottle—communin' with the muse for days at a time, but the hut is near enough that it sometimes is only for a few hours. I pushed the matter of the madman's caper entirely from my thoughts and decided to spend a few days at my hut findin' the shape of my heart with pen and ink. Upon my return several days later I was surprised to find a bank-draught made out in my name from a well-known London lawyer confirmin' the proposition. The amount staggered me. Enough to pay off my creditors, rebuilt Owlpen Hall, and more besides.

"And the proposition, as I have said, was simple: I was to take a small part in a prank played upon an old man who had for the entirety of his cruel life been a squeezin', wrenchin', graspin', scrapin', clutchin', covetous, old sinner—several men of considerable wealth who had been whipped by this man when they were boys were wantin' to teach him a lesson. I was told that they would stage a robbery and that just before a pair of *faux* highway-men were to do him harm, I was to step forward and frighten them away.

Nothin', I was told, could be simpler.

"When I arrived at the designated time I was horrified to see that a beatin' had been takin' place and the man was about to be either mutilated or murdered. The operation didn't strike me as bein' entirely benign from the beginnin', and so I took the steady Clarence along with me to act as reserve, and by Heaven ain't I jolly glad I did?

"I, of course, carried you, Mr. Scrooge, to my home after I saw that you'd been gravely injured. I sent for my own family physician, Dr. Blake, but was sent a message that Blake was out of town and that Dr. Tobias Fluch, a new doctor to the City, was shoulderin' the doctor's duties while away. Dr. Fluch sent for Mrs. Claypoole to nurse you, and I dare say you know the rest."

The Spirit in Jack said, "Mr. Weston is being too modest. He became suspicious of your treatment and after examining the bottle of laudanum you were taking began diluting the doses so that you would not become addicted to the drug as was Fluch's intention."

Scrooge shook his head. "I am deeply in your debt, Sir," said he. "How can I ever repay you?"

Weston made a dismissive gesture and looked away embarrassed. "Never, old fellow! It was not so grand a role as I would have liked, but I am happy to have helped in my small way."

The Spirit in Miss Trellis said, "When it became clear that Mr. Levy and Mrs. Edelstein's lives were in danger, I visited Mr. Weston and explained to him the Truth. He immediately offered to provide a place of sanctuary for any who were threatened by the demons. We frequently met to co-ordinate our activities. Mr. Weston has been instrumental in all your successes."

"You should have come to us, Mr. Weston, and explained. You could have prevented us all a great deal of grief," Miss Goosegrass said.

Scrooge said, "No, Jane. Do not blame Mr. Weston for playing his part as the Spirits directed him. The only person who is blameworthy is me. I see now that all this has been entirely my own fault. Oh, how many flaws of personality can one man possess? Greed, meanness of spirit, gluttony, pride. It is no wonder that I attract demons from Hell like honey attracts flies.

"I am culpable of so many crimes." Scrooge held his temples in woe. "I am guilty of ignoring those who asked for my help when I assigned them their duties. Milton expressed himself quite clearly that he did not feel comfortable in handling the development of the charity alone. I did not listen and brushed his concerns aside. I believed he lacked confidence whereas he wished only to create a collaborative working relationship with me. True, I wished to see to Tim Cratchit's medical treatments, but that could have been satisfactorily arranged in any number of other ways.

"The second thing I have been guilty of: ignoring my friends when they offer their advice after I've asked for it. Milton understood intuitively that Salvation Mitchell was untrustworthy, but I ignored him. All of this could have been avoided had I simply listened to my friend and not pretended that I knew more than he.

"Worst of all I have been guilty of deceiving myself than I am more important than everyone else. We are all the same in God's eyes: rich or poor; Jew, Hindu, or Mussulman. I am no better than the people I serve at the charity. I am luckier to be born with opportunities, but I am no better than and in some ways far worse than the lowest beggar. I have been blind for so long. Can such a number of serious derelictions ever be forgiven?"

Topper said, "We have all made horrible mistakes in these events, Mr. Scrooge. Be not hard on yourself. I cannot claim to be without fault, and I am not one to judge. I forgive you your weaknesses as I hope others will forgive me mine."

Scrooge sighed and clasped his hands together for a long moment before continuing. "My soul may be saved by the sacrifice and efforts of all who stand before me," he said, sadly, "but I am very much afraid that I shall end my days in debtor's prison. That might be a fitting end to the career of Ebenezer Scrooge, but it also means the end of the charity."

The Spirit in Mary-Martha smiled and slipped a hand into her apron. "Please, Sir. I found this. I thought you might be interested in what it has to say."

Scrooge held the sheets of paper in the winter light.

"What's this?" he said and gave an old dog bark of a laugh. "What is it you've given me, dear girl?"

"These are the records of the accounts to which the Reverend Mitchell diverted your funds. You may have it all back any time you wish," she said.

Scrooge and Miss Goosegrass stood to their feet and danced together in a small circle. "Such news! You don't know how that makes me feel. We can be married now," he said. "Did you hear, Jane? We can be married. I am so happy."

"I give you joy," said the Spirit in Jack.

Scrooge stopped and caught his breath. "That is wonderful news. That means I can give up the charity."

"Give up the charity?" Topper said, with a frown which struck silence in the room. "Haven't you meant to save it, Sir? Isn't that what this has been all about?"

"Of course, of course! Let me explain. I know that in saying this I am breaking a pledge I made earlier, but it cannot be helped. The charity won't be abandoned, however. I intend to give it to you to operate, Milton. And don't worry. I will see to it that you are completely funded for many decades to come."

Topper shook his head and said, "Mr. Scrooge, I'm afraid you still do not listen to me. Have I not said many times that I do not feel adequate to the task?"

"So you have, and thus I propose that Mr. Trumbull be your partner," Scrooge said. "He is from all that I can tell a very remarkable man, and the two of you already have much experience working together. There is no challenge that the two of you cannot meet."

Trumbull smiled shyly and said, "That is an interesting proposition that I'll need to give some thought. Now that I've found Annie I can turn my life in any number of directions."

"I do hope that you give it serious consideration, Mr. Trumbull," Topper said. "I would be honoured to continue to work with you at the Charity, although I would suggest that Mr. Scrooge play a greater role than sharing the weight of his purse."

"My purse? Its weight is more a burden than I can say." Scrooge narrowed his eyes in thought.

"But what will _you_ do, Mr. Scrooge? Return to Europe? Germany? Italy?"

"What will I do?" Scrooge said. "I should say _we_. Yes, we will travel in celebration of our matrimony as may be customary, but only for a short time. I am eager to return to this City for a purpose to which I shall devote the rest of my life. I have had no opportunity to discuss this with my dear Jane as I feared my fate lay in the workhouse, but I desire with all my heart to establish a school for the needy. Education! There is no greater cure for poverty. While there will always be a great need for charity to support those who are experiencing desperate times, there is an even greater need for educating the ignorant. Charity fills an immediate need. Education builds for the future.

"Miss Goosegrass has helped me see that the difference between success and poverty is not hard work. No group works harder than the poor. They work endlessly, but receive only low wages in return. The cycle of poverty can only be broken with education—teaching people useful skills, teaching them to make good decisions, teaching them to think. That is what we will do. We cannot save every soul, but we can lift humanity one child at a time."

Scrooge ran a hand along the edge of his jaw feeling the scratch of his whiskers as a measure of the passage of time.

"My own memories of school are not always fond ones, I will not deny. I was a good pupil, learnt my sums and letters, but the Masters were cold and often cruel, truth to tell." He placed his hands on his hips as if recalling the impact of a cane.

"School should be so much more. Instruction should be given with compassion and humanity. We must keep the good, cast away the bad."

Miss Goosegrass's eyes glistened. She could make no sound but only nodded her head in agreement.

"Three cheers for Mr. Ebenezer Scrooge," Topper said standing to his feet.

Three cheers shook the walls like the peals of a bell.

"We must take our leave now," The Spirit in Jack said. "Our hosts' bodies will be returned to themselves. They will in all ways be as they were

—none the worse for our occupation."

"Before you go I have one small request," Scrooge said.

"What would that be?" the Spirit in Jack said. "I will grant it if it be within my power."

"You must tell me where I can find a can of the brightest, merriest yellow paint made. Before the sun sets on another day I have a door which I fully intend to paint with mine own hands!"

Epilogue

ᔕᕈ

SCROOGE'S ROOMS GREW COLD IN SPITE OF THE COALS PILED HIGH IN THE hearth. Dr. Fluch clasped his hands under his armpits, raised his shoulders and pulled his chin into his collar. He paced a small circle. He paced it again and again.

There was food aplenty if one liked gruel. There was nothing to read, nothing to occupy his senses and little to reflect on save his uncertain fate.

Dr. Tobias Fluch rested his eyes on the leather-covered bottle. Should he partake a few dozen drops to pass the time or perhaps drain the bottle to put an end to his life? He picked up the bottle and turned it over in his hands. It gurgled merrily. The bottle appeared to contain enough of the common tincture of opium for him to choose either option. There was not so much that he would long have the second.

Fluch poured himself a glass of water, dribbled twenty-five drops and drank. He seated himself before the fire, threw a shawl over his shoulders and a wool blanket across his lap. He closed his eyes and ran his left hand over his unshaven chin. Oddly, for the first time, he missed his little finger. Sleep would come soon. Gentle, relaxing sleep where—at the very least— he could escape into his dreams.

The clock ticked steadily, but Dr. Fluch was unaware of any change in his senses—no increased acuteness of, say, hearing and certainly no drowsiness, nor sense of fantastic visions.

He uncorked the bottle and spilled more of the tincture in a glass, poured in a small amount of water and swallowed. A lock of hair strayed in front of his eyes.

No effect. He reached for the bottle again, but found it missing.

A thick animal stench filled his nose.

Fluch fell to his knees and averted his eyes. "Master," he said in a gasp. "You are here at last."

"You have been avoiding me, Magician," the Prince said.

"No master, I have not. Due to...due to my inexperience I allowed myself to become trapped in a prison of my own design. I have been a fool. Can you forgive me, Master?"

"No," the Prince said.

The words were not unexpected, but they shocked nevertheless. He said, "I understand. I will perform any act of penance to atone for my weakness. You only need name it, and it shall be done."

"You do not wish forgiveness?" the Prince of Darkness said.

"No," Fluch said. He knew better than to attempt to bargain.

"You do not wish to blame my Servants for your failure?"

"The truth cannot be hidden from you."

"To the contrary: there can be little truth in my presence, but let us not quibble over subtleties. I require from you a sacrifice—that is all."

Fluch breathed a sigh of relief.

Moments later the door to Scrooge's rooms swung open wide. Lucifer clearly was not subject to any trivial magic which Fluch may have cast. Swinging at the Beast's side, gripped lightly in its claws were long strands of hair attached to an egg-shaped object with eyes frozen wide in unspeakable horror.

FIN

About the Author

Glen L. Bledsoe lives in Salem, Oregon with his wife and an unusually large number of cats. When he is not teaching or writing he is practicing his sleight-of-hand.

For more information:

http://glenbledsoe.com

http://www.charityofscrooge.com

www.ingramcontent.com/pod-product-compliance
Lightning Source LLC
Chambersburg PA
CBHW070402260626
47161CB00001B/236